# The Visitor

## A Novel

Eric W. Gershman

With an Afterword by Joaquim do Espirito Santo

THIRD WORLD PRESS FOUNDATION
Established 1967

Chicago

Third World Press Foundation
*Progressive publishing since 1967*


Library of Congress Cataloging-in-Publication Data on file

ISBN: 978-0-88378-441-9

Printed in the United States of America

Cover design and interior book layout by Relana Johnson

# *Praise for* The Visitor

"I was pleased to discover that the historian and author Eric Gershman would choose to tell a powerful story of the connection between Angola and the United States. Mr. Gershman's gift for research and narrative has produced a thrilling tale of mystery, time travel, and explosive story telling."

**– Joaquim do Espirito Santo**
Angolan Ambassador to the United States

*"Eric Gershman has written an ambitious, sweeping first novel that takes an African girl, a child soldier in a brutal inter-tribal Cold War conflict, on a journey through America's slaving past, the politics and cultural confusion of international adoption and modern-day racism in this country. A compelling tale of war, escape, reckoning and revenge,* The Visitor *is worthy and engaging fiction that will open your eyes to the historic and historically brutal links between America and Africa."*

***– Biddle Duke,***
*The New York Times, The New Yorker online*
and *The Surfers Journal* contributor

*"Like the works of Colson Whitehead and N.K. Jemison,* The Visitor *uses the fantastic to find a deeper meaning in the wounds history has left us with. Gershman has written an ambitious, affecting book."*

***– Ashley Warlick,***
author of *The Arrangement*

"Anna is an unforgettable character with a captivating past. I will never forget the journey that she takes in present America and in her travels back in time. I was also fascinated with the research on Angola and its part in the history of American slavery, as well as contemporary America. I remain haunted by its piercing memory. A must read.

***– Ceneta Lee-Williams,***
*Former Sales Director, Penguin House &*
*Founder of CLW Editorial Consulting*

# The Visitor

*For my mother,*
*Carol Sue Gershman, who teaches me perseverance*

# Prologue

## *Tappahannock, Virginia, 1819*

The trial of the slave Jemmy for the killing of Kestin Kane took place on a Saturday in July. The deceased was the only son of the Master Leslie Kane, a much-respected local planter.

Judge Moore presided over the case. The overseer, Mr. A.C. Tomkins, served as key witness. He and Kestin Kane had only gone down to the slave quarters to check on the health of Jemmy's wife, who had been sickly that day. The overseer's reenactment of what happened next left the courtroom speechless, but not surprised. He dramatically pointed an outstretched arm directly at the accused.

"And then, Jemmy grabbed this big stick of wood and brought it down on poor Kestin's head, like this!" He then swung his arm down in a violent gesture that no one would soon forget. The poor Judge's wife promptly fainted in her chair and was carried out of the courtroom.

The only other eyewitness to the brutal crime was the nine-year-old daughter of the guilty man, who watched the scene from her perch in the loft. Neither side saw it in their interest to compel her to testify, as the girl was a slave and a mute.

The key evidence in the case was that the piece of wood found in Jemmy's hand matched the scar marks on the dead man's forehead. While that blow did not kill him, it clearly showed that Jemmy had struck his master in a fit of rage and then threw him against the wall, where death ensued.

After a brief appeal, Jemmy was hanged from the Ole' Oak tree as the Reverend Cooper conducted the service through clenched teeth.

Master Leslie Kane's plantation, Nottoway, was rightly compensated for the price of an able-bodied field hand, as was the Virginia state law provision. Jemmy was thirty-one years old.

"It's sad," commented one neighbor, "Old Man Kane lost his wife to consumption and now this."

He received the deepest of condolences from the goodly Christian community, and local folk even lent slaves to the Kane plantation to get the old Master through this difficult time, free of charge.

It would take two hundred years for the truth to appear.

# Chapter 1

## Luanda, Angola, 2002

Gate 7 had a roped-off area for youth traveling alone, and a fourteen-year-old girl sat by herself in the small section. It was her first time flying and while she fidgeted nervously, she was more concerned with where she was heading.

Her hands stroked a family heirloom, a sort of wooden doll called a *Ndimba* that had been with her throughout most of her life—and in her family even longer. A green amulet shaped like a heart hung from its neck.

Outside, a jumbo jet shone brightly in the Angolan sun. She watched as the workers lifted supplies on board. A conveyor belt fed luggage into the airplane's cargo section, its wide mouth swallowing the colorful bags. She wondered how such a massive machine could ever lift off the ground. Next to her sat a pink wheeled suitcase, which she kicked playfully. Except for a backpack and the heirloom figurine on the seat beside her, the suitcase contained almost all the possessions she had in the world. Most of its contents were not even her own, just collected and given to her at the orphanage. She wore a yellow dress with a purple bow, tights, and a pair of black shoes that were a size too big.

"These clothes are what the girls wear in America," the Mother Superior had said. The Sisters stood gazing into the mirror at her, shaking their heads in agreement. She felt like a character in a school play.

Her destination had two names, Washington and also D.C., and it was in the country of America that she would begin her new life. She stared at the passport in her hand and opened it again to her photograph on the first page. She gazed at the large gap between her two front teeth and wondered if that was typical for a girl her age. Her long curly hair was pulled cleanly off her face. Her eyebrows were curved up at the ends before disappearing into her temples. Was that normal? Even the name on the document was unfamiliar to her, *Anna White*.

"This is an American name. You will grow accustomed to it," the

Mother Superior had said while helping her pack her small suitcase. The girl understood of course, but her name was Zarkhanna, not Anna. This was just one of the many changes she had been forced to accept over the past months as the year 2002 was coming to a close.

"Why did you call me Zarkhanna, Mommy? It is a long name!" she had asked her mother while washing clothes by the river three years ago. It was a brilliant Sunday morning in February, before the soldiers came and destroyed everything, when they were doing chores together before church. Both were wearing red headdresses, and they were excited to see neighbors at the service, which was to be followed by a dinner in their village of Caxito.

During the sermon, the priest would speak about the men who disappeared in the Angolan civil war. He asked for the Lord's work to be accepted, not understood, as he stood beneath a small cross of Jesus. She always imagined that it was Jesus who gave the priest his words, because he always knew what to say to make everyone feel safe, if they followed the Lord.

Her mother had stopped cleaning for a moment to look upstream where the rushing water weaved through the colorful rocks. "You are named after your grandmother, who was smart like you and knew things. And you are also named after the great Queen Anna of Angola. But mostly because your name starts with a Z, and you are my little zebra!" Her mother had playfully splashed her with water, and they both laughed.

"I'm not a zebra, Mommy! You are!"

Zarkhanna had accepted her name's origins, and she thought of it often—in school, and when inventing private games with her friends, reading a person's thoughts, or knowing what would happen next. To do this, she had only to close her eyes and breathe the air, or stare at a person's eyes when they were looking away. She could see if neighbors would recover from their illnesses or fall further into darkness, and she could see which of her friends was telling the truth and who was telling lies. She told her mother about her ability.

"Everybody in God's world has a special gift, Zarkhanna," her mother said, as she combed her hair before school. But Zarkhanna was not sure if her mother understood.

"She does have a special gift," Auntie said. "Like Momma did." Often

Zarkhanna felt that Auntie understood her in ways that her mother did not.

Later, she would be able to sense which villages would survive and which would be burnt to the ground as she entered them, AK-47 in her hand, pushed along by soldiers not much older than herself.

Her name was Zarkhanna, named after her grandmother, and of this she had always been proud. But now, sitting in this airport, she was to accept her new name, *Anna White*. She spoke this new name softly to herself as she watched the activities in the gate area around her.

The hanger for Flight 319 to Washington, D.C. was busy with travelers readying themselves for the fourteen-hour journey. An Angolan family—a mother and father and one child—were putting half-eaten sandwiches into their backpacks. The mother was struggling to put a light coat on her daughter, who wore a red dress. The young girl stared at Zarkhanna as her mother twisted her body into the jacket.

A tall White man transferred bottled water into a large carry-on, his cell phone cradled on his neck, his large backpack covered in stickers of flags from many countries in Africa. An old couple held hands, looking forward, and a book slipped off the woman's lap and fell on a broken tile floor, damaged during the years in the war. Plywood separated some of the rooms nearby and men with construction hats fractured the air with loud drills, trying to rebuild the war-torn building.

Zarkhanna looked outside into the sparkling sunshine as she held tight to her Ndimba doll. She remembered it had been given to her by her Auntie when she was only eight years old. It was embroidered with beads that went from a deep yellow to a bright red; and it had blue stripes separating the major colors from section to section. The Ndimba itself reminded Zarkanna of her fashionable Auntie. It even wore sandals laced up the ankles, just like Auntie would have worn. The figurine's eyes seemed expressive, shaped like little suns, with pupils made of small bits of granite painted ruby red. She toyed with the heart shape that hung from the doll's neck.

"This is your Ndimba that one day will give you luck to have healthy babies of your own," she had said to her quietly on All Souls' Day. "It has been in our fom'ly for a long time," she said in English. Auntie often spoke in English to Zarkhanna. "Portuguese is a dying tongue, chil' and you mus' learn the language of the world, if you want to see the world, my little zebra."

Zarkhanna did want to see the world, but not in this way.

Zarkhanna continued to sit in the gate area admiring her doll. The heirloom was embroidered with beads that went from a deep yellow to a bright red; and it had blue stripes separating the major colors from section to section. The Ndimba itself reminded Zarkhanna of her fashionable Auntie. It even wore sandals laced up the ankles, just like Auntie would have worn. The figurine's eyes seemed expressive. Shaped like suns, their pupils were made of small bits of granite painted ruby red. She toyed with the heart shape that hung from its neck.

Whenever Auntie would come by bus to visit Zarkhanna and her mother, villagers looked at the fashionable woman with disapproval, especially the old Mrs. Proud, who was the local promoter of initiation schools for girls like Zarkhanna. Mrs. Proud did not appreciate unmarried women from the city roaming her village. She looked disdainfully at Auntie's fancy handbag, wedged heels, and designer blue jeans. The sixty-kilometer distance from Caxito to Luanda might as well have been ten thousand.

Auntie spoke to Zarkhanna's mother as they tended charcoal behind their adobe home. They had covered the patch of raw ground with a yellow-and-green patterned rug which they had transported from inside the home.

"Wanda, why don't you leave this old village and come live with me in Luanda?" she asked. They sat on brightly colored chairs as her mother prepared the *arroz de garoupa ilha* for lunch. Auntie had brought fresh meat and vegetables from the city. Zarkhanna had been instructed to go down to the river to obtain a mixture of sand and water and place it at the base of the large clay pot to keep the food from spoiling. Auntie had also brought a treat: fresh prawns. While the food cooked, Zarkhanna went back to weaving a sweetgrass basket to be used to store clothing. Auntie kept an eye on her handwork. It was clear that Zarkhanna had a natural skill. Her nimble fingers released the grass's hay-like fragrance, mixing with the scent of cooking in the air. She would finish each basket by stitching small white triangles along the base, a sort of family signature she had learned from her Auntie.

"And what do I do when Richard returns?" Wanda had responded. "What is he to find? His family gone? This is our home."

"Your daddy is not returning," Mrs. Proud told Zarkhanna when she had gone to the old woman's small farm to fetch goat milk months ago. The men had begun to go missing a year before. They disappeared when they went to find work on the highway. They disappeared when they went to the market. They disappeared when they went to help friends build a house. The missing fathers all left in the morning for different reasons, but come evening, they shared the same mysterious fate.

"Yes, Wanda, let's go live with Auntie in the city!" Zarkhanna had seconded, sweetgrass spilling onto her lap as she expertly wove it into a basket that someone always bought.

"Do not disrespect me chil'! I am your mother, and you will call me like that, or you will not see your friends for two weeks!" But she spoke with a smile because there was little the girl could do to distress her.

Zarkhanna smiled at her Auntie despite the warning from her mother and continued her weaving. She thought back to the one time she and her mother had gone to Luanda with its tall buildings. She remembered storekeepers sweeping the streets as if they were floors. Cafés were busy with colorful food and drinks. The children her age wore clothes with names like Nike and stayed out until almost dark, the girls leaning against cars, talking to handsome boys.

"Well, you and the little zebra can come live with me and give it a try," Auntie replied. "The apartment I go to on weekends has more than enough room. You would be safe there. Everyone says that Luanda is safe in this horrible war because neither side wants it destroyed."

People knew that traveling anywhere was becoming more dangerous. The checkpoints now had more soldiers, and the soldiers were getting younger and less disciplined. The radio said that people should only leave their villages if they had to, and the messages from the MPLA and UNITA were like two sides of the same piece of bread.

"We are safe, here," Wanda answered. And that was that.

Now, as Zarkhanna sat in the airport watching families that once looked like her own, she wondered what kind of new family awaited her and to whom she now belonged.

Her own mother was surely dead, she had heard the screams, and her Auntie was surely dead as well. Her father had been gone a long time now, but it was all going to be OK, she was told. She would now have a new mother and father, and the nightmares would go away forever; Mother Superior had promised. She would be someone else's daughter, like the girl in the gate area whose mother was now brushing her hair.

"Zarkhanna, go and hide in the ditches and place the sticks on top of you," her mother had instructed her as the trucks came rumbling into the village one morning. Auntie had been staying in the house for close to a month now and the three of them busied themselves with cooking, teaching, and dancing the *kuduro*. They had also invented their own dance, imitating the dying, springing to life from the floor and mock-scaring one another.

Auntie had pushed her through a narrow window, as ambush soldiers were already crawling over the village. Zarkhanna moved slowly on her belly to the safety ditch she and her mother dug in case the soldiers came, as she had practiced three times a week. She watched through the grass like a leopard as the soldiers destroyed her home, and then Caxito itself.

It reminded her of when she and her friends had built make-believe villages in the dirt and then jumped on them when they were called for dinner. But in those games, the neighbors were not running and screaming as they were now, and the dogs were not barking as the soldiers shot them dead.

Boom, boom! Dust was everywhere. A wandering cockcrow bird sat on the branch of a willow tree, watching the scene as Zarkhanna did. They glanced at one another like fellow witnesses at the scene of an accident. She waited in the ditch for her mother and Auntie to join her as they had practiced. But the only accompaniment she found was the sound of the screams, a sound she had never before heard come from her mother. She peered through the blades of grass as boy soldiers dragged Auntie from their home to a place out of her sight. She too screamed in languages meant for animals about to die.

She closed her eyes and covered her ears, the Ndimba heirloom in a basket she had been weaving when she was upended. This is how the commander found her and took her away from the village. She was ordered to carry supplies for the UNITA fighters. It was May 7, 2001.

Zarkhanna did not know how many nights she had slept in ditches with an AK-47 as a pillow and a machete as her best friend. She learned to obey the commander's every order and was smart about providing for herself. She made sure to eat enough and to ask to see a doctor for her wounds. She had been careful to hide and protect the Ndimba heirloom throughout the ten-month ordeal, and like her, it had somehow survived the ordeal.

Some of the UNITA soldiers had tried to take it away from her, taunting her by making her choose between food and the only belonging she had from her old life. The soldiers never did to her what they did to some of the older girls, but they enjoyed their cruel teasing.

"*Você quer sua comida, ou você quer seu brinquedo, garota?*" A tall soldier had goaded, using his long rifle to try to pull the heirloom away from her. Zarkhanna had swatted the gun away with her hand, grabbing a loaf of bread with meat while still holding the precious heirloom close to her chest.

"Leave me!" she ordered, staring coldly at the soldier.

The soldier laughed heartily. "Tough girl! Maybe one day you will fight for UNITA like a real soldier!" he said, allowing Zarkhanna both the meal and her treasured object. She ignored him and ate the bread quickly, as food did not come regularly.

The Sisters at the mission had helped her clean the heirloom in the days following her rescue. Now, in the airport, it looked worn but clean. A woven blue headdress adorned its head, and she wore an orange dress. Zarkhanna did not know how the figurine could one day help her. She only knew that Auntie had told her to keep it close when she received the gift, and, somehow, she had managed.

In the gate area, Zarkhanna caught the eye of the girl who was traveling with her family to the *Estado Unid*. The mother noticed the direction her daughter was staring and followed her gaze toward Zarkhanna. The three of them looked at one another before the mother turned the girl's head away from the lone traveler. The mother did not want her daughter to see that life, the life of so many lost children in Angola these days.

A woman in a uniform entered the roped-off area. Her dark-blue dress and black tie were clean and sturdy, like the low black pumps she wore on her feet. A small blue cap rested on her head with the logo for the TAAG Angola National Airlines stitched on top. She introduced herself as Miss Alecia.

"*Anna, estaremos embarcando no avião em breve, meu caro,*" she said in native Portuguese, looking into her eyes. "*Você embarcará primeiro, então junte suas coisas.*"

Zarkhanna nodded, not recognizing her new name, and began to ready herself to board the aircraft, even though Miss Alecia had said there was a two-hour delay.

"Thank you," she responded in English, then watched as the employee walked back toward the passengers waiting to check in. She put the heirloom down on the seat next to her, opened her bookbag, and took out a small journal and pencil. She drew the letters of her name in the notebook, turning the letters into pictures. She drew tents and trucks, trees and a river.

She would miss the land where she was from. It was beautiful, even though...Her heartbeat faster as she started drawing pictures of the brown-and-white house at 186 Tidewater Street that Mrs. Carolyn White had shown to her when she came to visit the Catolico Missionary. Zarkhanna had been escorted by one of the mission nuns into the garden for yet another interview with another stranger for adoption. Today, it was an American lady who had been speaking to the Mother Superior for some time. Zarkhanna sat in the garden watching the two women conversing. She could tell that the Mother Superior was angry, gesturing with her pointer finger at the American lady in the manner that she used when she was displeased. Zarkhanna waited until one of the younger nuns came out and handed the Mother Superior a letter, which ended the conversation, and she stormed away.

Zarkhanna caught the Mother Superior's eye as she passed and waited until the American lady called her over. Zarkhanna walked slowly in a white dress that was too small for her body. Approaching the unfamiliar woman, she felt as if she were invited into a lifeboat that may or may not be able to float.

"Zarkhanna, my name is Mrs. White." The woman reached out and touched Zarkhanna's hand. "But you can call me Carolyn if you like. That's what my friends call me." It felt like the woman was practiced.

Zarkhanna looked down and nodded but did not speak. She did not want a new mother. But Mrs. Carolyn White was kind, and her skin was pinkish white, and her hands were soft, and Zarkhanna knew that she could not stay in the orphanage, and that children younger than she needed her bed. The Mother Superior had told her so.

Then Mrs. Carolyn White had talked about the snow in America and high heels that girls wore and pizza as big and wide as your arms held out. Mrs. Carolyn White told her that she could go with her to America, if she wanted. Her short blond hair was so well placed, and her sleek outfit looked like she had taken it off a shelf and fitted it perfectly to her body.

"We can start out as friends, and maybe one day, I will be like a mother to you and help you, like, like a *mother.*" Mrs. Carolyn White's voice became choppy and Zarkhanna looked into her eyes and saw that they were filled with water. "Also, you will have a real brother and sister and two other children who also come from other countries."

"How old are my brothers and sisters?" Zarkhanna asked. They were the first words she had spoken.

Mrs. Carolyn White sat up straight. The girl named Tabitha and her brother Wyatt were eight-year-old twins. Simanto was an energetic five-year-old boy from Bangladesh whom everyone called Simba. The older girl, Juanita, was from Brazil, and everyone called her Nita. Mrs. Carolyn White was committed to helping children around the world and bringing them into her home and giving them a loving family.

"We all live as a family and we want you to join us," she said. The matter appeared to have been settled, and Zarkhanna could only smile in agreement.

"But we will take one step at a time," Mrs. Carolyn White said, pulling away and smoothing her dress which fit snugly to her frame. "And Mark, who is a very nice man, is so looking forward to meeting you in person!"

The gate agent made an announcement on the loudspeaker, reminding passengers to check around their seats and get ready to board. She put her backpack in her lap, her mind traveling across the ocean to a life she could only imagine.

Zarkhanna reminded herself of what the Mother Superior and two Sisters had said to her last night at the orphanage. "Zarkhanna, tomorrow will be the start of your new life, a wonderful life," the Mother Superior had said, sitting on a wooden chair in the large bunk room of sleeping children. She held Zarkhanna's hand in the dim light as the girl stood in a white nightgown.

She did not answer.

"But, child, there has been a small problem with your flying tomorrow. Mrs. White will be unable to come pick you up and fly to America with you. But this is normal, and everything will be OK."

Zarkhanna had tensed at the news, but the Mother Superior soothed her. "It is not a big problem, just something with her visa, which people need to travel. We just received word that Mrs. White will now meet you when you get off the airplane in America."

Zarkhanna's eyes widened as she imagined herself on the airplane. Where would she sit? Would she stand the whole' time?

"Do not worry, sweet child. The nice ladies on the plane will take very good care of you and let you watch television."

"It will be fun," the Sister behind her added, shaking her head up and down. "And you are going to fly in first class!"

Zarkhanna nodded and then looked at her feet. She did not know what first class was. She did not know if they would give her food. She did not ask.

Then the Mother Superior added, "Do not be afraid, child. You have seen evil and, God willing, you will never see this evil again, sweet child. The Lord Jesus will protect you, as he brought you to us." The Mother Superior had spoken these words as she gently pulled Zarkhanna's chin up to meet her eyes. She felt like the puppy that had once wandered into her village, remembering how the children had surrounded the confused animal.

Was the Mother Superior right? Was there nothing to fear? She remembered vaguely how it had once been in her village of Caxito—the smell of the green grass and manure, and how the smooth hills also gave off a scent like the earth itself. She remembered the cattle, the sable antelope, the small pools of cool water the children drank from even though the village women forbade them from drinking it. The men, the fathers, were gone to the war. She drew the image of the national animal that she had drawn in school dozens of times, a giant black sable antelope. She then vigorously scribbled it out.

"How long have you been with these soldiers?" a nun asked her when she had stormed the church alone. "What village are you from? Where did you get those scars?" The Sisters examined her arms and back and found bruises, many from sleeping in the dirt for nearly a year since the UNITA soldiers had come to Caxito. She had killed during this time, twice by gun and once with her own hand. Then one day she had wandered into the church to steal food, ready to shoot anyone who did not give her what the commander wanted, as she had been instructed.

As a girl soldier, she was punished for the most innocent of crimes. She would be slapped for failing to forage enough food, or failing to find meat, or for dropping an egg on her mad dash before sunset when she was required to give the food to the commander's chef.

No matter the physical hurts, hunger was always the deepest. Bruises on her body she could handle, but the pains in her stomach and weakness in her head sank her deeper into the ditches. At least she was not ever touched by the soldiers. Another girl two years older was brought into the army around the same time she was. The girl was the same height, but the soldiers liked her body because she had bosoms like a woman while Zarkhanna's were still like a boy's. A UNITA fighter had taken the girl from her sleeping place one night and hauled her to a lieutenant's tent. In the morning, the girl told her she was leaving with the lieutenant, her new husband. As the girl quickly gathered her belongings, she said she did not know where she was going.

Zarkhanna's days involved securing fresh meat and produce for the commander. As he wanted only the best, her job was to go to the houses in search of the finest food in the village.

She recalled once stealing cucumbers from a garden, when an old Mbundu woman had confronted her. Zarkhanna's rifle had been placed against the side of the adobe house, or she would have shot the old woman like she was told to do if anyone, including an old woman, refused to give food. There was a softness to the woman that made Zarkhanna feel easy, and in the old woman's eyes Zarkhanna could see that she knew things. The woman knelt next to her as the girl held several cucumbers greedily to her chest, dropping one in the dirt. They both gazed at it before the old woman gently picked it up and placed it into the Zarkhanna's arms, like a gift.

"This fight of men, this Angolan Civil War, has nothing to do with Angola," the old woman had said. She stood up and motioned for Zarkhanna to follow her into her home. A cat and several kittens, all black except for a single gray one, slept inside in the late afternoon sun. The woman had given Zarkhanna milk, which she drank quickly while the kittens crawled on her. The woman told her about the war and America and the Soviet Union, and Cuba and Portugal, and South Africa and the ancient Mbundu people. It was as much schooling as she would have in a year's time and

Zarkhanna listened, not speaking, watching the sun set over the vast fields, milk running down her chin. She knew she must be back at her post before the sun touched the horizon, but she didn't want to leave. She wished that she could stay with this woman and go to school. She wanted to sleep.

A stray gunshot, probably a few soldiers hunting antelopes that came too close to the military camp, startled Zarkhanna. She stood up abruptly and began to walk in the direction of camp, forgetting the cucumbers she had stolen. She did not have to worry. The old woman had prepared a sack full of pork and potatoes in addition to the cucumbers, and she handed Zarkhanna a piece of carob for a treat. Zarkhanna peeked inside the sack and, murmuring a quick thank you, ran back toward the tree cover, stopping once to look back. The old woman watched the girl from her garden, hand on hip, a gray headdress adorning her head like it was her own hair.

Days were spent huddled under the shade of mopane trees, waiting for the signal from the commander to march. Zarkhanna would spend these hours weaving baskets so tightly that she could carry water in them. As the soldiers watched movies in tents wired with generators, she wove baskets for the army to use. On occasion, she was able to finish a few baskets with the white triangles that were her family emblem.

"Use all of your fingers, Zarkhanna," she remembered her Auntie saying. "Pay special attention to the handles and use sweetgrass only, for its flexibility."

One day, as the UNITA soldiers awaited a crucial battle with the MPLA, she was ordered into the city of Benguela to find food. Upon entering the small city, she had immediately approached a clean white building on the outskirts and kicked the door open as she was trained to do. Inside she found a group of women sitting in a circle. She pointed her AK-47 at them. "Give me your food! I am a member of the UNITA fighters for the National Union of Total Independence and my commander orders you to give me your food!"

The women all looked in her direction. Ammunition was strewn across the girl's small frame. She wore the cap of the UNITA fighters and army shorts, and she was barefoot.

The radio was playing a *kuduro* dance song, the pulsating beat at odds with the tranquil scene. The women were doing the dance of prayer to the music. She could see that there was no food in the building, and that whatever the Sisters had would need to be obtained somewhere else. Zarkhanna's eyes were drawn to the image of the cross in the simple structure. It took a strong will for her to utter commands in a place where only the Lord's words were to be heard, but she had learned to trade a past she no longer needed for food she wanted now.

"Now! Now! Now!" She screamed in the voice she had been trained to use. But the nun in a long gray gown, who seemed to be the leader, stood up and walked slowly toward Zarkhanna.

"Do not come closer to me, bitch!" Zarkhanna ordered, but the woman walked up to her and gently took the rifle away. The girl did not fight this action. No one had ever done such an act, and she thought this woman knew something that she did not. She looked into the Sister's eyes, and they rested on one another for a long moment as the woman placed the rifle against the wall. She saw in the woman's eyes a vision like she had never seen, a vision in which she, Zarkhanna, was safe in a home far from this place of war.

Later, when two soldiers came storming into the building looking for her, the nun told them in a light voice that there was no girl there, that they had no business at this place, and that they should leave. Zarkhanna watched slivers of the scene through the floorboards, her eyes darting out in all directions.

"Now leave this house of God," she instructed. "Or I shall call General Nunda! Tell me your name!"

The soldiers cursed at the woman and looked at the young nuns seated on the ground, smiling. They took steps toward them, walking above the floorboard that Zarkhanna lay beneath. "What is your name, girly-girly?" one of the soldiers asked a young nun in Portuguese.

"Leave now!" The Mother Superior ordered. "General Nunda will strip you and beat you like the dogs you are!"

"Okay, lady!" The men spat on the ground and left the building, laughing.

So Zarkhanna was no longer required to spend her days hunting for food, raiding villages, and doing what the commander wanted done. Many things would be buried deep in her mind, and that is where they would remain. Like the time they raided a school dance, arriving to find teachers and students in happy dress, and leaving with their blood on the dance floor.

"Do not worry, sweet child," the Mother Superior had said in the months after Zarkhanna's rescue. "You are safe now." But Zarkhanna had other memories too. Dreams of people long ago, Mbundu people who lived even more simply than she did in with her mother. The dreams of these quiet, familiar people came to her on occasion and gave her relief from the visions of wars and guns and killings and bombs and rivers of blood. She did not know why she had these dreams, or who the people were, or why they seemed to know her.

Miss Alecia stood over her in her TAAG uniform, her hand outstretched. "Are you ready to go, Anna?" She nodded to the kind stewardess and stood up, adjusting her backpack and grabbing her pink suitcase. Outside, in the distance, she saw the soft green hills surrounding the airport, the sweet earth and cold waters that she and her mother and Auntie walked in, washed in, lived in. Two sparrows were caught in the high ceiling of the airport, unable to escape. She caught a glance at the family now standing in line waiting to board. After saying a quiet farewell to the hills, she walked with Miss Alecia through the narrow tunnel that led to the entrance of the aircraft.

There was a specific seat for everyone, and the fashionable Miss Alecia held a piece of paper that identified hers as seat 3A, which was close to the entrance. Miss Alecia placed her rollaway bag in a hidden compartment above her seat, and Zarkhanna sat down beside the window. Although the seat in between them was free, no one sat there. She watched as a long line of passengers moved past her. As the line stopped and started, Zarkhanna felt they were staring at her, as if seeing her were the purpose of their coming on board.

The family from the gate area made their way up the aisle and the girl in the red dress stopped in front of her seat. They eyed one another. They could be schoolmates, and for a moment Zarkhanna wished that it were she who was walking up the aisle with her family, going anywhere.

Zarkhanna wore no watch and had no idea what time it was. She had been told that the flight from Luanda to Washington, D.C. was fourteen hours, but not what time of day it would be when they landed in America. It took a long time for the plane to begin to move, as speeches were made by Miss Alecia and the General who was in charge of the airplane.

At one point she was given a heavy pamphlet with cartoons of life rafts and directions on what to do if the plane were to go into water. She knew that these speeches and diagrams were like the directions the commander gave before they entered villages, but what actually happened was always different. They would warn the assembled soldiers about the dangers they might encounter but had only seen them on occasion. Besides, Zarkhanna could often predict whether they would use their guns in battle or simply carry them as they stole supplies. She could also sense when the soldiers were given drugs, which affected the amount of carnage there would be.

It was best to be prepared as the pamphlet showed, but she was distracted by thoughts of her fate in the world of America. She sensed it would somehow be more than joining a new family in a foreign land.

She sensed that there were people there who already knew her.

The plane finally made its way down the runway, speeding faster and faster as if trying to get away, then lifting off in order to succeed.

She pressed her face against the narrow window and looked for the outline of the irregular coastline of Angola. To her, it resembled a puzzle. She now saw boats, some small that appeared to be fishing in nature, others large and holding containers, bobbing their way in the water toward destinations she could not see and would never know. Then, as suddenly as the plane was sucked up into the sky, a jolt of panic passed through her veins as she remembered something.

She picked up her backpack and began rifling through it, searching for the Ndimba, throwing aside notepads and a comb onto the seat beside her. She pulled out a book that one of the Sisters had given to her that morning to read on the plane. She found the sealed envelope with $40 of travel money allocated to her with a receipt from the Angolan Ministry for Displaced Persons, but still she could not find what she was looking for. She thought back to the last time she had seen the heirloom, the part of her own body that she now realized must have fallen off the seat beside her at the airport.

The Ndimba was gone. It was not in her backpack. It was not on the floor of the airplane. It was not in the compartment in front of her that held magazines and cartoons of slides and life rafts. Her blood pumped and she tensed like she did when she held onto her weapon or when her mother was angry at her and kept her from seeing her friends. Her breaths became faster as her eyes widened with helplessness. She wanted to get up from her seat and tell Miss Alecia that the plane must go back, but as she jolted up, the seat belt locked her in place. She realized that there was nowhere to go except where she was going, and now without anything she knew or wanted.

She looked down at the book that was now flipped open beside her and noticed a hidden pocket on the inside back cover. She picked up the book and looked around, as if she had found a piece of fruit that no one had noticed back at the base.

Miss Alecia had taken out a television screen from a pocket beneath her armrest, and the screen stared back at her with instructions she could hardly understand. Zarkhanna told her about the heirloom and Miss Alecia said she would call the Angolan airport about it as soon as they landed.

Zarkhanna then turned her attention back to the book's inside pocket. She pulled out the piece of paper that was folded neatly into it. Whoever had put it there had taken great care to fold it many times before hiding it in the compartment. Her mind raced back to the moment when the paperback was handed to her by a young kitchen worker at the orphanage in the minutes before she left.

Zarkhanna had been packing alone in the bunk room when the woman entered, as if on an errand. The orphanage often hired local women to help prepare the meals, but she had never noticed this one before.

"Hello Zarkhanna," she said, pulling the book from inside her simple gray dress. Handprints from baking were visible on her apron. The woman peered anxiously over her shoulder.

"This is an important book, and it would be a *good* idea for you to read it as soon as you can." They locked eyes. "Pay close attention to the end of the book, *minha querida?"* It was a thin paperback, frayed at all corners, with the title *The Outsiders* on the cover. She had been surprised that the woman knew her name.

"*Sim*," Zarkhanna had replied, shaking her head and stuffing the book into her backpack. She felt as if she were being given a sacred document, like psalms in church. But the thought passed quickly, as she was consumed instead with the news that Mrs. Carolyn White would not be joining her on the flight. The woman had kissed her on the cheek, then disappeared as quickly as she came.

Zarkhanna now opened the letter completely. The handwriting was familiar in a way she could not easily pinpoint. At first glance, it reminded her of her own mother's style. She looked at the note with questioning interest, knowing that whoever wrote it was someone she knew well.

The plane once again bounced in the sky and someone spoke over the loudspeaker, first in Portuguese, then in English, but Zarkhanna could barely make out the words besides 'experiencing turbulence' and 'seat belts.' She noticed that whoever had written the letter had continued on the other side of the paper. As she turned it over, Miss Alecia checked to make sure that Zarkhanna's seat belt was fastened. Zarkhanna nodded, holding the letter in her hand, like bread.

"Is everything OK, Anna? Do you need anything? This is just normal bumps in the air. Very normal." Zarkhanna nodded and managed a smile, the space between her teeth letting in slight amounts of air from the cooling vents above her head. "Thank you, yes," she managed to reply in English as Miss Alecia headed toward the back of the plane.

She returned to the letter, unable to understand its meaning even though the words were in plain sight. They could have been written by someone as alive as Miss Alecia, or long dead.

She sat frozen as she realized who the sender was, the last words written in Portuguese and the unmistakable signature. She felt an elation and a panic, not knowing if there was a difference. She re-read the last line as the plane held itself in the sky, screeching toward its unseen destination. It read:

*Be a good girl and know that I am with you. Love, Auntie*

If Zarkhanna could have placed the letter in a hidden pocket in her heart, she would have. But the date of the letter was six months prior. Whether Auntie had survived the war or not was as unknown as her destination.

# Chapter 2

Anna was awakened by the General of the airplane speaking over the loudspeaker. The plane had begun to shake and swerve in swoops. A squeaking sound came from beneath the floor as if someone were grinding a machine. As she looked out into the gray sky, she heard the sound again, and then again.

Outside her window, land was everywhere, populated by houses of all types, sizes, and shapes. In between the neatly laid out homes and neighborhoods, large fields loomed in perfect squares separated by roads. She could now make out vehicles moving along, some alone on roads, others on highways, where trucks and cars formed rows stretching for kilometers in all directions. Water and rain streaked across the airplane window. Anna felt like a cat peering out from under a bed, unsure whether the world was safe or hostile. She watched water droplets fall off of the wing, evaporating into the afternoon air only to be replaced by more droplets. They clung onto the wing like the tiny fish attached to a whale she had once seen in a schoolbook.

The clouds thickened, turning her view into nothing more than a gray curtain. She tried to calm herself by focusing on the other passengers in the cabin. Miss Alecia gave her a reassuring smile and a thumbs up. The plane now rocked steadily back and forth as it hurdled downwards in an oddly coordinated manner toward wherever it was going. Anna noticed that the vents above her head began to emit a tasteless vapor that was visible for only a brief moment before disappearing into the air.

The wisps began to thicken in the cabin, so much that it was hard to see the other passengers. Still, there was no smell, no taste, no alarm from the General, just a cold mist that stuck to her face like the wet bandages soldiers apply to their compatriots to soak up the blood from their open wounds. Unable to make out human forms or any sense of place in the airplane cabin, she turned her panicked attention outside. Immediately she noticed that the weather had cleared and the rain was gone.

The plane leveled and continued on a path which Anna was no longer sure had any destination at all. The land below was now completely in view, but it had transformed and was nothing like what she had seen only moments before. A dryness hung over the land as if everything pleaded for water, desperate for hydration. Every field. Every tree. Even the veins of brooks and rivers that now hardly filled their channels. It was as if some giant in the sky had taken a straw and sucked the water out of everything in sight.

And then she saw them.

At first, they looked like small machines working the fields, slow moving, in pairs or often by themselves. It was impossible from her altitude to see who or what they were, but there were hundreds of them in each of the square fields that she could make out. As she looked farther into the distance, the sun now shining brightly, she saw thousands of these moving creatures in all directions. The many homes and highways she had seen just moments ago had disappeared entirely, and all she could see now were green-and-brown fields separated by thin lines of trees. As the plane moved closer and closer to the earth, she started to make out what they were. Staring out the window, the scene beneath her began to take a disturbing shape. She looked around the cabin of the aircraft. Strangely the clouds which had once been outside had somehow penetrated the interior of the plane itself. She still heard the engines roar and felt the chaotic movement of the aircraft making sudden turns, but the other passengers were no longer visible. Miss Alecia was nowhere to be seen. Anna felt a sudden chill as the cloudy wisps covered her face and body so that she could hardly make out the seat in front of her.

She fanned the vapor away from the window and again tried to make out what was in the fields.

They were not machines at all.

They were men in tattered clothing, dirtied, ripped, and holding tools that hacked the soil. There were women too, sometimes with the men, by themselves, or near children. They also held tools for working in the fields. Some of the women wore long skirts and simple headdresses that lacked color, lacked any semblance of fashion, and were worn only to keep sweat from pouring down their skin, their black skin. For a moment, Anna thought the plane had returned to Angola, for everyone she saw in the fields shared her skin color, but the scenery was utterly unfamiliar.

Sometimes huge trees the likes of which she had never seen broke up the landscape, their tentacles reaching out toward the fields, offering havens of shade from the sweltering sun.

Anna looked into the distance for the many homes and highways that she had noticed only minutes ago, but the only buildings she saw were sporadic mansions, enormous in stature, mostly white and pillared with large green lawns and looming trees. These manors were far from the fields and Anna wondered why the people did not simply stop and walk toward the magnificent homes that offered shade.

Suddenly Anna detected a terrible scent; a musky odor combined with human sweat. As she held her breath, fear crept up her spine. The scene terrified her in a way that even the bloodied corpses of unknown villagers who had been hacked to death did not, because she felt this vision was somehow directed at her.

The people in the fields were all looking up at the airplane.

And she knew why they were looking.

They were looking at Seat 3A.

Hundreds of souls, perhaps thousands, were standing in these waterless fields and staring up at Anna. They were leaning on their tools and watching the plane, their heads moving slightly with the movement of the aircraft. She felt as if the plane were slowly passing by, like a leaf making its way down a river. If it were only the sight of these strange workers looking up at her, Anna would have observed them with no more amazement than when she noticed the television screen fold out of Miss Alecia's armrest. But Anna could read the feelings of these people in that special way that she knew about herself, and that Auntie had recognized in her.

It was as if they were locked in a collective prison with no walls. She felt waves of tears and winds of anger, and fatigue, oh, so much fatigue. It was a tiredness beyond how she herself felt on the thin ground cloth after carrying jugs of water for the army along dirt roads for endless kilometers. This fatigue she was seeing was beyond sleep, and something far more dangerous. These were people yearning for a rest so long that they might never wake up and be glad if they didn't. And as these collective emotions reached her body, they came with a profound sadness in a language she had never heard before.

And they were speaking to her. Their words were as audible to her as the roar of the airplane engines.

*Help us.*

*Help us.*

And then, as quickly as they came into view, a swirl of clouds once again took over the sky and droplets of rain crashed against the wings. The other passengers were once again completely visible, casually reading their books and magazines. Highways, roads, neat fields, and enormous parking lots sped by at increasing speed. A fire engine sat dormant on a runway. A yellow crane clawed at a large pit of dirt. The plane gently tilted from side to side.

"Ladies and gentlemen, we are in our final approach to landing in Washington, D.C. Please make sure your seat belts are fastened and that your seatback is in the upright and locked position."

Anna grasped the armrests and tensed her small frame.

Where would she find Mrs. Carolyn White?

The passengers around her seemed to be at ease, like they were in a car about to arrive at a friend's house. One woman held a makeup mirror and applied lipstick.

Anna pulled her backpack onto her lap and hugged it. She did not dare look out the window. But she could not ignore the motion outside. She now noticed other airplanes standing on the runway with their lights blinking, like iron birds waiting to join their flock. Large fields of pavement came into view and the plane landed at breathtaking speed against the tarmac. First it touched the ground and then bounced up twice before settling onto the pavement, as if unsure it had come to the right place.

Ronald Reagan International Airport was enormous. The TAAG plane rolled around the airport for what seemed like hours. It passed other airplanes that were connected to skinny passageways leading into the larger building. They reminded Anna of feeding tubes.

Small, motorized vehicles zipped between the aircrafts, some with rubber runways attached, and were driven by men dressed in orange jumpsuits, as if they were all on the same football team and taking their supplies to the big game. Another fire engine stood off in the distance, its hoses spraying randomly in all directions, practicing for a fire that was nowhere in sight. A dome-like building and large monuments stood in the distance. Anna knew Washington, D.C. was the capital city of America and wondered if that was the president's palace.

She was told by Miss Alecia that she would be escorted off the plane after all the other passengers left. They filed past her, and this time took no notice. Some were disheveled, stumbling with luggage and sleep. Others were perfectly dressed, like teachers going to a school graduation. The familiar faces she had noticed back in Luanda, the family, the old couple, the young backpacker, walked past her in fits and starts as the line moved awkwardly forward. The girl dressed in red followed her parents down the aisle. When her eyes fell on Anna, she waved goodbye and then exited the aircraft with her family.

Anna followed Miss Alecia and a group of other flight attendants off the airplane. They all wore the blue uniforms of the TAAG airline and tiny, small red caps concealing hair which was wrapped neatly beneath. The General of the aircraft walked alongside and spoke to Anna in Portuguese, and she responded with mostly yes and no answers. Her yellow dress and shiny black shoes felt ill-fitting. Teenage girls walked by dressed in jeans and carrying backpacks adorned with company logos she had seen in magazines. Her feet felt awkward in the loose shoes that now gave her a slight blister on her right big toe. Her long curly hair was no longer tied back, as she had fashioned it back home, and now hung loosely around her face, parted in the middle, black as her shoes.

"You are a very lucky girl," the General said in Portuguese.

Anna caught his eye and smiled, then darted her eyes toward the passing girls around her age.

An enormous hallway came into view, and she became conscious of the sound of many voices merging in the glass-enclosed space. She looked around at the mostly White people, their lips moving in conversations with husbands, wives, children, and airport workers dressed in jumpsuits, some carrying brooms. Televisions hung from the ceiling broadcasting news shows and sporting games. Anna became distracted by a newscaster talking about Halloween approaching. Her mind flashed back to the horrible Halloween Massacre which had killed so many UNITA supporters, making the commanders so angry, promising revenge. She dragged her pink suitcase behind her.

They walked down roads of carpeting and moving rubber mats. She had never seen so many White people before. The smell of sugar was everywhere.

"Her name is Carolyn White, is that right, Anna?" Miss Alecia asked as they approached a moving staircase.

Anna stepped carefully on the metal steps and pulled her suitcase onto the steel ridges. "*Sim,*" she answered, and then repeated the name of her new family mother.

"I'm sure she is right up there waiting for you. You must be very excited!" The group moved onto a moving staircase going upward and Anna took a small misstep before recovering her balance. The other flight attendants looked at her from their positions on the moving stairs.

On the opposite descending staircase, a White man dressed in a suit moved evenly down staring at a cell phone. When she looked up, she recognized the American lady whom she had met at the orphanage mission in Luanda. The woman was standing in a glass room looking out at her.

As Anna reached the landing, the American lady came through the glass doors and embraced Anna without speaking. Anna held onto her suitcase and allowed herself to be hugged.

"Anna, Anna, Ann-a!" the woman repeated. She held her by the shoulders and looked at her as if she were a piece of art. "Anna," she had tears in her eyes. "Welcome home, Anna."

Miss Alecia watched the new mother and daughter greet one another below posters of customs procedures printed in English, Spanish, and Chinese.

"We had a very good flight, didn't we Anna?" Miss Alecia said, handing Mrs. White a folder. She bent down on one knee and looked into Anna's eyes. She had on red blush and her perfume gave off a scent of ripe oranges. "Everything is going to be fine," she whispered. "You are a lucky girl to be here in America, but you will always be from our homeland."

*The people in the fields.*

Anna nodded without speaking and looked back at Miss Alecia and then up to her new mother. The American woman listened to Miss Alecia's words, but then began to separate the two travelers. Miss Alecia told Mrs. White about the lost doll, and information was exchanged between them.

Miss Alecia kissed Anna on the cheek and gave her a wink. She then walked toward a police booth where a single officer sat behind thick glass. Miss Alecia handed papers to the officer, and he stamped them with a loud bang. She turned once more toward Anna, gave her the same warm smile she had shared on the long airplane flight, and that was the last person from her country Anna would see for a long time.

"Anna, there is so much to tell you, and we are so excited to have you here. I am so sorry that I was not able to be with you on the flight, but it was beyond my control! Terrible!"

There was no luggage to collect, and they walked into an enormous garage. Anna entered the back seat of a blue car, and they began moving down a busy road. She missed her Ndimba doll. How could she forget it after managing to hold onto it for so long? She wanted to tell Carolyn, and she did.

"Your doll? Oh, yes that! The stewardess mentioned it. That's terrible!" Carolyn said. "But don't worry, your sisters Tabitha and Nita have lots of old dolls and I am sure that they would not mind giving you one." She caught Anna's eye. "Or we can go to a great big store and buy you any doll that you like! Would you like that?"

No one in the cars they passed looked familiar, or happy.

"Anna, the reason why I didn't travel with you is because of my visa. There was a last-minute problem. Do you know what a visa is?"

"Yes, Mrs. White. It's the papers that are needed to travel."

"You do not need to call me Mrs. White anymore, OK? You can call me Aunt Carolyn for now, and maybe mom one day, OK?" She spoke as if the matter were settled.

The sound of the phone ringing stopped her mid-sentence. "That must be Mark!" Carolyn pressed a button.

"Well, hello, hello!" Carolyn began.

"Hi Carolyn. Are we good?" a man's voice asked through the speaker.

"We are great! Anna is sitting in the back seat. She looks adorable! You can say hi to Mark if you like, Anna!"

Anna smiled and clicked her toes together in her shoes. She pulled on her curls. "Hi," she said in a little more than a whisper.

"Well, hello there Miss Anna, and welcome-welcome-welcome! Wait, can you guys hold on for a moment?"

Carolyn and Anna waited. Mark spoke away from the receiver, but they could still make out most of his words.

*"Take a look at the script. It's all in there. I told you that we need a character actor, someone who looks like a terrorist from...not someone who looks like someone's father."* Carolyn gesticulated to Anna as if she were trying to figure out to whom Mark was speaking. The phone was tussled on his end, and he returned to the line. "Carolyn? Sorry! Oh, yes, Anna, tell me, how was your trip?" he asked.

Anna and Carolyn started talking at the same time. "It was..." They both laughed and started to answer simultaneously again, stepping on each other's words. Carolyn took the lead.

"I cannot begin to tell you what I have been through! When was the last time I spoke to you?"

"We spoke in London, yesterday when you were trying to fly to Luanda and pick up Anna."

"Well, who knows what day it is with all the time differences. What time is it now?" She glanced at the clock on the dashboard. "5 p.m, so I guess it's 11 p.m. for me, and five in the morning for poor Anna here!"

"You must be exhausted," the man on the speaker said, but Anna was not sure to which one of them he was speaking.

Carolyn was dressed in a white suit that seemed similar to what the navy sailors wore in the city streets of Luanda. Her white sneakers had gold laces. A green-and-black silk scarf was wrapped perfectly around her neck. Her short blond hair was rounded like a helmet, not a hair out of place. She appeared to Anna to be about her own mother's age.

The man on the speaker continued, "So what happened in London? They wouldn't let you get on the plane?"

"I thought my visa was all set when I left the States, but when I checked in for the flight I was denied, and the plane left before I could get it sorted out."

"Jesus."

"But something amazing happened in London. Incredible. I went to the West End theater district and caught that ridiculous show with the... Mama...whatever." She thought for a moment. "I think there are some actors in that show who would be perfect for your film!"

He then spoke many words Anna understood but didn't know what they pertained to. She heard *film* and *script* and *character* and *shooting,* and *must travel tomorrow,* and Carolyn just shook her head and drove faster and faster down Highway 17.

Anna stared out the window as the cars and people passed by. Occasionally she saw a cross planted along the side of the road, sometimes by itself, sometimes surrounded by flowers, and she wondered if these were signs for nearby churches.

"Can you still hear me, Anna?" the man said.

Anna was jolted from her thoughts and sat up straight, as if caught napping by the commander. "*Sim!*" she said in Portuguese and then corrected herself.

"Anna, we're having pizza for dinner from Mario's! Are you hungry?"

"*Sim,*" she repeated and again corrected herself. On the plane she had eaten all the food that was given to her on plastic trays but was never sure if it was dinner or lunch or something else.

"Where are you guys? Are you close?" the man said.

"Close, we are just coming along the Rappahannock. Anna, that is the river we live near. We're almost home!"

"Ok, then. We'll see you soon, honey. The twins and Nita and especially Simba are all excited to meet you. And so is Chowder!"

"Do you like dogs, Anna?" Carolyn asked. "You are going to love Chowder!"

"Welcome to the family and welcome to 'ginia!" the man said. "Get ready for some of the best pizza in the world! I wish I didn't have to travel this week, but I do. Anna, I make movies. Do you like movies?"

The word brought back images of the movies that the UNITA soldiers sat around watching at night, smoking marijuana. They would go on vicious raids and then come back and take up the film where they had left off.

"Mario's!" Carolyn repeated, looking over her shoulder. "The best pizza on the 'tire planet! We should be home in ten minutes honey." The man on the speaker clicked off.

Anna leaned her head against the car window. As the vehicle began to round a long curve, Anna could make out a small mountain with two oddly shaped summits. "That's called the Camel's Hump," Carolyn said. "The trails are right near our house. We hike up there with your brother and sisters." On the opposite side of the highway, happy sailboats bounced on the river. A group of kayakers wearing wide-brimmed hats paddled by, waving to one another. Carolyn pointed as if she were a tour guide. "And that's the yacht club, Anna. I learned to sail there," she mulled.

The car turned off Highway 17. A large sign with the image of a river came into view.

Welcome to River Hills
Life as it should be
Please drive slowly, children playing

The vehicle turned onto a street, and the homes began to look like the ones Anna had been shown in photographs. Multiple cars populated the driveways. Basketball hoops were numerous, as were flowers and winding walkways leading toward the homes that, upon closer examination, appeared almost identical. Only the windows, doors, and placement of garages varied.

Carolyn swung the car into a driveway where a man and four children stood. She parked, turned off the ignition, and turned toward Anna.

“Welcome home,” she said.

The address on the house was 186 Tidewater Street.

# Chapter 3

The oldest of the Whites' adopted children was a seventeen-year-old from Brazil named Nita who came to the family when she was eleven years old. Her birth name was Juanita, but Carolyn had adapted it when the girl landed on American soil. Carolyn still called her by her birth name in the confines of the family household.

The new sisters were lying on single beds separated by a nightstand in the room they now shared. A lamp stood on the narrow stand and a digital clock was blinking A.M. although the hour was close to 11 p.m. Outside the window, old growth trees belonging to no one helped provide some privacy in the clean and clustered development.

"Você gosta de rap?" Nita asked. Although the girl's Portugese gave Anna a sense of familiarity, her Brazilian dialect made her old life seem that much further away.

"Sim. I like...a lot of rap music," Anna said, trying to pull her into English.

Nita took the que. "Well, if you don't have any music you really like, and I'm guessing you don't play sports or have a boyfriend, you might find it kind of hard here." The older girl stared at the ceiling. Her words were spoken gently, like a friend.

"I like boys," Anna offered.

"Really?" her new sister asked. She turned toward Anna and propped herself up on her elbow. "Tell me about one of your boyfriends."

Anna proceeded cautiously.

"Well, he's a boy in school. He plays soccer and is on the team in our village."

"Village?"

"Yes."

"You come from a village?"

Anna looked over at her. She felt like she had given the wrong answer in class. "I think, yes, I guess," came out.

"I'm from Rio de Janeiro. It's a city."

No one spoke.

"Well go on then. What's he like? I guess he's Black, right?"

She tried to think of a boy in Caxito or the army who she thought was handsome, or who was skilled with a soccer ball, but all the faces now jumbled in her mind and no one clear winner emerged. She was only twelve when the soldiers came to Caxito and took her mother and Auntie... and her. Years ago, there was a boy named Randall who had also gone to the initiation school and learned the ways of men, as she was taught the ways of women. They had spoken a few times, sitting on a rock.

"Randall," Anna offered.

"Randall? Do you mean Randy?"

"Randy, yes," she said.

"What does he look like?"

She tried to remember his physique, the length of his hair, the outline of his jaw. The moments clicked on.

"You don't have a boyfriend, do you?" Nita was now looking directly at her.

Anna looked at the ceiling and noticed the shadows of tree branches creeping across the ceiling.

"Well, whatever. You better get some clue if you want to survive middle school and make it to River High. I'll let you listen to my iPod. We can start with Beyoncé. She's Black, too." She rolled over. "Also, you'll need to get some new clothes. I assume you don't have any money." Nita's long hair fell toward the floor, a barrier Anna wasn't sure she wanted to cross.

"I have some money," Anna answered, remembering the $40 in American money given to her by the mission when she left. She told Nita the amount, and the teenager laughed.

"Like I said, no money. But don't worry, I know how to get you some nice stuff."

The hour crept toward midnight, and she felt the weight of the time difference. Still, she could not sleep. Thoughts of the people in the fields she had seen from the sky kept her awake, as did the softness of the bed.

When Nita fell asleep, her light breathing became deeper and longer. Anna got out of bed and walked down the hallway to the bathroom. The twins, Wyatt and Tabitha, slept in a room to the left. Five-year-old Simba slept in the room next to Carolyn and Mark's. She walked into the bathroom and stood in the dark, looking for the toilet before realizing there was a light switch.

She gazed at herself in the mirror and saw her reflection had somehow changed. Everything about her seemed bigger. Her upturned eyebrows seemed more pronounced, the space between her teeth had grown wider. Even her curly hair looked thicker, more unkempt and weird.

Voices startled her as she moved back toward her bedroom. Mark and Carolyn were speaking to one another downstairs, and Anna edged toward the staircase and quietly stepped down to the landing. She could just see their lower legs against the couch.

"We are going to have no problem getting this film picked up," Mark said.

"Uh-huh," was all that Carolyn responded. They talked for a while, using words like 'actors' and 'distribution' and 'location.'

Then there was silence. After a minute, Mark spoke up. "Carolyn, tell me. How many is enough?"

"You talk about them like they're cupcakes," Carolyn said. "I don't know. How about a baker's dozen?"

"Just trying to survive here, Carolyn."

"And so are children in the world who need homes. I just got a voicemail tonight about that Chinese boy we spoke about. I'm going to go to Richmond in a few weeks to do the interview."

"What about our family? Could you maybe just stop collecting kids and pay attention to ours?"

"There's nothing wrong with doing our part. Besides, the $10,000 adoption credit doesn't hurt, Mark, if money is the issue."

"Money is an issue, but that's not what I'm talking about."

"Then why are we talking about money?"

There was a pause as both sides tried to gather their thoughts. Then Anna heard words like 'subsidies' and 'adoptees' and 'disabilities.'

"There was nothing wrong with checking the box on the form to get the per-child subsidy. Simba was psychologically scarred and there's nothing inexpensive about taking him in and giving him a home, Mark. And the same goes for Anna. What that child has been through!"

The family dog, Chowder, now walked toward Anna, letting out a small yelp as he stared up at her while wagging his tail. He had a long snout and friendly eyes that peered out under yellow fur. The Whites both turned in the dog's direction before resuming their conversation.

"Carolyn, did I tell you that my movie's being looked at by Miramax?"

"Mark, it hasn't even been made yet."

"Yeah, but Barry spoke with someone at Miramax who said he loves the idea."

"Let's keep Priscilla and Barry out of our money troubles, Mark. Priscilla's daughters are all set to be Anna's welcome wagon. They don't need to be involved with every nickel of our lives." One leg rested over another, and a gold-laced sneaker swung freely. "Besides, I thought you said Barry was pretentious."

"Well, he thinks there's going to be a bidding war between Miramax and Universal for foreign rights, and he offered to do the legal."

"That so?" Carolyn said, a statement, then, "When's that day, Mark?"

Her husband ignored the remark. "Until then, we're living on the funds I'm raising for the movie plus this government money you somehow seem to find for these kids we take in."

"I resent that," Carolyn said. "We're doing important work. We're helping the world."

"What world is that, Carolyn?"

No one spoke. Anna could feel the tension between them.

Mark continued. "I'm on the road for the rest of the week. There's an investor group in L.A. that's taking me to lunch, and I expect to be signing papers by the end of the meal." His voice rose in a crescendo.

Carolyn batted it down. "Well don't forget your wallet, Mark, just in case you have to pick up the check."

Chowder barked again, inviting Anna to play with him. When his yelps became slightly louder, Mark and Carolyn looked in his direction.

"Do you really, really think that now is the time to make a sympathetic film about a terrorist?"

"Carolyn, if you weren't so busy traveling the world looking for your next adoptee, you'd know that *Invasion* is neither sympathetic nor about a terrorist. It's a comedy that shows the absurdity of any radicalized religion. It's funny!"

"Hysterical. I think I'll keep helping kids," she let out a quick laugh.

"But you never answered me, Carolyn. How many is enough?"

Chowder barked louder and they both looked over at him. Mark stood up from the couch and started walking over toward the staircase. Anna's breath quickened. The dog stared at Anna as Mark came into view.

"Well, hello, Anna," he said.

Carolyn jumped up from the couch. She hustled into the foyer and the two of them looked up at Anna on the landing. She was wearing a long nightgown and her feet were bare.

"Is everything OK?" Carolyn asked. The couple looked at one another. A painting of a Virginia scene hung next to an antique clock, seconds tapping away in sync with Chowder's tail.

Anna looked down on her new parents. Carolyn's green-and-black silk scarf was still wrapped around her neck. Auntie and her mother would have used it as a headdress.

Mark was the sort of man who had two completely different looks; one that was studied and confident with his eyeglasses on, and the second, thin and frail when he removed his glasses to rub his eyes. He and Carolyn seemed more like relatives living in the same house than husband and wife. She noticed that they rarely touched one another.

"*Sim*," she said and then translated quickly 'yes' into English. All three smiled.

Mark walked up the stairs toward her. "You must be jet-lagged," he said. "Tired from the time difference."

Anna stood in place.

"Are you hungry?" asked Carolyn.

And she was.

The air was taking on a chill as the days moved into November. In Caxito, rains would appear like a brief visitor, saying hello and then slipping quietly away. Here, rain moved in for days at a time and took over everything, penetrating deep into the skin.

"Winter in Virginia," Nita counseled. "A shitstorm."

"Yeah," Anna said, imagining snow. It was a Tuesday morning. Anna and Nita prepared to walk to school together, diverging at the end of their route toward two sides of the River Hills School—Anna to her eighth-grade homeroom and Nita to the high school cafeteria.

Out the front door of the White household, the girls turned left down Tidewater Street toward the Clubhouse, which was up on a hill overlooking the neighborhood, the largest by far of all the houses in River Hills. Behind it was a pool and a rolling golf course that was part of the River Hills Country Club.

An enormous oak tree had stood for more than two hundred years between the Clubhouse and the neat homes along Tidewater Street. The tree spread out across the road. One low-lying branch was supported by an iron pole lodged into the ground. Near its base, an old cemetery was surrounded by an iron gate with no latch. The headstones leaned in crooked directions.

The golf course extended everywhere, rolling fields covered by a perfect green carpet. Anna imagined it as an ocean transformed into a jade velvet landscape she could walk on for miles. The fields felt familiar to her, as if she had crossed them a thousand times.

"The Clubhouse sucks," Nita commented as she skirted its wide porches. "Totally shit-ass lame. Can't do anything. We go out on the golf course and get high, that's about it." Nita looked at her. "Do you get high? They do that in your country?"

"I think," she said. The soldiers had once forced her and she remembered throwing up behind a tent, another girl holding back her hair.

Nita picked up a stone and threw it at a tree. "My friend grows it, so I can get it for you at a good price. Keep it in mind." She was wearing another new pair of jeans. Anna noticed that Nita rarely wore the same pair twice. Her closet was stuffed with clothes, many with the tags still attached.

As the girls continued through a wooded area, the school came into view through an opening of the trees. It appeared to be made of brick boxes pasted and stuck together by a black membrane on top. Satellite dishes sprang from the rooftops, and a massive one sat in a grassy area encircled by a metal fence. A building that looked like an old church stood next to the school. The faded lettering on the side was still visible.

*Rappahannock Baptist Church*

A few service vehicles were parked in front of the old structure, now converted into a maintenance shack. A falling steeple tipped at an angle atop the church like an antenna broadcasting a long-ago sermon. The girls walked along the sidewalk that circumvented the school until it came to a T. Nita took the one to the high school and Anna the one to the middle school.

It was the last period and the third day of Ms. Romoldo's geography class projects, and some students had brought food typical of their assigned countries. Anna sat next to Mary Kane, who was assigned to Anna as a welcome wagon together with her older sister Cassy. They were the daughters of Priscilla and Barry Kane, close friends of Carolyn and Mark White.

"Our family has been in Virginia forevah," Mary told Anna on her first day of school, sucking in a breath from her asthma inhaler. "Whatever that means." Anna had just started to hang out with Mary and her sister. They had the same type of cell phone, a Motorola Razr. After Nita taught her how to text, Anna found herself wanting to start a conversation only to erase it, not sure how much was too much or too little information. She was hoping that the girls had moved beyond a forced friendliness to an actual friendship.

At 125 kids, the size of the eighth grade seemed enormous to Anna, but Mary claimed it was actually pretty small for Virginia. There were five homerooms, but most of Anna's day took place in one classroom overseen by Ms. Romoldo, a woman who Anna thought was too young to be a teacher.

Anna sat next to Mary amidst multiple rows of students. The air conditioning unit was loud, and she sometimes had trouble understanding her classmates' English. The make-up of the class was more varied than any school or restaurant or building she had been to in Angola. It struck her as a larger version of Carolyn and Mark's household, with white kids, Black kids, a few Spaniards, a Chinese girl, and a boy from India who looked like an older Simba.

Even so, when she entered the classroom, she often felt the thirty-odd students looking at her. She sensed them taking notice of her outfits, her hair, and her accent. Although her English was excellent, she felt as if her enunciation was always on display, with the other kids ready to pounce on any mispronunciation. She felt she was different for reasons only she could understand, but that these reasons were somehow different than what the other kids thought. She tried to laugh at what others laughed at, or wince at what others ridiculed. She wondered at times if she was the object of their jokes. Her loneliness grew with the hollow realization that no one in her class—not even Mrs. Romoldo—could point to Angola on a map, or even guess which African coast in lay.

She had taken to wearing a pair of blue jeans Nita got for her which had silver beads running down the legs. This week she wore her hair in a braid. Last week she had put it in a high ponytail like Cassy's. She tried to hide the space between her two front teeth by rarely smiling. A lot of her classmates wore braces, and she meant to ask Carolyn where they could be found in America.

Ms. Romoldo called on Mary, who pointed at herself in surprise before standing up in front of the class. Mary unfolded a large map of England and dropped it on the floor before picking it up again and taping it to the wall behind her. Mary shared with the class that her family was originally from England, and she passed out chunks of scones she had cut up before class. Other students spoke about countries in South America and Asia. A Chinese girl gave out small cakes which everyone ate quickly and then asked if there were more.

A week before, Ms. Romoldo had asked Anna to stay after school. Anna stood across from her teacher, pressing a pile of books against her chest. "Why don't you tell the class about the Congo, where you're from?" Ms. Romoldo said.

Anna stood in place, confused. "Okay," she said slowly. "I can do my project on the Congo. But I am from Angola, Ms. Romoldo."

"Did I say Congo, Anna? I'm so sorry! I meant Angola. Can you show me on a map where you're from?"

Anna studied the map of Africa hanging up on the whiteboard, narrowing down the regions before finding Angola halfway down, hugging the coast. She felt as if she were choosing a color for an art project no one would ever create. "Here," she said, pointing to the green shape.

"On the ocean! How nice! You must love going to the beach!" Ms. Romoldo exclaimed.

Anna nodded politely and walked out the door. In the hallway Mary leaned against her locker talking to some of the boys in their class. No one noticed Anna as she fiddled with her locker, put some books in it, and headed to her art class in the basement.

"Angola is a country on the west coast of Africa," she began when it was her turn to give the geography report. "It is the seventh largest country in Africa, bordered by Namibia to the south and the Democratic Republic of Congo to the north. It is on the Atlantic Ocean."

Many of her classmates were not paying attention. Some glanced at the clock above the door, waiting for school to let out, some carried on sign language conversations. Mary sat in the third seat of the row to her left, tossing a crumpled piece of paper toward Reggie, a Black student who sat toward the back of the room next to a boy named Port Moore. The boys laughed and tossed a plastic basketball at each other when Ms. Romoldo was not looking.

"Today, I have brought some *funje* for you all to try. In Angola, we have this with many of our meals. It is made from cassava flour, water, and salt." She wanted to explain how she and Auntie used to peel and grind the locally grown casava root—a sort of potato like staple—but she sensed that the other kids simply didn't care how flour was made or where it came from. Most of them just pulled it down from a shelf in their pantry. On the teacher's desk was a wide basket Anna had woven with a large Tupperware bowl inside. Ms. Romoldo prepared samples of the white porridge, spooning it into small Dixie cups. Mary balanced them on her science book as she handed them out.

Anna stood in front of the class. She could hardly conceive of her homeland as a foreign land. The people who inhabited Angola were diverse and varied. They spoke over forty different languages, whereas the people of the United States seemed to speak only one or two. Angola is enormous, whereas the state of Virginia ends just across the Rappahannock River, where it is bordered by other states with their own rules. Anna wondered if back home she would ever be assigned a report on America, and if so, what she would say. To her, America was a foreign country, not Angola, and it felt strange to speak of her homeland as a place so far removed.

The kids in the class tasted the *funje*. The purpose of the side dish was to even out the intense spices of many of the traditional dishes eaten for dinner. She could see several of the kids sneer as they sampled the bland food. Port Moore in the back pretended to gag.

"Are there bugs in this?" he asked from the last row. A few of the other boys laughed.

"Excuse me, Mr. Moore?" Ms. Romoldo asked, standing up.

"This tastes like grass," he said.

Someone coughed as he said something. It sounded like "ugga-bugga." Reggie and Port both laughed out loud.

"Mr. Moore if you cannot be respectful to your classmates, I will send you down to speak with Principal Dumont."

The boys stifled their laughter with fists to their mouths. One blew a raspberry which was audible to the entire class. A few of the girls put down their samples and looked over at the group of boys at the back of the room.

Mary spoke up. "Maybe you can use it to stick your mouth shut so it can't talk," she said with her back turned toward him. "Sorry it's not McDonalds!" She was a thin girl with hair down to her waist that she had never cut since childhood.

"That's enough," Ms. Romoldo interrupted. The students seemed to take sides.

The bell rang, and Mary helped Anna pack up the remainder of the *funje* and throw away the paper cups.

"Port Moore and Reggie Cooper are dumb as rocks. Don't listen to them," Mary said as they walked to their lockers.

"Totally," Anna learned to say.

"I hate them. You know Reggie's in love with Cassy."

"Well, that'll never happen!" Cassy interjected, approaching her sister from behind. She had come over from the high school so the sisters could walk home together.

"Want to come to our house for a while?" Mary asked Anna. "You can stay for dinner. My dad is grilling. He's really good at it."

The three girls walked side by side toward Mary and Cassy's house, which was within sight of the school. With the golf course visible in the distance, it looked as if the houses and streets were part of the game itself. The strong roots of gnarled centuries-old trees broke through the wet sidewalks, as if reminding them that they were there first. Anna matched her steps with the sisters.

Mary wore a long jean skirt that seemed stapled to her narrow waist. Cassy had boyish looks and wore a River High sweatshirt over her strong frame. The differing figures of the two sisters made them seem unrelated, but they shared the same unmistakable laugh, a giggle that came out of nowhere which accented their speech. For Mary, the laugh made her seem nervous, but for Cassy, it was a mark of confidence.

Mary and Cassy's mother, Priscilla, was gardening as the three girls approached. "Hi girls! How are y'all doin' today?" Her red hair, pulled back in a ponytail, was damp from the misty rain. Like Carolyn, she favored colorful attire that could be worn to an aerobics class, and her southern accent was strong. "Anna, sweetheart! It's so nas' to see you coming by so often!" She turned quickly back to her gardening. She reminded Anna of one of the Sisters at the mission, not so much for her looks, but because she asked questions and never listened to the answer. The Sister had been in charge of bedding.

"Now how are you today?" The Sister seemed so warm as she handed her the weekly linens. But when Anna would start to answer, the Sister had always moved on to another girl.

"Tell Carolyn I say hello," Priscilla offered. "Your mom, I mean!"

"I will, ma'am," Anna said, entering the house.

Now Priscilla addressed her younger daughter as Mary opened the front door. "How is your throat feeling, Mary? Still sore from coughing?"

"I don't feel great, Mama. I had to go lie down in the nurse's office again today." Mary was so thin that her backpack seemed to weigh her down.

"You go on upstairs and rest," Priscilla said as she stood up. "I have some errands to run in a lil' while."

The Kanes owned several houses in the neighborhood, and the one they entered was older and statelier than the newer construction River Hills homes, such as the Whites'. Mary mentioned that her great granddaddy had once owned most of the land where the neighborhood was built.

Entering the home, Anna could see the swimming pool in the backyard collecting drops of rain on the surface. Next to the pool stood the largest barbecue grill she had ever seen. In the living room, past the staircase, a giant sable antelope's head was mounted above the mantle, a trophy Mr. Kane had brought back from a safari.

"My dad got that in Tanzania," Cassy had said the first time Anna visited. "Is that near Uganda?" Anna didn't know.

Now she looked at the animal's head on the wall. She had never seen the Angolan native on display like this before. She knew the soldiers would shoot one for supper, illegal as it was. One evening, a sergeant with a deep scar on his scalp brought a slain antelope back to camp and carved it on the bare earth, its blood pooling in all directions.

"Isn't it against the law to kill giant sables?" Anna had asked, transfixed by the animal on the ground.

The sergeant stopped his carving and looked at the twelve-year-old girl. "In war, what is right is why we are fighting to begin with," he said, returning to his task. Anna had eaten the meal with the other soldiers, children, and commanders in the big tent. The captured villagers from the morning raid ate whatever was left.

The three girls now settled in Mary's bedroom.

The sisters sat on a white platform bed sharing a pair of Apple earphones. The tinny sound of *Stacy's Mom* by Fountains of Wayne escaped from their device and reached Anna's ears across the room. The air conditioner in the window hummed. An iMac sat on a white desk and the light fixture had the motif of a sailboat. Abstract posters in metal frames hung on the walls with costume jewelry hanging from them.

Anna was beginning to feel queasy, which had been happening often since her arrival in America. Not serious enough to make her have to lie down, the feeling just seemed to hang in her body, as if she had drunk bad milk without realizing that it was more poison than protein. Nita and Carolyn both thought it was the American food, or the weather, or simply all the changes.

She began to feel dizzier as the sisters talked about a prank they were planning to play on Reggie.

"Why don't we send him a note that says you want to meet him at Friendly's? Then we can all go, except you, and stare at him and then ask him who he's waiting for..."

"Is he dumb enough to think I like him?" Cassy was sitting up straight.

"Reggie? Did I tell you what he and Port were saying during Anna's report today?" She relayed the story.

"Well, I don't want to hurt the guy," Cassy said with some hesitation.

"We can say anything we want to Reggie or Port," Mary countered.

Anna looked up toward the air conditioner in the window, which had been making her feel cold. Strangely, some cloudy wisps started to come out of the vents, eerily similar to the mist that took over the cabin on her flight to America. She looked out the window and saw brazen sunshine.

Now she began to feel hot. Sweat started to bead on her forehead. She felt perspiration trickle down her neck and oozed into her body. She felt the vapor affect her breathing, and her nostrils filled with the dusty scent of an old forgotten room.

"We can say anything we want," Mary said. "What's today? Tuesday? OK. So tomorrow at school I'll put a note in his locker saying that you like him and that you want...."

The vapor in the air began to wisp through the bedroom, obscuring Anna's vision. She could hear more than she could see.

"...to date him and hook up this weekend but you don't want him to tell anybody...and then he will...be waiting...like...we'll call the other boys to see..."

The girls on the bed paid Anna no mind, caught up in their clever plotting. The white cloud continued to fill the room and Anna could only see through an occasional clearing. She was conscious that her friends were still planning their scheme against Reggie, but the details seemed to change, and Anna no longer recognized the boys' names, nor the location where the encounter would take place.

But then somehow, someway, Anna heard an entirely different comment. Like a distant memory, it came from the past but echoed in the present. Mary was still speaking, but the words no longer made sense.

Anna was struck by the musky odor in the room, like that of an attic of a long-abandoned house. The vapor from the air conditioner now reached every corner. Anna felt the weight of her upset stomach as she found herself gazing into a world that she recognized but could not name, like seeing a familiar flower in a brochure for a land to which she'd never traveled. It reminded her of when she was small, and a playmate had moved away. When the girl and her family returned years later, they stared for a long while before recognizing each other.

Sitting on the floor surrounded by the fog, Anna clearly recognized Mary and Cassy, but they looked like they were from another time. Mary turned toward Anna and smiled like a friend, but in that face Anna saw something else entirely. The expression was neither warm nor hostile, welcoming nor rude. It was the face of a girl who always had her needs met in every way.

Like a stage set that changes before the audience's eyes, Mary's room shifted dramatically. The platform bed that was there moments before was now an ornate maple bed frame adorned with a yellowish canopy. Instead of the white desk with an iMac stood an oak roll-top desk with parchment paper and a fountain pen like the ones Anna had seen in antiques stores in Luanda. The abstract poster on the wall had been replaced by a Virginia scene with horse-drawn carriages and oak trees standing along an old Highway 17, Camel's Hump in the background. The light fixture was now a candelabra.

Gone was the jean skirt on Mary as well as the River High sweatshirt on Cassy.

The sisters now wore printed cotton dresses, stylish in a time long past. Mary's had small daisies and Cassy's had purple rosebuds. Both were high waisted, billowing more fully as they traveled down their bodies and showing little beyond their ankles. Their necks were hidden by the high stitching of their dresses. They both wore lace-trimmed bonnets.

Anna closed her eyes tight so that the familiar, normal setting would reappear, and her queasiness would disappear. But when she opened them again, the sights and dusty scents only joined together with one another like raindrops on a dirty pane of glass. The modern double-hung windows now appeared as divided panes. Outside, the rain had ceased, and piercing sunlight now illuminated distant fields with scores of figures bent over endless fields of crops. The room had a musky odor.

Intense fear took hold of Anna. It was not the kind of fear she had experienced witnessing the butchering of villagers huddled together, nor was it the kind of fear she sensed when the Commander gave orders to drug-induced soldiers to carry out missions. Those were atrocities that were happening to others. This was something else entirely. It was the fear that she had fallen into a place where she did not belong, from which she could not escape. The fear was personal, and it spoke loudly. Her very life depended on the whim of these two girls from another time, and Anna's role was clear and unmistakable: complete servitude.

And then they began to speak.

"I saw yesterday that nigga' boy look twice at you when you were out taking air."

"To whom are you referring, Mary Louise?"

"Why Calvin of course, that son of the nigga' that killed our dear brother. Why don't we send that boy a message that you favor him, Sistah, and want to meet him at the shed?" the girl who was once Mary said through the mist.

"Why Mary Louise!"

They both glanced over at Anna who stared back at them. Her words were gone.

"Tell him that I like him and want to give him a kiss," Cassy said, her energy suddenly returning.

"Yes, a kiss! Then we will tell Mr. Tomkins that he's got a darky on his hands who likes to look at Kane girls. He knows how to deal with that kind," Mary said.

"Well, I don't want to get in trouble with Daddy though!" Cassy said.

"We can talk to any nigga' on this plantation we want to, Sistah, as lon' as it's not Sunday," Mary Louise said. "And if a slave boy is lookin' at one of us Kane girls, then we have the right to apply the kinda right disc'pline that Daddy in his day would rightly administer himself!"

They both glanced at Anna sitting across the room. "Don't mind Annabelle," Mary Louise said to her sister. "She's a half-wit, hasn't spoken in five years. And I bet that Calvin ain't even her real brother given the way those people breed!"

"But she do listen!" the girl who was once Cassy said. "Annabelle, go fetch some water for my sickly Sistah!" The girls giggled and went back to their conversation.

*Annabelle*?

Anna sat frozen in time.

That very morning, Anna had put on Nita's blue jeans with beads of silver for her class presentation, but now her outfit had changed into an itchy gray woolen dress that suffocated her skin beneath its coarse texture.

On and on the two sisters spoke, holding hands within the white haze that now encompassed the room. Once again, the queasiness welled up in Anna, but this time it had nothing to do with the vapor filling her nostrils. She now detected the smell of a land desperate for rain or water but, having none, sank deep into its own arid stench. It reminded her of the time she crawled under her church into a hiding spot full of dead insects and petrified rodents.

At that moment, the sisters looked back at her from beneath their bonnets. The reality of it all raced through Anna's veins like speeding horses.

The musky odor, the nausea, the strange outfits and spinning decor, all of it now overcame her in a wall of confusion. Without warning, her body tumbled out of the chair, and she hit her head on the hard floor.

Scenes and images from home, wherever home was, flashed beneath her fluttering eyelids. A soldier nudged her with the butt of his gun. "Time to get up, princess," he sang, muddied, laughing.

She felt hands on her face.

She felt water, perhaps a wet cloth, dampening her skin.

She heard voices she knew.

She felt a pillow beneath her head.

She opened her eyes and saw Mary and Cassy standing over her, like helpless nurses frantically wiping her brow and fanning her face.

"Anna!" someone said. "Anna!"

She felt her vision begin to return. The room was clear. There were three people, and she was lying on the floor. Looking toward the window, she saw that the rain continued.

"Anna, honey, are you OK?" asked Priscilla.

"Mary, go downstairs and fill a bottle with ice wata'!" Priscilla directed. Her red ponytail had come undone, and a single strand hung over her left eye.

"Carolyn is on her way. She said that you haven't been feeling well. Why would you go to a friend's house when you're sick, dear?" She did not wait for an answer. "Sick girls ought not to be spreading things around."

Cassy handed her mother another damp cloth and Mary returned with a fresh water bottle. The three formed an assembly line of care.

"Thank you," Anna managed. She began to sit up, but Priscilla pushed her down.

"Girls, can you go down to the kitchen and fetch me some crackers. She needs salt. I still need to run to the store before dinner, so please hurry!"

"I'm sorry, Mrs. Kane," Anna managed to say.

"Now, now, it's nothin'," Priscilla returned. She wiped Anna's forehead with force. Anna could still hear the distorted music of the Fountains of Wayne playing out of the earphone speakers, and she tried to focus on the music. She tried to take the towel and wipe her own brow, but Priscilla removed her hands. Outside, a bluebird hung on a branch and turned its head toward her before flying away.

When the girls returned with crackers, Carolyn was with them.

"Anna, honey." She was sweating and slightly out of breath.

"I would have called an ambulance, Carolyn, but she woke up as soon as the girls touched her," Priscilla said. Then, she whispered her concern. "I do hope it's not something foreign!"

"Well, she hasn't been feeling well, but I've been taking her to the doctor regularly to follow up on her shots. He thinks it's just the change in weather and diet." Carolyn put her hand on Anna's forehead.

"She'll be OK," Carolyn said. "Do you think you're ready to come home,

Anna?"

She nodded.

They started down the staircase with Mary and Cassy walking backwards in front of her, their arms outstretched as if ready to catch her fall. She still felt uneasy as there was no way to explain what had just happened, especially since she couldn't understand it herself.

"I think it must be something I ate," Anna offered. She was hoping that they would pass along this plausible story via text rather than the mystery that it was.

Mary and Cassy walked outside as Priscilla stood at the door. The girls walked beside Anna, holding out helpful hands that she did not need. The blue Audi was parked with the engine running, Wyatt waiting in the backseat and Tabitha in the front.

Carolyn stood by the driver's side door and called out across the roof of the car to Priscilla, who stood in front of her house's front door.

"I'm sorry about all of this, Prill. I'm sure all the girls will be fine. As I said, she's had all her shots, so there's no need to worry." Carolyn got into the car and lowered the car window on the passenger side. "Are we still on for dinner this Friday?"

Anna did not hear the answer. Instead, she got into the backseat beside Wyatt. Carolyn drove away while Mary and Cassy waved goodbye.

"Mommy said you were sick," Tabitha said. Today she wore a blue dress and gray stockings, similar in style to Carolyn.

"I'm OK," Anna said. "I think I'm just still getting used to things."

"We don't want to get sick," Tabitha said.

"Tabitha, do not speak that way to your sister," said Carolyn.

"Why not? She's not our sister!" Wyatt defended his twin.

No one spoke.

Anna looked at Carolyn in the rearview mirror. The twins' eyes darted toward their mother to settle the matter. She quickly switched on the radio. An ad for Mario's restaurant was playing. *For over 40 years, Virginians have enjoyed the great food and warm ambience of Mario's Italian Restaurant.* An accordion accompanied the dialogue.

"Why don't we have take-out dinner from Mario's tonight?" Carolyn suggested. "Are you kids hungry?"

Wyatt slammed himself against the back of his seat. "I'm not hungry."

"I'm hungry!" Tabitha blurted from the front seat.

"I guess I am a little," he said.

"Mom, you said you don't want us to catch whatever Anna has!" Tabitha said.

Carolyn turned to look at her daughter.

"Tabitha, I didn't say that your sister's sick. She's a teenager and, well, things happen with teenage girls."

"She's going to make us sick!" Wyatt whined.

"Wyatt White!" Carolyn snapped.

"Well, are you sick?" Wyatt turned to Anna. Slight in stature, he was gawky with large ears, which made him seem younger than his age. "You shouldn't cook for us if you are."

"Wyatt, I do not like the way you are speaking to Anna, and she is not your cook. She helps around the house like you and your sister should. If this attitude continues, you're going to your room as soon as we get home."

The ride home continued past the clean and organized homes of River Hills. Bicycles were toppled over in driveways and soccer balls littered lawns. A man sat on a riding mower talking to a neighbor who was walking his dog. Service vans from pest control and cable companies were parked in a few driveways.

The Audi pulled into 186 Tidewater Street.

Mario's would be fine with her.

# Chapter 4

It was the twins' birthday, and the entire family was enjoying a barbeque celebration in the backyard of their home.

Mark tended the grill. A supermarket cake sat on the outdoor table with a box of candles. A pitcher of lemonade stood beside a wooden bowl filled with potato chips. The twins and Simba loaded hamburgers and hot dogs onto paper plates and ate them standing up. Carolyn and Mark were saving their appetite for a date night with Priscilla and Barry. Nita watched the scene like a reporter, unsure if she wanted to participate in the scene.

Five-year-old Simba pointed a disposable camera at the family and took many pictures. Anna posed for him with her hair up and then with her hair down. She was wearing a blue velour sweatsuit, which she borrowed from Nita.

"Anna, why is there a security tag on your shirt?" Carolyn asked.

"It mine," Nita said, walking over. She moved to Anna's side, grabbing the security tag as if it were a strand of fabric that did not belong. "They must have missed it. I can take it off." She pulled a large safety pin from her purse, and easily removed the tag. Simba took pictures of Anna, Carolyn, the cake, and his watch, which had a fish motif. Under the table, Chowder waited patiently for scraps.

Anna had spent part of the morning preparing Auntie's *sambal* sauce for the barbeque, but it sat untouched on the table, except for the flies gathering around.

"Everyone has to try Anna's sauce," Mark said.

Tabitha stuck her finger into the bowl and brought it to her lips. Anna watched for her expression.

"Gross! I'm not eating that. It's spicy. I want ketchup!"

Anna looked at her closely, thinking that she must be joking. Everyone loves *sambal* sauce.

Carolyn stroked Tabitha's hair. "Anna or Juanita, can you please get some ketchup from the pantry?"

The two older girls headed inside, bumping into each other as they went through the screen door.

"I'll get it," Nita said.

"Also, the mayonnaise!" Wyatt yelled.

"And pickles!" Carolyn added.

Nita opened the refrigerator door. "Get ready to clean the windows next. They always have something for us to do."

The modern kitchen had all the latest appliances surrounding its island. A small vintage sign, *You don't scare me, I have kids,* was propped above the oven. A poster of vegetables, photographed and phonetically named, hung on the wall above the kitchen table. Untouched cookbooks were stuck together on a shelf below the TV cabinet.

"I have more chores than any of my friends," Nita lamented.

"There doesn't seem to be that much we have to do," Anna defended. "Doesn't everyone help out?"

"Everyone except the twins," Nita said. "They're sacred."

"What about Simba?"

"He may as well not even be here."

The two went back outside, Anna with a family-size bottle of ketchup, Nita with the mustard and mayo. Mark had grilled more food than any normal family could consume. Everyone sat down at the table, Mark and Carolyn at each end, disconnected, with the twins and Simba on a bench facing the house. Nita and Anna on the other side.

"Now that you two are nine years old, what do you want?" Mark asked. Maybe a trip somewhere?"

"I want my own bike with two wheels!" said Simba.

"It's not your birthday!" Tabitha scolded. "I want to...go to a rodeo. In Texas."

"Horses, Dad! I want to ride a real horse!" Simba exclaimed.

"First you have to learn how to ride a bike," Wyatt pointed out irritably.

"Why don't you teach him?" Mark suggested.

"He's too little," said Wyatt.

Carolyn spoke up. "He's not too little. You learned to ride when you were the same age, and he's almost as big as you were."

"No, he's not," Wyatt countered.

"I can try," Simba said, sitting up straight. He was going through a growth spurt that made his head seem too large for his body.

"Can I learn to bicycle too?" Anna asked.

Mark and Carolyn glanced at each other.

"It's not your birthday, Anna," said Mark.

"When it's your birthday, then you can ask for things," Carolyn explained.

Nita gave Anna a soft kick under the table. "Told you," she whispered.

"Told her what...Juanita?" Carolyn blinked steadily.

"Nothing, Mom," Nita retreated.

"When *is* it my birthday?" Anna asked, tilting her head to the side. She was not sure if, like her name, Carolyn had changed that too. She had thought it was in May.

"December 7," Mark replied.

"November 17, Mark," Carolyn corrected him, looking at Anna.

Tabitha stuck her tongue out at Anna.

"That's rude," Nita said as the oldest sibling.

Carolyn closed her eyes and turned to Nita. "Where on Earth did you get that shirt?" she asked. The low-cut halter top had tiny gold and silver flower-shaped beads.

Nita looked down at her chest. "The mall," she said. A small price tag hung from the side. "I might return it," she said.

Mark had an announcement. "Everyone, I have to travel on business tomorrow." No one spoke.

"But you just went away," Tabitha whined. "Where are you going now?"

"I'm going to..." Mark spun the ice cubes in his soda while his eyes wandered. "Where am I going?" he asked no one. "Florida! The investor group that put together the funding for *Erin Brokovich* and *Almost Famous* saw some of the dailies we shot and..."

"I'd love to go to Florida, Mark," Nita interrupted. "To the beach.

Could you please take us to the beach?"

"It's a business trip, Nita. I'll be busy working on my film."

Carolyn looked past Mark's head at the trees growing over the screened-in porch and made a note to call the gardener, but she'd have to check the cost.

"When will we get to see your movie?" Wyatt asked.

"When it comes out next year, right here at the movie theater!" Carolyn raised her eyebrows and took a sip of her Seven Up, which hid a small amount of white wine. A hummingbird bounced around a nearby butterfly bush. The shrubbery hid the neighbors' house, which was only steps away. Amid the cluster of homes they lived in, privacy was less about what could be seen than what could be heard. Many a private backyard conversation was later whispered about at the Clubhouse bar.

The family, full, continued to pick at their food, and the conversation lulled. For a moment, Anna felt like they were at a public park where no one knew each other.

"So, kids, your father and I are going out tonight with the Kanes. Ronnie is coming at five o'clock," Ronnie was a heavyset Jamaican woman who had worked for the Whites since the twins were five years old. "And I'd like Juanita and Anna to help out."

"I'm going to a concert," Nita said flatly. "What concert?" Mark asked, surprised. Carolyn looked hard at Nita, who didn't respond.

"Well, Anna will be here at least," Mark said.

After the twins held their breath, made their birthday wishes, and blew out the candles, everyone ate cake. There was no song.

Tabitha turned and looked around her. "Is our birthday over?" she asked.

Carolyn got up from her chair, went over to her daughter, and hugged her from behind. "Your year is just starting! This is yours and your brother's weekend!"

Tabitha had been promised a manicure and Wyatt a trip to the bowling alley.

Nita stood up and started picking up the plastic forks and paper plates. Anna grabbed the condiments. Carolyn took a phone call on the back corner of the patio and Mark sat staring into space. Simba followed Anna into the kitchen with the empty pitcher while the twins played tag in the grass beyond the patio.

"Of all the families in the world to be parachuted into," Nita lamented as she threw the plates into the trash, "I had to land in this one. Try arriving at a senior party on a bicycle. Then you'll know what it's like to be me," she said.

A bicycle of her own sounded good to Anna.

Later that afternoon Simba and Anna watched an episode of *The West*

*Wing* together in the living room while the nanny could be heard opening and shutting cabinets in the kitchen. When the episode ended, the two walked into the kitchen hand in hand. The twins were eating Ritz crackers with butter, which they had arranged into a checkerboard on the kitchen table.

"Can Simba and I go for a walk before dinner?" Anna asked Ronnie. Tabitha looked over, wondering if they were invited.

"Why don't you kids neaten up da playroom first?" Ronnie suggested. The heavy-set Jamaican woman had worked for the Whites since the twins were five years old.

Anna flicked on the basement light and descended the steep, carpeted stairs. The room was scattered with games, toy soldiers, and boxes overflowing with trucks and dolls long abandoned by the growing twins. A small trampoline sat in the middle of a pool of blue cushions. A handwoven fanner basket, started by Anna, sat in the corner.

The outline of Camel's Hump could be seen through one of the narrow basement windows near the ceiling. The room smelled of new carpet and cool cement. Simba played with a yellow construction truck, pushing it toward Anna in an attempt to engage her. But Anna was focused on the basket she was making to store Simba's toys in. Although she had been able to find sweetgrass in the woods nearby, she had mixed in some local bulrush, which seemed like it would be durable. She touched one of Auntie's signature triangles that she had placed around the base of the basket.

When she weaved, she found herself wondering about Auntie and her mother. She knew that death halted the body, she had seen that with her own eyes, but what happened to their souls? Like Jesus. She put the basket back in the corner and strode up the stairs with Simba trailing.

"Can we go for a walk now?" Simba asked Ronnie, whose green-and-white apron said *We be Jerkin*. She had one hand on her hip as she stirred a pot of chicken soup. She nodded and wiped her brow with her forearm, pushing her hair net slightly askew.

"You always askin' me what you know your own momma and daddy say no to!" she said, continuing to stir. "You kids lucky I good to you, but you be back on time for your supper, or I forget you asked!" she said. "Or else!" she finished as the two headed for the door with a peanut butter and apple sandwich that Anna had prepared for her little brother. Tabitha watched her half siblings walk out the door.

Simba and Anna headed right out the door toward Camel's Hump trail, which began at a cul-de-sac at the end of the development. Frequented by joggers and walkers, the ten-minute climb to the top was just long enough to get the heart beating. Nita hiked up with her high school friends to get high at night. Carolyn fast-walked it with Priscilla. Teenagers used it as a lovers' lane. Even climbers honed their skills on the opposite side, where the steep cliffs toward the east fell down to Highway 17.

"I want to go to the top!" Simba said.

"Think that you can make it?"

"Yes! I'm strong!"

"I know you are."

With a surprisingly fast stride, Simba bolted ahead. The trail was wide and worn by decades, no centuries, of people, young and old, following in each other's footsteps. Large boulders covered by carpets of thick moss hugged the trail, which headed straight up before cutting sharply to the right at the top. Anna walked steadily while Simba galloped around the corner ahead of her whistling.

She noticed her heart beating harder than it should for such a short hike. She knew that just on the other side of the hill lay the curve in the highway where she thought she had seen the man in the ill-fitted suit standing by his cross with a broken neck. She could hear the echoes of the cars speeding by, but she wanted to conquer her unfounded fears.

Anna tuned into the movement everywhere around her. A sudden rustling startled her, but it was just chipmunk scurrying home. Tree branches swished in the breeze. Birds warned each other of her presence. Critters jumped from foliage to rocks, escaping to and from their hiding places in the crevices of the small mountain.

But for what she saw next she could not ever be prepared.

Up above, through the woods off the trail, two Black travelers were walking. It was an old woman followed by a very large man walking in line. They descended straight down the hill, undisturbed by any obstacle in their path. She thought they might have traversed right through the trees. When they passed by her, they did not look up and were silent, as if she were not there.

She noticed the man had enormous hands and appeared like a gentle giant. The older woman was slight in nature, perhaps five feet tall and she carried a bundle of clothes in her arms, like laundry. Her faded dress looked like it had been dragged in the dirt for some time. Her headdress, once a fine one perhaps, looked like a rag dotted with holes.

"Anna! Where are you?" Simba called.

The wind brought a musty scent to her nostrils that was as familiar as it was disturbing. It was the same musty odor she noticed in the airplane when the people in the fields came into view and later when she saw Mary's room transform. The mustiness was mixed with the scent of sweat from working in hot, arid conditions.

Her eyes followed the two travelers on their silent journey to nowhere, perhaps down the hill toward a home they no longer inhabited. At that moment, the couple stopped and looked back up at her. Anna froze, not certain if they could see her or not. Perhaps they were just changing direction. Or maybe, she thought, they were looking for someone, anyone, to guide them back...to where, she did not know. They did not make a sound. Even their footsteps in the woods were silent. Like the man with his cross along Highway 17, their mouths were still, but Anna thought she heard them speak. Their message echoed liked Simba's whistling, bouncing in the small valley between the two peaks of Camel's Hump, searching for a response.

*Help us,*

*Zarkhanna,*

*Help us.*

No one in this country knew her by that name. Carolyn had assigned her a new one upon arrival, as she had with Juanita and Simanto. And when others are admitted to the White family, in Carolyn's quest to make right with the world, they too will receive suitable names to remove them from their heritage and insert them safely into the America they now belonged. It felt so strange to be called by her name by these timeless strangers wandering the woods in search...in search of...?

When Anna walked past a tree with an enormous trunk, the couple failed to appear on the other side. They were gone. The musty scent had dissipated, leaving only the fragrance of Virginia bluebells. This time the confusion that she had felt was replaced by a sense of purpose, a sense of responsibility toward things she both knew and couldn't yet know.

The first among them was making sure Simba stayed safe. As she picked up her pace, she felt her fear fall behind her. The old couple meant no harm—no way. They were lost and seeking something from her, as if she were some kind of religious person and they were her followers. Admittedly, their appearance had initially frightened her, like when her corps of soldiers entered a new village. Passing the villagers in the streets, she sometimes feared they would shoot her, when in fact they were fetching water or even, one time, tying ribbons on trees for an upcoming wedding.

Simba's whistling stopped and Anna hurried her step. She glanced quickly over her shoulder to where the wandering couple had been but saw only trees.

She caught up to Simba.

"You're slow, sister!"

"No, you're just fast, little brother."

They reached the top of Camel's Hump and cheered. Anna looked at Simba's fish-themed watch. A grouper pointed near six o'clock. Ronnie would expect the two of them back soon, but the view of the Virginia sunset was too captivating to walk away from. Anna had to take a minute or two to admire its beauty.

Although she had been to the top of Camel's Hump several times, including once with Cassy and Mary to share a warm beer they had found in their garage, every time there was something new to see. In the direction of River Hills, she could make out the winding layout of the mostly white homes and black driveways. Although the Upper Hills section was a twenty-minute walk, from here the neighborhoods blended together. The golf course stretched in all directions, capturing every hill, every brook and landscaped feature in its color war. Isolated clusters of magnolia trees stood firm against the onslaught. The Clubhouse was at the center, master of the fields, master of the greens, master of all the houses. Golf carts wandered up and down the fairways in the twilight.

"My great-grandfather and great-great-grandfather or something lived there," Cassy had pointed out when passing the Clubhouse on a few occasions. "And we owned all this."

Anna had followed the sweep of Cassy's arm motioning across the fields. "It was a plantation called Nottoway," she said, shaking her head up and down. "We had slaves, lots of them...Isn't that messed up?"

*"Totally,"* Anna had said. It was a word she had picked up. It meant lots of things.

From where Anna and Simba now stood, the enormous oak tree stood guard in front of the Clubhouse, marking the spot between the smaller homes of River Hills, where the Whites lived, and the statelier residences of Upper Hills, where the Kanes lived.

To the east flowed the Rappahannock River. Down below, Highway 17 hustled its way toward the nearby town of Tappahannock. Across the curved highway they could see the River Hills Yacht Club, where boat instructors motioned to rowers adorned with bright orange jackets and sailors caught the breeze.

"Are you a good swimmer?" Simba asked, looking toward the river. A few jet skis sped along, avoiding the small sailboats.

"Yes, yes I am," she replied. "Knowing how to swim is important."

The boy continued to stare at the river below. "Can you teach me to swim?"

It was less of a question and more of a plea. Anna touched Simba's hand. His smile was gone, and she wanted it to return.

While there were a handful of siblings at her orphanage who looked out for each other, most were on their own. All the children knew that the adults, however kind, were not the same as parents. Most had never had a sister or brother to play with or care for them. The adults were responsible for them. They fulfilled all the children's basic needs, except for love, which had been stripped away from them in a thousand different stories. There were many children she came to know there, but none felt like a brother or sister. This new attachment she felt toward Simba was as foreign to her as the state of Virginia, but closer now, because she was there.

"I will teach you to swim," Anna promised. "We'll ask Aunt Carolyn to take us to the pool and I'll give you lessons." The boy looked satisfied.

Anna excused herself to go to the bathroom in the woods. She knew this infraction was not typical in Virginia, and was definitely not practiced by Cassy or Mary, but toilets in Angola were far more primitive. During her year in the army, they did not exist at all. For her, going in the woods would always be a habit, neither good nor bad, just familiar.

In search of a suitable spot, she noticed a deer path going off the summit and followed its narrow ribbon to a small clearing. The open rock face, about six feet wide, was encircled with vegetation.

As she crouched, a baby chipmunk darted in between two rocks. When she was ready to leave, she saw the chipmunk again. Anna knelt on her knees and peered into the crevice, hoping to see the critter staring back at her. Instead, she saw something pushed way toward the back. She couldn't tell what it was. When she reached her hand in, the tips of her fingers touched something smooth and soft. She reached in farther, rotated and tugged it until it broke free of its hiding place.

It was a small leather pouch that appeared very old. She tugged at the leather string that held it closed. When the string did not give easily, she gently grasped the bag to try to discern its contents. It felt like nothing more than some sticks, stones, and dead leaves. She touched the leather to her nose. It smelled organic and musty. She held it in her hand, trying to decide whether to take it with her or leave it behind.

"Anna!"

Through the foliage, she saw Simba waiting for her on the bench put there by the River Hills recreation crew. He stood up and waved.

"I'll be right there!"

"Hurry!" he said.

She experienced a head rush as she stood up and she stumbled back against a thin tree. Finding her balance, she saw that the tree leaned over the edge of the sheer cliff she had often seen from Highway 17. She remembered noticing rocks tumbling down it to the boulders at the base right off the highway. She grabbed the tree as she found herself leaning toward the precipice. The cars below looked like toy trains rounding the curve. A few loose stones hobbled down, ricocheting off sharp boulders as they made their way to the base. One boulder protruded up like the tip of an arrow. She started to feel vertigo.

"Coming, Simba!" She called out as she ran back down the deer path, reaching him moments later. His mood brightened quickly, and he smiled all the way down the trail toward home, the leather pouch tucked securely in Anna's pocket.

"I found something cool today." It was just after 11 p.m. and Anna and Nita lay in their twin beds. The light from the streetlamps created a soft pattern on the ceiling and closet. A Forever 21 bag stuffed with clothing sat beside Nita's bed.

"Cool," Nita said.

No one spoke.

"OK, tell me," Nita said. A trace of cheap alcohol from her night out hung in the air.

"I took Simba for a walk up Camel's Hump, and I went off the trail for a minute to...see the view. And I found this really old sack hidden deep in the rocks."

Nita took in the information.

"I hope you didn't bring it in here," she said in a monotone. "I don't want bugs in the room." Her breathing became heavier.

The sprinklers started up on the lawn and the whoosh of the water sounded like rain splashing in the wind. The volume went up and down as the sprinklers spun in circles, whipping the porch with loud splatters. As Anna listened to the rhythmic spraying, her mind traveled back to Caxito, to her home, and to her journey.

"Are you awake?" Anna whispered.

A quiet murmur came from Nita. Her head moved on her pillow as she exhaled. Her long braids fell off the side of her bed.

"Are you sleeping?" Anna whispered more loudly. The night was her private time, and she used it to sometimes explore the house. Tonight, she wanted to find the letter that she had discovered in the book on the plane, one of the few connections she had to her former life.

She had to read it again.

She swung her feet toward the floor, keeping an eye on Nita, as if Anna were still a soldier stealing in the night.

*This is an important book, and it would be a good idea for you to read it on the airplane,* the kitchen worker from the mission had said.

Anna opened her closet gently. The light automatically came on as she entered the tiny compartment and quietly closed the door behind her. In the months since she had arrived, it had been stashed on the top shelf of her closet, the letter tucked into the back pocket. She reached for the book on the back of the shelf where she had also put the leather pouch she found on her walk and retrieved both items. She opened the book to the hidden sleeve in the back. She unfolded the letter and began to read, translating the Portuguese into English.

Zarkhanna,

The woman who gave you this letter is someone I know, but I have no idea if it will ever reach you. She has information on the missing children of the war, and she promised to look for you, and to keep looking.

The afternoon you were taken away, I managed to escape and spent six months with the army. I am in a hiding place too secret to reveal in a letter. I never wish to think about the evil I saw and experienced, but, like you, I have survived until now.

If there is a way to find you, I will.

Be a good girl and know that I am with you.

Love Auntie

The letter was dated April 8, 2002, six months before Zarkhanna left for America, after everything and everyone she loved was taken away. Carolyn, Mark, Nita, Simba, the twins, Mary, Cassy, and River Hills...this was her life now.

Whether Auntie was alive or dead depended on how hard Anna prayed.

Anna refolded the letter, brought it to her lips, and kissed it. She noticed that Nita was stirring and got quickly back in bed, taking the book and the pouch to bed with her, and rested it on her chest. Nita got out of bed and headed toward the bathroom as Anna pretended to sleep. The letter made her feel every possible way, from deep sorrow to a joy that had no words. Nita returned to her bed.

"I can't sleep," said Anna.

"Cool," Nita replied as she pulled the covers over her head.

The night brought a stillness to the room. Outside, cars occasionally rolled by the residence, the sprinklers continued to slap the back porch, and a single dog barked.

"Does getting your period hurt?" Anna asked. Maybe it was the circumstances of the last few years, but she had not yet experienced this sign of womanhood.

"No, it just kinda sucks. Don't worry about it, you'll be OK."

"Back home, we learned about it in initiation school," Anna said.

"I'm tired. Going to sleep...What's initiation school?"

To Anna this was like asking what food was for, but she took the question. She wanted to talk about it, to bring herself back to her people and her past. She had never told anyone except Auntie and her mother what happened at the initiation school. Now she was feeling a need to share who she was and where she came from, for herself most of all.

"It's a school that prepares girls for growing up by teaching about our culture and native traditions. They give lessons on all sorts of things, like how to dress and act, cooking, and dance, and stuff like that."

Nita was quiet. After a pause she asked, "Is that where they cut you down here?" She pointed in the darkness toward her crotch.

"Sometimes," Anna offered, and Nita gasped.

"Growing up, this woman named Mrs. Proud sold us vegetables in our village. I had noticed that she spoke mostly toward the children in her presence, so I wasn't surprised when I later learned she was the local promoter for this school. She was a teacher, but Auntie said that there was nothing that woman could teach me."

"Mrs. Proud," Nita said with a laugh. "And Auntie. Ha!"

Anna continued. "One day when I went to her house to buy potatoes, she told me that I'd be joining her school. She was heavy set, and no one knew why she was so heavy because she was no different than anyone else in Caxito. But people in the village looked up to her because it was said she could speak with the ancestors."

"Sounds like voodoo to me," Nita said, half asleep. Her breathing had been heavy, and Anna had not been sure if she was listening. Either way, she wanted to tell, and so she did, even if it was just for herself.

"One night I heard my aunt and my mother arguing in the kitchen. I'd been sleeping in the next room. I remember there had been a meeting at the church that evening about the war and what was happening everywhere. Women were not allowed, but a few had gone anyway, and word was spreading quickly. People were arguing in the streets, and I remember a few women yelling at the men. I was wide awake when I heard my mother and aunt enter the house. They kept their voices down, but I heard them anyway..."

"Wanda, why would you let that crazy old woman teach Zarkhanna? What exactly is she going to teach her anyway? You and I didn't go to these schools. Mother and Father forbid it!" Auntie said.

"And what of it? The problem with this country is that we have all these governments telling us how to be. The Portuguese government is one thing, but now America and Russia and who knows what's next. Zarkhanna needs to learn about our culture, our heritage, and who she is," said Wanda.

"I understand, but you are not really going to allow your daughter to be cut and butchered? To have her labia stretched like some farm animal?" Auntie objected.

"I want her to learn and to respect the traditions and values of the Mbundu people. Richard and I discussed it when she was young. He felt strongly about this and set aside money specifically for her initiation.

"I listened to my mother and Auntie and wondered what exactly I needed to learn. I had heard about procedures being performed on girls, and I lay awake that night wondering why."

Nita was now fully awake, Anna's words like a cold splash on the face. "Did they...do anything to you?"

Anna was quiet.

"I ended up going, and Auntie and my mother continued to fight over it the whole time. Auntie pleaded to let me go with her to Luanda to attend the International School there. She said that because I was smart and had done so well in school I could go there for free. She argued that the initiation school was primitive, that the world was changing, that Angola was changing, and that's why there was so much talk about war. Once again, my mother told Auntie to stop trying to interfere. She said she didn't have the right to tell her how to raise her daughter.

"I am just asking you to be supportive, Samara. Zarkhanna looks up to you, respects you, and this is what her father and I want for her."

"The next day, Auntie took me to the school, which had to begin that day because of the full moon. This was related to menstrual cycles, but since I hadn't gotten my period yet, I was confused," said Anna.

"So, when you got there, this Mrs. Proud...did things to you?" Nita probed.

"It was a rainy day, and we had to get there very early. Auntie wanted to stay but wasn't allowed. When she addressed Mrs. Proud, the teacher barely looked her in the eye. Auntie wore an orange handbag, wedge high heels, and a colorful headdress that flowed into a scarf. And she was unmarried. I knew Mrs. Proud did not approve. She told Auntie that she didn't belong in the village, that she should go back to Luanda."

"So what? Women can't wear what they want? That's crazy!"

"Women are allowed. It's just that Mrs. Proud didn't think they should be."

"Then what's the problem? It sounds really screwed up. You must be glad you're out of there." Nita's voice had risen in anger before once again cooling down.

"I think sometimes Auntie waited outside the school because she worried they'd do something to me."

"Well, did they? Is that what they do in Africa?"

She did not know what happened in Africa. She only knew what had happened to her.

"The students came from villages throughout the region. A few other girls from Caxito were there too. We dressed up in sheepskin skirts with grass hoops, which we had seen women wearing along the riverbanks. My mother had made a clay necklace for me to wear, oooand the other girls wore similar ornaments. Our skin was painted with white and black soil, *phepa* or *pilo,* depending on which community we came from. Then, Ngaka arrived.

"I was surprised because I recognized her. My friends and I thought she was strange and made fun of her behind her back. We were taken to a lodge outside of town. It was more of a shelter really, with straw walls and roof supported by trunks of mopane trees. Inside it looked like any other classroom with chairs and a table in the front. Sitting in our grass skirts with painted faces, we listened to the Ngaka tell stories of our ancestors and the terrible things that happened to them. She explained that suffering is woven into our lives and is an essential part of our personal identity, as with all people.

"The Mbundu people were sold as slaves for centuries and the Ngaka believes the sweat from our bodies represents their tears. She told us we would all remain slaves until we shared the agony of our ancestors. We were allowed to ask questions. One girl wanted to know if her father would ever come home, but the Ngaka did not have answers to these types of questions."

Anna looked over at Nita, facing her, eyes wide.

"I went there for at least a month, maybe longer. Auntie walked me every morning in silence, and I think that she stayed close by while I attended the classes. She did not approve of my being there and sensed that she needed to stay close by. Since my father was no longer in the village, and my mother was neither divorced nor a widow, I was assigned a lower-level group called Senkoyhi, three levels down from the top. We made masks and figurines, and I remember giggling with the other girls during a lesson on marriage. They taught us a dance called the Ngoron, whose steps were very particular. It took forever to get it right as we were corrected at every turn. Once this dance was mastered, it meant we had completed the initiation and would be free to return to our families."

Anna wondered what Nita thought of all this. She had not heard of anything like this in the United States. In Caxito, the customs were something most people valued or at least accepted, and, in a weird way, Anna was proud of them.

She paused to see if the older girl was still awake and looked over to find Nita propped up on her elbow, looking as if Anna were telling a ghost story.

"One morning, after I had slept in the lodge for a week, Mrs. Proud took each girl one by one to a small nearby hut where the Ngaka was waiting. Eventually, it was my turn.

"The Ngaka was a tiny old woman with a slight figure. She was barely five feet tall and looked more like a large child, but she had they grey eyes that were sort of dull. Up close I could see that she was younger than the hard years showed on her face. A wooden necklace in the shape of a crescent moon hung around her neck.

"She did not speak like other women, which Mrs. Proud said was because of her powers. She gestured for me to lie down on the table."

"Why didn't you just run away?" asked Nita.

"I wanted to. Especially when I saw the knives laid out on a clean white towel, and the spots of blood on the table. Mrs. Proud took my hand and assured me the procedure would be quick, that this was an important part of the initiation into growing up, and that she was there to help me, not hurt me.

"I lay down on the table holding Mrs. Proud's hand, closing my eyes tightly. The Ngaka stood over me and I braced myself for what was to come. When no one touched me, I peeked through my eyelids. I could see the Ngaka's hands spread over my body, like she was kneading bread without touching the dough. Eventually, Mrs. Proud asked her if she was going to do the procedure, but the Ngaka was silent. After some time, Mrs. Proud pulled me up to a sitting position facing the two women.

'This girl is a Kimbanda,' the old woman said. 'A Diviner.'

"I looked into her eyes, which had been dull but were now bright and clear."

"But how could the old woman's eyes...?" Nita questioned.

"I can't explain it. Maybe they were only clear for me? They reminded me of the the eyes of a child who was born centuries ago. They seemed to be smiling, crying, talking, singing, and seeing me all at the same time, and when my eyes met hers, I felt no fear. She seemed like a friend, a friend I had never met, or once knew but couldn't remember. I can't explain it."

"Obviously," Nita said.

Anna surprised herself by how much she was telling Nita about what had happened to her. She had never really talked about it, and only Auntie and her mother knew what had really happened.

She again looked over at Nita, whose eyes were still wide as she lay on her side. Anna looked at the ceiling and continued.

"Mrs. Proud looked at the Ngaka woman and me as if realizing that she was no longer needed in the room or the conversation. People from distant villages were filing into the room carrying candles through doors I could not see. The flames created white wisps that made the air hazy. They wore clothing from another time, but they all seemed familiar. A man with a lazy eye smiled at me with so much kindness. Beside him was an enormous man in green overalls, gentle as a kitten. Other people seemed as connected to me as my own parents. It reminded me of All Saints' Day. We were all there to celebrate. The Ngaka looked at me and started speaking in Kimbundu, which I don't speak, but I can understand a bit.

'Speak to the spirits, Zarkhanna. These people were taken from this place and forced to work as slaves. They need you. For what, I cannot say. So, speak to the people here and ask them what it is they want you to do.'

"A white fog filled the room, and I could no longer see Mrs. Proud at all. I felt that everyone there had something to tell me, but there was no time to listen to them all. The Ngaka herself joined the group and began to talk about rain or the lack of it.

"Something like 'there was no rain, there had been no rain, it would not rain.' The large man gestured with his enormous hands as he spoke about crops and his family dying somewhere far away. They all seemed to be close and I knew them as they knew me. They told me I could help them as easily as I could sweep a floor, but I had lost my voice and had no idea what to say even if I could."

"Weird." Nita said.

But Anna was now as much talking to herself as to her new sister. Her words became animated as she recalled these events that had happened so long ago, but so vividly close to her memory.

"The Ngaka repeated that I was a Kimbanda and told me that I could feel the stress and strain of whole communities, and that I could ease the suffering of my village, even the entire province. I didn't know what she meant. I only knew that I had seen the people in the room and they could see me.

"Then she took my hand and told me what awaited me. She said that I was going to be asked to travel. She said that a Kimbanda from long ago had misspoken and the community at large was suffering. I would go to this place, and I would understand what needed to be done—and it would happen at the base of a certain tree. I would know when the time and place was right.

"After a while, the old woman's eyes became dull again and it was just the three of us in the room. The old woman told me to take off my sheepskin skirt and had me lie back on the table. I do not remember much of what happened next, but I may have screamed when they touched me. The next thing I knew Auntie had rushed into the hut. Mrs. Proud and the Ngaka looked up as the door swung open and Auntie just started yelling at them. She ran to me and blocked me with her arms out wide. She told them in no uncertain terms that I was not to be touched.

"Mrs. Proud became angry and argued with Auntie. She said that I would not be able to complete my initiation, but Auntie would have none of it. There was a lot of yelling, but Auntie was even more adamant than Mrs. Proud and the Ngaka and eventually I was taken back to the lodge."

"Did they kick you out of the school?"

"Since it was so close to the end, I was allowed to continue. We finished making our masks, which had meanings and symbolism related to the various lessons. I remember some were about how to act around boys," Anna laughed.

"We finally mastered the Ngoran dance and on the last day Mrs. Proud presented each girl with a cowhide dress, beads, ornaments, a new blanket, a colorful towel, and red ochre to rub into our skin and braids. Then we all stood outside the lodge, and it was deliberately set afire and burnt down to the ground. Afterward, we were allowed to return to our villages. I remember my mother hugging me. Even Auntie had tears in her eyes." As Anna finished her story in the darkened bedroom, she felt as if she had lived the initiation all over again, the mixture of warmth and happiness she felt. It seemed so long ago.

So much had happened so quickly in her country. Maybe something had gone terribly wrong, and the spirits had been disturbed from their slumber and took out their anger on her village and her family.

When she turned toward Nita, she saw that the older girl was fast asleep. The shadows of branches stroked the ceiling. A door opened down the hall and someone turned on a faucet. Anna listened as the water went down the drain and quiet pumps engaged somewhere in the basement of the house. The washing machine beeped on another floor. Somewhere in the neighborhood, an electric garage door opened, and the distant sound of sirens rose and fell with the wind. Anna's breathing steadied, her chest rising and falling under the soft weight of the book and the leather pouch under her covers. She moved them carefully to the floor.

She wanted to keep them safe. The book was her only connection to home. And the pouch...intrigued her. When she had untied the leather string hoping to find money or something valuable, she was disappointed to find nothing more than some odd rocks, bird bones, and a piece of bark. She thought of discarding it in the garden, but something about the little bag and its contents seemed worth holding on to.

This book and the pouch were secrets she could keep, even if they were worthless. She didn't want them to be found by Carolyn or Nita. Keeping them in her closet was risky, as Carolyn often added clothing to their wardrobes and Nita sometimes borrowed her shoes. Anna wanted to find a better hiding place for the contraband, so she got out of bed and crept down the hall with her treasures.

Anna's bare feet fell softly onto the carpeted stair, and she took each step slowly so as not to wake anyone. Chowder opened one eye as Anna passed him in the foyer, and his tail slapped the floor twice. She heard the dishwasher humming and the furnace kick on. She figured the basement was as good a hiding place as any, perhaps under the fanner basket she was making. She held the book and the pouch in her hand and opened the basement door.

After descending halfway down the stairs, she felt the plush landing give way to a crude and splintered plank that heaved slightly under her weight. The light went out and she found herself standing on a dimly lit landing with a ladder leading down to a floor below.

The room had the musky odor combined with human sweat that she had experienced now on several occasions.

Yesterday, Simba had hid behind a water tank in the basement playing hide-and-seek. Now the tank was gone, as were the cement walls, the mini trampoline, and the boxes of forgotten toys on the carpet. Instead, the wooden ladder descended to a crude dirt floor. Moonlight streamed through windows, which were little more than square openings roughly cut into the wall. As she reached the base of the ladder, she saw a chimney with an open hearth and iron cooking implements beside it. A cane chair had been propped against the front door. A yellow-and-green patterned throw rug that resembled ones she had grown up with in Caxito covered a portion of the floor.

Through one of the ill-framed windows, she could make out the outline of Camel's Hump, which helped orient her. She knew she was still on the site of the Whites' River Hills property.

Looking around the room, she became aware that she wasn't quite herself. Her frame felt smaller, her chest flat, and her hands and feet looked like they belonged to a younger girl. Her arms and legs looked shorter too, and her vantage point was that of a child of nine or ten, and not a day older. But she was physically there in every other way.

Gone were the familiar sounds of the White household. Instead, a dog barked in the distance and toads gurgling in the night. She looked around and saw that she was standing in a rustic cabin, so roughly built that she could see between the slats in the walls. As she took the last step off the ladder she lost her balance, landing on the floor with a thud.

And then she saw them.

A woman and a man in a bed in the corner had been awakened by her clumsy step. She walked over and stood at the foot of their bed. The woman nudged her partner as she sat up and looked at her. Anna blinked at them, frozen. She felt caught, but had no idea what she was caught doing, or not doing.

"Annabelle, have some water, child, and go back to sleep." If the sound of the woman's voice surprised her, she did not feel any fear. It was the calm, gentle voice of someone who knew her.

"Annabelle?" The man lying beside the woman said, smiling warmly. She noticed that one of his eyes seemed to stare into space. It did not scare her.

Anna remembered one time, when she and the soldiers invaded a village, she came upon a cement shack and burst the door open. The man inside had not even bothered to look up at her. One of his eyes wandered. She raised her gun, but there was nothing in the old man to hurt her. As she turned to leave, she apologized. She felt the same urge now—to say she was sorry for waking them, that she did not know where she was. But the distance from her thoughts to her words seemed like centuries, so she said nothing. She grabbed a jar of water that was sitting on the table as if trying to blend into the strange surroundings. She took the jar, less because she was thirsty and more to call less attention to herself.

"Good girl, Annabelle," the man said.

*Annabelle, again.*

She looked back at them and saw they had turned their backs and returned to slumber. Although this tired old cabin was as foreign to her as the land she came from, she felt that she had dug her toes into its dirt floors before, and it was a place she once somehow knew. As sure as she felt the splintered ladder rung in her hand, she knew this couple cared for her—knew her, even, dare she admit, loved her.

She began to once again ascend the ladder and stopped halfway. Someone was sleeping in the loft. It was a boy sleeping with one hand hanging over the side of his crude bed, his fingers slightly spasming as he dreamed. She looked back down below and scanned the cabin further. Dirty grey clothing hung from thick nails in the cabin. The remnants of severely worn-out shoes rested on the floor. Bottle flies buzzed in and out the windows. The place was clearly a home, but it lacked the most basic features of even a poor residence in Caxito.

She sucked in her breath as she caught sight of a small doll hanging against the wall. She recognized its shape immediately, but it was so out of place that she felt it might as well be floating in the middle of the ocean. The ornament-like wooden doll had embroidered beads that went from a deep yellow to a bright red. Its eyes were shaped like suns with pupils painted a dull ruby eye. A green amulet shaped like a heart hung against the doll's neck down to its heart.

Anna's own heart leapt.

There was no mistake, and no possible explanation for what she saw. It was hers. It was the Ndimba doll she had left behind at the airport in Angola.

Her family heirloom.

# Chapter 5

The next morning, Anna awoke to the sound of a lawnmower whirling outside her window. She looked over at Nita who was beginning to stir in her bed.

She thought back to the encounter in the basement. After ascending the ladder and then walking onto a platform that led to stairs, she had found herself back in the normalcy of the kitchen. Chowder slapped his tail as she emerged from the basement. She remembered stashing the book with Auntie's letter and the leather pouch under the cushions of the loveseat that sat in the foyer area between the kitchen and the living room. Now, she breathed in deeply and took in the sweet bluegrass that was being kicked up by the mowers. But it was mainly the Ndimba heirloom on the wall of the shack that she remembered this morning, despite the impossible nature of it being there at all.

She thought back to the look in the eyes of the people in the bed. It was clear that they both recognized her as someone they expected to see in their space. But as bewildering as the brief scene was to her, the entire experience had a familiarity to it, as if it were a mural painted on a building that she had walked by a thousand times, but only now stopped to notice that the painting was in fact of her own house. As much as she thought it must have been a dream, she had only to look at the floor in front of her bed to see the obvious trail of dirt footprints she had brought from one world to the other.

It had now been six months since her arrival in River Hills. Sleep was difficult. Whether because she was still on another continent's time, or the flood of changes, she couldn't say. She would lie awake at night listening to the sounds of the neighborhood and wonder, or speak with Nita on a myriad of subjects, whenever the older girl welcomed conversation.

Whatever was on Camel's Hump, or roaming in the woods, or even in her own basement, she didn't know. But as baffling as these experiences had been, she was convinced that they were as real as the pillow she now rested her head on. She now felt that she belonged on Tidewater Street, and that whatever it was that kept trying to get her attention was in no way out to harm her.

It was as if she were playing nurse in a hospital filled with people she knew, only they were behind closed doors, and she had only to knock to see the familiar faces and find out what was wrong. And if that really was her cherished Ndimba hanging on a hook in the very basement of the very home she lived in, wasn't it hers to go retrieve? She began a plan to revisit the basement cabin, if for nothing else than to get a closer look at the heirloom she had lived her life holding, protecting, and cherishing until ultimately, she lost it.

She got out of bed and ended up spending the greater part of the day over at the Kane girls' house, but Mary had become obsessed with Port Moore and Cassy had started up with a junior. Most of their banter now concerned plans to either meet or avoid the boys, and they rarely asked Anna's opinion. Last week was the middle school dance; Reggie had asked Anna to be his date, but she declined because she felt like he had been pushed into asking. Next thing she heard he was going with a girl from another school, whom everyone thought he'd wanted to go with all along.

"You are my date tonight," she had said to Simba as she weaved her basket on the night of the dance. She promised herself she would finish each basket with the white triangles that Auntie had taught her, now just an instinct in her fingers. Ronnie had fallen asleep in a chair and the twins were both on sleepovers.

"What's a date?" he had said, concentrating on a building he was making with his blocks.

Nita had not been asked to her senior prom, which was being held at the Clubhouse. She had sat outside in the parking lot with a few of her friends, drinking rum and waiting for the after-prom parties to start out on the fourth green of the golf course.

The next evening, Anna had returned from Mary and Cassy's house to find the entire family, except for Mark, sitting around the kitchen table.

"There she is," Carolyn said when Anna entered the house.

"I was at the Kane's house," Anna responded, then realized that no one had asked. She put her windbreaker on the loveseat. Underneath the cushion sat her secret.

"Everyone, I have good news," Carolyn began. Wyatt and Tabitha were seated at the table eating spaghetti. Whenever Simba ate pasta, he tended to spill it all over the floor, so Carolyn had asked Ronnie to go out to McDonalds and get him a cheeseburger. It was a like a gift for the boy, and he unwrapped it slowly with eyes wide.

The bowl of pasta they had laid out for Anna sat untouched on the table. Nita opened and closed her flip phone as if it were a make-up case.

Carolyn began her speech. "Your father and I have found another child that we think would be perfect for our family. He is from China! We all can learn the language! But he is also a star soccer player, Wyatt. You love soccer!"

"Great," Nita murmured. She looked at Anna and rolled her eyes.

"Why?" Tabitha asked.

"Why what, Tabby?" Carolyn's perfect strands of hair encircled a blond helmet on top of her head. "There are boys and girls in this world that need the kind of love and caring that we have in this house. Your sisters Nita and Anna, and your brother Simba..."

"They're not our brother and sisters," Wyatt interjected.

"Are too," Simba said, looking down. He stuck out his tongue toward Wyatt. It was pink against his dark brown skin.

"Here we go again," Nita said.

"Excuse me, Juanita?"

"I said...that's great Mom."

Carolyn blinked several times and held her stare at the oldest girl. Anna looked down and noticed a folder on the kitchen table labeled International China Concern. The folder was thick, and a paper form jutted out that Anna could see had been partially filled out by hand as well as a photo that was partially covered.

"Does anyone have any questions?"

"I do," Nita said. "Is he a brat, like Wyatt?"

"Mommy!"

"Shut up, *Juanita*," Tabitha jumped in, saying the name with disdain.

Simba took another bite of his hamburger and began to chew slowly. He sipped on some water and spilled it on his chin.

"When is he coming to our family?" Anna asked.

"Thank you, Anna. Thank you for that kind question. At least you have the manners I expect, even though you have not been feeling well. Let that be an example to all of you." She raised a finger in the air and pointed it around the table, as if casting a spell.

Carolyn took the stage. "The answer is...we don't know yet. We just know that he has been preliminarily approved to come to us, but we need to go through the visas, same as what we did with Anna." She paused in the story. "Just like we did with our wonderful Anna," she corrected. "But it will be lovely, and I know that all of you will welcome a new brother to our home." At this, the phone rang, and everyone recognized that Priscilla was on the line.

Carolyn spoke into the phone as if to broadcast her triumph. "Yes, everyone seems excited." She cupped the phone. "Aren't we?" she asked the family. She sipped on iced orange juice and nodded her head. She continued into the receiver. "The world is so full of need, and we are so blessed here in Virginia that I just feel that it is our responsibility to look up from what we are doing and to widen the narrow vision that is ourselves and say that there are children...."

Anna looked toward the door to the basement. The sight of it held more intrigue than any fear she felt about anything that was or was not down there. After all, as unexplainable last night's journey had been, the door also held toy chests and wooden blocks for Simba and a fanner basket that still needed Auntie's signature white triangles.

Carolyn spoke about her new adoption plans to Priscilla, and neither the twins nor Nita noticed when Anna walked away. She opened the door to the basement and began descending the steep staircase.

The light flickered for a moment before coming on strong, whitening the concrete walls. The trampoline sat in its place with a purple ball on top, deflated. A yellow construction toy crane sat with its bucket lifted in the air, a few marbles trapped inside. Outside one of the basement windows, she could make out the exact same view of Camel's Hump she had seen from the old shack that she had seen during her night journey. It was the only thing that connected the old wooden shack in the night to the modern envelope she now lived in. But one thought was clear. Here, there was nothing more to see, and there, there was nothing more to fear.

She looked up to see Simba descending the stairs. He was carrying a bag of pretzels that Carolyn did not see him take from the cupboard. Food was not allowed to be eaten anywhere except the table. Breaking this rule always received swift reprimand from Carolyn and Mark, but when the twins disobeyed, the scolding was more of a reminder, whereas when Simba and Anna transgressed, they were more likely to face punishment, such as having to throw the food away.

"Simba, you are not allowed to eat down here!"

"I know, but I forgot." His brown eyes rested on Anna.

"OK, I won't tell anyone. You can play for a while," she offered.

"Yay!" Simba opened the bag of pretzels and spread out a few of them on the floor. He started to stack them and then placed a few against the tower so that it formed a pretzel sculpture. Anna watched him, neither wanting to play nor wanting to leave, because if she left, Simba would follow, so one place was as good as the next.

The boy had been raised by his father during his brief life in Bangladesh. He was due to enter kindergarten in the fall, but since he had not attended preschool in River Hills, he had few if any friends. The twins preferred to play with one another, and during those times that Anna preferred to be alone like the teenager she was, she saw that he played by himself in the living room, usually making forts out of the cushions and hiding with Chowder in the soft caves. He would often be found asleep in these chambers. Carolyn tended to get angry that the living room kept getting disturbed.

"Let's play school, Anna! You be the teacher, and I will do what you tell me!"

Anna sat cross-legged on the floor. The stale odor of the cool basement felt natural compared to the air-conditioning that filtered through the house.

"OK, brother. How about we do math?"

"Yuck!" he said, then reconsidered. "OK, then!"

The boy looked at her as if she were a magician about to show him tricks. She placed a few of the pretzels from the stack into a separate pile and asked him how many were in each group. The boy watched her hands move and answered her questions correctly. As she was unable to stump him with addition and subtraction, she playfully tossed the pretzels at him. This quickly escalated into a full-on pretzel fight with both laughing and eating half the ammunition. They both lay on their backs and looked up at the ceiling, a maze of white plastic pipes that fed the home.

"You're my real sister," the boy said, and he swung his leg over hers.

She turned her head toward him, but the boy kept staring up at the ceiling. The words crept from her ears into her mind and then through her body, tingling her fingers and then shooting down her legs toward her toes before racing back again through her.

"Well, you are my real brother, and I will take care of you."

"I know," he said and then sprang up and ran toward the stairs. He stopped on the first step, and then turned and stepped toward her as she pushed her hands against the floor to sit up. He had only to lean down slightly to find her cheek, and he kissed her quickly before running back upstairs. She followed after a few minutes and walked past the twins and Carolyn, who was talking to them about activities this summer. Anna went up the stairs and entered her room, where Nita was sprawled on her bed tapping on her cell phone.

"Welcome to Carolyn's orphanage," she said without looking up. Anna sat down at the computer desk. She had hoped to never hear that word again, but here was Nita bringing it across the ocean from her old world to the new one she had joined. It made perfect sense to Anna for Carolyn and Mark to continue to adopt.

Carolyn's happy news reminded her of those announcements she would hear from Mother Superior that such-and-such Catholic boy, or such-and-such Protestant girl would be joining them. The feeling Anna had then, as she had now, was neither joy nor surprise. It was more like scraping her knee again in the same spot.

She never chose to come to Virginia. She was told by the Mother Superior that she was leaving as if she was being told that she was having chicken for supper. If her father were alive, or her mother had somehow slipped through another window, or Auntie had managed to make it through the war, then, yes, she would easily choose any real family. But short of anyone she knew or loved appearing at the front door of 186 Tidewater Street, she would have to start making choices about her own life. Going back into the basement and finding out whatever it was that was happening was going to be her first step.

She placed her fingers on the keyboard, called up Netscape, and searched for books about Angola on the bookstore Amazon.com. She thought back to everything that had happened last night and retraced every step, from lying in bed telling Nita about Mrs. Proud to noticing the time when she returned from the basement.

She had been in her nightgown. She had been carrying the book with Auntie's letter in it. Could the book have been the trigger? One afternoon she had been in the basement with the book, and everything was as it was supposed to be. She searched her memory and came to the leather pouch, which she also had with her last night.

The relic seemed as old as the shack that had appeared before her eyes. She had had the item in her hand when she descended the basement steps, and it was the only possible explanation of how one world disappeared and the other emerged. Most of all, she wanted to know what was so familiar about that place, who the couple in the bed were, and most of all, how they knew her. She began to devise a plan based on what little she knew. She remembered what the woman in the bed had said to her.

*"Annabelle, have some water, child, and go back to sleep."*

Nita interrupted Anna's thoughts. "One day, I'm going to go back to Brazil, she said. "There is a little town called Parati where I am going to buy a house. It's not so hot in the summer like it is here."

"Oh?" Anna responded. She was now clicking away on the computer. Her teacher had told her that there was an Angolan embassy in Washington, D.C. and suggested she should visit it sometime. It was odd to think that her entire country could be reduced to a single building, but here a photo of the building appeared, and she clicked through the ambassadors and diplomats that represented her home country. Ndalu was a football player whom she remembered her father talking about. She stared at his image.

"Have you ever been to Washington, D.C.?" Anna asked her sister.

"Duh. Where else do you think we go? Of course, I've been to D.C. You really should learn about the United States."

"Can't we go with Mom and Dad?"

"Don't call them that, Anna, trust me." She looked up from her phone. "You'll be disappointed."

"Well, can't we?" Anna persisted.

"This family is always too busy adopting the next kid." She had her legs up on the wall with her arms outstretched, one hand holding her phone. "I can take you there myself. Why do you want to go?"

"There is an Angolan embassy, and there's probably one for Venezuela too. I want to go."

"Really?" The girl now walked over to the screen and looked over Anna's shoulder. Anna pulled up the Venezuelan embassy on the screen. It was on Massachusetts Avenue, a twenty-minute walk from the Angolan one.

*"Embaixada Do Brasil Em Washington*, his excellency, Ambassador Cristobal R. Orozco," Nita read slowly. A photo showed him shaking hands with the United States ambassador in front of the flags of both countries.

"Cool!" said Nita. "Let's go sometime, you and me! There are buses that leave right from the courthouse in Tappahannock. It's easy."

Anna was clicking on different rooms in the embassy. "We'll need to have money for lunch and tickets, and they probably will charge us to go into these places."

"I know where there's some money in this house," Nita offered.

It was the first time that Anna ever heard Nita suggest anything to do together besides walk to school. Anna had come to believe that she was an embarrassment to the older girl. She was too young to hang out with Nita's friends, and she wouldn't fit in with them even if she weren't. Cassy and Nita knew each other from the high school, but the senior and junior classes were like neighboring countries with few words between them and even fewer visits.

Nita's friends would wave to Anna as they drove away as if she were a bystander at a bus stop. Anna could never tell Nita about the strange visions that she had been experiencing. She sensed that Nita felt as out of place as Anna felt in this country. Once, Nita had mentioned how awkward it was to hear her friends talk about Spanish class as if the language were a disease that had infected the grade. She was embarrassed to speak Portuguese in front of them, so she rarely spoke the language at all. Mrs. Munoz had asked her once to give a presentation, but she had declined. Nita did, however, tell Anna that she would sometimes hang out with Mrs. Munoz after school and speak in her native tongue, enjoying the sweet words spilling from her lips. It ended with her walking out alone into a world she never asked to be in, but now found herself immersed in. Now, the two girls looked at the computer screen, scrolling around for what was left of Angola and Venezuela in the girls' minds.

They heard a car pull up and honk twice. "Going out!" Nita said and flew out of the room. Anna heard a car door closely followed by the sound of the engine disappearing down the street. She hit the back button on the screen and looked again at the Embassy of Angola. She thought it would be joyful to visit the embassy. Maybe the kitchen in the building had the sweet scents of *mufete*, palm oil, and yucca in the air. She imagined entering and being instantly transported to a busy street in Luanda or to a forest of mopane trees standing beyond fields of brush. People would be coming and going, bringing water, cultivating onions, and talking amongst each other. There would be children attending school and she would walk by and peer inside a window. And then, after roaming through the great building, brilliant sunlight would shine onto a tranquil garden where she would come across her mother and her father sitting behind their simple home, preparing *funje* to eat with the tilapia they had prepared for supper. She would stare at them from a distance until they noticed her, and then, waving, she would raise a single finger as if to say that she would be home soon. They in turn would blow her a kiss and maybe her father would say, "Come eat, Zarkhanna. You can play after supper."

The sound of the large brown truck that delivered packages brought her back to where she sat. The blinking image on the computer screen still showed the Embassy of Angola. The light, cream-colored brownstone on 16th Street in Washington was so close to her, yet a million miles away. She searched the site and found the "Contact Us." She clicked on the link and began to write a lengthy email about herself. She described her life in America, the White family, the differences between Angola and the United States, and even problems she was having with friends.

She remembered how she had provided the details about her life at the Catholic mission, and that it had won her safety, and for better or worse, a new home. She was sure that the embassy needed this information if they were going to invite her to visit.

It was almost 1 a.m. when Nita came back and quietly entered their bedroom. Anna lay in bed facing her and pretended to sleep. The night was her friend. It gave her nine or so hours that she did not have to be anything other than who she was, and that, to her, was feeling more and more like a girl who had lost everything. Friends like Mary and Cassy were fine, but they did not know her, and she never dared to go into any detail about her days in the army with them.

"You were in an army?" they would ask. "Like, the *army* army?"

Anna was no more the daughter of Carolyn and Mark than she was a bird flying in the sky searching for a nest. 186 Tidewater Street was a house that contained nothing that was truly hers. Sisters and brothers were invented, and it was only Simba, the broad smiling five-year-old child, who she looked forward to seeing every day, but even he was like a visitor here himself.

Now Nita crawled into her bed, and after texting friends, she was soon sleeping, her long hair falling over the bed. Anna stepped out from under the covers and headed out the door of their bedroom. She stood for a moment in her nightgown and listened to the pulsating sounds of a house sleeping. Carolyn and Mark's door was closed—he was still away, and the twins' door was slightly ajar. The door to the room where Simba slept was also ajar and she looked inside. A nightlight with the image of a whale gave a yellow tint to the room. He lay sprawled on the mattress with his arms and legs contorted in a child's slumber. She closed the door softly.

Downstairs she walked, her feet sinking into the carpet. She walked toward the kitchen and Chowder once again opened a sleepy eye and gave her the benefit of two wags of his heavy tail. She went over to him and bent down on her knees and stroked the golden dog behind his ears, which caused him to stretch his limbs before realigning his head and returning to his sleep.

She walked over to the loveseat and lifted the thick cushion to find the only possible ticket that allowed her to move from this world to the other—a world that she had found on her own, without help from anyone. She ignored the book with Auntie's letter and instead picked up the leather pouch and placed it in a pocket of her nightgown. It contained nothing more than smooth rocks and shattered bones but, real or imagined, she had convinced herself it had the power to make one world go away and another to appear. So, with the pouch stuffed into her pocket, she opened the door that led to the basement.

The kitchen clock read 1:30 a.m.

She stepped from the carpeted stair onto the coarse wooden planks that seemed to be the last steps before this otherworld appeared. Her skin felt a stickiness as she descended. Upon reaching the landing, she looked down from the loft where she crouched. She was hit with the musky odors combined with human sweat that was now so familiar.

Perhaps it was the light, but she could now see more of the cabin than on her previous visit. Woven baskets were strewn about the cabin, some holding clothing, some holding vegetables. The same chimney stood in the middle of the room. A white water jug sat on a table which had three legs and a makeshift post. The moonlight illuminated the outline of Camel's Hump through one of the openings that served as a window, the same view from 186 Tidewater Street. She could even smell herself, as if she had not showered or bathed in days. Most odd was the feel of her own body.

Once again, she looked down at her wrists and feet and was surprised to see that they resembled a girl of ten years old, perhaps even younger. Her fingers were thinner, her entire body just smaller in every way. There was no doubt—it was her body; it was just a younger girl's version of it.

She heard breathing close to her and noticed the same person who was sleeping in the loft on her last visit, this time with one foot sticking out from under a wool blanket strewn with holes. Downstairs, she could see the man and woman in the bed, but they were now startled themselves, as if Anna had woken them, which seemed impossible as she had made no sounds. A pattering of rain could be heard on the thin roof above her head.

Then, as she turned to descend the ladder so she could speak to the couple in the bed, she heard loud voices coming from somewhere outside, so she froze without going down.

The man and the woman looked up and met her gaze.

"It's all right, Annabelle," the man said. "Go back to bed, child." She could see that his one eye was lazy and that the other had all the intelligence of his thoughts.

"This is nothing for you, Annabelle. Listen to your father and go back to sleep."

Your father?

And then the voices from outside became clearer.

"Risey up y'all!" a man called out from somewhere nearby. "Me and Mistah A.C. Tomkins comin' for a visit!"

Then a second man outside the building said, "Petunia! How ya feelin'?" said a second man from outside the building.

The door swung open, and the chair that served as a doorstop was kicked over, just like she had done with soldiers in the past. Two men entered. One had a thin beard that resembled the unshaven faces of the soldiers she had served. He appeared small for his age, and she could make out a scar on his cheek, its outline catching the unstable light of a kerosene lamp held by the other man.

The second man, who must have been A.C., wore a large floppy hat that shielded his face. Both men were smiling, and even from her perch in the loft, she could smell the familiar odor of alcohol—just like the way the soldiers stunk after drinking as they stole into people's homes. Anna moved to where she could see but not be seen. The boy next to her did not wake or stir.

"What cha doin', Jemmy?" the man called A.C. said. Anna looked down and caught sight of the Ndimba, checking to see if there was some mistake, and that she had no place here. But the beads went from yellow to red. The eyes, hand painted the same ruby color she had stared at a thousand nights in Caxito, and three hundred nights in the army, caught the light of the lamp. What erased any doubt was the green amulet shaped like a heart hanging around the doll's neck.

The woman was still in bed, but the man, clad only in a gray shirt, had swung his legs off the side of the bed and leapt up. The woman began to pull the blanket over her frame and Anna noticed the fear that had entered the room, buzzing like a swarm of mosquitos. The man with the lazy eye now spoke.

"Missus is resting her and the chil'ren are in the loft. Maybe you gentlemen can get on home and let the chil'ren sleep." The man pointed toward where Anna peered down, but no one looked in her direction. He continued to point toward her.

"Who you telling to go home, nigga'?" the thin man named Kestin said. He straightened the chair that had been kicked over and sat down as if this were his home. He made remarks to the now stricken couple claiming he was the owner of everything in this shack as well as the land that surrounded the structure. He was smiling broadly, and Anna could feel his power over the hapless couple, intensified by the man in the hat.

"Where is that sweet petunia flower?" the man named A.C. said. "I heard she wasn't feeling so good, so me and Kestin and Doc Kiley come down to see how our stock is making out!" The unwelcome visitors shrugged at one another.

"Ain't that right Doc Kiley?" A.C. called out to someone still outside the shack.

"Right as rain!" came back the response.

Jemmy had picked up a piece of wood that was leaning against the wall beside the bed and was holding it by his side and a little behind him so the men didn't notice it.

Now the three men in the shack stood staring at one another until Kestin stood up and placed the kerosene lamp on the chair. The man with the hat walked over to the bed and pulled at the blanket.

"Found me a petunia, Kess!"

Jemmy looked up to the loft and caught Anna's eye. She noticed the amulet of his necklace in the shape of a crescent moon. A.C. followed his gaze.

"Ain't nothin' down here for you to see so get your eyes back to where they belong." A.C. commanded.

"Children need sleepin' if they be workin'," Kestin echoed. "You hear me, girly?"

A.C. again said they just came to check on the woman in the bed because she'd been sick that day. Anna had seen this type of confrontation before. When she and the soldiers entered towns controlled by the MPLA and the General Pina suspected collaboration, the routine cutting off of limbs was not the worst of their punishments. Women were taken into homes and men ripped off their clothing so their breasts were exposed, and then the men would do things that made the women scream. She had even seen girls her age being similarly attacked.

Here in this cabin, Anna could feel the hot hand of violation taking its form. Jemmy held his ground.

Jemmy spoke up. "My wife is fine now and she don't need to see no doctah!" He took a deep breath. "Where is Massuh Kane?" looking directly at the thin man.

"Why, nice of you to ask, Jemmy," Kestin offered. "My daddy had business up in Baltimore and he lef' just this afternoon. He put me in charge to make sure everything works hunky-dory."

A.C. was now kneeling on the platform bed, stroking the woman's form beneath the blanket. She let out a small cry. "Now, now, Madia honey, we ain' gonna hurt cha."

"Hands off her!" Jemmy yelled.

A.C. looked up over his shoulder at Jemmy.

"You say somethin' boy?" he said. He now pulled hard on the blanket and the woman's form appeared. Anna could see that the woman was perhaps thirty years old, the age of her own mother, and she had hair similar to her own, which now fell in damp ringlets around her sweating brow. She gave out a cry that even startled the boy sleeping next to Anna, but he returned to his slumber.

Jemmy began to move the piece of wood from hand to hand and both intruders noticed his threatening manner. The husband then raised the weapon over his head.

And then the man named Kestin stepped forward. "What you got there, Jemmy? You want to fight or somethin?"

"They hang niggas' for fightin' their mastas', ya know," Tomkins said, looking up.

"Mr. Tomkins here asked you to step outside," Kestin said, and he grabbed for the piece of wood in the husband's hand.

It was then that the weapon came down on Kestin's forehead. It was a solid blow, but only served to daze the man. The altercation seemed to snap the man out of trance. He felt for the trickle of blood and offered a quiet laugh, as if it were the evidence he was looking for.

"Let's get out of her, Ace, go have us another drink." He pointed at Jemmy with the trickle of blood on his hands. " This nigga' gonna be flogged, or worse!"

Jemmy now took hold of the man on the bed and pulled him off of his wife.

"Get your hands off me, nigga'!" A.C. spoke slowly, the words like commands, instructions to the lowest-ranked soldier. "I asked you all nice to go outside. You work for me on this farm and now you gonna watch me show this pretty little thing how a man be." He again grabbed for the blanket and it revealed her form.

"Look at that beauty laying all pretty!" he yelled.

Anna had seen this kind of scene many times before when fighters would storm a village and massacre husbands in front of their wives, and rape wives in front of their husbands.

Then Kestin stepped toward the commotion. "Ace, we don' need to have none a' that. We gonna whip this nigga' tomorrow for how he act. We done here for now."

But A.C. acted as if his accomplice had just taken a drink out of his hand. "This 'ere nigga' ain't nothing but a lazy field hand and I'm the one that git short pay 'cause a' him. So, If I wanna come down and give him lil' reminder..." He stopped to bury his face in Madia's hair, sniffing loudly, "then I gonna have myself a little playtime." He reached for his pants.

"I said, let's get on outta 'ere, Ace, we don't need to get into things," Kestin shot back.

A.C. gave the younger man a shove. "I'll be jus' a minute."

"No, you ain't."

"Jemmy," Kestin said, "why don't you go ahead and help Mr. Tomkins back on his feet."

A.C. looked in the direction of the half-naked husband. "That nigga' touch me, I'll kill him," he growled. "As for you, Kestin, you just a boy 'fraid of your daddy. You ain't man enough to run this here plantation and everybody know that your sister Cassandra got the smarts. You ain't even a Kane by birth! Bet your mama was a hussy down at Mrs. Malone's whorehouse! Ha!" Tomkins turned and glared at Kestin. "I ain't gonna listen to no coward who doesn't know a hogshead from a hog. You spend yo time countin' the money I make for you. Now leave me be, Kestin. I'm more of a Kane than you ever will be."

Jemmy did as the younger man instructed and approached A.C. and grabbed him from behind. A struggle began and A.C.'s hat fell off as he wriggled and broke free. Outside, the night animals in the forest could be heard calling to one another. Kestin now rushed his fellow intruder. Hands swung in the night, mostly punching air, but the younger man was gaining advantage against A.C.'s drunken motions. At one point A.C. fell backwards on the bed and rolled over toward the woman who let forth another scream. The woman covered her head in the blanket again and looked away, a witness to everything but not with her eyes.

Anna could clearly see what was happening below, and she watched as Jemmy stood off to the side, trying his best to stay away from the fighting men.

A dog barked in response to the calls of the night creatures. A.C. now sensed what was happening to him and Anna could see his chest rise and fall and his muscles tense. It was the younger man who stood over A.C. as he tried to assert his role as the owner, and the leader he was supposed to be.

A.C. would have none of it. "Eat the hairs off my balls," he said, and then, with a swift motion, he jumped off the bed and took the younger man by the shoulders and threw him with great force toward Jemmy who shielded Kestin from falling to the ground. As he bounced off of Jemmy, A.C. took Kestin by the shoulders and shoved him like a ragdoll into the wall.

Anna watched carefully as Kestin's eyes became wide, and he stopped moving, his expression moving from hatred to fear and finally to terror. He began to flinch uncontrollably, and it was clear that whatever was on the wall was holding him there.

And then she saw the blood.

It oozed down the man's neck, first in a thin line down his right side and then a gush that began to circle his neck like a red bandanna. His arms began to slack, and his eyes opened to colossal size before collapsing in their own sockets. His head remained fully impaled by whatever was holding it against the wall—a nail, perhaps, which had been driven into his skull.

No one spoke.

A.C. grabbed his hat from the ground, stumbled toward the door, and called out for whomever was waiting for them outside. Before exiting, he looked at the man called Jemmy.

"You killed your masta' and overseer, Jemmy. Look what you don!' He looked up into the loft but Anna had moved out of view.

Jemmy stood tense in the dim light. His shirt was stained with sweat.

"Doc," A.C. called out. "You better get in here. We got a nigga' who gone murder his masta'." He pointed at Jemmy, arm outstretched.

The woman in the bed screamed out. "No, no! My husband don' murder no one!"

The man who had been outside now came into the shack. A.C. hunched over and rested his hands on both knees. The man whose brain was embedded with the nail hung in his place like an ornament. Anna tried to calm herself. Where was she to go, and who was she to tell?

In the distance, a chorus of animals continued to trade calls. In between the cries, their mates answered them. Anna heard voices in the distance. It was a group of men, at first only audible through the collective rumble of their voices. They became louder as their pace quickened. Then they were within sight outside the window and Anna could see the lanterns and torches lighting their way. Soon, the small mob of men were directly outside. They opened the door slowly, as if they did not want to disturb what had happened.

"Jemmy Cudjo," a new man with a smaller hat said, "you are under arrest for the murder of Kestin Kane." The man walked up to Jemmy and placed handcuffs on him. A.C. tended to Kestin as if he were his own brother. He did not seem to notice or care about the arrest taking place.

But then, as Jemmy was being hauled out of the shack, A.C. turned to him and spoke. "You're going to' hang like a well bucket for this, Jemmy."

Now more men came into the shack as the woman in the bed cried full and inconsolable tears. The sound of her wailing awakened the boy in the loft.

As the woman cried and the coyotes howled in the early dawn light, Anna stepped back on the platform which made stairs appear, and she began to ascend them back home. She had moved too quickly and felt her forehead crash hard into the splintered ceiling. The sound of the impact caused the persons in the room below to turn their heads upward, but she was now completely out of sight. She felt a trickle of blood on her forehead and wiped it away.

In moments that she could hardly decipher, she opened a door at the top of the stairs and found herself in the familiar kitchen.

Chowder wagged his tail and stretched again.

She checked the clock in the kitchen. She felt sure that she had spent at least three hours in that other world.

The clock read 1:35 a.m.

She had been gone barely five minutes.

# Chapter 6

Anna awoke the next morning with blood on her pillow.

It was a Saturday in early July. She felt her forehead, where she had collided with the ceiling on her way out from the underworld, and a small smear of blood stained her hand.

But while she was everything from confused to angry about what she had seen last night, she was not frightened. She had come to accept unexplained circumstances and her role in them. Once, back home, the Ngaka had told her that she could expect such encounters, and now, after her life was disassembled through war and adoption, she was piecing it back together with the help of the unexpected.

"This girl is a Kimbanda," the old Ngaka had said.

Now, lying in bed she listened to cars rolling by in River Hills and garbage cans being dragged from garages to the sidewalk.

"Breakfast everyone!" Carolyn called.

"Breakfast!" one of the twins repeated.

Anna got out of her bed. She caught sight of herself in the mirror as she took off her nightgown and put on gym shorts and a River Hills High sweatshirt and checked her reflection.

American girls made their mirrors a sort of destination. In Caxito, gazing at herself was a sometimes event and she would really gauge her appearance by the look in her mother's eye. The church had a small bathroom with a mirror she would sometimes look at, noticing over time the pronunciation of her dramatic eyebrows and the thick curls that framed her face.

As she entered the kitchen, Ronnie was placing a plate of bagels on the table. Anna noticed that the basement door was open, and the light was on. She peered down the stairs and saw Simba sitting at the bottom, unaware that he was being watched. Other than the square shape of the room, there was nothing even remotely similar to the altered place that she had been in only last night. Simba rumbled his voice, imitating a truck as he whooshed the yellow toy in front of him. Tabitha was running around the table touching each chair in a solo game of tag. Wyatt sat on the kitchen counter kicking a cabinet with the heels of his sneakers.

"You look tired." Tabitha said.

"Maybe she didn't sleep that well last night, and it's none of your business anyway," Nita replied. She was headed for work at the Clubhouse as a hostess and her khaki pants and a polo shirt fit the part. Her job gave her privileges to the pool, but Anna had yet to be invited.

Carolyn swept into the room.

"Good morning, good morning," she sang. Her motions were swift and her look was clean. "Is everybody good?" It was a question no one could answer, so no one did. The children all looked up at her. She poured a cup of coffee and leaned against the counter. Wyatt played with her hair, and she shrugged him off.

"I'm leaving for Richmond again today, but I'll be back tomorrow. Your father leaves for Nevada in a few hours," she informed them. "Juanita, are you working today?"

Nita nodded without looking up.

"I should hope so with all of the clothes you buy," Carolyn commented into her coffee cup.

"Sure thing, Mom," Nita replied flatly.

Now Carolyn went down the line, assigning places. "You kids are with Ronnie," she said, pointing at the twins. Anna, what would you like to do?"

"I don't know," she answered.

"Where's Simba?"

"I saw him in the..."

"Here!" a voice from the basement shouted.

"Come up here for breakfast!"

"He already ate," Wyatt said.

"A lot," Tabitha added.

Nita stood up. "Gotta go! I'm not sleeping at home tonight. Party I told you about."

"Juanita, make good decisions. Anna, can you spend the day with Simba? Maybe you two can set up a sprinkler in the backyard or go for a walk?"

"Sorry, I already made plans to go over to Mary and Cassy's," she said. "I was going to sleep over at their house tonight, remember?"

Carolyn sipped her coffee. “I'd like you home to help with your brother.” Ronnie could handle the twins but could hardly keep up with Simba's high energy.

“I'll be back tomorrow,” Carolyn repeated. “We're getting closer with your new brother. I just need to finalize the papers.” She headed upstairs to pack and ready herself for the trip. She turned toward the kids. “Maybe I'll even learn a few Chinese words that we can all practice when I get home.” Anna forced a smile, but her brothers and sisters ignored their mother's comment.

“Can I go?” Tabitha asked. She was standing on her tiptoes.

“Maybe next time,” her mother said. “I'll be going to Richmond often over the next few weeks to take care of the details.” She was talking to herself.

Anna sat at the kitchen table and pushed around the eggs on her plate. She was tired from all that she had seen and experienced last night, and besides, good sleep was a friend she left behind long ago. Gone forever was the sound of her mother whisking *funje* as she woke from peaceful sleep. Gone forever was the sense of belonging she felt when she listened to the evening sounds in her village. Now she seemed to have everything except for what she wanted most. She was like those lost pieces of luggage circling on the carousel when she arrived at the airport. Most nights she lay awake wondering what her life would be like years from now.

She looked over at the basement door as she heard Simba ascending the stairs. One thing was clear, this underworld which she had now visited twice was situated right here at 186 Tidewater Street. The view she had seen of Camel's Hump on both occasions proved this to her without a doubt.

If she returned there to tell someone about the terrible crime she had seen and to vouch for the innocence of the man named Jemmy, she knew she was not going to some far-off place. She would be right here, and she believed she could return safely whenever she wished. She sensed she could come and go as she pleased to that queer world, which was her own secret.

She looked over at the loveseat where the leather pouch was again stashed after she emerged last night.

“Anna, why are you bleeding?” Carolyn asked, noticing Anna's forehead. Carolyn walked over and examined it carefully. The blood had dried, and it looked like a discolored blotch above her right eyebrow.

The twins circled her.

"Eww!" Tabitha shrieked.

Carolyn took a cloth and ran it under the sink, returning to Anna to blot the wound. "What happened?"

"I think I hit it on my bed," Anna fabricated.

"You think?"

Carolyn looked at Anna as if the girl were on trial. "Hmm, fainting at your friends, hitting your head, feeling sick? I'm worried about you, Anna." She looked more carefully at the wound. Well, it doesn't look like it needs stitches, but...Ronnie, can you take care of this? I really have to get on the road." Carolyn kissed the top of Anna's head. "Poor girl," she said, then disappeared up the stairs.

Ronnie patted her head with a piggy-shaped ice pack the family used for minor injuries. Tabitha chased her mother up the stairs. Nita left for work without saying goodbye, and Simba sat on the top stair of the basement ready to play with anyone who asked.

Anna watched from the front porch as Carolyn pulled the Audi out of the driveway. Mark went upstairs to pack. She heard him talking quietly on the phone to what she assumed was a man.

"I want to see you again," he said. "We are all going to the game but maybe afterward you and I could...."Anna did not catch the rest of his sentence. She went out the door and started walking in the direction of the Upper Hills section where a pool party was being held at Port Moore's house. The air was so misty that a cloud appeared to hover in the very street where she was walking.

She turned left toward the Clubhouse and walked the clean streets. Several neighbors waved and kids on bicycles had set up a small jump with a plastic ramp. One of the mothers watched from the porch as the kids lined up to take turns. Each step brought her closer to the enormous tree, the Old Oak, said to be over 300 years old.

Anna did not understand how anyone could count the rings of a tree so ancient, but the sheer enormity of the wooden giant spoke of age. The tree was less tall than it was wide, and it swayed in the warm breeze. A rush of wind gave it a voice, one that could tell stories without interruption if anyone cared to listen, Anna imagined as she admired its gnarled branches.

Anna stopped at the iron gate to the old graveyard behind the tree and looked at the tombstones. Most of them were small and unmarked, giving the sense that the dead who lay beneath them had neither names nor importance.

A small sign that looked like a grave marker stood just outside of the cemetery. Black lettering covered its white face.

Anna walked into the old cemetery. Most of the tombstones were no more than markers, low to the ground. There seemed to be no planning as to how the graves were laid out, but she sensed that there were more bodies beneath the earth than stone markers on the surface. She walked between the gravestones and bent down to read what she could. Most of the markers were too weathered and darkened to make out words, but it seemed as though a few were etched with just a single name. She saw one for a woman named Beatrice. The name Arthur was engraved on another. The largest of the tombstones seemed to be in honor of a person of importance. But the letter J was all that remained, as well as the year of his death, 1819. She placed a pebble on this tombstone, exited the cemetery, and continued on in the direction of Port's house.

She passed the Clubhouse with its huge porches and oak trees framing it, admiring its elegance. She noticed that someone was sitting on the porch.

An old man.

Sitting in a chair, rocking, drinking what appeared to be a cup of tea, a red-checkered blanket covering his frail legs and a large felt hat obscuring his face.

Did he just wave at her?

*Hello Annabelle.*

Anna stared at him as the rising mist swept through the scene. On the other side of the white blur, the old man had disappeared. She told herself it was just an illusion, nothing to worry about. Her thoughts now returned to Carolyn and her plans to bring in another adoptee into the household.

*Your father and I have found another child that we think would be perfect for our family.*

'I understand, I suppose,' Anna told herself, defending Carolyn and

Mark. There was no reason for her to think she was overly special. Lucky perhaps, but clearly not special, she thought. She realized she had just said the words aloud and a squirrel was staring at her. She continued on her way toward the party.

Port's home had an indoor-outdoor pool that started in his basement and went out into the backyard, which was encircled by a cedar fence. A weeping willow tree was rooted just outside the fenced in area of the pool, its drooping foliage hanging into the yard. Port's father was a judge and senator, and the Moore name was as old as Virginia itself.

Anna joined Mary and Cassy on colorful towels next to the pool. She and Reggie were the only Black kids, but by now Anna was used to being in the minority. In Angola, White people stood out like solitary trees in a field, but here in America it was the Black kids who stood out on an otherwise white sand beach. She had not spoken to Reggie since he had texted his invitation to the prom. Anna had learned that, in America, it was normal not to talk to boys who texted girls out of the blue, and that such texts were like jewelry, to be collected and compared with one another. Cassy and Mary's plan to humiliate Reggie at Friendly's had misfired when other boys accompanied him, spoiling the ruse.

Now the boys were jumping off the diving board and making varying twists while catching a small rubber ball in the air. Each time they landed in the pool, water splashed closer to the girls.

"Let's move away from these idiots," Mary said irritably. The three girls went up a small hillside overlooking the pool and laid their towels on the grass. They sat leaning back against their hands as the boys attempted to extend a garden hose and spray them.

"Idiots," Cassy said.

"Total," Mary said. She put her forearm over her eyes.

"So immature," Anna added.

No one spoke as the spray from the garden hose sprinkled their feet.

"Stop it Port!" Cassy yelled.

Then Anna thought she heard one of the boys murmur something that sounded like...*ugga-bugga*.

Port got out of the pool, dropped the hose, and walked up to the girls. His blond mop-top hair fell over his forehead, and his nose was too large for his freckled face.

"Do you guys want to go to the Clubhouse and take out some golf carts?"

"We're not allowed to drive the golf carts," Mary objected. "We could get into trouble." She looked over at the other girls for support.

"I have a shirt that the groundskeeper wears and nobody says anything," Port countered. His braces flashed in the sunlight when he spoke.

Anna remembered Mary telling her that she had gone for a ride in a golf cart with Port and that he had tried to take her bra off. He had simply reached around her back and tried to unhook it. When Mary pushed him away, he laughed and bragged at school that he had taken her bra off. All the girls knew it was a lie, but Port had convinced a few of the boys. Mary and Port were kind of going out, but it was not official, and she had told Anna and Cassy that she planned to say no when he officially asked, if he asked.

"Oh, he'll ask," Mary bragged, her eyes wide.

"I think yes" Anna offered.

Now the three girls looked at Port, who stood with both hands on his hips. Mrs. Moore walked from the kitchen onto the back patio and put down a plastic bowl of chips, together with a liter of Pepsi and several red plastic cups. Reggie ran up to the bowl and stuffed a handful of chips in his mouth.

Cassy spoke for all the girls. "We don't want to go steal golf carts and ride around."

Anna tensed at the words. The Whites were members of the Clubhouse and could attend events, but the tennis courts and golf course had additional fees and Mark and Carolyn said that they did not want to pay this year while they were raising money for the film.

"Well, my dad is a charter member, and our names are on that plaque near the entrance when you walk in," he offered.

"Oh, you are so rich and cool, Port Moore," Cassy said. "There are a ton of names on that plaque. Who do you think you are, like a Kennedy or something?"

"Well, we're going in a few minutes, and you girls can come. Even Miss Uganda." He gave Anna a thumbs up.

"What did you call her?" asked Cass.

"Miss Uganda. Isn't that where you're from or something?" He looked at Anna.

"Angola," she said quietly.

"Whatever," he said. The other boys overheard and laughed, their eyes avoiding Anna's.

Cassy's eyes widened and she shook her head. "I think we are going to go home." The girls sat on their towels in perfect alignment with one another, facing the boy. "But maybe..."

"I should be getting home," Anna interjected, remembering that she was supposed to help take care of Simba.

Mary looked over at Anna and grabbed her hand. "If Anna can't go, then we can't go."

Anna could sense that her friends wanted to be with the boys and that for whatever reason she did not fit into this puzzle. "I have to go anyway. My mom wants me home."

"Your mom? I didn't think you had a mom," Port said, feigning pity.

"Shut up, Port!" Cassy said, and Port turned quickly and did a cannonball into the pool.

"Jerk," Mary said.

"Total," Cassy agreed.

The boys were now softly chanting *ugga-bugga, ugga-bugga, ugga-bugga.*

None of the girls spoke.

"They're idiots, Anna. Don't pay any attention," Cassy said.

Anna looked over at Mary and Cassy. "I don't, they're dumb." But she could still sense that the girls wanted to go with Port and the boys to the Clubhouse.

A few of the boys jumped back in the water, but Reggie started to pack up his backpack to leave. Mrs. Moore came back outside with a tray of hot dogs and stood with a hand on her hip wondering if her food would be eaten. A white puppy sneaked past her and the screen door banged.

"Let's play 'Tell Me Something I Don't Know'," Cassy suggested. It was a game they had played before, but only in the cafeteria.

"I kind of think Port is cute," Mary began.

"We know what you think," her sister said. "Tell me something I don't know." Her eyes rolled.

"Well, I think I might say yes if he asked me out," she said, mostly to herself. Her long hair shielded her face.

"Tell me something I don't know," Anna said.

"I have one," Cassy said. "My mom saw your teacher Ms. Romoldo drunk at a bar in town, and she couldn't walk straight."

"Really?" both girls answered. "That's crazy."

"Yeah, so you should get an empty bottle of something and put it on her desk," Cassy suggested.

No one spoke, but the two sisters now looked over toward Anna. "Tell us something we don't know," Cassy asked, tapping her on the arm.

"OK," Anna began. She wanted to say something the girls would find interesting, but she had no boys to talk about, no secrets about teachers, and no stories about growing up in Virginia to share. Her mind was more occupied with the strange goings on that had plagued her since she came to River Hills. The bizarre episodes were beyond comprehension. The man with his cross, a couple walking through trees? Bedrooms transforming, and fainting and making a fool of herself in front of Mary and Cassy? A murder witnessed from a loft? She felt there was no way she could share these experiences with anyone. She had once told Carolyn that she had strange dreams but all that her new mother said was that dreams were normal and they tell you about who you are.

But Anna dared not tell Carolyn that they were more than dreams, that the people who appeared in the basement were as real as the furniture in their home, and that men had come there, to their property, and attempted to do terrible things to a woman, and that Anna had seen it all from a vantage point in the basement that did not even exist. Yet the place and the man and the woman there all seemed so familiar, and didn't the man called A.C. refer to the man named Jemmy as her father?

She could not tell Carolyn about any of this, especially because she did not wish to admit that the strangers gave her a sense of connection she could not explain. It approached the warmth she felt from her own mother, and from her father before he disappeared. Before she was taken away for good. Before the only world she knew became a kind of Hell, and eventually a terrible dream she only remembered in glimpses.

"Do you guys ever have weird dreams?" Anna looked over at the two sisters.

"Oh yeah," Mary said, exchanging hand signals with Port.

She paused and considered her words. How much to tell, she asked herself. Explaining it all seemed ridiculous, like the time she told them she was a soldier, but then quickly retracted. All it did was make her seem more alien, more different.

She was tired of being different. She wanted to be like Mary, just a girl in a town worrying about immature boys and parties. But she felt that 'different' was permanently stamped on her forehead. Before she could worry about boys and parties, she would have to forget being stripped of her parents, Auntie, and her homeland. She would have to forget being taken away from her village and forced to put down her baskets and pick up a gun. She would have to forget that she knew how to shoot with an AK-47 rifle, and that she may even have killed someone. Yet here she was, with the sense of being different embedded within her, longing for real friends like a bee longs for nectar in summer. She wondered what the girls would say if she shared any of the strange goings on she had seen since her arrival, and even before—like the people she saw from the plane who had stopped their work in the scorched fields to gaze up at her in seat 3A.

She began, cautiously. "You know in that *Freddie vs. Jason* movie where there are people walking around that are like dead or something?"

The two friends looked at one another and crunched their eyebrows.

"Yeah," Cassy replied.

"Well, sometimes I think I see those kinds of people walking around in River Hills. I know that they're not real, but sometimes I think that I see them. One time, when we were driving on the highway, I thought I saw a man in an old-fashioned suit standing next to that cross in the woods, you know, where there must have been a car crash or something? Do you ever wonder what happened there?"

The sisters stared at her.

"And then sometimes I think I can see the past. It's kind of weird. Maybe I should just stop watching scary movies." Anna forced a laugh and shot a glance at them. The girls did not speak. Their eyes darted about as they searched for what to say. Anna had hoped to hear words of understanding, like *I sometimes think the same thing*, or maybe, *I had that happen to me once but I...*but nothing of the sort came from them.

"That's weird, Anna," Cassy finally said.

"Um, maybe you should tell your mom and go see a doctor or something," Mary added.

Anna forced another laugh but felt her body tighten. She used to feel that rigidness in the early morning hours in the army camp when they were getting ready to mobilize. She would wake up on the ground, her head resting on a dirty rag covering her rifle, and she would hear the soldiers moving all around her. She would know that whatever came next, she would have no control over its outcome. Day after day, surrounded by soldiers, she remained by herself in a brigade of loneliness.

The girls turned their attention to the boys who were now drying off, getting ready to go to the Clubhouse.

"Maybe you should get a diary or something, Anna," Cassy suggested, trying to be helpful.

Mary spoke. "I'm going to go to the Club. Are you sure you don't want to come?"

"I have to watch my brother."

"Well, I'll call you later then," Mary said, drying her feet off.

Anna smiled and nodded. The two sisters walked over to where the boys were waiting for them, but Cassy stopped and turned toward Anna. She did not have her sister's feminine features, but she stood confident with her short hair and a freckled face. "Don't mind those boys and what they said about, like, Africa or Guyana or whatever. They're stupid and they've never even been to Europe."

Anna gave a quick smile and shrugged her shoulders. She watched the girls walk away with the other kids, like they were heading to a fun movie as Anna went home to watch TV. "We better be getting community service credit for this," Anna thought she heard Cassy say.

A few mockingbirds chased one another in agile patterns through the air, skimming the surface of the pool before shooting skyward toward the weeping willow that reached for the water's edge. They called out in quick succession, piercing the air. Underneath it, Anna thought could also hear something else—the sound of the kids chanting as they walked away.

*Ugga-bugga. Ugga-bugga.*

Who could blame them, she asked herself. She came from a different continent. She spoke differently, she thought differently, and she looked different. This was not her real home, and her parents weren't even her parents. She did not belong in America. Everyone in River Hills knew she was the adopted girl from Africa, and nobody could even remember the name of her country. She wondered if *ugga-bugga* also meant ugly. No boy seemed to like her, that was true. As hard as it was to imagine a boy liking her, it was even harder to imagine liking one of them. They were rude and mean. If a boy ever did like her, would she even care?

*Ugga-bugga.*

She would ask Nita what it meant. She was sure it was not a compliment. She would also look it up on Netscape.

That night, with Carolyn away in Richmond again and Mark off on another of his business trips—although it did not sound like all business—she went back to the computer. There was an email in her inbox, and it only took a moment to realize it was from the Embassy of Angola. She devoured it as if it were a letter from a friend back home. It was even written in Portuguese, but she translated and spoke the words quietly to herself.

> *Srta. White:*
>
> We are always pleased to assist our countrymen with any of their needs while in the United States of America. Please feel free to email me directly.
>
> Sincerely,
>
> Ambassador António Santos França
>
> "Ndalu"

Anna read the email a dozen times. Ndalu! The famous Angolan soccer star who became a politician. And he sent an email to her! She closed the laptop and rested her head on the desk. Angolan people in the United States, and only a bus ride away! She opened the email and read it again, crafted a reply, deleted it, and then decided on the right words to respond. She would love to come to Washington, D.C. and visit, and yes, she would contact his assistant, Mr. Marcus Neto, and set a date and time.

She closed the computer before sending her response. She could envision her visit, watch it unfold in her mind. She would take the bus and then walk to the embassy where she would speak and ask questions in Portuguese. She vowed to only tell Nita, never Carolyn. She wanted the trip to be her own, an escape hatch that she could perhaps use from time to time—just to remind her of home before returning to...whatever River Hills was to her.

She closed her computer and started to go to her bed, but then she remembered the phrase the boys were using back at the pool, and she returned to her computer.

'Ugga-bugga,' she typed. She clicked on the first search.

*A derogatory name for foreign people, sometimes African.*

Anna closed the computer and looked toward the window. The house was quiet, the children gone, the parents gone, her friends...doing their thing. Outside, the sound of fire engines swirled around the nearby hillsides. It sounded like they were coming toward her and then away from her before disappearing.

A month passed, and in addition to looking forward to her visit to Washington, D.C., Anna thought about her inevitable return to the scene of the murder she had witnessed in that other world. She did not know if or when she would go back, or for how long if she did.

When she witnessed the murder, the kitchen clock said she had only been gone for five minutes, even though it felt like she had been gone for at least three hours. So, days in that other world would translate into no more than a few hours in this one. A whole day there would be equal to less than an hour in real time in River Hills, she figured. She felt a pull to return and wanted to be free to come and go as she pleased. So, she made a plan.

It was a Saturday night, and it was quiet throughout the house. Carolyn had again left for Richmond for a special conference on adopting Chinese children. Mark had departed yet again to try and collect the last of the funds needed for the movie he promised everyone would be coming out in the cineplex next year. Or maybe he preferred to be with someone other than Carolyn, although Anna never saw him look at women as other men did. Nita came home at around midnight, and she would be the only one to know if Anna was home, since Ronnie had gone to sleep early and believed that Anna was staying the night at Kane's' house.

After Nita fell off to sleep, Anna tiptoed downstairs. Chowder greeted her with more excitement than she would have liked, so she grabbed a piece of cheese from the fridge to calm him down. Ronnie was asleep in the guest room off of the living room and the lights had been turned off.

As Chowder stretched on his bed and closed his eyes, Anna gathered the leather pouch from under the loveseat cushion and opened the door to the basement. As she descended the stairs and stepped onto the wooden platform, she noticed that she had not changed this time. This time she did not transform into a younger version of herself, the body of the girl who had witnessed the tragedy. She felt in every way the 14-year-old girl that she was.

But she was clearly back in the underworld again.

# Chapter 7

As she stepped onto the loft in the underworld, she could now see that the sleeping figure was a teenage boy, older than herself. The light, the air, and the sounds outside told her that it was early morning, not much past seven o'clock. She heard the whoosh of a bird's wings outside. The rhythmic breathing of the boy's gentle slumber gave her a sense of ease. She noticed a loose plank in the wall perfect for hiding the leather pouch, which she did.

A ray of sunlight came through a window, and she noticed the yellow-and-green patterned throw rug that resembled ones she had grown up with in Caxito. There were small wooden stools throughout the small structure. She stared down from the loft and her eyes met those of the familiar woman, who smiled at her. The woman seemed to mouth some words to her and her alone.

*Good morning.*

Anna heard the goings on outside the shack. Men talking, someone singing, dogs exchanging yelps. Smells of food, bacon mostly, found its way to her nose and reminded her that she was hungry. She had not gone over to Mary's house that evening and had not had dinner. She had no idea what to do or where to go, so she listened to her senses. She felt a need to come down from the loft, a need to eat, and a need to relieve herself, although where she did not know. First, she found a loose plank in the wall and placed the leather pouch inside, concealing it from plain view.

"Child, go and get us our share of water. Today is a special day," the woman called.

Like an actor in a school play, Anna followed the script and descended the ladder. She wanted to ask the woman what they were having for breakfast. But when she tried to form the words, none came. It was as if there was no connection between words and sound in her throat. Her ability to speak had simply vanished.

The woman did not appear to expect an answer. Instead, she continued giving light orders. Anna looked around the shack for some sign of Jemmy, a piece of clothing, shoes, anything, but it seemed like he was no longer there. Several of the handwoven baskets she had noticed before sat on the floor, one overflowing with carrots and cucumbers, another filled with rags. The baskets were expertly crafted. She moved to pick one up, when the woman distracted her.

"Eggs outside with Ole' Beatrice, so go do your business and come back soon."

Outside the cabin, a small village was coming to life. Trees were everywhere in all shapes and colors. She found the place to relieve herself—far more crude than anything she experienced in Caxito, but serviceable.

As she walked, she noticed that the land gave the strong odor of a desperate dryness, as if no rain had come for a long time. That morning, the few clouds in the sky had gray linings.

Two young boys were playing a game of leapfrog. One of them, clad in a white shirt, pointed at the sky. "Maybe it's raining!" one said to the other.

Others in the awakening village also looked upwards.

"Nah, that ain't rain," said an enormous man wearing green overalls and a straw hat. "Rain gon' from this land." Despite his huge size, he gave off a gentleness that put Anna at ease. At his mention of rain, a few people walking by also looked at the sky.

Anna knew that the land she was on was clearly the same terrain as River Hills. The view of Camel's Hump was the same as from 186 Tidewater Street, but it could no longer be described as a street. It was more akin to a row. It was as if the modern house that she normally lived in had been removed and replaced by this simple structure, comforts all taken away. She looked around the village coming to life. Unmistakably, she saw the white Clubhouse with its wide lawn at about a half mile's distance to the left.

She watched the comings and goings of the people, African people. She passed children much younger than she, others closer to her age, old women, young men, infants—people of all ages. Some walked directly by, others greeted her with a nod or a wave of recognition. Anna took in the fragrances of breads, rice, and even the unmistakable smell of fish cooking as she passed families eating breakfast on their small front porches. Pens held hogs and sheep for the villagers to use in various ways. Chimneys gave off steady streams of curling smoke, filling the air with the scent of burnt wood.

Her instinct told her to take the road heading away from the Clubhouse. Soon she came upon a shack identical to the one from which she had emerged, except the porch was covered.

"Mornin' to you, Annabelle. Nice to see you on this special day." The old woman had white unkempt hair and deep wrinkles. She was slight in nature, perhaps five feet tall. She leaned forward in her chair with her hand resting on a cane and squinted her eyes. She handed Anna a basket of seven eggs. "Ole' Beatrice," the woman said, pointing to herself, "she not forget you on this day, even if I can hardly see anymore." A Black girl slightly older than Anna was attending her with a glass of milk. She was dressed in a cream-colored dress with a collar.

"Drink this Nanny," the girl said, but the old woman ignored her.

Anna began to thank Beatrice, but the words did not come. She could not utter the phrase. Her eyes expressed, her body language conveyed, and her mind knew what it wanted to say, but there was no voice to carry the message.

The old woman nodded and smiled. Anna managed to do the same before going back into her...home...to see what was next in store for her.

"Now get ready for church, you two." Madia started cracking the eggs into an iron skillet over the fire, inviting Anna over to slice a loaf of crusty brown bread. She picked up the knife to cut the loaf. Upstairs, the boy looked down from the loft with sleepy eyes and a disoriented look.

"Calvin, come on down here and do the man's work. You got to get it done before church." The woman's oval eyes, graceful neck, and distinct eyebrows resembled her own.

Anna noticed her Ndimba doll on the nail beside the door. She walked past it and stared at it as if it were a photograph of someone she once knew. Anna thought it best not to touch or alter it in any way as she believed it created some order between her two worlds—three worlds if one were to include her homeland. The figure on the wall reminded her of everything that was good in her life and gave her the feeling of being close to something resembling...home.

"Annabelle, your dress is hanging there on the hook. Ole' Beatrice wash it for you during white week. This week is dark week so whatever dark you got, she wash it for you." Following her direction, Anna took hold of a green gingham dress, which resembled Madia's. It was a dress from another time, reminding her of photos she had seen of women in the 1800s. The notion flew across her like wind, covering her whole body with goosebumps. The dress flowed out from the waist, its wide skirt reaching the floor. Like Madia's, the collar encircled her neck with a hint of lace. The dresses reminded Anna of the matching outfits she and her mother wore when Anna was a child. As the woman fixed Anna's hair into a bun, Anna listened to her speak of many topics—from the weather ("A bit cool, don't you think, Annabelle?") to church ("I hope that the Reverend Cooper don't go on and on!") to chores ("Think you can finish up that basket soon, Annabelle? It be one of yer best!).

She could feel the love in Madia's fingers—the love of a mother taking care of her daughter.

The boy named Calvin descended the ladder from the loft. He seemed eighteen or nineteen years old. His body was powerfully built, but his face—heart-shaped with high cheekbones and long eyelashes—had almost girlish features.

"Mornin'," was all he said before exiting the cabin and coming back minutes later with wood stacked in his arms.

"Go on and get ready, Calvin. We got church at half past nine."

Anna stood barefoot and Madia gestured toward a row of shoes. Anna walked over and put on a pair of simple leather sandals.

"What choo doin' chile' with those old things? It's Sunday! Put on your Sunday shoes! Whatsamatta? You don' sleep right last night, sometin?" Madia gave her a playful slap on her behind and pushed a pair of closed-toes shoes with a wide heel and two buttons on the side.

Anna sat in one of the chairs and buttoned the shoes. There were small chunks of dirt stuck to the wooden sole and one button was missing from the left shoe. As Madia fried up the eggs over the fire, the oil mixed with wood smoke making its way up the chimney. Oddly, Madia did not ask her to do much other than sweep the dirt floor, so she sat on the chair after completing her task and observed. It was as if she were ill and no one wanted to disturb her. Calvin brought in firewood and Madia continued cooking, cleaning, and dressing. Finally, it was time to go.

Outside, a group of perhaps fifty villagers converged, walking together in the direction of the Clubhouse. It was on this very spot of earth, Anna thought, that she had walked countless times past the immaculate homes of River Hills. Now, there were only shacks where tidy, well-built houses existed just yesterday. The shacks lined both sides of the street, neatly laid out about fifty feet apart on both sides of the dirt avenue. Many had porches and some had a few glass windows. It seemed like they were built by poor people for even poorer people to live in. Nonetheless, they formed a community, and on this particular day everyone seemed to know where they were going.

As the procession continued, Anna noticed the women were dressed mostly in bright-colored cotton dresses and white handkerchiefs that were neither African headdresses nor casual bandannas—it was an entirely different look. Men wore indigo-dyed patchwork shirts tucked into baggy wool trousers and worn shoes.

The two young boys she had met this morning walked with their father, the enormous man still clad in his green overalls who she noticed everyone called Big Arthur. There did not appear to be a wife with them. Entire families of people ranging in age from a few months old to well into their sixties all walked together. Many of the men wore formal vests, however frayed from age.

They passed the Old Oak and Anna noticed that it was far younger in years than she remembered. The small cemetery at its base was manicured and the headstones were even and well-marked. Older hemlocks and oak trees grew to spectacular heights. Anna could hear the sound of horses in thc distance, and it seemed like animals were everywhere—dogs, stray cats, chickens, sheep, hogs. The sky whipped around with fast moving clouds, nonthreatening, but as if they were being stirred.

Madia reached for Anna's hand and squeezed it as they walked.

"Maybe you start talking again, child. Maybe this be the day."

Anna wanted to respond and attempted to find her voice. Her questions were too numerous to count, but as hard as she tried, the syllables failed to come together. Her eyes moved in their sockets as she found herself utterly devoid of vocabulary.

The woman who everyone called Ole' Beatrice chimed in. "Poor child, poor child. She seen too much." Her wide kerchief was wrapped low on her forehead. "Say my name, Annabelle. *Say Ole' Beatrice to me.*" The woman was familiar to Anna but she could not place her name or face.

Anna looked at Beatrice but still the words did not come, and she could tell that neither Beatrice nor Madia expected them. They cast their eyes on the road and continued walking, eventually coming to an intersection, the same one she had come to with Nita more than a hundred times. One direction went toward the Clubhouse and the other toward the high school. But the procession continued straight ahead, through a brief stretch of woods that opened up to the vast fields.

Gone was the golf course and its luscious green rolling hills. In its place were endless fields of giant plantings. The crops had broad leaves and appeared at first glance to be healthy. There was a strong smell of tobacco mixed perhaps with a touch of leather.

But the leaves were brown and dry.

Anna thought there was something sickly about these fields. She quickly noticed the brittle, wilting leaves as she walked through the rows. As her shoulders brushed past the tobacco plants, a few leaves peeled right off their stalks.

The people around her looked up instinctively toward the now cloudless sky. She remembered what the large man with the two boys had said.

*"Rain gone from this land."*

Every once in a while, a patch of green would appear in the field and one of the men would examine the crop and either smile or shake his head. But these green crops that occasionally appeared were like small puddles in an otherwise brittle field. The plants swayed in the breeze, giving off their own chattered sound. A few men began to sing, then others joined in, and the singing continued as the procession made its way through the lifeless crops. The song rose in volume as the slow traveling group moved along.

*Judgement, Judgement,*
*Judgement day is-a-rolling around.*

A church steeple came into sight. It was in the exact spot as River High School, where the old church beside it was a maintenance shack. But the faded words on the side of the building were now clear; *Rappahannock Baptist Church,* freshly painted and welcoming.

The group followed the dirt path that ran to the entrance of the church. Its windows were made with individual panes of glass. A piece of tin at the apex of the spire caught the sun and momentarily blinded her. Into the building the procession went, and Anna soon found herself sitting between Calvin and Madia in a wooden pew with prayer books peeking out from pockets on the backsides of the benches. Behind them sat the people she came to know as Ole' Beatrice and Big Arthur. Villagers who had walked alongside her to church were seated throughout the simple structure as well as other people she had never seen, yet everyone was dressed in clothing from another time. The only sameness was the color of their skin, for all of the people in the church, and everywhere she looked, were Black.

A man stood up toward the front of the congregation and approached the simple pulpit. The church itself was little more than a large house and the gable of the roofline went down the center of the structure. Behind the pulpit hung an image of Jesus, and Anna felt the warmth of his love, even if it was just a symbol she had seen on a thousand occasions. There was nothing about her Christian core that had anything but good feelings for her. In Caxito, the church was in the center of the village where all of the bargaining and bickering of normal life would flow into an hour or two of togetherness. The church in Golungo Alto was also where she had burst in with her rifle demanding food for Commander Pena and ended up being overcome by the image of Jesus and the dancing, praying nuns.

The man on the pulpit today was dressed in a long black frock. He cleared his throat, took a sip of water, looked out over the crowd from his perch, and began speaking in a thunderous voice, far louder than one would expect from his appearance.

"When our Divine Savior sent his apostles and his disciples throughout the whole universe to preach to every creature," he began, "he laid down the conditions of salvation thus..." The man spoke in tempo as if singing the words and Anna felt herself lost in the familiar images that he invoked—*Savior, Son of God, Salvation, Heart, Lord.* These words were like a lullaby to her, bridging worlds. The sermon continued for what felt like an hour, and at one point, Anna caught Madia's giggling eyes indicating that the sermon was getting too long. Members of the community would occasionally shout out encouragement and agreement, a practice she had never seen in Angola. Eventually, the sermon came to a close, and there was a long pause.

All were quiet. An unspoken and heavy tone entered the church. It felt as if someone or something unnatural was making its way through the air and through the bodies of all who were present, and the next words that the preacher spoke confirmed the feeling.

"It has been five years since the rains were last seen...and we all saw the strange silver bird in the sky moving like it were a machine, around the time of a hanging of an innocent man and the start of our long drought. We never used to think twice about rain because having rain was like having chil'ren, until…" He looked out over the crowd. "Until that chil'ren is taken away from us. Since that time, all we see is blue sky. We ask God for forgiveness. We ask for his help. We ask that the rains return to this land."

The congregation murmured in acknowledgement.

"God commands me under the pain of eternal damnation to believe all that He has taught, and He gives me the means to understand. And now we in this Essex County know that five years ago to the day—on July 24th in the Lord's year 1819—a great crime took place."

*1819? Five years ago?*

Anna gulped a deep breath.

Madia squeezed her knee and Calvin put a hand on her shoulder. Now it all began to make sense. The old roads, the clothing, these people—who she now realized were not Africans, but Americans speaking English and living in what she knew was a time of terror for Black people who had come to this land from Africa and were forced to work as slaves.

She lived now in the year 1824.

"We all know the story of Jemmy Cudjo, whose wife and children sit before us. He was a man who could see! A man who could heal! A man who could give answers in everyday ways that sometimes we as Christians must wait lifetimes to know! He was a conjurer…our conjurer."

The congregants shook their heads and voices of agreement echoed through the hall. Hands clapped and feet stomped, shaking the pews.

"It was five years ago today that this man was executed for a crime that he did not commit. We all prayed and prayed that our friend's life would be spared, that the Lord would see fit to step in and save him, but nothing could stop the cruel hand of injustice that bears down on our souls. And as the tobacco crop has dried on the earth, it's been hard times for everyone. We pray for God's mercy."

Amens circulated through the congregation.

The doors of the church were suddenly opened and the presence of the men who entered could be felt. Reverend Cooper momentarily stopped his sermon and looked at the back of the church where the men stood. Anna turned her head.

The man in the hat stood out to her, not so much for his white skin in a church full of Negroes, but more because his face that had been seared into Anna's memory on the night she witnessed the murder in the cabin belonging to Jemmy and Madia.

A.C. Tomkins stood at the back of the church. Next to him stood what appeared to be his assistant. This other man wore overalls and a small hat. Both men were smiling.

"Morning Reverend," A.C. called out. "Just making sure you don' need no help with your nigga' teachin'."

"Your nigga' teachin!' the man in the overalls mimicked. His name was Wendell, now in A.C.'s old role as junior boss of Nottoway Plantation.

The Reverend looked at the men. "You may take your seat in this house of God, gentlemen," he said. The men sat in the last pew, removing their hats.

"This church will be treated with respect, Mr. Tomkins," said the Reverend. "You may now be the overseer from Monday to Saturday, but you are a church member on Sunday, just like these fine people." The church was built with the funds from the local plantation owners, and the preacher's own salary was paid by the masters themselves to bring order and religion into their valuable enterprises.

A.C. put out his hands in a mock gesture of submission. Anna noticed that his skin looked irritated with red blotches that were covering his face. Whatever disease it was, the irritation was also traveling down his neck in mean patches. Anna looked away.

Madia put her hand in Anna's, and she could feel Calvin move closer to her. The people in the church had become silent and a certain feeling of fear now hung in the air, less from the intruders who now occupied the rear of the chapel, and more from the strangeness of the occurrences over the five years that the man Jemmy—her father—had unleashed.

"We do not pretend to know the workings of God, but we ask him today, on this five-year anniversary of the death of a man—a conjurer man—who took the rains with him from Essex County, to bring us back our water. We have watched our cattle die, our piglets fall over in thirst, and the crops have wilted as we have toiled. We too have suffered, and we have buried children in the harshness of our new climate. We ask our Lord to bring the waters back to the Essex County and to release us from this curse, because we know that the words the conjurer spoke at his hangin' were not intended for the slave people."

At this point, A.C. stood up and dropped a copy of the Slave Bible[1] on the wooden pew. The sound echoed through the chamber and jolted those who were enrapt by the Reverend's words. A.C. put on his hat and walked out of the church, slamming the door against the wall and leaving it open. The Reverend watched him depart with his assistant.

"The crops have wilted, and we have been blamed by the people that God has sanctioned to look over us. Until we find our salvation and the Lord Jesus Christ delivers us to freedom, we suffer under the master who we must serve in order to find our true masters, to whom we will once again return."

"Return!" A man yelled out, and others joined him, the words moving through the congregation like a donation offering. Hands clapped and feet clamored throughout the building, and it appeared to Anna as if they were dancing.

"The cruel sun bears down on us day after day with no rain to quench our thirst. We do not understand the workings of God or the curse of this draught, but we ask that the spirits of our brothers and sisters, and of Jemmy Cudjo in particular, be lightened and joined with you, mighty God, so that we may all live amongst the waters again." Outside, Anna saw the bright sun tear through the narrow windows that went all of the way up the walls.

Anna could see that a small wooden bucket filled with water and a tightly woven basket containing the same was making its way in opposite directions to the worshippers. She watched as the basket moved up and down, from hand to hand, child to elder. It disappeared behind bodies and then reemerged.

"As we have been doing now for five years, we will once again pass the water. Today we ask that the waters come. Five years is long to wait." Eventually, the basket containing water landed in her lap.

She examined it and saw the water swoosh in the container. The surface of the water reflected her face. She raised the basket and scrutinized its construction. The tight coiling was crafted expertly.

And then, a more careful look.

White triangles went all along the base of the basket.

She gasped and her eyes rolled in her head. There was no doubt in

1 Slave Bibles were used to educate and convert slaves in the 1800s and only included 232 chapters. They were heavily edited doctrines that removed any passages that could spark rebellion or thoughts of liberation.

her mind who had made this basket. But when? And how? She turned to Madia to ask but, once again, words failed her. Madia smiled knowingly at the handiwork.

Big Arthur put a hand on her shoulder. "It is alright, Annabelle," he said, and she looked back at him. It was clear to Anna that the man was a friend. His hands were oversized, and his scent was like fresh earth.

"Arthur is right," Madia said, standing up and looking at the large man. "We will find right in the wrong. It is God's command."

Big Arthur spoke in a deep voice. "Your daddy died under the Old Oak, we know that. He said before he died..." Arthur stopped in his speech, trying to remember the words.

Ole' Beatrice spoke up. "A.C., you will burn in suffering as the slave people suffer," she quoted.

Arthur nodded in appreciation to Beatrice, and then continued, as if reciting a poem. "The rope that he hung from I still have in my home, because that rope one day I will use to hoist a bucket from a new well of my own filled with the water from our Lord, when we all be free."

Others around him overheard. "Amen," they said together, gathering their belongings.

Arthur continued. "Your daddy was a good man. A conjurin' man. He buried behind the Old Oak in the slave people cemetery. He don' get no fair shake from the masta' or from A.C. Tomkins, who is..." and now the man looked over at the pew where A.C. had been sitting not long before "... liar, Annabelle. They say you seen what happened to your daddy, and that he don' kill Kestin Kane. You seen that. Nobody else can vouch for your daddy but you and your mama. One day when you ready you tell wha' happened. It maybe not bring your daddy back, but maybe it bring back..." Here both Beatrice and Arthur looked up at the ceiling and seemed to look straight through it to the sky. "Maybe it bring back the rains."

In a whirlwind of confusion that came over her, Anna began to understand that what she was experiencing was real. As real as the touch of Arthur's hand and the look of love in Madia's eyes.

Beatrice chimed in. "And the poor girl has not spoken a word since she seen what she seen five years ago." The woman had the look of a large child, barely five feet tall, but her face was weathered and strong with dull eyes. She wore a wooden necklace in the shape of a crescent moon around her neck. "Your daddy was what we call a Diviner, and he had powers!"

"Nobody should be seeing their daddy hang from no rope." Beatrice reached over and cupped Anna's chin in her hand. "Nobody." She breathed in deeply. "Maybe they believe you if you talk. Maybe they believe you..."

Beatrice released her and Arthur took his hands off of her shoulder, but not before Anna could feel the concern of these caring souls who held a sort of love for her that she had not felt anywhere in River Hills. She felt she had met them in a sort of dream...somewhere in her past. Maybe it was a vision, maybe a visit of sorts. Anna scoured her mind for an answer and then, as she heard the parishioners' footsteps on the wood floor, it hit her.

The Ngaka from the hut whom she had met in the initiation lodge. Beatrice looked just like the old woman who had called her a Kimbanda, and then the vision that followed. And Arthur also was in her vision that day...a man from another time. No, it could not be, but there she was and the resemblance was beyond just physical...it was complete and total. These were the people she had met before on her initiation back home in Angola. Beatrice wore the same necklace as the Ngaka woman, a crescent moon.

They began to make their way out of the church and her new family led her away from Arthur and Beatrice. "Come Annabelle," Madia said. "You don't need to listen to folks making you 'member things you want to forget. You talk when you are ready." She stopped and looked at her daughter.

"But you need to start talking again in your own words, Annabelle. You must." Standing outside of the church, they both looked up at the cruel blue sky. Whatever gray-lined cloud that had passed by earlier that morning was now gone. They began to walk with the others who were making their way back to Nottoway. Madia turned to Calvin.

"She talk when she good and ready."

"Yes, Mama," Calvin said. The pain on the boy's face had been building for years.

"We will get masta' Kane to listen to what happened to my Jemmy," said Madia.

Anna's mind went back to the scene she had witnessed weeks before. They were weeks for sure—certainly no longer—but in this world five years had passed.

"Today we go visit your daddy's grave to remember," Madia said to Calvin and Annabelle.

The procession continued in meandering groups toward home. The outline of Camel's Hump peaks grew larger as they approached.

# Chapter 8

Inspired by the Reverend's sermon, the churchgoers returned to Tidewater Row with a lightness to their step.

Annabelle walked beside Madia and Calvin while they conversed about the service and the Sunday tasks, they hoped to accomplish that day. Arthur and Beatrice caught up with the family. Their destination was the old graveyard behind the Old Oak, where they would pay their respects to Jemmy.

The dirt cracked under her feet and the trees were either wilted or on the brink of death. Some fenced-in horses hung their heads with their tongues protruding, while others fought amongst themselves for wooden buckets filled with meager amounts of water.

The mourners soon came upon the Old Oak. Behind the tree, the long and sloping lawn led up to the magnificent Federalist estate with its rows of tall white columns.

Smaller oak trees surrounded the residence, whose beauty could be painted from almost any angle. The mansion's driveway wisped up the side of the lawn and then curved toward the impressive entrance. The driveway circled at the apex and then descended back down past various outbuildings, from sheds and outhouses to barns and warehouses. A lone carriage stood under the awning at the entrance to the estate. On the generous veranda, Annabelle could make out an old man in a white hat and suit sitting in a rocking chair. She sensed the quality of his attire from her distance of around thirty meters (almost 100 feet, using the measuring system she had come to know in America). Like so many others here, she had seen him before.

The mourners talked about the sermon about Divine faith, the unwelcome interruption by the overseers at church, and the past five years of scorching sun with only intermittent drizzles of rain. The morning dew was the only consistent water that appeared at Nottoway. As they lifted the heavy latch of the iron gate to the graveyard, Arthur called for silence. They now stood fully under the shelter of the tree, and he pointed up toward a particular branch. "They hung your daddy right off that branch. You were there, and you'se know, but no one understands why he took the rains with him, or how to bring them back."

Annabelle looked up at the branch and felt a sense of déjà vu.

*A certain tree.*

Although no remnants of the rope were visible, she looked at a flat section of the hulking tree's branch, and knew it was the spot where Jemmy, Annabelle's father, had been hanged. A sense of sadness overtook her and she found herself wondering if she could have done anything to prevent his suffocating death.

How could five years have passed in barely a month? It made no sense. But nothing made any sense to her since she had been taken from her home in Angola years ago. Why should anything suddenly begin to make sense now? A few steps later the group found themselves standing amongst the unmarked graves. Several of the granite stones had small pieces of crockery sitting on top—some organized in the shape of hearts, others in straight lines.

Beatrice touched a few headstones as she passed, citing the name of the body that slept beneath. "Horatio. Caesar. John." Her fingers graced the tops of the stones. "Hello darlings," she said. "You two died toiling in the hot sun, and my tears will fall for you forever...." Annabelle's heart went out to this mother as she spoke to her dead children.

Madia and Arthur touched the children's tombstones before continuing toward a simple, unmarked grave resting under a redbud tree that was flowering a brilliant purple.

It was as if everyone gathered there were whispering the name of the man, who lay for five years in his pine coffin beneath the dusty earth.

Jemmy.

Calvin stepped close to Annabelle and took hold of her hand. Annabelle could feel the hand was of someone who cherished her, natural in every sense.

The mourners looked down at the earth beneath their feet.

Calvin spoke first. "He was my daddy. Our daddy." He gave Annabelle's hand a gentle squeeze.

"He was my friend," said Arthur.

Annabelle could feel the words in her throat as she tried to form them.

There was so much she wanted to say, so much she wanted to ask.

He was innocent.

A chipmunk came to rest on Jemmy's gravestone, and as the sun appeared as a sudden visitor to this scene, she thought back to that night when A.C. Tomkins and Kestin Kane had come crashing into the cabin where Madia and Jemmy lay in their bed.

*"Risey up y'all!"*

He was innocent.

*"Look at that there beauty laying all pretty!"*

He was innocent.

*"You don killed your masta' and overseer, Jemmy. Look what you don!'"*

Annabelle felt the words forming on her tongue. They had been lost somewhere inside her, like water trickling down a thirsty throat and disappearing somewhere into the intricacies of a body. And then she felt the words make their way from her throat, into her skull, and finally to her tongue.

"HE DIDN'T KILL ANYONE." The words spilled forth and came out in her voice, Annabelle's voice.

Madia gasped and turned toward Annabelle. Arthur raised his hands skyward. Calvin's eyes grew wide. Only Beatrice kept her focus on Jemmy's grave.

"Of course he was, child," Ole' Beatrice said.

Annabelle felt a dizziness flash through her body and her head went light. The sunshine had now taken hold of the graveyard.

"I saw everything. I had woken up…and I looked down to see…my mother and father in the bed…they were speaking…and then, then…" Annabelle's heart started to race.

Madia looked down at the grave, "Jemmy, my love, listen to our daughter Annabelle speak again!"

The sound of the iron gate made the group suddenly turn. Reverend Cooper stood at the entrance to the graveyard. He had heard the rebirth of Annabelle's speech.

"And the Lord said, 'Behold, I have put my words in your mouth.'" The Reverend's confident voice was assured as he stepped forward and placed a hand on Annabelle's shoulder. "What befell your father, and our friend was a tragedy for us all. We have always had faith in your father's innocence, Annabelle. If you can tell me what you saw, I promise I will get the word to Masta' Kane."

Even the air seemed to hold its breath. Nothing moved, even the chipmunk sat still on the tombstone. "Go home now, child, and I will come speak with you about what you saw. For now, we pray to the Lord that Jemmy finds peace, for we know his soul is troubled and our community has been troubled with him."

Beatrice looked up at the ceaseless sky. "It's a haunt. The spirit of Jemmy can't rest. His suffering troubles the living, and now everything is dying along with him."

Annabelle looked at the small animal on top of the tombstone, which appeared to be listening to the exchange. Its reddish flesh hung loose on its frame, and she could see its anemic suffering. Everything struggled for thirst in this county, and everything was dying before its time. So many of the slaves of Nottoway had passed on these past five years—not so much for the lack of water, but for the illnesses it generated.

Arthur spoke up. "There's a rumor that many of us at Nottoway are to be sold so the masta' can make ends meet. The crop ain't worth nothin' this year, and the only thing worth anything is us slave people."

This was not surprising to the group as there had been lots of talk about the troubles Nottoway had seen since Jemmy's hanging.

Money was the water that kept the plantation flowing, and as it dried up, so had everything that trickled down with it. The hogs didn't live long enough to grow the fat needed for sufficient meat. Blackleg had attacked the cattle population. No spring rains came to water the tobacco seedlings, so back-breaking canals needed to be dug from the Rappahannock River. In normal seasons, slave people were expected to transplant one seedling every two minutes into the rows on the hills, but now the pace was cut in half and the crack of the whip insured its discipline. The only sure signs of life in the tobacco fields were the infectious worms with their fierce-looking horns that sucked the life out of the plants. There was not a field hand amongst them who had not brought these vicious creatures into their beds.

As the group made its way back to Nottoway Plantation, Annabelle noticed the hollowness in the cheeks of the people that made up this village. The disappearance of water had first afflicted their mouths, with dry tongues and cracked lips. Then it showed on the skin, which was visibly dry and sometimes peeling. Next it affected the earth, which stank of dung and cracked dirt.

And finally, it was everywhere in sight, from the birds that clung to dead branches to the Old Oak itself, which seemed to hold up its enormous branches with the greatest of effort. The dearth of water was drying up the spirit of every living being at Nottoway in the year 1824.

Anna did not belong in this underworld.

These people, whoever they were, lived in their own time, in their own lives, and somehow, someway with God's help they would find peace in their lives. It was not her place to stay, contribute or interfere. She had her own life with people she had come to know, and she vowed to live it.

She lay next to Calvin in the loft whose fingers twitched with his dreams, perhaps inching his way toward a distant Jemmy, or away from this dilapidated shelter for good. Dreams, Anna thought, were the only true escape for the enslaved, temporarily freeing them to wade in the cool waters of their imagination or help themselves to the love of long-lost relatives. She hoped that Calvin—kind Calvin–was in such a happy place right now, and she gently kissed his hand. After a few hours in the silence of the night, she gently maneuvered herself away from him, retrieved the leather pouch from behind the loose plank, and ascended the platform that would lead her home.

How long she was gone from Carolyn's world she did not know. The smell of bacon from the morning breakfast hit her as she came out of the basement door. Dishes were left in the sink that she knew Nita was expected to do. Ronnie may have had the day off. She closed the door behind her as if sneaking out of a museum that had closed hours ago. She placed the leather pouch underneath the loveseat.

The clock read 3:10 a.m. and the night had its full grasp over the house. Even Chowder, laying half on his bed and half on the floor did not stir. Anna stood in place, neither hungry, tired or confused. She was just there, and she felt that if she headed back down the stairs to the underworld or upstairs to Nita's room, neither decision was right or wrong. Still, she knew that whatever she would do, it would be her choice and no one—not a general, not a soldier, not a dead mother or one who claimed to be her new Mom, no one could make decisions for her.

Someone had forgotten to turn the TV off, and she stood on the landing and watched the images. There were cowboys and well-dressed women in what appeared to be the 1800. The sound was turned low. The actors spoke to one another with moving lips and little action. At one point, a sheriff walked into the room. The scenes struck Anna as nothing more than the going on of a time long past. She thought of the people she had met in her brief journey to the underworld, going about their business, making small decisions in a maze of uncertainty that she knew would ultimately lead them out. She wished them well.

The doors of the hallways where the family slept seemed to reflect the inhabitants inside. The door to the room she shared with Nita was closed tight. The twins were wide open, and Simba's was ajar, as if he didn't want to acknowledge that he was in fact alone. Carolyn and Mark's door seemed as if they were not even there. The dull light of the hallway ended at their door, and she could hardly even make out the doorknobs. Whether Mark was home or traveling she did not know. Whether Carolyn was there didn't even seem to matter. But as Anna put her hand on the door of her own room, she felt an urge to check on Simba.

As she opened the door of the five-year old's room, she was alarmed to find that the boy was not in his bed, and Anna moved quickly into the room. She looked in the corner where he sometimes slept rolled up in a tent made up of blankets, but the room was empty. She had a disturbing thought that he had escaped through the window and was wandering the streets looking for her, and she actually moved to the window and looked out on the dead quiet neighborhood.

"Anna," someone said behind her.

Anna whirled around and placed the back of her hands on the windowsill, as if caught.

"Simba, Simba," she said.

"I had to pee," he said. "But I think I missed. I missed the toilet. Tabby hates it when I miss the toilet. I'm sorry I missed the toilet."

Anna stared at the boy and he in turn did not move. She just knew that she was back where she belonged. She walked across the room and took the little boy's hand.

"You won't tell her will you Anna?"

"Let's go to sleep, Simba," and just like that she took the boy to his bed.

"Anna, where were you tonight? No one could find you. I thought that maybe you went to the Camel's Hump where you and I go. Did you go there? Don't go without me when you go." But he was no longer seeking a conversation or an answer. His breathing became heavier, and Anna held the little boy in her arms. In moments, he was asleep, but Anna was not tired. She was still living in another time. Her belly was full from a dinner of eggs and chicken that Ole' Beatrice had prepared for everyone. Her body was hyper alert from the newness of the long-past underworld. Her mind was intrigued from the aliveness of the people she had met, from Calvin through Madia through the Reverend. She thought of Big Arthur raising his boys with no help from anyone, except perhaps the kindness of the village and God himself.

And she thought of A.C. Tomkins who had perpetuated a lie that now seeped its venom onto an entire community. It was a sad affair mixed in with the real life and hopefulness of people who seemed to have a place for her as Annabelle, or Anna, and yes, even Zarkhanna. She wondered if she had made the right decision. After an hour of lying awake, she moved her arm out from under Simba. The boy seemed to come awake at that moment. He raised his head and looked in her eyes.

"Don't go, Anna," he said. "Please stay with me." And then he fell back asleep.

Anna relaxed her arm and fell into the pillow. Someone sneezed in another bedroom. A red flash from the ceiling smoke detector gave off its signal and Anna stared at it as if moved from right to wrong and then back again.

Tomorrow at Carolyn's 186 Tidewater Street, the morning would come. Breakfast would be served and the people that were trying to be a family would gather around and eat the food, and then disperse themselves as far away from one another as they could.

Simba would be alone, and only Anna could save that. She wanted to take him with her and escape this place. It had the strangest kind of love that the world had ever known, neither affectionate nor alienating. It was like a butterfly that had gotten into the house but escaped to corners that no one could find.

She thought of waking him, walking him down the stairs, past the sleeping Chowder and into a world that she could share with him, their own world that they could live in forever.

But the work of the underworld that needed to be done did not concern him. It was full of danger. It would be as cruel as a roving, drunk army recruiting 11-year-old girls to do the most terrible of all work.

Yet A.C. needed to be stopped, and a world of beautiful new friends needed to be helped, and with a kiss to Simba cheek and a silent promise that only they heard, she slipped her arm out from under his neck and headed again for the basement of 186 Tidewater Street.

A month passed in the underworld, and the talk of the village was that Annabelle was once again speaking after living in silence for five years. Doc Kiley said that it had been a form of consumption, but the local conjurers knew better. Ole' Beatrice claimed that the girl had been with spirits. Some said that a hag had got her, a sort of evil that feasted on her blood. But the general belief was that whatever she had seen on that fateful night she had long forgotten. On the night of her father's arrest five years ago. Annabelle had knocked her head so hard on the loft ceiling that she stayed asleep for two days, and when she finally woke up she was unable to talk. Now, it seemed like a miracle that she was speaking again, and all the slave people at Nottoway rejoiced, feeling as if a part of her had been away.

At night, she lay in the loft next to Calvin. It had become their habit to talk with one another on the large bedstead that they shared. She used the time to find out more about Jemmy, and the hard life that was his, as well as what kind of world she had joined.

"I miss Daddy," Calvin confided one night. "Remember what he used to call you, Annabelle?"

"I remember," she lied. "What did he call you?"

"Ah, he had lots of names for me, don' you remember? But 'specially liked to call me 'little strong man.'" He paused and took a breath. After what seemed like minutes he said, "I liked when Daddy called me 'little strong man.'"

She had carefully hidden the small leather pouch back behind the loose piece of timber and assured herself that she could use it at any time to return to River Hills, once she had told the entire story about what she had seen. She wondered if anyone back in River Falls would really care that she was missing, but only Simba came to mind.

Annabelle thought back to the first time she came to this underworld, when she had spent nearly three hours here and emerged back into the kitchen to find that she had been gone only for a few minutes. If that were still true, even a month here would only be one or two days there, she figured. Besides, Mark was traveling, and Carolyn was preoccupied with her next adoption in Richmond. She knew that her absence would be noticed, first by Ronnie probably. But she also knew that she needed to be here to meet with the Reverend and tell him exactly what happened to Jemmy. She needed his assurance that he would tell the authorities or Masta' Kane so that A.C. would be forced to admit the truth. Annabelle had seen men die for lesser crimes, and this was among the worst cases of deceit she had ever seen, even in her days with the army.

Only then would she be ready to return to her own time. But the weeks she had spent in this life, even with the terrible conditions and relentless work, had made her wonder to which world she belonged. She had been a slave in the army, and in a way, to the will of others for years now. She vowed to find her own freedom.

Her answer to this question could be summed up in one word: Simba. She had made a promise to him that she would care for him. By now, people back home would know that she was gone. She knew that he would be looking for her in all of the places where a five-year-old boy thinks his big sister might be hiding, and she longed to hold him and tell him that she would come back soon. Sometimes when Calvin and Madia were sound asleep, she whispered to Simba from the loft, assuring him she would be back soon. She pretended that he heard her words.

Days began at dawn with a flurry of chores, for the entire plantation, as slave work in general was on a ruthless task system. Then she would go to work in a large room with women who she recognized from her first day walking to church. It was a room given entirely to basketmaking next to the house kitchen, which was slightly downhill from the Great House and near the main stable. The smell of meat and starchy rice floated past her through the air as she worked the long days. They sat at wooden tables filled with baskets. Some were broken with tobacco stalks stuck to the bottom while others were near completion. An entire table was devoted to hand-coiled fanner baskets used for winnowing rice. Many were more practical than beautiful and were made for carrying food and other items that were needed. Annabelle could not help but turn her expert eye toward their manufacture.

The women who worked in the weaving room wore bandannas or

headdresses. Gone were the clean white kerchiefs that the women had worn to church. Their dress was industrial and practical. A Black woman who evoked authority walked up and down the tables, examining the work. She wore a red bandana and her squat figure. Her singsong accent reminded Anna of Ronnie back at Carolyn's house.

"Y'all responsible for getting two inches done today and don't think I ain't measurin'." Her name was Glennie, and she was the overseer of all of the domestic servants at Nottoway. She reported to A.C. Tomkins directly on the day's progress. "We got two inches done weaving on twelve baskets in the weaving room," or "since it be white week, we washed all the sheets and replaced 'em in the big house." She spoke in a voice so loud that sometimes the women in the weaving room gave a slight jolt at the sound of it. Her job as house overseer gave her privileges such as better rations and clothing and, especially, a hidden closet in the big house for sleeping, an unheard-of privilege that she protected with her entire being.

Annabelle had been sitting next to a girl named Lizzie, a few years older than she, who had no natural knack for the intricacies of basket weaving. A thin girl with very dark skin and large eyes, Lizzie lived with Ole' Beatrice about the time that the poor woman lost the last of her own family through a story that Annabelle could hardly follow. Lizzie was acquired by Masta' Kane when she was just four years old in exchange for two cords of lumber, and grew up with Cassandra Kane, the eldest daughter of Nottoway Plantation. When she was not working Lizzie helped Ole' Beatrice, whom she called Nanny, with the aging woman's needs. Beatrice would also help with the laundry at the big house and the two of them sold eggs to the other slave people on Tidewater Row.

"Use all your fingers," Annabelle instructed Lizzie. "When you get stuck, you can use your teeth to hold your place...like this," she said before demonstrating the technique. But Lizzie was a daydreamer and would wince when Glennie came by and tapped her shoulder. "Two inches is your task and you ain't done till I see it," she warned the girl. It seemed to Annabelle that Lizzie had been placed in the wrong room. Throughout their days together, the girl spoke of wanting to work in the kitchen where she could learn to bake, like her mother who had been sold a year ago, and to eat some of the cakes and pies and peaches that for whatever reason never made it to the Great House.

The hour was nearing three o'clock, quitting time, and the group of women were nearing completion. Annabelle had noticed that Glennie liked to start and end the day on time. She was, after all, just another slave, and she remembered how important it was to have the day end when it was supposed to. This little detail Glennie never forgot to give back to her poor flock. But in between the morning start and the afternoon quit, she loomed over the workers and was quick to report infractions to Mr. Tomkins. She was not going to have her privileges revoked. It was all she had, what with her family sold off and gone now for almost seven years.

With nothing else to do but weave all day, the women who made the baskets were able to talk sometimes, sharing rumors they had heard about the plantation. Those who had been issued tickets to neighboring plantations shared stories of friends, husbands, and lent slave people.

"A.C. tryin' to be more than the overseer of Nottoway now that Kestin out of the way," Lizzie started. "If it weren't for Miss Cassandra, he might do it."

"Change g'wine come," said Ole' Beatrice, who was allowed to help in the weaving room, although she did little.

"He don' have the smarts to run all masta' Kane's business," said a heavyset woman named Martha who was able to weave with incredible speed. "He try to put his hand in everything. My money on Miss Cassandra, if I had some money to bet y'all."

"Ain't no one makin' no money," Beatrice replied. "We ain't got no rain and no rain mean no good tobacco. I start to think about all the bad things that A.C. do that masta' Kane knows nothing 'bout."

"I like Miss Cassandra," Lizzie said dreamily. "We were friends when we were young. We used to play together on the porch." She paused, remembering. "But then we both grew up and we are not friends." She put down her work whenever her mind drifted, which was often.

"This here plantation got nothing but hungry worms and parched throats," Martha said. "Mr. Tomkins going to have no choice but to order that more trenches be dug from the river and require all the slave people to help out. Betcha they even make Ole' Beatrice here lift a shovel!"

"I ain't lifting no shovel and I tell masta' Kane that myself!" the old woman said.

"Alright then," Martha said, laughing, "maybe not Ole' Beatrice, but every slave on this land going to be digging soon, and we all know that digging nigga's makes for dying niggas. We seen too much dying on this plantation already. God help us!"

Annabelle listened and remembered the overflowing cemetery where the slave people ended up, many without any grave markers at all. She knew even their names would fade to nothing over centuries of time.

"I hear Mr. Tomkins get ready to start selling the good slave people," Martha said as she held a basket up to the light to check the tightness of her stitch. "Maybe not only the good ones," she said. "Bet cha they even try and sell Ole' Beatrice here if they can get a good dollar for her. Not sure there'll be much choice since there ain't much money for food and all."

"People ain't got no business trying to be God," Beatrice said quietly. She had been working on a winnowing basket for weeks. It was more beautiful than functional, but Glennie allowed the regress. The old woman made sure that Lizzie showed up on time, with breakfast in her belly, and that was enough for Glennie, who considered herself fair-minded.

As the quitting hour approached, two men entered the weaving room. Annabelle quickly recognized the once-handsome face of A.C. Tomkins. The disease that affected his skin now manifested in open sores on various parts of his face. It was impossible not to gaze at his oozing affliction. Annabelle watched as he spoke to Glennie out of earshot.

She had come to know A.C. well in the month and a half she had been in this world. He had become a familiar figure in their small cabin. He would come late at night to lie on Madia, who would turn her head to the side with a dead gaze Annabelle could see from the loft.

She recognized the second man as the one who entered the church with A.C. and interrupted the service. He was short, wore a pair of overalls, and went by the name Wendell. A.C. spoke up so that all could hear. "How'd we do today?" His voice tended to be overly friendly, like a new lieutenant trying to get everyone to appreciate him.

"We got the full two inches from most," Glennie replied.

"Most? Who ain't included in 'most?'" He walked between the tables examining the baskets. His concern was production, not quality. It was how he got paid by Masta' Kane.

He moved toward Annabelle. "Might it be the pretty one?" He stood over her and she could feel his breath on her neck. She looked up and caught a glimpse of his straight teeth gleaming under his broad hat. Over the previous week, Annabelle noticed that he walked around with the butt of his whip visible to all of the workers. She had never seen him use it, but the sight of the stinging instrument was intimidating enough.

"This 'ere the one? Madia's child?" He put the butt of the whip under her chin and snapped her head upright.

"No, not her. She is the best darn girl in the place. She teaches the whole school how to weave. Not a drop of water comes outta what she makes."

A.C. seemed disappointed and released her. "That's good, Glennie. Masta' Kane looking for good nigga's he can sell for even better money. What with all these hard times and no rain." He looked at Wendell, showing the junior overseer how to be in charge.

"How much dollars you think we can get for a fast-weaving nigga' girl with a pretty mama?"

Glennie spoke up. "She my best, 'twasn't her who was short. You leave her alone."

A.C. shot a glance at Glennie. "Don' you go tellin' me what's boss!"

Glennie looked away.

"Who den was short?" Wendell asked.

Glennie jutted her head toward Lizzie, who was looking down at her work. Annabelle reached over toward the girl to quickly correct a stitch. A.C. slapped her hand away.

"Why don't you finish your task, Lizzie? You lazy like your mother? We don' turn her into money because she wasn't worth anything on masta' Kane's good plantation. You no good like your mama?"

"No sir," the girl said. Then, confused, she added, "Yes sir."

"Mr. Tomkins," Beatrice said. "She all right. You leave her to Ole' Beatrice." Her comment came out like a defense and a plea. Annabelle knew that Beatrice would try her best to protect the girl whatever the case, but A.C. was fixated on her.

Glennie began shutting down the operation for the day and returning tools to the tool drawer. She instructed Martha to sweep the floor of the stray tobacco and sweetgrass that had found its way to the ground. A.C. waited and watched as the women collected their belongings and headed out of the workroom while he and Wendell stood guard over Lizzie. The men had other jobs to check on to fill in their registers for the day, so they needed to be quick.

"Git up girl!" A.C. demanded.

Annabelle watched from the edge of the adjoining kitchen while Lizzie continued to attempt to finish the task. Annabelle knew that Tomkins was capable of anything. She had seen him kill and blame another with her own eyes. And she had seen what he did to Madia.

"Man said git up," Wendell added. "So, git up."

Lizzie dropped her work and looked straight ahead. Annabelle attempted to walk toward the scene but felt Glennie's hand on her shoulder.

"She gotta learn what she gotta learn," Glennie said.

The men raised the girl by her elbows, and she dropped her work. She stood with her head down. Her once white headdress had gone grayer with each day.

"Which part about two inches don' you understand, you dumb nigga'?"

"I…I understand. I's sorry," Lizzie said.

"Sorry don't get masta' Kane his two inches." A.C. looked at his accomplice who stared at the girl as if she had just let the horses out of the barn.

"Sorry ain't good enough. Work is what we do here, and masta' Kane is good to you. Feed you. Sell your mama to a good house. This what you give him in return?"

"I's sorry," she said, her hands folded in front of her.

There was a back door where raw materials were loaded into the weaving room, and the men began to push Lizzie toward the opening. "Girl, you know any arithmetic? You know what two times two is? Cause you get double the number of lashes than what you miss in your work."

"Maybe that ain't enough, A.C.," Wendell suggested.

A.C. stopped and pondered the idea. "You know, every once in a while, you come up with a good idea," he said. "Why settle with four when we can do eight?"

"No!" Lizzie cried. "Please, no! Please!"

Annabelle was struck by the fact that the men did not seem to take particular pleasure in dishing out punishment. Instead, they acted like it was just a job that needed to be done, like throwing hay to the horses in the barn. They ceased their smiling as they escorted Lizzie out the service door. Her cries turned to whimpering and after a few minutes, Annabelle saw Ole' Beatrice head for home, her closest companion being thrashed in a crude shed. She knew loss well and Annabelle could see it in her step. The snap of the whip against Lizzie's skin sounded nearby. Like thunder following lightning, the girl's screeching cries were slightly delayed as the pain shot through her body.

Many of the slave people on Tidewater Row took their meals in a kitchen next to the smokehouse, the closest outbuilding to the Great House. The room held benches with no tables. The benches looked forward, like in church, but here they faced hot stoves and chimneys. The slaves of the plantation row mingled their rations together on Sunday evenings, mostly rice, so that the cooks could know what rations would sustain the community for the coming week. Times were hard because of the lack of rain, harder than they had ever seen, and death and dying was everywhere. Mostly short rations was what they expected and short rations was what they received, but now they were down to half rations at the order of A.C. Tomkins.

Annabelle sat with Madia and Calvin. As they finished their meager meal, Reverend Cooper entered the room. The slave people looked up at him. The mood was somber, what with not enough food and no good news to be had. The Reverend wore plain gray clothes with a buttoned vest. He walked around the room greeting parishioners but kept nodding toward Annabelle as if to make an appointment. Glennie sat at an adjoining table speaking with Lizzie. She had been calming the girl after the lashes she had received and nodded lightly to the Reverend as he approached Annabelle and her family. Glennie walked up to the Reverend in front of Annabelle and her family.

"Evening Reverend Cooper. What brings you to Nottoway?"

"Now, now Glennie. You know it is my job to look after these here slave people. Why you asking questions you know I ain't gonna give no answers?"

"Well don' be upsetting everybody with yer talk of freed slave people and such. We got enough trouble here."

The Reverend removed his top hat and stroked his whiskers. "Good evening, Glennie, and don' be telling no Rev Cooper his business."

The woman turned on her heels and headed for the door.

"Tell masta' Kane I give my regards," the Reverend called after her. He watched her disappear out the door of the smokehouse.

"May I join you, Mrs. Cudjo?" he said, addressing Madia. The Reverend sat down and began to speak about his recent visit to Philadelphia. He had bought a new top hat, and he allowed Annabelle and Calvin to stroke its smooth finish. After a pause, he suggested that they all go somewhere private so that they could speak.

Madia nodded. They collected their plates, dropped their scraps in the pig bucket, and went outside and headed down Tidewater Row and entered their quarters. Red coals in the fireplace gave out a warm light. The Ndimba doll made it feel like home to Annabelle in a way that Calvin and Madia would never understand. Outside the window, they saw Glennie walking in their direction.

"Watch out for that one," the Reverend said, listening to her footsteps come closer and stop for a moment in front of the cabin before continuing on by. The assembled group waited till they heard her resume her footsteps.

The Reverend drew a chair in front of the fire. "Now Annabelle, tell me exactly what happened that night, what you heard and what you saw." He held his hand out and she took it in her own. As Madia and Calvin looked on, Annabelle described what she witnessed from the loft. Calvin sat down next to her, placing a hand on her shoulder in an effort to comfort his younger sister. She welcomed him next to her.

"When Jemmy...my Daddy, stood up to stop the bad things they were going to do to Mama..." she began, calling Madia by the name that made sense in this two-act play in which she was the star, "the men...Mr. Tomkins and Kestin began to fight. It was quick, but I know that Jemmy... my father...did not kill that man. I saw Mr. Tomkins grab Kestin by the shoulders and throw him into that wall." She pointed toward the very spot of the occurrence as if giving indisputable evidence.

"So, you are sure that you definitely saw Mr. Tomkins kill Kestin Kane?" the Reverend asked. "These are very serious charges, my dear. Are you certain that you saw it as you tell us now?" His face was grim, but in the firelight, she saw comfort in his eyes.

Annabelle took a moment to run the memory of that evening back in her mind. "Yes, I am positive—positive Mr. Tomkins killed Kestin Kane," she said. "I remember what he said. Something like 'I ain't gonna listen to no coward...You spend yo' time counting the money I make for you. I'm more of a Kane than you ever will be.' And then Mr. Tomkins pushed Kestin hard—hard—into a nail, right over there. That nail over there!" She pointed and spoke as if solving the crime once and for all. Her voice was loud, and the Reverend quieted her with a hand gesture. Outside, horses neighed, and a group of slave people passed the house, talking quietly to one another.

Madia held her head low. “What’s the difference, Reverend? No one believe her anyway and even if they did it wouldn’t bring Jemmy back to his family.”

“You’re right as rain that it won’t bring nobody back to life, but we know that since the masta’s only son died, Tomkins is vying to be in charge of all the masta’s affairs. He is a bad man and will continue to do bad things to the slave people of Nottoway, and these people are my flock. We need masta’ Kane to know who killed his son, and once he know that, Tomkins is gone from this land and maybe…” The preacher looked up at the ceiling, beyond the crude wooden frame to the clouds and sky above, “maybe the suffering will end, and things will get better for our people. Maybe your daddy’s soul can rest. As it is, he troubled and he place a curse that he don’ mean, but that curse is what is haunting this land and stopping the rain. We start with telling the truth to masta’ Kane and getting A.C. Tomkins off this land and easin’ the suff’rin.”

Annabelle had been listening intently to the wise Reverend. Whatever she thought she could solve by coming back to this past world and telling the truth now seemed doubtful. She was reminded of the time that she had gone looking for food for the commander and came across the old woman in the garden with her cats. She had felt the comfort of the woman’s simple cottage and cool milk, but in the end it did nothing to stop Annabelle from continuing her servitude to the UNITA fighters. The truth about Jemmy might not do anything to change what needed to be changed. Life was so hard here, so cruel and unjust. For the first time, she desperately wanted to go back to River Hills.

She looked toward the loft where the leather pouch was safely hidden. She thought of running up right then until she remembered that she felt no more destined for that world than she was for this one. At least here there was a chance she could make a difference and possibly ease some of the pain that was everywhere in this year of 1824. Stuck in this dilemma, she found words falling out of her mouth, the question she had been desperate to ask since her first visit here.

“What happened to my father, Reverend?”

No one spoke for a long time.

Calvin broke the silence. “Don’ cha remember, sister?”

“Calvin, you know she hit her head on the ceiling and was knocked out for two days. Den’ she stop speakin’ ’cause of what she see,” said Madia.

"Maybe you have heard it in the kitchen or the weave room, Annabelle. But if not, I'll remind you." Calvin bent over and added some kindling to the fire. It sparked up and they all became mesmerized by the small flame. "Our daddy was tried twice in a court of law at the old courthouse in Tappahannock. Judge Moore presided over the trial."

"Judge Moore's a friend of mine," the Reverend said, and the preacher now picked up the story from Calvin. "He has a good heart, but this one... well this one got away from his goodness.

"The trial took place in the Essex County courthouse just like Calvin says. He had a lawyer that Masta' Kane provided for him. His name was Mr. Quentin and he tried to allow for Madia to testify, but the Slave Codes don' allow for no slaves to serve as witness against a White person."

Caught between the two worlds, one of which she had seen by happenstance and one in which she now knowingly entered, Annabelle wondered why she was not somehow more involved in this trial the Reverend spoke of.

The Reverend continued. "Annabelle was said to be awake during the murder, but neither the prosecutor nor Mr. Quentin felt that putting a nine-year-old slave child on the stand would further either of their cases. Besides, Annabelle had lost her ability to speak after the murder." The clergyman stared into the fire as Annabelle tried to think of way to explain, but there were no words for what she had been thru.

"In the end, Mr. Quentin called two witnesses, Mr. Henry Wilkins, the night watchman, and Doc Kiley, who Madia knows was present that night, but that Wilkins man is a coward and Doc Kiley is a drunk. Neither man had any intentions of standing up for a Negro field hand against the Kane family.

"Then, A.C. Tomkins took the stand on behalf of the prosecution saying that they had gone down to Tidewater Row with a doctor to check on the health of one of his own and that Jemmy attacked the men. It didn't help that Kestin had an abrasion on his head that the detectives matched in shape and size to the piece of wood that Jemmy hit him with," the Reverend concluded.

"Even though that little nick didn't kill Kestin," Madia said, as if testifying.

No one spoke.

"What killed Kestin was A.C. Tomkins throwing him against a nail on the wall," Annabelle said.

"There were no credible witnesses to advocate the lawyer's claim of reasonable self-defense, unless one were to allow for the testimony of a mute slave girl," the Reverend said, remembering the trial's written court documents, and the punishment was according to the slave codes.

Madia recited the awful words etched into her memory. "This court finds the defendant Jemmy of Nottoway Plantation guilty under the Slave Laws Proposition 19d, section 2. The sentence shall be hanging until you are dead. May God have mercy upon your soul."

"And that was it?" Annabelle asked, incredulously.

"They took Daddy to the jail cell," Calvin said. "Masta' Kane visited him and made sure he was as comfortable as possible. He knew there was some wrongdoing on the part of someone. He just didn't know who. There was so much talk going against Jemmy."

"He knew," Madia lamented. "He knew." She placed her forehead in her hand. Outside, the night ticked away with the clicking of insects and the chirping of fox squirrels. Bobcats were always nearby, and the occasional howl of the creatures echoed up the crevices of the nearby Camel's Hump.

"I went to see him too. To say goodbye," Madia finally said.

No one dared to ask for more information on her private memory with her husband, but Madia continued. "He said that Masta' Kane came down and talked about the old times, when Jemmy was jus' a boy and Master Kane was learning the ways, but those men remembered the old times in different ways. Then Masta' Kane said he would look after us, his family and he left."

A long silence ensued.

"And then?" Annabelle said.

"You saw the tree, child," the Reverend said, taking her hand. "Tomkins had all of the slave people watch. I presided over the service."

"The murder!" Calvin interrupted.

"Was Masta' Kane there for the...hanging?" Annabelle asked.

"I saw him on the porch of the Great House in his rocking chair with that red checkered blanket over his knees," the Reverend responded. "So, you can say he was there, or that he was not there. I don' think he approved, but these are bad times for our people."

"People ain't got no business trying to be God," said Calvin. It was

Ole' Beatrice's line, but many of the slave people used it these days.

At this point, Madia began to weep softly. The Reverend knew that these memories hurt her, but Annabelle had been a witness to important events, so he continued with the thought that the truth needed to be ripped from the ground, like rotten tobacco.

"What did my daddy say, before they...?" Annabelle asked.

"I asked your daddy...is there anything you wish to say before you meet your Lord?" The Reverend looked into the fire.

"Your daddy looked around at the crowd assembled and repeated that he was an innocent man. Tomkins then called your daddy a liar as he stood on that four-legged stool with the rope around his neck, dressed in the same suit that Masta' Kane had given to him for the trial."

The image sent Annabelle back to the vision of the man in an old suit standing beside his cross along the curve below Camel's Hump.

"Tomkins again claimed that your daddy viciously killed Kestin for no reason, but I looked at Tomkins and told him to hold his tongue before the Lord. So, I asked your Daddy again to speak before Jesus, if he so wishes."

Madia lifted her head off her lap. She looked at Annabelle and the Reverend. "Yes, then he speaks. He say something," she said.

"Your daddy was what they know in these parts as a conjurer. He was known to heal people who were sick, and make it rain when there was no water in the skies. He had a leather pouch he carried that had certain things he would heal people with. I never looked inside, and I never asked about it. But your Daddy did heal people, and he got his power from Camel's Hump, that much I know. He was no ordinary man."

Annabelle's eyes widened and she looked up the loft toward the leather pouch lay hidden.

"Now he stood on that stool in an old suit Masta' Kane gave him and he looked directly at A.C. Tomkins. He looked at that man and he said these words that I never forgot... 'You ain't gonna git what you want by doing away with me, 'cause I ain't going nowhere,' your daddy says.

"A.C. now walk right up to your daddy and he call him a no-good nigga', and even I could not stop A.C.'s rage at your daddy. But Jemmy kept staring down at him as the rope dug into his neck. And then I'll never forget his last words.

"He says, '*A.C., you will burn in suffering as these slave people suffer, but I release them from....*'

"But he never got all the words out. As he was speaking, A.C. screamed out 'Let's be done with this murderin' nigga'!' and before the executioner could stop him, A.C. done kicked over that chair mid-sentence, before your Daddy could say the final words that he was going to say. The rope then snapped tight, and your Daddy writhed and gasped for a long time, until all the life and breath gone out of him. But we all knew he wasn't able to finish what he was saying, that he meant to say something else."

"Release what?" Annabelle asked. "What was my daddy trying to say?"

Madia spoke up. "He wanted A.C. Tomkins to suffer for his lies, not the slave people. Not his own people."

Calvin finished the thought. "But A.C. interrupted him and the nature spirit in the Ole' Oak captured his words before they got out and conjured them all up. Folks believe that whatever our daddy wanted to say got buried in the thick of the branch that he hung from, which is what nature spirits do. It was unfinished business. Now the curse is buried in that tree and the wind spread it every night throughout this county. Five years now."

"Five years," Madia repeated, throwing a log on the flame. "And a' course A.C. become head overseer at Nottoway with no Kestin around to get in his way."

Calvin stared into the fire and then looked at everyone as if he wanted a different end to the story. He had lost his father and what was left of his boyhood.

"The process of dying may not be complete for five years. God help us," Madia concluded.

Annabelle listened intently. "Is there anyone else I should tell about what I saw?"

The Reverend thought about her question. "Yes, I believe so. I will speak to Masta' Kane and ask if we can all meet. He is getting on in his years. He don' want any more trouble than he got, and if A.C. done what you say, and I know he did, Masta' Kane and Miss Cassandra will deal with it. People ain't got no business playin' God." He looked at Calvin and smiled. "Maybe some good come of this after we speak with Masta' Kane."

Madia took the Reverend's hand and thanked him for coming and he left to return to his church. The widow was too exhausted to speak any further. Calvin retrieved wood for the hearth and brought in a bucket of drinking water for the night. Madia lay down and Annabelle placed a blanket over her. When she saw that she was quietly crying, Annabelle climbed in next to Madia, held her, and they both cried for different reasons, but with tears as real as one another's.

The next day, the Reverend sent word that Master Kane and his eldest daughter could meet the coming up Friday at noon on the veranda of the Great House. Although the Reverend had requested that the meeting be sooner, it was not possible because Master Kane was scheduled to travel to Philadelphia on business. They would have to wait three days.

Annabelle lay awake in the loft thinking of the words she would use to tell Master Kane about what really happened to his son. She knew that when she told the commanders about the wayward actions of some of the soldiers, there were consequences. But that was in her own time. What would happen in this time and for a moment, she could see that it might make little difference. Still, she vowed to tell the old man what she saw.

Directly following that meeting on Friday, she planned to use the leather pouch to return to Carolyn's home.

Forever.

Madia worked as a servant in the Great House, reporting to Glennie. Her primary job was to attend to the daughters of Master Kane. Mary Louise and Cassandra had lost their mother at an early age, and they relied on Madia for both their most intimate and public needs. The younger Miss Kane, Mary Louise, had been ill with yellow fever. It seemed that everyone at Nottoway had at one time or another contracted the disease and had been able to ward off its more severe symptoms, but Mary Louise was a frail girl with a constitution that made her prone to falling ill. At times she had to be carried to the chamber pot, her brow continually wiped with a cool cloth that needed to be replenished from the icehouse.

It was Wednesday, two days before the meeting with Master Kane was scheduled to take place. After making breakfast for Calvin and sending him off to the tobacco fields with the other field hands large and small, Madia walked with Annabelle along Tidewater Row to begin their workday. It was August and the weight of the heat hit the residents of Nottoway.

"You are growing up so nice and strong," Madia said, slowing her walk to extend their time together. "I wonder, what kind of work will you do when you all grown?" She spoke in a hopeful tone, but like a visiting teacher to a remote village who knows that the students will never leave.

Annabelle had the benefit of having studied history in school, and she knew that speaking of a future was of little consequence. For whatever reason, she was now this woman's daughter, and she knew that this bond was almost all that Madia had left in the world. Given the love that Madia had shown her—helping her get dressed, brushing her hair, singing softly as she and Calvin fell asleep in the loft—she wanted to give back what she could.

"I want to be like you, Mama," said Annabelle, squeezing her mother's hand.

No one spoke but they brushed shoulders as they walked at a comfortable pace.

"I love the smell of flowers in summer," Madia said, even though there was nothing to smell other than dry earth. They walked on in silence for some minutes.

"I ask Glennie if you can help me today with Miss Kane," Madia said. "I can hardly lift her with my back, and you can make your weaving in the next room. If I need you, I will call you, but you work in the Great House this week. Glennie says it alright."

"Yes, Mama," she answered.

Annabelle went to work in a small room that was adjacent to Mary Louise's room and listened to the conversations throughout the day. Whereas she could hear the moans as Mary Louise endlessly called for Madia to bring her water, or flowers to smell, or bread with 'light butter,' Annabelle would also hear the older Cassandra bound into her sister's bedroom with her fierce energy like the horses she was known to gallop near the tobacco fields. It was said that Cassandra was the favored daughter of Master Kane, and he was grooming her to be well-versed in business affairs, including the family's interests in all the businesses for which Master Kane partook.

Annabelle worked on a fanner basket that was to be used to cover food and rice grain. Although light sweetgrass was plentiful around the area, she could not help herself from finding darker shades of bulrush and finishing her work with at least a few lighter triangles in the tradition she had been taught by Auntie. Her midday meal was brought to her by Lizzie as Glennie had succeeded in reassigning the girl to kitchen and house duties. The whipping that the young girl had taken at the hands of the overseers had little effect on making her more adept at the intricacies of weaving a sweetgrass basket.

"Mary Louise is in a bad way," Lizzie said. "Best you stay away. Your Mama in there dealing with her. Anyways, Miss Cassandra in there now helping your Mama attend to her needs." At that moment, Annabelle heard Madia's voice.

"Annabelle, child. Stop what you're doing and come in here and help me out with Mary Louise."

Annabelle and Lizzie looked at one another as if they were playing a game and got caught. It was not proper for Annabelle to shout out in the Great House, so she left her weaving on the table and entered the bedroom where Madia was attending the younger Miss Kane. Cassandra stood nearby, impatiently observing the servants.

"Thank you, Annabelle," Madia said. "Miss Kane is not feeling herself and she needs help getting to the chamber. Help me lift her up, child."

Annabelle walked over to the bed. Mary Louise lay on her side facing the opposite wall. She was a thin and sickly-looking girl with hair down to her waist. It was said that she had not cut her hair since her mother died. The girl lay in a white dressing robe with small strawberries weaved into the fabric. The older sister, Cassandra, a quick-moving picture of health, watched the scene from an adjacent chair. She had the athletic build of someone who could lift a carriage out of a mudhole' if the moment required. There was a rumor that it was she, the elder sister, who was to take over the plantation when Master Kane passed, and this fact was one that A.C. Tomkins knew well. Now, Annabelle and Lizzie began to retrieve the sick girl from her bed and bring her to the water closet. Madia guided the three of them, taking Lizzie's elbow.

"Oh, oh," Mary Louise said as she was picked up and led across the room. "Is my daddy still here? Tell my daddy to come and see me. I feel so weak today!"

"Yes, Miss Kane," Madia answered.

When they had returned the girl to her bed, the young mistress sat on the edge of the mattress. Her hair covered her face like brush in a forest. She had the look of a girl who would grow thinner as she grew older. Her complexion was clean and young, but her body moved like an old woman. They then helped the younger girl change into her day clothes.

Miss Cassandra got up off of her chair in the corner and walked over to her sister. She swept her sister's hair off her face and applied a wet towel to her forehead, wiping off the sweat that had formed from the brief excursion to the water closet. The girls began to speak of a planned vacation to the Carolina coast.

"The Parsons are heading to their summerhouse in a week, and Daddy says I can go with them. Maybe you should come with us. It will be good for your constitution Mary-Lou."

"How can I travel when I am so very ill?" the girl responded, looking up at her sister.

"I'll take care of you, and you will ride with me in Daddy's carriage. We'll play cribbage and before you know it, we will be at the seashore with our toes in the sand. They say it rains all the time down there. Let us get out of this cursed county!"

Annabelle watched as the two sisters interacted, and whether it was the heat, or her breakfast this morning, she began to feel queasy and dizzy. A vapor began to fill the room, like a mist. It danced and hovered around the sisters as they spoke. The conversation between them crawled around her skin like the tobacco worms from Calvin's work clothes at the end of the day.

"Get me some more water, Annabelle," Cassandra ordered without looking at her.

Annabelle stood frozen in place.

"Annabelle, get me some more water for my sister!"

"Go get some water, child," Madia softly urged.

It could not actually be, but Annabelle felt like she was listening to Mary and Cassy months ago. Here they were, in this other world, in another time, and interacting with her in a completely different way. As Annabelle returned with a crystal pitcher of water handed to her by Lizzie, she found the two sisters sitting next to one another on the bed. Madia waited outside the room as the girls talked amongst themselves. They were not concerned with Annabelle. They had not heard the news that the slave girl had regained her voice, so they felt that their secrets were safe.

"I saw yesterday that nigga' boy look twice at you when you were out taking air."

"To whom are you referring, Mary Louise?"

"Why Calvin of course, the son of the nigga' that killed out dear brother. Why don't we send that boy a message that you favor him, Sistah, and want to meet him at the shed?" Mary Louise said. "Then we'll inform Mr. Tomkins that one his darkies is casting an eye at a Kane sister!"

"Why Mary Louise!"

They both glanced over at Annabelle.

"Tell him that I like him and want to give him a kiss," Cassandra said.

"Yes, a kiss! Then we will tell Mr. Tomkins that he's got a darky on his hands who likes to look at Kane girls. He knows how to deal with that kind," Mary Louise said.

"Well, I don't want to get in trouble with Daddy though!" Cassandra said.

"We can talk to any nigga' on this plantation we want to, Sistah, as lon' as it's not Sunday," Mary Louise said. "And if a slave boy is lookin' at one of us Kane girls, then we have the right to apply the same kinda right disc'pline that Daddy in his day would rightly administer himself!"

They both glanced at Annabelle sitting across the room. At this point, Ole' Beatrice, half blind, dragged her feet into the room to drop off laundry. While the woman's hands and body were no longer what they once were, she kept careful watch and ears over the slave people. She nodded in the direction of the Kane sisters and then departed, but Annabelle could feel that she was just outside the door.

"Don't mind Annabelle," Mary Louise said to her sister. "She's a half-wit, hasn't spoken in five years. And I bet that Calvin ain't even her real brother given the way those people breed!"

Annabelle sat frozen in time.

On and on the sisters spoke, holding hands within the white haze that now encompassed the room. Once again, the queasiness welled up in Annabelle, but this time it had nothing to do with the vapor filling her nostrils. She now detected the smell of a land desperate for rain or water but, having none, sank deep into its own arid stench.

"Annabelle, where is that water?" Miss Cassandra repeated.

The room began to spin in time.

"...That slave Jemmy was a murderer who killed our big brother. He hung like a well bucket and I'm glad for it! It's up to us to teach our servants how to act around decent folk!"

Annabelle watched as the words tumbled out of the girls' mouths. She felt the blood rush to her temples, blinding her in a whiteness that made her uneasy on her feet, but the girls failed to notice. She could hear that Mary Louise was speaking, but the words were no longer making sense.

Outside the window, she saw the sunshine shedding its torturous light over the tobacco fields where she could make out small figures toiling over the dried stalks that were crawling with insect-infested leaves.

She now recognized this room from the time she had watched Mary's bedroom in River Hills transform before her eyes. Up above, the yellowish canopy draped over the bed. There, the oak rolltop desk with parchment paper and a fountain pen. On that wall, the painting of a local scene with horse-drawn carriages and oak trees standing along the old Highway 17, Camel's Hump in the background. The girls themselves wore cotton print dresses; their necks hidden by the high collars. Lacy bonnets topped off their outfits.

"Maybe Glennie or Mr. Tomkins will see us talking to him and ask what we are doing," Cassandra said.

"Remember, this is our right! We must protect the 'tegrity of Nottoway!"

"Tell me Sister, 'cause I know it's true, don't you have other business with Mr. Tomkins? I know that you have caught his eye on more than one occasion! He is most handsome!"

The younger girl blushed and brought her arm to her forehead, a sickness coming upon her, but she smiled. "I cannot help who requests visits with me, dear Sistah!"

Their plans set; the girls moved on in their conversation about the upcoming holiday trip to Pawleys Island. To them, it was as if Annabelle were not present.

Whether these girls were friends of hers in another time, she did not know. But she felt she needed to do something, and the thought of it alarmed her. If she were to tell Master Kane on Friday of the girls' prank, word would get back to them and who could tell what would happen from there? He would surely protect his daughters. She must warn Calvin about this plot. Telling him could be a matter of life or death.

She had to warn Calvin of the plot to entrap him. Then she would return to the other world she came from, even if it held little for her.

But the conversation to warn Calvin would never take place.

Nor did any such meeting with Master Kane.

Tomkins had learned from the eavesdropping Glennie that Madia and Annabelle planned to speak to the old man and point to him as the real killer of Master Kane's son. He made quick plans.

The next morning Tomkins descended upon Madia and Annabelle as they were starting their day. They were forced onto two separate wagons.

"You two troublemakers are leaving Nottoway for good. You been sold. We don't need no bad hands on Masta' Kane's land," he said, pushing them along. They had no belongings with them whatsoever. Annabelle found herself helpless at the hands of a man who had the power to keep her permanently in a world she did not belong in, a world she could no longer escape.

She would never see Madia again.

# Chapter 9

The Jefferson Hotel in Richmond, Virginia, was holding a two-day symposium on Chinese adoptions. It was the second day of the conference, Monday morning, and Carolyn White sat in the back row of the ballroom. Her phone was on silent when she noticed a vibration in her purse. She fumbled for the device and looked at the caller ID.

"Hello Juanita," she said. "I'm in my conference, can I call you back?"

"Sure, but I just wanted to ask you something."

Carolyn stood up and the conference speaker, an immigration attorney, momentarily stopped his PowerPoint presentation as she exited through the function room's double doors.

"Everything OK?"

"Yes. Just calling to see...if you know where Anna is. No one can find her."

"What do you mean? Where is she?" Carolyn asked.

"We thought you'd know."

"Who's we? Isn't she home?"

"No, Mom."

"Have you checked Mary's?"

"Mary doesn't know where she is either. Anna didn't come home last night. When I call her mobile it just goes to voicemail."

Carolyn felt a rush of panic sweep through her body. "Where's your father?" she asked, thinking back to his schedule. Mark had left home Saturday and was scheduled to fly back from Vegas on Tuesday. He was at an investor conference, organized by the Sundance Festival. It was an event where screenplays were being auctioned and filmmakers could make the deal of a lifetime, or head home no better off than the retirees who stuffed their last nickels in the airport slots.

"I don't know where he is, and I don't know where Anna is, which is why I called you, Mom."

"Where's Ronnie?"

"I don't know, Mom. I have to go to work. I was just calling to see if you knew where Anna was. I'm sure she's fine. I have to go."

"Juanita, don't hang up! Go get Ronnie."

"I'll tell her to call you. I gotta go," and she hung up.

Carolyn took in a breath, called Anna's cell phone, and was immediately sent to voicemail. She tried to sound calm. "Anna, dear, can you please call me as soon as you get this? We're all wondering where you are. Please call as soon as you can." Carolyn closed her flip phone, then opened it again, and tried Anna a second time.

The wide hallway outside the conference room was deserted. Coffee stains ran over the white tablecloth on the refreshment table. An easel held a large placard advertising *Adopting the Chinese Child.* Next, she called Mark and left him a message to call her when he had a second. She did not want to appear panicked. She then called the house. It rang and rang. Finally, someone picked up. It was Tabitha.

"Hi Tabby, how are you sweetheart?" Carolyn started down the escalator toward the lobby. A towering chandelier hung over the room. A bus was parked outside the entrance and elderly people were slowly disembarking.

"I'm fine, Mommy. Are you back?"

"No sweetie, but I will be soon. Is Ronnie there?"

Carolyn heard Wyatt in the background. "Let me talk to her! Tabby, no!" The boy grabbed the phone.

"Hi Mommy! We can't find Anna!"

Tabitha grabbed the phone back. "Mommy, guess what? There was a fire at the end of the street and an ambulance came."

Carolyn tried to focus. She tried to go through the revolving doors but became trapped when an elderly man halted the turnstile midway, waiting for his wife.

"A fire?" Carolyn asked, flustered.

"There was a fire truck!" yelled Wyatt in the background.

"Tabitha, please go get Ronnie. I need to ask her about your sister."

"She's not our sister, Mommy. She's adopted."

"Tabitha White!" Carolyn raised her voice. "This is no time for games. Anna didn't come home last night!"

The girl fell quiet, and Carolyn realized she was not helping the situation. She fumbled in her purse for her parking ticket and gave it to a high-school-aged bellhop in a white button-down shirt and bowtie who then jogged down the drive toward the underground lot.

"I don't know where Ronnie is, and I don't know where Anna is either," Tabitha replied, starting to cry.

"Tabitha, listen to me carefully, OK honey? Go find Ronnie and tell her to call me immediately."

Carolyn tipped the bellhop, jumped into her car, and started driving down Route 650. She tried to calm herself. There must have been some miscommunication. She pressed her foot on the pedal to pass the car in front of her. She fumbled with her phone, and it slipped out of her hand and landed in between the seats. Soon after the speedometer hit 86 mph, Caroline noticed blue lights in her rearview mirror.

"God damn it!" she cried and tried unsuccessfully to reach for her phone, scraping her hand on something metal. She pulled over in front of a national historical landmark which was adjacent to a sign indicating she was headed west, away from Tappahannock.

The plaque for the landmark was for the sight of the Tuckahoe Plantation. It resembles a tombstone along the highway, its white lettering raised against a black backdrop.

***Tuckahoe Plantation***

*Boyhood home of Thomas Jefferson, 3rd President of the United States*

*Thomas Jefferson spent part of his youth on this land in the late 1700s. Tuckahoe Plantation served as a tobacco plantation from 1740 through 1900. 86 enslaved persons worked this land until 1864.*

There were so many plantation sites in Virginia, but like a New Yorker who had never gone to the Statue of Liberty, Carolyn had never visited any of them. That era was far gone, and good riddance. What was the South thinking? She gazed at the sign as a female trooper stepped up to her car. Carolyn's phone rang and she searched for it, jamming her hand between the seats again. The trooper tapped on her windshield as Carolyn fumbled with the window switch while feeling for the phone.

"Officer, I need to take this phone call," she said before the policewoman could speak. “My daughter is missing!”

“Do you know how fast you were going, ma’am?”

“Officer, I don’t know.” Her phone continued to buzz. “I’m sorry, but I have to take this call.” She grabbed the phone between two fingers, dropped it again and then pushed it forward between the seats before unflipping the receiver.

“Hello?”

Ronnie had hung up.

“Ma’am, your license and registration please.”

Carolyn ignored the request and redialed Ronnie, who answered on the first ring. “Ronnie, hi, how are you? I got a call from Nita who said she hadn’t seen Anna. Do you know where she is?” She could hear the twins yelling in the background.

“I thought that she slept over at Mary’s house last night,” Ronnie replied. “But Nita says she didn’t, so we’re looking for her now, Mrs. White.”

“Ronnie, where the hell is Anna? I’m in Richmond for God’s sake. Where is she?”

“I am checking around, Mrs. White. I’m sure she is fine.”

“Hold on Ronnie, I was stopped by the police. Give me a second.” Carolyn put the phone to her chest and looked up at the policewoman.

“May I see your license and registration please?”

Carolyn reached into her purse. “My name is Carolyn White, and I live in Tappahannock. I was rushing home because I was just told that my fourteen-year-old didn’t come home last night.” Carolyn handed her license to the officer. She did not look at it.

“OK, OK. Finish your call, please.”

“Ronnie, I’m on my way home. Please let me know if you hear anything. Wait, where’s Simba?”

“Simba right here,” Ronnie said.

“Good. Did she tell anyone where she was going? Could she be at a sleepover? Does Mary or Cassy have any idea where else Anna could be?” The officer looked on.

When Carolyn hung up, the trooper asked her to get out of the car, escorted her to the cruiser, and sat her in the front seat.

"Now tell me what's going on. How long has your teenage daughter been missing?"

"I don't know. I have to get home!"

"Mrs. White, I can be of assistance. Let's start with your daughter's name, age, height, and weight."

Carolyn tried to calm herself, beginning with her breathing. A school bus passed slowly and made an awkward turn into the plantation entrance, which her Audi was partially blocking. She gave all the details she could think of to the officer, who then reported to dispatch. After several minutes, the information was reduced to "Possible missing minor, 14-year-old African American female, 5'5", approximately 125 lbs., long dark hair, goes by the name Anna White, last seen in the River Hills area."

The officer spoke gently. "I'm sure your daughter's fine, Mrs. White. We'll contact the Tappahannock Police Department to make them aware of the situation. These things usually sort themselves out in a few hours. I'm sure everything will be OK. About the speeding, I'm going to let you go with a warning. You're actually headed in the wrong direction anyway. You need to take 650 East back to Richmond and then take Highway 360 East to Tappahannock. Your local police will contact you with any further questions. Go take care of your family, and please, drive safely."

Now headed in the right direction, Carolyn drove along the road and was soon held up by a ten-car traffic jam caused by an overpacked hay wagon following a Kubota tractor. Shortly afterward she had to wait for a construction crew to allow the cars in her lane to cross a narrow bridge. While she waited, she called Mark, who was heading for a meeting and knew nothing. Words poured out of her of what little she knew, and the conversation ended with Mark saying that he was heading home anyway.

Next, she called Priscilla. As she fiddled with the phone, she looked up to see that she had crossed the double yellow line and a Ford Taurus coming toward her veered away and leaned on its horn. Carolyn recovered her car.

"I am sure Anna is just fine, Carolyn," Priscilla drawled. "Don't worry, we will find her. Wait, hold on." Then, speaking off the receiver, it sounded like she was checking in for a spa appointment.

Carolyn now realized that she should never have left five children to Ronnie. The Jamaican nanny was getting older, and it was too much to ask to look after three young children and two teenage girls. This much she knew: Anna had slept at home on Saturday night but was missing as of yesterday morning, and nobody said anything. Everyone thought she spent the night at Mary's, including Nita, Ronnie, and Carolyn, although she realized that she never called yesterday or checked on the kids. "Anna would surely be found soon," she told herself, but now she was beginning to worry that word would be getting around that she had lost track of her child.

As five o'clock rolled around and Nita returned from work, Carolyn had made no more progress than she had on the roadside under the purview of the state trooper. The only difference between then and now was that the entire town probably knew that her daughter was missing. She had forgotten to ask Priscilla to keep it quiet, but she didn't want it to be kept quiet. She wanted to find Anna, just not in a way that was too public.

As she pulled into the driveway, Mark called. He had taken the first available flight and was driving in from D.C.

"Where on Earth could she be?" Mark asked, the cell service intermittent as he spoke. She had no news to tell him. The baffling set of circumstances was as hard to understand as why Ronnie couldn't keep proper track of her kids.

Detective Ted Washington came from a long line of policemen, but to Carolyn he was just a guy she knew from high school who never went anywhere. Someone once mentioned that Ted had tried out for a Redskins farm league. He was rumored to have had a child with a local White woman, but no one knew who or even if it was true. She had heard that he lived with a sister in a house they inherited when their parents passed on, which overlooked the Rappahannock River. In high school, Ted was a well-liked football player who happened to be Black. He had always wanted to date Carolyn, and she did nothing to inhibit the infatuation. But when he asked her to the prom, she had declined.

The detective now sat with Carolyn and Mark in the kitchen of their home in River Hills. It was now almost eight o'clock on Monday night. Under the circumstances, Ronnie had agreed to sleep over. She had succeeded in getting the children to bed, a chore that Carolyn greatly appreciated her doing. It was not her fault.

Anna had now been missing for close to thirty-six hours. The last person to see her was Nita, who said that Anna was asleep in their room Saturday night when Nita had come home around midnight. She had assumed that Anna was sleeping over at the Kanes' house on Saturday night. But when Mary called the next morning, they came to the realization that everyone thought that Anna was with someone else.

Priscilla had stopped calling, not wanting to intrude, but other parents were now calling to offer help. Carolyn felt as if someone in her family had been diagnosed with cancer and no one wanted to get too close, or too far.

"Can you think of any reason she might have run away? Or anyone she might have gone to see? A relative, maybe a boyfriend?" the detective asked. Carolyn looked to Mark for any kind of good idea between them. Her eyes widened. She could think of nowhere the girl would go, and the idea of an abduction in this neighborhood was inconceivable.

"We can't." Carolyn and Mark both shook their heads.

"When did you leave town?" the detective asked, looking from one parent to the other.

"Saturday afternoon around two o'clock," Carolyn muttered. It seemed like a week had passed.

"Also Saturday. About 10 a.m.," Mark replied. It came out like a question.

The detective took notes. For Carolyn, it was after lunch, just before she left for Richmond. For Mark, it was when he was packing for his trip to Vegas. He had just come downstairs for something when Anna told him she was going to Mary's house.

"Priscilla's daughter. You remember Priscilla Martin, Ted? Now she's Priscilla Kane." She stated the facts as if trying to convince him of the normalcy of the situation and their parenting, and how inconceivable it was that a child of theirs would go missing.

Nita entered the kitchen holding a sheet of paper in her hand.

"I may have found something," she said.

The three adults looked at Nita, who had dyed part of her hair pink. It did not make her look better. Neither wanting to seem too desperate nor too aloof, Carolyn gave Nita her undivided attention as she stood at the table.

"I checked the computer in our room to see where she's been surfing and saw that Anna recently contacted the Angolan embassy in D.C. Here's a printout of her email to them."

Carolyn studied the email before handing it to the detective, who read it before handing it to Mark. It was a lead for sure, and the words were clearly Anna's. But Carolyn was bewildered. Why would Anna want to run away to an embassy?

"Anna and I talked about the bus to D.C. that leaves from the courthouse. She said she wanted to go sometime. Maybe she took the bus there and got lost or something," offered Nita.

Mark looked at Carolyn. "Actually, I did just notice that there was some money missing from my bureau."

"How much?" Carolyn asked. Stealing? Anna?

"I think around $300."

Nita shifted in her place and looked away. "You should also talk to the Kane girls," she suggested. "Anna's been having problems with some of the kids in her class. They've been calling her names and stuff."

"Who? What stuff?!" Carolyn exploded.

"Just some immature morons saying something like 'ugga-bugga.' Because she's from Africa, I guess. Stupid middle school stuff."

Mark confronted Nita as the detective watched the family interchange. "Why didn't you tell us about any of this? You share a room with her, Nita."

"Mark, this is not Nita's fault," Carolyn defended.

"I didn't say it was her fault. I'm just asking our oldest and smartest daughter why the hell..."

"This information is very helpful," Ted interjected, picking up the email printout. "Maybe Anna took a trip to D.C. for the day and got lost. Maybe she has been trying to contact you. We can check the cell towers."

"Actually, our youngest son Simba found her cell phone in the basement," Carolyn said, realizing she should have mentioned this sooner. "This afternoon."

This did not seem to faze the detective. "I see. Well, we'll contact the embassy. If she did go there, they may not give us much information except for the basics, especially if for any reason your daughter felt she was in danger."

"Danger? What are you talking about?" demanded Mark.

"I'm sorry, wrong word. I meant unsafe. If what Nita here is saying about the recent bullying is true."

"Nita, is that true? Anna felt unsafe?" asked Mark.

"I don't know," Nita exclaimed as she turned abruptly. "I'm just trying to help!" Nita left the kitchen and ran up the stairs, slamming her bedroom door.

"Nice job, Mark, "Carolyn said.

Mark looked like he was assembling verbal ammunition. Carolyn could sense his frustration, feel his reproach. All of these kids. All of this responsibility. Something was bound to go wrong eventually. It was just all too much. Factoring in the complexities of international adoptions, it was only a matter of time before these kids developed serious problems. Who knew who their parents were, what was in their genes? They could be predisposed for God knows what. Simba could grow up to be a successful businessman or a troubled felon. Who knows what can happen when you pluck these kids from the middle of the world and put them in the middle of River Hills, Virginia? Why weren't Tabitha and Wyatt enough? The look in Mark's eye said all these things to Carolyn. She reminded herself that he was scheduled to fly back to Atlanta this week to finish pre-production. Trailers had been hired, actors reserved, catering companies on call. She suspected there was something or someone else, but it was only a feeling.

"I do need to ask you for a recent photo of Anna." The detective looked at Carolyn. Any excuse to look at Carolyn he took.

"Of course." She removed a photo from the refrigerator door that had been taken by Simba on the twins' birthday. With her head cocked slightly to the side, Anna's expression was more inquisitive than happy. The space between her teeth and the unique curve of her eyebrows were unmistakably Anna. Carolyn handed the photo over to Ted.

The detective held it up closer to the light. "I'm sure there's a perfectly logical answer as to where Anna is. In the meantime, we'll look into all possibilities. A missing person bulletin will go out statewide, which includes all bus and train stations and airports."

Detective Washington got up and started for the front door. Carolyn and Mark followed him as if he were a dinner guest, asking him if he needed a drink or to use the bathroom. He grabbed the doorknob and held it briefly before opening the door halfway. "I think we've made acceptable progress, Mr. and Mrs. White." The formal exchange seemed appropriate and helped defuse the tense situation. "We'll find your daughter," he assured them. "Get some sleep. I'll call you as soon as we get in touch with the embassy. In the meantime, if any of your children or Anna's friends think of anything—someone she met, a place she was interested in, a new boyfriend—please let me know." He handed Mark his business card. "Call me anytime," he said, and with a silent thank you, he left.

It was now after 9 p.m., and Carolyn was too exhausted to call Priscilla with the astonishing request for information on her own daughter. She knew there were rumors about what was known as her predilection for adopting needy children. The common language among mothers in River Hills consisted of the goings on of their children, and Carolyn knew that they were confused about the kids in the White household—how many there were and from which countries, not to mention their names and ages. Even Priscilla and Barry would on occasion forget the names of the Whites' children.

Carolyn looked at the house phone on the wall as if it were a thirty-pound barbell. Picking it up, calling out for help, blaming Priscilla's girls even though she didn't blame them. It was all too much. She decided to wait until morning. Perhaps more information would come in from Ted.

"I'm going to try to get some sleep," Mark said. "She hasn't even been gone for thirty-six hours. Let's try to stay calm. I need to tell you about some good stuff happening with my film."

"Mark, please," she begged.

But acknowledging how little time Anna had actually been unaccounted for slightly eased her mood. But, like applying pressure to a wound before the pain begins again, she realized that any amount of time for a child to be missing was too much.

Carolyn sat down on the couch and Mark stepped behind her and put a hand on her shoulder. She placed her hand on top of his, the rare touch offering a connection bridging some of the distance that had worked its way into their marriage. She did not want to admit that they had not been intimate in years. It was not always like this. Mark White, running communications for political campaigns, a producer of movies, a person going places with his own set of tickets. There was a connection between them that did not need words. They shared a ticket to a destination that did not need to be discussed. Daddy liked him. Everyone did. What was not to like?

As Mark turned to go upstairs to bed, it occurred to Carolyn that she had not spoken to anyone else in his creative circle about the film. As far as she knew, it was fully funded, had a distribution deal, and was heading into pre-production with no foreseeable issues.

She admitted to herself that over the years she had been happiest when he was bringing home a regular paycheck from the Virginia Republican Caucus, a position from which he was let go for reasons that, according to him, had nothing to do with his performance. They both knew the $25,000 adoption credits allocated for both Simba and Anna were quickly being depleted. The funds were more than just a displacement allowance. Carolyn knew she really should just be spending it on essential items for each child, but expenses were expenses, and what was the difference, really?

She'd grown up as Carolyn Jenkins in a house overlooking the Rappahannock River, the third of six children. Her biological mother was not discussed, but she was a relative on her mother's side who was institutionalized. This much she knew.

Carolyn was the only blonde in the mostly Greek family, but if anything made her stand out more from the rest of her siblings, it was her tall stature. Her father ran an insurance agency and had a knack for investing, which allowed Carolyn a life of private schools and sailing lessons. But, although she came to the family when she was barely three years old, she always felt as if she were a cousin visiting from another state who might be leaving soon. Even her age gave her an odd place in the Jenkins household. She was sandwiched between the other siblings and her parents often struggled to remember her age.

"Carolyn's sixteen," her mother would say.

"Danny's sixteen, Mom. I'm fifteen," she corrected.

"Oh, yes, Carolyn is fifteen."

The children's birthdays were acknowledged with a dinner at Baxter's Fish House and a homemade cake from Famous Frey's in Richmond.

The Jenkins children were expected to gain their footholds by being quiet and overachieving, never calling attention to themselves. She remembered when her younger brother caught a touchdown pass that won a state title, he declined to speak at the celebratory dinner, raising his arm in appreciation but avoiding the spotlight. That was the Jenkins family. It seemed to Carolyn that all of her siblings had gone on to get the same, second-in-command type of jobs. All were technically successful, but none were the stars of anything. CFOs, vice presidents serving under the CEO, registered nurses working for doctors...these were the careers of the Jenkins children.

When Carolyn ran a high-profile campaign for state senator in Virginia, her mother, sitting on the outdoor furniture overlooking the river, eked out, “That’s nice, Carolyn, you got my vote,” and that was the last anyone in her family said about it. Of course, she had lost miserably, but she had gained a husband, as the campaign is where she met Mark.

Mark White was full of everything except himself. He was talkative, interesting, and talented. He had studied film at the University of Virginia, and one of his projects, a short, won accolades for its stark commentary on relationships. The film, which he adapted to summer stage theaters, was called *EXIT*. It featured both a split screen and split stage that showed two people going through other relationships before literally bumping into one another center stage in the final scene. The other lovers, dumped and departed for all kinds of reasons, went through the blinking EXIT door. It was hailed as a stark commentary on how a slew of relationships can come and go in our lives until we settle on our choice. Carolyn thought it was brilliant, and she told him so over sushi on their first date.

Hollywood, the emerging studios in Atlanta, location shoots, interesting friends. It all made for a perfect sounding life, and as the appetizers made their way around a creative conveyor belt in the Japanese restaurant, and Carolyn and Mark made joint decisions on what to consume and what to let pass, they both felt that they were staring at the same menu and there was no need to go anyplace else, except, eventually, the Greek Orthodox Church where they were married eleven months later. She was not really a Jenkins after all. There was nothing wrong with calling attention to oneself, if that self had something to say. She and Mark would make a life, and so, they began.

Later her passion for adopting needy children was tolerated by her siblings and parents, but the adopted kids tended to be treated as unrelated to the Jenkins clan at best. Mark, Carolyn, and the five—soon to be six—kids could hardly fit comfortably into her parents’ house, and that was just fine with Carolyn. Everyone was welcome to visit her at 186 Tidewater, where they could squeeze in. Although her parents rarely came, checks from her father did, addressed and made out to her personally, and they were quickly put to use. Mark knew, but rarely said anything.

The hour grew into the early morning, and Carolyn stared at an infomercial for a rotisserie oven by Ronco. In went the basted turkeys, chickens, and pork loins. Out came the perfect food.

"Just set it..." the announcer taunted, "and forget it!" the audience responded.

Where in God's name was Anna? How dare that child run away? She felt a surge of anger well up inside her, a rage at the loss of control of her own life when everything had been...going so well. Wasn't it, before all this?

The fact that money had been taken from Mark's drawer was a good sign, a clue. As dark as the thought was, Carolyn did not know if she felt more worried or embarrassed. She had a sixth sense, a mother's feeling, that the girl was safe, and that imagining the terrible things that could have happened was inviting fear into a situation that no doubt had a perfectly reasonable answer. The facts were that the girl had been thrown into a completely strange environment, felt ill since arriving, and was being bullied at school. And she had the added haunting of having been a child soldier, with all of its unspeakable horrors. She came not only from a different country, but a different world. She very likely had gotten on that bus in downtown Tappahannock and gone to the Embassy of Angola where she thought she belonged. It all made perfect sense. Yet, how could Carolyn look anyone in the eye and admit she didn't know where her daughter was? What kind of mother loses a child?

"Set and forget it," the TV infomercial chimed.

It even made pizza.

Carolyn awoke in her bed alone just after 9 a.m. Her first thought was of her missing child, which created a caving-in feeling in her chest. She had no desire to face this challenging day. She knew that if Anna had been found, someone would have woken her and told her the news. She sat up and stared at the closed bedroom door and felt the dread of what lay before her.

Mark walked into the bedroom holding a cup of coffee. He shook his head in anticipation of her first question and sat down by her side. An unsaid dialogue sat between them, like dialogue boxes in a cartoon, that spoke of Carolyn's save-the-world quests and Mark's stay-away travels. Anna was missing and the circumstances that had allowed it to happen were buried so deep that neither could begin to address them. Instead, they moved straight to more questions, and fewer answers.

"Ted called this morning. He said that they've contacted the embassy, but there were no reports of Anna or anyone requesting asylum. He spoke to the ambassador's office, Franca's his name, who confirmed that they received Anna's email a few weeks ago. A file had been opened on her when she contacted them, which is apparently just a formality. The embassy is now involved in the search. They said that there are more than 3,000 Angolans living in America. On a separate note, we also need to talk about money, because we're running out. I know this isn't a good time to bring it up, but *c'est la vie.*" Somehow, Mark had combined the two pieces of information like medicine that no one wanted to take.

It all came at Carolyn like a radio broadcast at the top of the hour. *Give us five minutes and we'll give you the world.* The night had been long, and she vaguely remembered Mark retrieving her from the couch. The whole situation felt like a bag of old board games found in the basement, with missing pieces and the instructions all mixed up with one another.

Simba and the twins burst into the room. "Can we go swimming today?" they all asked.

"Give your mother time to wake up," Mark said. But the children circled in closer, and Carolyn looked at them as if they were trick or treating for candy. She could see either Mark or herself in the twins, but Simba was growing into his own features, and it occurred to her how foreign the boy actually was.

Nita entered the room as well, staying near the door. Carolyn got up and Tabitha followed her into the bathroom, and she relieved herself as Tabby watched. Carolyn could still hear the other children talking to Mark.

"Any news?" Nita asked.

While Carolyn sat on the toilet, she heard Wyatt jumping on the bed. Her headache felt less pounding than thick. She always knew where to start her day, but today she could not find the first step. She knew that she needed to call Priscilla to ask about what had been going on with the kids in Anna's class. The thought of bringing other mothers into this was as revolting as the toilet that needed to be cleaned, but there was no money for housekeepers.

"I hope nothing's happened to Anna," Tabitha offered in a way that she hoped would be helpful. Through strings of hair flopped in front of her face, Carolyn gazed blankly at her natural daughter.

"Everyone, go downstairs," Mark ordered. "Your mother and I will meet you in the kitchen in a few minutes. Although we haven't been able to find Anna yet, we're sure she's alright. We'll talk more, but please leave your mother alone right now." At this, the children filed out, Nita being last, staring at Mark with an expression of concern.

"*Bad parents*," Carolyn thought.

It was a windy day, and Carolyn could hear the gusts pick up and subside. She walked over to the window and looked out at the street coming to life. A BMW sedan crawled by at the five miles per hour speed limit before stopping for a ball that had made its way into the street. A man was picking up after his dog.

"What are we going to do?" she asked Mark.

"What are we going to do about Anna, or what are we going to do about money?"

"About Anna, for God's sake!"

"We'll find her. But we also need to find money today because those subsidies we counted on are not enough with all these mouths to feed. Can you call your dad?"

"Mark, this is not the time, and the kids are not just mouths to feed. They're our children." She was holding her head in her hands like it was a soccer ball someone handed her.

"Your children, Carolyn."

She grew angry. "Why the hell are we talking about this? You can use the goddamn money you've been raising for the film!" she blurted out.

Mark crossed his arms. "Look, the police are on it. Even the embassy is involved. The neighborhood is aware. When a child goes missing, it's everyone's business."

"Are there going to be search parties in the neighborhood?" asked Carolyn.

"I don't know. Just, please get dressed and come downstairs. We need to talk to the kids about what's going on," Mark said.

Carolyn walked into the kitchen where Mark and four of her five kids were waiting for her at the table. She had pulled her hair into a tight bun and wore fitted pants that ended where the Jimmy Choo wedges began. Today this was her war outfit, and while her head still pounded from lack of sleep, she felt in charge. She sat down and Mark, the assistant director, took over. The hour was moving toward 11 a.m.

"Everyone, as you know, Anna is still missing after two nights now. We want you to know that your mother and I are doing everything we can to find her," said Mark, from the script.

The children took in the information in varying degrees of concern.

"We think she may have gone to Washington, D.C. We're piecing together everything we can, but we believe she's safe and maybe just lost. Her cell phone was in the basement, so either she'll find another way to reach us, or we'll go find her ourselves. Either's possible, but we expect to have your sister back home tonight."

The children all asked questions, the youngest three having trouble with the concept of having to forgo their activities, and Nita feeling the weight of being the oldest, the one who knows the most but says the least. As the questions dissipated in light of invisible answers, everyone dispersed except for Mark and Carolyn, who sat alone at the table.

"The ambassador is going to come here tomorrow afternoon, around 2 p.m.," Mark announced. "He apparently has some information, not about Anna's whereabouts, but about something he thinks could be relevant, so who knows. In the meantime, the police are organizing a search party in the neighborhood tomorrow afternoon. Everyone will meet at the Clubhouse at 1 p.m. I'm not going, and I actually don't think you should either. It's too much."

"Mark, how can this be happening?" Her headache, the lack of sleep, the confusion, everything began to seep through her skin. "Damnit, where could she be? Why was her cell phone in the basement of all places? Why didn't she tell us about...?" Her voice trailed off. Mark reached over and put his hand over her forearm. She appreciated his touch, a source of warmth in this cold conundrum of unknowns. She also felt the pressure of his upcoming production in Atlanta, now only two days away. Her priority was of course finding the child, but she sensed that Mark saw the matter as more of a chore.

The day ended with no more answers than when it began.

The doorbell rang the next morning and Priscilla and Barry Kane appeared. The two couples went into the living room and sat down. To Carolyn, it felt like a couple's therapy session in which she and Mark were the patients.

Barry began. "In my law career, I have some experience, unfortunately, in these situations. I've seen kids disappear, husbands disappear, wives, you name it, and most of these situations are resolved in a day or two. It's usually a misunderstanding, plain and simple." He was hunched over as he looked at Priscilla. "Right Prill?"

"As rain," she chimed.

Barry continued, "We came because we want you both to know that we're here for you, in fact the entire community is here for you." His polo shirt with the River Hill Golf Club logo was tucked into his khaki pants. He had the look of someone who was always ready for a pop-up meeting. Just give him a conference room, or even a golf cart.

Priscilla tried to cradle them. "If there's anything either of us can do—watch the kids, drive them to a lesson..."

"Bring you dinner," Barry chimed in hopefully. The words felt empty as the enormity of the situation hovered over them.

Priscilla now took the lead. "I also want you to know that I had a long conversation with both Cassy and Mary last night. They told me there were some boys from school who were making fun of her—rude, unacceptable behavior—but they assured me that Anna is popular and that the kids really do like her. Of course, neither of the girls took part in any of the boys' nonsense." She finished her statement as if she were giving a closing argument in a courtroom.

"Oh, we never thought your girls had anything to do with this," Carolyn assured them. For a moment the Kanes looked taken aback and Carolyn felt as if she had misspoken. "Anna is clearly a happy teenager and has been doing well, which is in part thanks to your daughters who took her under their wing. We're delighted that they've become friends over time." She paused. "Mark and I want to thank you for that."

Barry put a hand on Mark's shoulder. "We're going to find Anna. In the meantime, call me if there's anything you need, pal, anything."

Then two couples conversed briefly about Mary and Cassy's plans for the rest of the summer, but the visit was obviously a stopover for the Kanes. Their body language signaled they were ready to leave and as they headed toward the door, they whispered to one another about an estate sale they wanted to investigate. Their visit ended with quick hugs rather than kisses and the couple left, leaving Carolyn and Mark alone.

A meeting with Ambassador Franca was set for 2 p.m. in a private dining room at the River Hills Clubhouse. Carolyn and Mark were only adjunct members of the club and only had access to the public spaces and the restaurant. Still, the situation warranted an exception. As they approached the grand entrance under the veranda, they were met by a young man with striking jet-black skin, dressed in a suit with a perfect Windsor knot.

"Mr. and Mrs. White?" he asked, extending his hand. "My name is Marcus Neto and I am assistant to Ambassador Franca. He asked me to greet you. He will be joining us momentarily. Please, follow me."

Carolyn and Mark followed the man down the foyer toward the back of the club. Outside the windows the river grew larger and more prevalent. He opened the door to a drawing room and allowed them to enter first.

"Please," he said with a wide and welcoming smile.

Red velvet function chairs were arranged around an oval-shaped antique table. Marcus Neto took a seat halfway down and gestured for the Whites to sit on the opposite side. He picked up a silver pitcher brimming with ice and poured five glasses of water.

"We wanted to meet you here instead of your home as we did not want to bring spectacle to the situation. I want you to know that all of us at the Embassy of Angola are ready to assist with any resources you may need." His voice looped up and down in a colorful accent.

The Whites looked at this man who was speaking about their daughter like an admissions officer at a preparatory school. The parade of people who were now involved—Detective Washington, Priscilla and Barry, the Embassy of Angola, the ambassador, his aide, the entire neighborhood—just added to Carolyn's sense of helplessness.

"Ambassador Franca will brief you on the details. He has gathered some intelligence from Zarkanna's background which he hopes will be helpful to you in this...ordeal. In fact, we have discovered an important piece of information that may be relevant."

Carolyn and Mark looked at one another.

"We understand that the police are now involved, and the FBI have been alerted, and we fully expect that Zarkhanna will return home to you shortly."

"Anna," Carolyn said.

"Excuse me?"

"Our daughter's name is Anna."

Marcus looked down at his papers and moved to the next page, wetting his finger as he proceeded. "Zarkhanna Cudjo, native of Caxito, Angola in the province of Bengo. Abducted by UNITA soldiers on May 7, 2001, when she was twelve years old and served as a child soldier for ten months before being rescued by the Catolico Orphanage, where she spent one year before she was adopted by Mark and Carolyn White. She has no known living relatives." He spoke as if reciting a dossier.

"Yes, that's all true, but her name is now Anna, her American name is...Anna."

"Yes, sorry! It does say that here. I see now, Anna White," he said, pointing down at the papers he was holding. Outside, they could hear the high-pitched hum of electric golf carts and the murmuring of players arranging lunch dates.

"As background, Ambassador Franca is actually the first ambassador to the United States after our country's civil war, which unfortunately you know something about. You will be glad to know that there is now peace in our country. General—excuse me—Ambassador Franca is a true hero in our country. He was a great football star on our national team before joining the war effort. He is widely known by his nickname, Ndalu, but many of our countrymen know him as the general of the generals."

Carolyn had studied enough about the country to know that he was referring to the UNITA rebels who had fought the Soviet-backed government troops, leading to an uneasy truce.

Someone knocked on the door and all three were glad for the interruption. Carolyn and Mark turned their heads as a man dressed in a fitted silver suit entered the room. He had the look of a bodybuilder who had donned the suit for an interview. As he approached the table, Marcus stood up and exited the room, turning briefly to reiterate to the Whites that he was available to them day or night.

The ambassador went over to the White's side of the table and embraced their arms one at a time in a solidarity gesture, looking deeply into their eyes. He did not speak as he returned to the opposite side of the table. There was another knock at the door and Detective Washington entered. Carolyn was pleased to see a familiar face in the midst of so much foreign formality.

"I wish that we were meeting under better circumstances," the ambassador began. "I have come to understand that your daughter is a remarkable young woman of great courage, and we are confident that this situation will be quickly resolved." He turned toward Ted, whose badge was visible on his blue blazer. "Detective Washington has been keeping my team fully abreast of the situation."

The detective then informed them that search parties were being arranged as they spoke. A flyer with the photo of Anna had been printed up. However, the media had not yet been notified as the FBI declined to accept the case until Anna was missing for seventy-two hours, which was still thirty hours away. Dogs were being brought in to scour the neighborhood for any signs or clues. Special attention was being given to both the river and the Camel's Hump trails.

The ambassador watched the detective with a sense that he himself was only able to handle complex situations such as this.

"I do have one piece of information that may be helpful," Ndalu interjected. "When we received her email at the embassy, we began conducting a standard background investigation—nothing that we would not do for any Angolan citizen living in the United States—but you may be interested in what we have found."

"Anything," said Mark.

Ndalu took a deep breath, which stretched the buttons on his white shirt against his powerful frame. "Are you aware that Zarkhanna..." He shuffled some papers in front of him.

"Anna," Carolyn corrected.

"My apologies. Yes, Anna." He smoothed out his jacket.

"When you adopted Anna from our Catolico Orphanage in Luanda, were you made aware that she had an aunt who was never confirmed as having perished in the war?"

"We knew about her aunt but, no, we didn't know that she was alive," Mark said.

Carolyn was silent. She had reviewed Anna's file. Born November 17, 1989. Her village had been attacked and her mother killed. Her father had disappeared when she was very young. Her mother had a sister, but no one claimed her after the allotted year that Anna had spent in the Catolico Orphanage.

Carolyn thought back to her last conversation with the Mother Superior in the garden just prior to her first conversation with Anna. She remembered the religious woman's stern words and having an argument with her just before Anna had appeared.

"Our country has been involved in a great war," the Mother Superior said. "No one knows for certain who is dead and who is alive...there have been inquiries about this girl. Maybe you can wait a few more months before taking her from her country forever?" The orphans under her care were more than her charges, they were her responsibility before God.

"What sort of inquiries?" Carolyn had asked politely.

The Mother Superior continued. "The International Committee of the Red Cross is reuniting families with the children who were forced to serve the UNITA and FNLA fighters. What we know about Zarkhanna is that her mother and father were killed. She has no siblings, but her mother had a sister who is neither confirmed dead or alive. The ICRC has put out a list of lost children whose relatives have not been ruled out, and Zarkhanna is included on this list."

Carolyn had stared at the religious woman and tried to hold her tongue. She had turned toward the mopane trees that looked like they were part of the landscaping. It was her first trip to Africa, and all she could say about the trees was that they *looked* African. An abandoned fountain still trickled green water from a rusty pipe and two stray dogs were drinking the dirty liquid. The *60 Minutes* series on Angolan War Children had premiered months prior and there were no national campaigns to rescue these child victims from their own war-torn society, which in itself was a sin, Carolyn had thought. If Zarkhanna did have a living relative, who knew in what kind of conditions the woman lived? Carolyn could provide a home, a safe home, and a new life for the girl. All of this had been arranged. Hers was a true humanitarian gesture.

During this trip, Carolyn had donated $5,000 to Catholic Ministry which she knew from experience made the international gears of the foreign motors move more swiftly. This she paid out knowing that the $25,000 subsidy Carolyn and Mark would receive was certain. She had also provided all relevant documentation prior to traveling to Angola. In talking with the Mother Superior she had wanted to explain that she and her husband were no strangers to international adoption and that she was not there to discuss country-wide searches but to make arrangements to get the poor girl on a plane to Washington, D.C. Five years ago, she had made a similar arrangement in Venezuela with another mission to obtain the then eleven-year-old Nita.

For each of the children the Whites had adopted, they had received the fully legal subsidies that were available to them. Usually reserved for children with physical disabilities, there was a box for psychological assimilation that served as a loophole and allowed them to obtain the needed monthly funding that was required in raising any child. She had made the same $5,000 contribution for Juanita's release to her desperate family. $25,000 in subsidies came back to her when Juanita arrived in Virginia.

Carolyn addressed the Mother Superior firmly. "Then why was the girl eligible for adoption?" Carolyn asked. If there were any issues or concerns, she would have appreciated it if they had been brought up and discussed prior to her flying 5,000 miles.

The Mother Superior had gotten visibly angry. "Our job at the Catolico Orphanage, Mrs. White, is to find homes for these children. We have hundreds of cases here. Please do all you can in the coming days to exhaust any possibility of reuniting her before you exercise your right to adopt her and pull her from our country forever." The Mother Superior was then handed a telegram that required her to end the conversation abruptly, leaving Carolyn to wait in the garden for Zarkhanna to arrive.

There was no time to scour the country looking for some elusive relative who may or may not be dead or alive. The life that Carolyn was offering the girl would be vastly superior to tending the national soil of a war-ravished land. The girl would leave with her before she had a chance to wonder why and begin her new life with a new name. She would always be from Angola, and of this, the girl could be proud and go back one day and help out in some way. She wrote down Zarkhanna's name in ink on the mission pamphlet she had picked up earlier in the day and examined the lettering.

Zarkhanna. What an unusual, interesting name.

But it would not go over in Virginia. She circled the first part of the name and played with several names, but then she noted the last four letters and circled them twice. *Anna*. She seized the familiar Western name with glee, as if she had just solved a *New York Times* crossword puzzle. Anna White, younger sister to Nita, older sibling to her natural-born children

Wyatt and Tabitha and the most recent addition to the family, Simba, from Bangladesh.

"How old are my brothers and sisters?" Carolyn remembered Zarkhanna asking in the garden.

Now, as Carolyn sat before the ambassador, remembering the conversation with the Mother Superior and her vague references to alive or dead relatives, she felt as if she were being chased by a false rumor that everyone knew contained a speck of truth. She did not need the added weight of some long lost relative. She had followed the adoption procedures impeccably.

She had actually never forgotten the talk with the Mother Superior, and it gnawed at her from time to time. Anna had been in the United States for close to a year now and she seemed, at least on the surface, to be assimilating. Ripping her from her war-torn homeland was a good thing, a humanitarian thing. To sit at this table now and have to defend the decision in the midst of her disappearance simply took more energy than Carolyn could muster.

Anna had of course spoken about her mother and her aunt, Auntie as she called her, but Carolyn and Mark were never sure how much of the past the girl wished to share. Through no fault of their own, Anna's mother and 'Auntie' had failed to protect her, and as a result Anna had spent nearly ten months as a child soldier. In what way did these well-meaning relatives give her the life she deserved? Why not just let her start over with a loving home, even if love from the heart took time?

Carolyn looked the ambassador in the eye. "Why would we be aware that she has a living relative back in Angola, Ambassador Franca? What are you insinuating?"

Ndalu was a practiced politician. "There is nothing I am insinuating, Mrs. White. I am well aware of the hardship you yourself endured to rescue one of our country's most vulnerable children, and the Angolan nation is eternally grateful to you and to your husband."

His comment washed over the Whites and cleansed the room. Still, Anna came from somewhere else, and Carolyn had the unmistakable sensation that there were tentacles reaching out and connecting the girl to another country, a country that Carolyn knew little about.

"Our common goal is to find your daughter wherever she is and at whatever cost we must assume. It is coincidental that she was in touch with our embassy only a few weeks ago, and we did what any embassy would do in a post-war scenario, which is to cross-reference our citizens with any known relatives. In doing so, we came up with this." He reached into his attaché case to take out two photographs and pushed them across the table.

"This is Anna's mother, Wanda Cudjo. She was killed on May 7, 2001, in her village in Caxito by the invading UNITA army, which I myself was involved in opposing."

Carolyn and Mark peered at the photograph of the woman, who looked approximately their own age. She wore a yellow headdress and had a bright smile. Her eyebrows, curved up at the edges, were distinctly like Anna's. They looked at the photo as if it were a mugshot.

No one spoke.

"And here is a photo of Wanda Cudjo's sister, Samara Gaia." This image showed a fashionable woman, slightly younger than Anna's mother, with large circular earrings and a graceful neck.

"We expect that Ms. Gaia, Anna's aunt, will soon request to be reunited with your daughter."

"Did Anna contact her or something?" Mark asked.

Sensing the investigative tone that the exchange had taken on, the ambassador put the photos back into his case.

"Not exactly," Detective Washington interrupted. "Anna contacted the embassy, and the embassy came into contact with this relative of hers, who is now aware that Anna is missing."

"How?" Carolyn asked, alarmed.

The ambassador turned and called over his shoulder for his assistant. "Marcus!" His voice was thundering and decisive.

The door opened and the aide came back into the room. "Ambassador?"

"*Por favor, nos informe sobre sua comunicação com o parente da menina em Luanda,*" the ambassador said.

Marcus seemed prepared for the question. He held a clipboard in his hand, and his perfect suit seemed like the only clothes he ever wore.

"On June 23, 2003, we received an inquiry from a Miss Anna White indicating assimilation issues with her new adopted family as well as those of her adopted sister, a Miss Juanita White, living here in River Hills."

"Assimilation issues?" Carolyn objected. "What kind of assimilation issues? We were not aware of this."

The aide's words still hung in the air though both Carolyn and Mark knew the answers to their own questions.

Still, the ambassador seemed uneasy with the process by which his aide was informing the parents. "Marcus, thank you for your thorough report, however Mr. and Mrs. White were not aware of the girl's aunt and her attempts to get in touch. Can you kindly skip to the section on Ms. Gaia's communications with our staff?"

"Yes, your excellency. I apologize." He nodded toward the Whites.

"Inquiries on the girl's background were made following the contact with our embassy. To make matters short, we began a standard investigation which uncovered this document." He pulled out a short memo which was typewritten on standard printer paper. He attempted to hand it to the ambassador who instead gestured for Marcus to read it aloud.

> Dear Ambassador França,
>
> I have received through the Center for Displaced Persons an inquiry about my niece, Zarkhanna Cudjo. I have recently learned that she was adopted through the Catolico Orphanage on October 12, 2003, and since then I have been unable to obtain any more information about her. I am the sister of her mother, Wanda Cudjo. I have a stable home and employment and am living in Luanda. Please contact me with any information that you have on my niece so that I might pursue adoption of her person through all proper channels. I appreciate all of your attempts to unite families separated by the war.
>
> Sincerely, Samara Gaia

As Marcus finished reading the correspondence the room became quiet. Outside the clean sounds of golf balls meeting wooden clubs could be heard. A dish shattered in the kitchen and everyone's head turned toward the startling sound before returning their attention to the meeting.

"What do we do now?" Carolyn asked Ted.

"We did get a message to the aunt advising her that her niece may be contacting her and asked her to immediately get in touch with us if she does," the detective responded.

"So obviously this woman now knows that Anna's missing," Carolyn said.

"She does," the ambassador replied. "And under our post-war retribution, we have an obligation to keep any living family member of a person affected by the Angolan Civil War abreast of a situation like this."

Mark spoke up. "Did anyone check the airlines? Could she be on her way back to Angola right now?"

The detective spoke next. "Yes, we've already checked into this and alerted customs, which has her photo. But it would be difficult for her, or for any fourteen-year-old without a credit card, to book a ticket and get through customs without somebody asking questions."

The comment gave the impression that progress was being made, but the heavy burden took the air out of the room.

"My God, where is she?" Carolyn asked helplessly.

"We don't know yet, but first we'll need to eliminate all suspects," the detective answered, looking at Mark.

# Chapter 10

It was early in the morning following Annabelle and Madia's meeting with Reverend Cooper when they were abruptly stopped by A.C. Tomkin's junior boss, Wendell.

"Mr. Tomkins like to have a word with y'all," the man stated. He stood with a hand on his hip and a hat low over his eyes. He went to grab Madia by the arm, but she wriggled out of his grip.

"Jeez, y'all don't have to get all hot and bothered!" He had brought an accomplice with him, and this larger man grabbed hold of the women and led them to two separate work wagons. One contained slave people sitting on benches beneath a canvas covering. Annabelle could not make out who they were. The other was just an open wagon covered with tobacco leaves left from the previous day's fieldwork.

Wendell pointed toward the crowded caravan. "Boss says young one suppose to get in dis one, and the mama is supposed to get it dat one."

"Where are we goin'?" Madia asked.

"You goin'! That's all you need to know!" He gave both Madia and Annabelle a shove and they stiffened at his touch. Two horses were hitched to the wagon that Annabelle climbed into, indicating that she was going far. Madia's had only a single horse.

Annabelle could now see that people were sitting on benches facing one another. As she placed one foot onto a step to the rickety wagon, she looked over at Madia, who now sat alone on her assigned cart. Only a dull gaze shared between them captured their connection. Words could not be said.

Annabelle felt a hand push against her backbone, and she turned toward her aggressor. "Don't you touch me!" Her eyes were narrow and her tone even.

Wendell backed away and put his hands up in mock surrender. "Whoa! Didn't know you was a talking nigga' now! I'm just doing what the boss sez."

The feel of his hand on her body reminded her of being pushed by the UNITA lieutenants, particularly one who delighted in dragging the children from their sleep with rough hands and jabs. Sitting in the wagon, Annabelle looked right through Wendell as a man rode up on horseback.

"Problem?" he asked.

"This girl thinks we got all day to get in the wagon," said Wendell.

Annabelle looked up and met A.C. Tomkins' eyes.

"That so?" he asked, then dismounted. He gave the reins to his deputy and walked up to Annabelle. He had sweat running out of the creases of his eyes. His skin on his face and hands were dotted by boils, some of which had recently burst. He wiped them with a filthy handkerchief.

"That man told you to get in that wagon?" he addressed Annabelle.

She looked over toward Madia, who was shaking her head in a silent dialogue between them, telling Annabelle that she was among dangerous people, and to think carefully.

"I was getting into the wagon," Annabelle said quietly.

"You were getting into the wagon, master-sir!"

The slave people inside the wagon pulled apart the canvas curtain to see the commotion. Inside, Annabelle saw the frame of Big Arthur as well as young Lizzie from the weaving room. A few other workers peered out and Annabelle saw that Ole' Beatrice was also among them. She turned her head back toward Tomkins, who was growing taller with piped-in anger as he stood over Annabelle.

No one spoke.

It was then that she felt the strike across her face. Tomkins had taken the handle of a bullwhip and crushed it against Annabelle's jaw. She fell to the ground, dirtying her simple gray dress on the manure-stained earth as she looked up at Tomkins.

"Who you think you are talkin' to nigga'? My man say get in the wagon, you get in the wagon. I say call me master-sir, you call me master-sir. I say shit, you shit!"

Annabelle felt the pain of her wounded jaw and collected her strength. There were many days with the soldiers when she was pushed, shoved, even struck. She reminded herself that some moments were to be acted upon, and others saved for more opportune times.

Once a young lieutenant dragged a girl not much older than herself into the bush and violated her, a habit the young officer became fond of and continued for weeks. One night, a group of young soldiers just like herself, four girls and a boy, decided to end the ordeal. They grouped together and snuck up on the sleeping soldier as he lay in the open. As four of them covered his mouth and held him down, a bayonet was jammed deep into the soldier's shoulder by the girl who had endured his abuse. His service was now useless to the army. The commanders knew the revenge that had been bestowed upon him, and with nodding approval toward the child soldiers learning the ways of war, he had the bloodied and screaming soldier executed in a nearby ditch by firing squad the next morning.

Although it was not Annabelle who had thrust the bayonet into his shoulder, it was as if the young lieutenant had shot her father, raped and killed her mother, and sent Zarkhanna astray from everything and everyone she cherished. She had not exacted the revenge, but she had assisted by holding the soldier down with the others and helped complete the task with the efficiency and expertise that she herself had witnessed in the maiming of the villagers whenever the UNITA commanders felt the whim to terrorize a rural community suspected of MPLA sympathies. She had decided later that it was not she who had helped commit the atrocity, but rather her hands acting in a kind of wild protection of herself and those that she had come to care for. She was not proud, but quickly forgot the incident as she carried the goods and scrounged for food in the endless military campaign.

Annabelle's nostrils flared as she looked up at Tomkins from the ground where she lay. His hat cast a shadow over her, providing a moment's reprieve from the hot sun. He grabbed her by the arm and dragged her across the earth. The boils and redness on his skin looked angry and Annabelle could not help but stare at his disfigurement in disgust. Suddenly she felt Tomkins grab her long mane of hair, and she screamed as he dragged her toward the same shed where Lizzie was flogged just days before.

"I got no time for disobedience, girl!" the overseer called out as he pulled her by the hair. His blue eyes looked like tips of arrows aimed at her. Wendell followed and picked her up off of the ground. She felt her legs fall beneath her and the two men now dragged her backwards. One of the stray dogs that hovered around the plantation's kitchen ran up to the scene and began to sniff at Annabelle's legs, which were trickling with blood. They came to the shed which, with its door hanging askew by one hinge, seemed like a shack worthy only of housing tools. Inside was a small, dark platform with chains. As they entered, she heard a voice that stopped the party in its tracks.

"Gentlemen." It came off as a statement and a question at the same time.

Annabelle was sweating, bloodied, and confused as she looked up to see the man dressed in white suit with a tie that disappeared into his blue cotton shirt. Master Kane stepped closer to them.

"What seems to be the problem here, Mr. Tomkins?"

Tomkins let go of Annabelle and stood up straight, brushed off his baggy gray trousers, and adjusted his hat away from his eyes. Wendell also stood, took his hat off, and held it to his chest in reverence to the owner.

"No problems here, Mr. Kane. We were on our way off the grounds to complete the sale of the Negroes when this one here acted up. We were just goin' to calm her down with a light brushin'."

Master Kane surveyed the young girl on the ground. "What is her name?"

Neither man spoke up. Annabelle filled in the space. "Annabelle," she said. "Annabelle."

"Annabelle, sir!" Tomkins corrected.

"That'll be enough, Mr. Tomkins. Let the girl regain herself. Now, miss, were you here givin' Mr. Tomkins trouble?"

"No sir," Annabelle replied.

The overseer glared at the girl. She saw the squinting of his eyes and a quick twitch of his upper torso. He started to speak, but Master Kane held up his hand.

"Mr. Tomkins, why don't you and your party 'accompany me to the porch so that we can sort this out. I have business matters to discuss with you." The man turned and headed past the kitchen toward the porch of the stately home. He stayed within earshot of Tomkins and Annabelle.

"Guess you got lucky today, girl. But you gettin' sold like the piece of property that you is, and I be glad for it."

Annabelle walked in front of the two men and about a dozen paces behind Master Kane.

*Sold? To whom? Where?*

Up to this point, she had felt that her coming to Nottoway had a purpose, but as she began to follow men whose existence held absolute power, she felt there was no purpose to the madness around her, and she had best learn to live with it. How she had come to this place and how she would leave became tangled in her mind without any hope of resolution. She knew only that moving forward had gotten her to where she was, and that some purpose existed for her—perhaps to tell more of what she knew of Jemmy, perhaps to provide answers to the rainless sky, perhaps to show someone in this world that a young Angolan orphan captured by a ruthless army could survive.

The party walked past the Old Oak where squirrels jumped from branch to branch in search of food they could not find. Its leaves turned their brittle skin toward a sky with no water. An audible pattering of critters could be heard as they scurried about the trunk. Annabelle felt a thirst in her throat. It was as if a dried ravine flowed through every living organism in the county. She looked for Jemmy's grave and saw the white gravestone protruding at an angle from the ground, as if even in death he could not sit still. Annabelle continued up to the house, passing a few slave people tending the gardens with buckets of water. She ascended the wide staircase and sat down in a wicker chair Master Kane pointed out to her. She was given a glass of water and a towel to wipe her face. Master Kane sat on his rocking chair and Tomkins sat on a wicker couch facing him. Wendell stood near Annabelle, acting as if he needed to guard her from running away.

The realization that she could no longer get to the leather pouch swept across her and a sense of panic stirred inside her chest. Every part of her body wanted to run back to the cabin, grab the pouch in the loft, and make it back to the safety and sanity of River Hills. She had been here for a long time—she did not even know how many days it corresponded to back home. Were people looking for her? If she were somehow able to get past this man guarding her, make a run to the cabin, and make it back to her time, what would she really be going back to? Wasn't her life over when she came to America in the first place? After all, her mother, her father, and Auntie were all dead and her country was destroyed. The home the Whites provided felt like little more than a collection of walls with people inside.

There was only one reason to return, and she felt it throughout her being.

*Simba.*

She could picture him now in the basement stacking his blocks, missing the only sister he ever had. If she were there, she would put down the basket she was finishing and take him for a hike up Camel's Hump. He'd be hungry and she'd sneak him a pre-dinner peanut butter and apple sandwich under Ronnie's watchful eye.

Annabelle could make out the two wagons waiting on the main road. She could see the figure of Madia sitting alone in the back of the smaller wagon. She was wearing a faded green headdress that had lost its color through excessive wear and washing. The wagon she was on started moving, and this mother Annabelle had known, a woman for whom she felt a queer sort of love, started to disappear down the road. Madia was stoic as she watched what was left of her world vanishing. At one point, Annabelle thought she saw her wave, and she stopped herself from waving back. Turning toward Camel's Hump, the cart became smaller and smaller, until all Annabelle could see was a thin stream of dust being kicked up behind.

*Mother.*

"What transactions are you fosterin', Mr. Tomkins?" Master Kane asked.

He had placed his favorite red checkered blanket over his lap. One of the gardeners nearby, a man well into his seventies, swore when he pricked his finger on a purple thistle.

"Excuse me, sir," the gardener addressed Master Kane. He brought his finger to his mouth then made a friendly gesture with his hand.

Tomkins cleared his throat and spoke as the businessman he longed to be. "I am takin' inventory of our assets, sir, as you directed me. Takin' into account the seventy percent reduction in tobacco harvesting that we expect for '24, this year will be inferior to the last. We have reduced to half rations to the population and are now requirin' that they grow part of their own. Ain't no reason we need to feed all these nigg...population like times er good."

"Go on," the old man said. "I assume you have met with Judge Moore's accountin' fellows to review our ledgers."

"I have, sir, as you directed. I have also taken it upon myself to recalculate wages and place the paid hands on a scale that reflects their productivity, instead of the weekly salaries that you so kindly offered."

"A.C., since the death of my son Kestin, you have become like a son to me. You are indispensable to Nottoway." The old man placed a hand on the overseer's shoulder and looked into his eyes. "I know that you have looked over my int'rests as if they were your own. Perhaps this is our destiny, eh?" The old man patted Tomkins' shoulder.

"Yes, sir, I do indeed look after this plantation here like it...is a foal that came from my own horse." He spoke with halting words and forced emotion that passed by the old master like the hawks flying overhead.

"Have you briefed Miss Cassandra on these details regardin' Nottoway?"

Tomkins was silent. He had been speaking with the confidence of a man in charge, but the mention of the master's daughter, a 16-year-old incompetent girl, seemed to startle him. He took out a handkerchief and wiped away a small amount of blood that had burst from one of the boils on his arm. It seemed the strange illness was spreading all over his body.

"Have you had Doc Kiley take a look at your skin there, Mr. Tomkins? Maybe he could be of some assistance." The sight of the boils was squeamish to any casual observer.

The overseer quickly covered the bloodied mark with his sleeve. "Thank you, sir. I will. It must be from the sun and being out in the fields overseeing our important work."

The old man nodded and brought up the subject of his oldest daughter again.

"Sir, she is but a girl...and while I have..."

"Mr. Tomkins, you are a fine overseer and a good man. In the midst of these ter'ble times, you have managed to squeak out a decent crop by creatin' the series of canals from the river that now feed our fields. But this 'ere is a family farm...." The old man looked out over the great lawn before him. In the distance, he could see slaves digging ditches that would connect to the main tributary of the Rappahannock River, skirting the north side of the big house in order to quench the thirst of the desperate tobacco plants.

"Yes sir, I understand."

"These matters were to be left to my son. But since his death, since that time and whatever happened five years 'go, we have had nothin' but bad luck—ter'ble times, Mr. Tomkins!"

"Yes, sir, I understand. Which is why I chose to review our assets and sell off the Negroes that we could command a good dollar for while still maintaining the productivity required at Nottoway."

The master looked at his overseer. "Mr. Tomkins...the Reverend Cooper, a man whom I admire, has requested a meeting with myself and my daughter. He said he had some info'mation that pertained to the wife and daughter of the slave Jemmy, the one who murdered my son." He spoke as if talking to the wind. "Do you know what would be the purpose of such a meetin'?"

Tomkins became quiet. "I do not know, sir, but I have heard that the Reverend has fallen ill." Tomkins smiled broadly as he delivered the news. "Also, as you may recall, sir, we have made arrangements for the murderer's wife."

Annabelle had heard that the Reverend was unable to get out of bed after drinking a cup of tea, tea that he normally drank every day, but this time had made him so ill that he was kept from conducting his business. Everyone knew that the Reverend hardly ever got sick. She looked over at Tomkins, who was now fiddling with his hands.

"Fallen ill, you say? Well, alright then. And where are the wife and daughter now, Mr. Tomkins?"

Annabelle fixed her gaze on the old man. When Mr. Tomkins did not acknowledge her presence, she decided to speak up.

"I am here, sir!" All heads turned toward her.

The heat of Tomkins' rage darted toward her, but she ignored it.

"I am the daughter you are referring to, sir."

The old man met her gaze. "Is that true, Mr. Tomkins?" he asked, turning toward the overseer.

"Yes, sir. This is the daughter of the slave who ruthlessly murdered your son and my friend with his own hands. She is of his blood," he responded, spitting off of the porch.

"Your name is Annabelle, is that correct, my dear?"

"Yes, sir."

"Annabelle," he repeated. "Is there somethin' that you would like to tell me?

"Yes sir."

"Then make it a point to visit with me. I would like you to come see me this evenin' just after dinnertime and tell me what it is that you wish to share."

Madia may be gone, the Reverend might be ill, but Annabelle would have her audience, and this man seemed to be the kind of man who would listen to reason, listen to the truth about the lying, wicked overseer he had in his employ. On the other hand, the truth was beginning to feel as useless to her as yesterday's weather. What pain would be eased by telling this man what happened? What dead would reappear? She wondered why she should even speak to Master Kane at all, still she felt there was a reason why she had appeared in this world, and she felt this was an opening she needed to seize.

Perhaps time *could* heal all wounds.

"Now, Mr. Tomkins. I have just traveled to Philadelphia to see firsthand the most remarkable discovery. I met with a great man, a certain man named James Espy[2], who is known as..." The old man retrieved a leather-bound notebook from his inside pocket. "He is known as a me-te-rol-o-gist. A sort of scientist that studies the weather. This brilliant young man is now engaged in the production of a machine that has the capability to produce rain. Yes, rain! His revolutionary experiments are bein' supported in part by the United States Congress, which is awardin' him a grant for his position at the Franklin Institute!"

Annabelle could just make out Tomkin's expression as he listened to the man who held all of the strings to his income, and his future, and although the science that the old man was discussing was so strange—and impossible—she could sense that Tomkins wished to give the master his supposed attention.

"I plan to hand over the supervision of this project to my eldest daughter. As you know, Cassandra has studied the books of scientists and engineers. Women can learn to be proper managers, Mr. Tomkins. Tis a sign of the times we live in!"

Tomkins shifted in his chair. "A machine, you say, sir? How does the machine make rain, if you do not mind me askin'? I too have great interest in books and...engineers!"

The old gardener stood up straight and listened intently. He had the look of someone who was once tall and strong, but now his old body just served to carry its hunkering size. His gaze was observed by the two conversationalists, so the old gardener went back to his work.

2 James Espy, 1785 –1860, Climate Engineer, proposed theories on how to make it rain, commissioned by US government

"Rain it can, Mr. Tomkins. Indeed, it can. I and the good Mr. Laurel from the neighborin' plantation, together with other Virginians, are providin' this young scientist with the capital he requires to build his rain machine. Progress, Mr. Tomkins! Imagine havin' all our wells filled with water on demand instead of requirin' our good labor force to dig these trenches!" He looked out into the fields where narrow lines interrupted the landscape. The irrigation system was dug with the muscle and excruciating pain of the slaves Annabelle had come to know. Smoke rose from outdoor furnaces used to create sluices to divert the water from the river. The man-made system required constant maintenance because the dirt walls regularly caved in and blocked the flow of water. In the past several years, men and women had died doing the work. Falling down in the field, their bodies simply gave out. Others deteriorated slowly, their searing back pain working its way into every bone of their bodies.

"In best of times," Annabelle learned from Ole' Beatrice one evening on their porch drinking tea, "of every hundred babies born on this land, twenty-five die before they reach the age of ten. Another twenty perish from disease or accident by the time they are twenty years old, then another fifty leave this earth before they are fifty. Only four in a hundred would see their sixtieth birthday. "Myself" the old woman said, pointing toward herself "I defy the odds!"

Beatrice and Arthur were also amongst those fortunate to survive, but survival as a slave had its own price, not the least of which was watching as children die as easily as old people. Beatrice had herself lost three.

"Farmers could produce perfect crops!" Master Kane continued. "Reservoirs could be created by diggin' out earth to store water for whatever purpose, includin' mills! Imagine, Mr. Tomkins, the important work that Mr. Espy is engaged in and with which we—includin' you as our overseer—are about to embark!" The man could not contain his excitement.

Tomkins looked up at the sun that stole the water from the clouds and plagued the plantation. He was a man who understood opportunity, and while he did not understand the mechanism of a machine, he knew how to encourage an old man.

"How does such a machine work, sir?"

"Air! Simple air! Nothin' more complex than a chimney system, although one reachin' far higher than any chimney in the South! Mr. Espy has based his research on the chimneys of London that, through their collective heat, produce an average of three to six inches of rain per month in the Thames Valley. The project simply requires the construction of a chimney on our plantation to produce a steady column of heated air reachin' great heights! Then the flames will control the exact temperatures needed to create rain!" Sensing the enormous undertaking of building such a chimney, and the oversight that would be required supervising slaves, Tomkins moved closer to the old man with keen interest.

"But does this scientist know why our county here has not seen rainfall?"

At this question, the old gardener who had been tending the bushes stood up. While audibly working close by, he had been listening to the description of the scientific discovery that so intrigued the elder master. He spoke up. "No rain has come since the curse. Five years we don' see no rain since the hangin' of the conjurer under that tree. Since the chair be kicked out from beneath him." He pointed toward the oak tree and looked at Tomkins, remembering that final blow. The steadiness of his voice felt neither intrusive nor welcomed. He spoke as if he were merely reciting facts.

"Just before the man was hanged, some of his words got caught in the thick bark of the Old Oak, and the wind spread it throughout the whole county these past five years. But he was gonna say something else, something that he never got to say...That's why there's been so much trouble..." His colorless shirt was buttoned to the top and suspenders held up his weathered pants.

"Thank you, Moses," Master Kane nodded with a polite smile. "I know that you people have your superstitions, and I don't mind the comment, but there is a perfectly logical explanation to the lack of rainfall in Essex County."

The old gardener stood listening with his hoe in one hand.

"Get on back to yer work," Tomkins said with an icy temperament.

"No, no, Mr. Tomkins. I've known Moses since he was a boy and we played on this very porch. He is welcome to listen in about this discovery. He can parlay this information to the rest of his people at Nottoway, as rain is indeed the topic on everyone's minds."

Moses now put both hands on top of the hoe, ignoring the overseer's frigid stare. Tomkins then turned toward Master Kane with a smile that he hoped displayed his overwhelming interest in the master's words.

"Mr. Espy had asked that I bring along some topographical maps from northern Virginia, which I obliged. After spendin' an evenin' studying them, we met for breakfast the following mornin'. He asked specifically about the two round tops at the edge of our property."

"Camel's Hump, sir?" Tomkins asked.

"Yes, yes, Camel's Hump. I have an amusin' story 'bout that," the master said with a laugh. He turned his head toward the two small peaks in the distance, and Annabelle followed his gaze. She had walked the trail with Simba in a time that she could remember, but not locate. She recalled the strange couple she had seen walking down the hill in their old clothes and shoes. She remembered how they had both gazed right through her as if it were she who was lost in the woods of time. And she remembered the man in the ill-fitted suit, staring at her with his withered neck beside a cross from another time.

She remembered walking away from Simba toward the clearing overlooking the steep cliffs that tumbled down to the highway. It was in this spot that she had reached into the crevice and retrieved the leather pouch—a move she wished had never happened. Now she saw a tiny cloud dance on top of the hills, as capable of bearing water as a newborn calf able to produce milk.

The old man continued his good humor. "When I was a boy, that hill was known as Tapp Hill, after Tappahannock. My daddy sat right here on the porch when I was a lad and asked me what I thought that mountain looked like, and without ever havin' seen a camel before or even knowin' what one was, I says it looked like a Camel's Hump, and the name has stuck to this day."

"The peaks are as part of Nottoway as the Ole' Oak," Tomkins said.

"Well, the two rounded tops on Camel's Hump have created what the meteorologist Mr. Espy calls a..." he referred again to his notebook, "a 'down-draft' due to an atmospheric change in the county's weather, brought on by the risin' temperature of the Rappahannock River from some of the industry that our northern neighbors are engaged in; namely the iron furnaces for iron smeltin'. You can lay the blame at the boots of the Maryland legislature's offerin' of 100 free acres to any man buildin' the furnaces and willin' to produce goods for the makin' of weaponry.

"Those forests are bein' clear cut at an alarmin' rate to produce charcoal, and burnin' timber is the favored method that our friends in Chesapeake have employed! Myself and Mr. Laurel intend to prove the theory in court and be reimbursed for our hardship these past five years, includin' loss of revenue, and even loss of Negroes that we have suffered due to the arduous task of diggin' trenches just to supply our fields with water! I would like a list of our lost assets, includin' the Negroes, Mr. Tomkins!"

"I have kept careful records, sir."

The old man paused as he considered his financial losses. "In the meantime, we have called for a cease-and-desist order against a few of the Maryland factories which we are filin' right here in the Tappahannock courthouse."

"As you should sir," Tomkins said.

The old gardener looked on warily.

Annabelle listened as if she were hearing a fable being told to her from a book about talking dinosaurs. The ancient theory Master Kane was proposing fit right in with the bizarre otherworld existence she was now a part of. She looked over at Tomkins, who was now feigning as much interest as he could.

In these past weeks, she had come to know Tomkins for the man that he was. She observed him when he went in to tally the tasks that Glennie oversaw in the weaving room, and she heard his grunts and posturing when he invaded Madia's bed at night, including long one-way conversations Madia was forced to endure, despite her fatigue.

"I'm a good man," he repeated to Madia only last week. She sat on the bedstead at an hour of the morning when all was quiet, waiting for him to leave so that she could sleep. "Before my daddy died in the war, he tol' my mama he wanted me to have good schoolin'. He had a big farm not too far down the other side of the river that he willed to me. Even had him a few niggas. One of them was named Stephan. He came up with a new way to cure tobacco leaves with charcoal that made the smoke more easy on the lungs. Just before my daddy passed, he was about to patent that there process, and I was gonna continue his work." He carefully pushed aside a stray strand of hair from Madia's face.

"Maybe sometime I show you that there farm I lived on, and you can see for yourself that I'm a good man."

She tried to manage a smile.

"That farm is in need of a woman. I ain't cleaned it for a year, no time ya know! A good woman who knows how to work is what I need, a petunia like you." He stroked her hair. "You come to know me, and maybe you don't think I'm so bad," he said.

*Petunia! How ya feelin'?*

"Uh-huh," she had uttered to the killer of her husband, a man who, upon entering the cabin several times a week, would as easily push her on the bed as he would sit on the crooked chair by her bed and tell her about his hopes and dreams.

"I ain't so bad, is I?" he asked before leaving. He had not touched her that night.

Madia had just looked at him with eyes that spoke of survival, without making so much as a gesture to give the overseer any reason to stay.

On another occasion, Tomkins had bragged to Madia about his skills. "I can manage Nottoway better than some schoolgirl, even if she is Cassandra Kane, phew! She don' like me one bit, but if I got to marry her dog of a sister Mary Louise to get the inheritance I deserve, I figure I can bear it. She's dumb as a doornail and as gullible as she is ugly, I tell you." He spit and Madia watched his saliva fly across the room. "Masta' Kane just got to give me the chance to show him what I can do."

He stared at his captive in the low light of the lantern that he had placed on the floor. As she listened, Annabelle felt as if she were gathering evidence to use at the right time to free her, to prove the innocence of Jemmy, and to make this intolerable world even a fraction more bearable for Madia.

"I never don kill your husband," he insisted. It was a line he often repeated, as if trying to convince himself. "I'm a good man," he repeated. "You a beautiful lass. Even though you a nigga', you a beautiful lass. Maybe you come to know that I ain't so bad."

When Tomkins visited the shack, he sometimes looked up toward the loft to see if Annabelle or Calvin were awake. Annabelle would sometimes make her presence known, but most times she would hide and pretend to sleep.

Now, Tomkins was ushering Madia off of this plantation, and Annabelle had a suspicion where she was heading. She would have blurted out the question to Master Kane, but she now understood that she herself was in as dangerous a position as Madia—soon to be silenced, and destined to disappear into the thirsty year of 1824, which was in the process of swallowing everything in sight—crops, trees, animals, and slave people.

The conversation concluded and Tomkins stood up and shook Master Kane's hand. The old man took the checkered blanket off of his legs and stood up slowly. He walked toward Annabelle, and instead of confirming their meeting that evening, he continued right past her as if he had forgotten it altogether. He stopped with his hand on the front door of the Great House and looked over at Tomkins.

"Have Doc Kiley take a look at that there skin condition, Mr. Tomkins. I need my overseer to be healthy. There is much work to be done." A blotch had developed on the overseer's face.

Tomkins watched the old man go into the house and listened to his footsteps subside into the wooden hallway. At that point, Tomkins sauntered over to Annabelle and snapped his fingers for her to stand up. His accomplice gave her a small shove in her back and the three of them headed down toward the remaining wagon.

"Stupid, old man," Tomkins said as they walked.

The comment made Moses look up and watch as Tomkins departed with his assistant and his captive.

As they walked, a young woman appeared from behind the Great House. It was the elder daughter of Master Kane, Miss Cassandra.

"Good morning, Mr. Tomkins. I have been looking about the grounds for you. I have just had the most horrid experience!"

Tomkins stopped and Annabelle watched as he removed his hat and held it to his chest in deference to the young lady. "That so, Miss Cassandra? How may I be of service to you today?"

"We have had an incident with one of your field hands, Mr. Tomkins. It seems he has been having improper thoughts about myself that are most troubling and are particularly unsettling for the frail constitution of Mary Louise, who is someone I know you care so deeply about!"

Tomkins was a man who recognized opportunity. He clenched his jaw and the veins in his neck began to emerge. Annabelle's presence was hardly acknowledged.

"It is that rude boy Calvin, son of the nigga' who killed our dear brother, Kestin!"

"Miss Cassandra, if you will only share with me the facts of the matter, I will see that the boy is dealt with properly."

"I had asked him to carry some potatoes for me, and when he placed the sack down near the shed, he bent toward me and attempted..." The girl began to fan herself... "He attempted an improper gesture toward my person, Mr. Tomkins!" The girl composed herself and looked at Annabelle, then pointed a crooked finger at the girl. "Don't I know you? You was in the bedroom with my Sista'! You are the halfwit!"

Tomkins let the comment pass, knowing that Annabelle would not dare speak, and the silence would serve to his advantage.

Annabelle looked at the ground, trying to think of whatever move or escape she could fathom. She wanted desperately to believe that she alone could make a difference, that her conversation with Master Kane would somehow make him see that the true killer of his only son was right under his nose. Tomkins would be driven himself from Nottoway. Then, afterward, she would make it back to the shack, get to the loft, grab the leather pouch, and return to River Hills—and to Simba. Maybe she could take Calvin with her. She would make a world right where so much of her own had gone so wrong.

"Thank you for seein' to that piece of business, Mr. Tomkins. My daddy would be...appalled at this disrespect from a slave to whom he has shown nothin' but kindness! Where would these poor souls be if not for the generosity of Daddy?"

"Let me assure you, Miss Cassandra, I will take care of the boy Calvin."

Annabelle tried to imagine a single reason why this plot should be devised by the Kane sisters but could think of nothing except the pairing of power and cruelty that were natural byproducts of a society that had lost its sense of right and wrong.

"Yes, yes," the elder Kane sister continued. "Where would they all be if not for the kindness of our family? And speakin' of ingratitude, I must report that our servant Madia did not show up this mornin'. I have spoken to Glennie, who is as equally perplexed. I fear a runaway! Might you check on that matter as well?"

Tomkins seemed to stir on his feet, and he looked into the distance as if he were searching for the missing woman. A junior overseer in the distance called for a temporary halt of work of a crew digging a canal to supply a back-up water system to the Great House. The sun turned up the heat on the earth.

"Miss Cassandra, regardin' the woman Madia, with whom I am acquainted as you know, she has been sold for a fair price."

"And why was I not consulted on that matter? I am the matron of Nottoway as is well known. The woman Madia has been 'tending to my sickly Sister!"

"I will be including it in my weekly report this coming Friday, along with the price of the Negroes that have been sequestered, as times require."

"Very well, Mr. Tomkins."

"Now how is that lovely sister of yours, Miss Cassandra?"

"That is none of your concern, Mr. Tomkins, and may I remind you that your charms do not work on me! I suggest you stay far from her so that you yourself do not catch her ailment."

"I might find that beyond my abilities, so please send her my fondest wishes for a speedy recovery." His brilliant blue eyes flashed.

"I shall indeed, Mr. Tomkins," she blushed. Then, her face became stoic. "I expect to be fully consulted on these matters regardin' the Negroes in the Great House. Madia knew the house, and served our purpose well, Mr. Tomkins, quite well." She looked at Annabelle.

"And wasn't that woman your own mother, girl?"

To speak struck Annabelle as inviting danger, so she just nodded her head.

"Mothers should not be taken away from their children, Mr. Tomkins, unless absolutely necessary," she scolded. "Your job is the overall well-being of the Negroes as much as it is the smooth workings of Nottoway Plantation." At this, the young mistress began to walk toward the Great House, stopping to greet the old gardener.

Tomkins steamed. He alone was familiar with the workings of this plantation, and Master Kane had made it clear that a dramatic new invention would fall under his capable hands. He would no longer have to waste his time looking over the shoulders of lazy and mischievous Negroes, or answering to a stupid girl, even if she was a Kane.

Wendell gave Annabelle a shove and they once again began their walk when Miss Cassandra again called out to them.

"Mr. Tomkins, to whom have you sold the woman Madia, and for what dollar amount?"

Tomkins turned toward his questioner, this time keeping his hat on his head. "Actually, Miss Cassandra, I have purchased the woman myself for twenty percent over the price that her skill commands, and I have already paid the down payment sum of $600 to the banker your daddy directed."

"You yourself have purchased the Negro?"

"That is correct," he said confidently. "Fifty percent with cash and the other fifty percent against my future wages. It's a fair deal that was negotiated with the aid of the accountants that assist this plantation with the ledgers."

"Hmm," the older Miss Kane answered as she seemed to contemplate the matter. She then marched toward the house to attend to her sister.

The three continued their walk toward the wagon. "That ugly Mary Louise ain't worth the parchment of a marriage contract, but a man must endure to get what is rightly his own!" Tomkins declared as he watched Cassandra disappear into the Great House.

The soon to be beating and possible death of Calvin, the sale of Madia to A.C. Tomkins himself, and Annabelle's own fate began to bear down on her like the unrelenting sun. She passed two dogs panting beneath the shade of a redbud tree, its purple flowers turning a dull pink as they searched for moisture that was nowhere to be found. A thickness formed in Annabelle's head. It dawned on her that whatever curse or haunt that was declared at the hanging of Jemmy was now being cast upon her.

*A.C., you shall burn in suffering as these slave people suffer.*

It occurred to her to question why Jemmy had chosen these words. Since he was a Diviner, as she herself had been called by the Ngaka in the small hut behind the initiation lodge, why would he call for the suffering of the slave people, for them to burn as Tomkins himself...burned. She looked at his face and saw the scarring.

She had no plan to help Nottoway out of the hardship caused by the ceaseless heat of a blue-blood sky. She knew how to get herself out, that had been as simple as grasping the leather pouch and disappearing up the stairs, but even that exit was now outside her reach. Still, there was at least the possibility of an escape hatch for her. The people burning under Jemmy's curse did not deserve this fate, and she had no idea how she could bring the cruelty to an end, and the rains to a beginning. As she was pushed along the road by the greasy hand of Wendell, she could not conceive of a single strategy that stood a chance of success, except to take another step forward.

They approached the wagon and Wendell motioned for Annabelle to get in.

"Where am I going?" she asked

"Where I tell ya," Tomkins responded.

"I can't go anywhere," she reasoned insistently. "The General asked me to visit with him tonight, Mr. Tomkins," she said, pointing toward the porch.

"You mean Masta' Kane? You ain't goin' to no meeting you stupid hog! He's as crazy as a coonhound shot full of quills! All he cares about is the money we get from selling y'all," and then, just as the words began to sink into her, he struck her across the face with his hand. For Annabelle, this assault brought back her first days in the army when she was directed to shoot an AK-47 into a thick forest at an unseen enemy, and then told later that her side had won the battle. She had killed before, and it was not hard.

He stared down at her. "Glennie don tol' me that you and that nigga' preacher were gonna tell Master Kane that I's the one that killed his son! What, you all smart now that you can talk? What you seen from up the ladder that night? I tell ya what you seen...you seen your nigga' father kill Kestin Kane!" He kicked her in the gut, and she fell over in the dirt. "We don' need no lying nigga' girls around Nottoway! Even the good workers, we sellin' y'all! Got us $1,200 for you alone! And you ain't never gonna see your momma again, ya hear? 'Cause I buy her for myself!"

Tomkins could sense her resilience, and his fury showed as clearly as the blistering boils on his face. His crystal-clear eyes gave him a power he never earned.

"You start to look like her with those pretty eyes, and that ain't a bad thing! Maybe one day I will come to gitcha and show you what I do to your momma, and what I will keep doin' to her as long as she's alive! Now git on up, unless you want me to chain you up!"

At that moment, a hand reached out from the canvas flaps and Arthur pulled Annabelle up onto the wagon, where she landed among people she knew. Less than four feet separated the slaves from the coachman, so the passengers' voices had to be kept down. Annabelle looked around at her fellow travelers. Ole' Beatrice met no one's eye. Lizzie quivered. Arthur rested his forearms on his knees and stared at the floor. A few other men sat on the crude benches turning their heads side to side as if searching for an escape.

Everyone was silent as the wagon jolted forward. Tomkins himself had joined the coachman. Then Annabelle noticed the chains. She had been so distracted; she had not registered the fact that their feet were coiled together in a rusty harness that looped through their ankles and was secured to a slat in the wagon. A thick lock joined the two final links.

The question of where they were going did not have to be asked because answers were not given to slaves. But a rumor had stirred up the prior night that a group of them were to be hired out to Wappocomo Plantation, a three-day journey away. No one thought that they themselves would be part of the convoy, so no one prepared, including Annabelle. Now they sat in the back of the wagon with only the clothes on their backs. It occurred to Annabelle that the slave times would eventually come to an end with the American Civil War between the states, but that was not for another forty years, so these people had no choice but to move toward their next indentured placement. Now Annabelle, at fourteen, had to accept that she was captured in this time and would die in this time.

The wagon moved steadily, occasionally dipping into a rut along the road that the travelers could anticipate by listening to the horses' steps. The elder Beatrice and Arthur grimaced in pain whenever the wagon dipped too aggressively, their backs objecting to the ruts in the road. The journey continued for hours with sharp turns that forced them against one another and stretches uphill that made them slide toward the back, where there was nothing to hold onto except one another.

The sounds of the Virginia woodland provided the only indication of where they might be. Peering outside the flaps revealed more dirt road and the occasional passerby—sometimes a Negro traveling alone on a wagon making deliveries, sometimes a stagecoach on a scheduled transport. Then it was the birds; the eastern bluebird chattering in sync with the rhythmic woodpeckers. Strangely, there was a sense of calm to the journey that reminded Annabelle of the slow, hopeful walks with the UNITA Army after her regiment had been idle for weeks. Perhaps they were going to a better place, she hoped.

Ole' Beatrice was a house woman and a launderer who had grown up in the tobacco fields. Arthur was a full hand in the fields. Lizzie was...a cook, perhaps. Annabelle had quickly gained attention as a master basket weaver. Like in the army, it only made sense to assign the people where it made the most sense. Perhaps the work would be easier...wherever they were going. But it was no coincidence, she thought, that she was with the people who knew her best, and about this, she was deeply concerned.

Annabelle now heard talking as an approaching wagon came into earshot. They could all hear the sound of chains rattling and quiet singing growing louder as the two wagons converged on the road.

"Top of the day, Bryce!" Tomkins exclaimed. Arthur peered through a slit in the canvas opening at the front of the wagon. As Tomkins was focused on the other driver who was heading in the opposite direction, Annabelle leaned toward the opening to see for herself. The other driver had a mustache that stood out from a distance.

"What cha got, Ace?" the other driver asked.

"Another day's work!" Tomkins replied. Annabelle could feel their wagon shift as the horses kicked flies off of their bodies.

"You buyin' or sellin'?"

"Don't know Bryce. That depends on the price of rice in Charleston, now don't it?"

"Where you headin'?"

"Over to Wappocomo Hill. We're gonna lend out a few niggas. Times hard, ya know and Masta' Kane needs to get some money rollin'." He looked up at the sky. "Don' look like rain coming anytime soon to make our tobacco worth somethin'."

"You got three-days ride to reach Wappocomo, Ace, unless you lighten your load of a nigga' or two? Then maybe you can beat it by an afternoon, huh? Whatdaya got, Ace?" The man pointed toward the back of the haywagon where Annabelle sat with her cohorts.

"Whatcha got?" he repeated.

"Three full hands and a lazy one."

The man named Bryce shook his head. Seated beside him was a sturdy man whose thickness reminded Annabelle of a tree trunk. He stepped down off the coach and began to lead their horses slowly past the wagon in which Annabelle and her friends were imprisoned. A train of people stood in a long line behind the cart that he was riding.

Now Annabelle could make out the human cargo that followed Bryce and his coachman's wagon. It came first as nothing but the sound of metal, a rattling that was unnatural in these Virginia hillsides. Then came the sound of shuffling feet, followed finally by the grunts and groans of exhausted men and women. The procession began to pass, then halted. There were over twenty-five people; men and women of different ages, including some around Annabelle's own age, clamped in chains and forced to follow behind the coach driven by Bryce. The sturdy man handed out canteens of water that worked their way through the silent walkers.

"Three full hands and a lazy one, huh?" Bryce asked.

"How old the lazy one?"

"She sixteen or something."

"Whatcha want for her?"

Tomkins began to weigh the question. "Well, jeez, I ain't sure that Masta' Kane wants me to sell nothing. I mean, I just supposed to rent 'em out for a good nickel. But she is pretty and maybe she can do something after a good floggin'. I done it myself once, but she just come back as stupid as before."

"Can I see the goods?"

"Don't see why not!" Tomkins came down off the coachman seat and moved to the back of the wagon. He opened the canvas flaps and stuck his head inside. His hat was pulled down just above his eyes.

"How's the ride, ya'll?" he joked, then looked over at Bryce.

"Lizzie, get on out and come outside where my good friend can take a good look at cha." He unchained the padlock, and the travelers began to rub raw blisters on their ankles.

Lizzie began to walk down the aisle between the low wagon benches, her chains dangling off of her person. Ole' Beatrice grabbed onto her person and a look passed between them they only they understood.

"No, not my Lizzie," Beatrice exclaimed.

"I'll be right back Nanny," Lizzie said, and kissed the old woman on the cheek. She climbed out of the wagon as Beatrice held her arm out toward her.

The sun shone on her skin and Annabelle noticed Bryce eyeing her. The slave people in tow paid little attention, seemingly relieved to have a break. Annabelle looked down at their ankles, which were bloated and bloodied from the jostling of the heavy chains against their raw skin.

"Whatcha want for that?" Brice asked.

"Ain't selling, I say."

"Now now there, Ace. The old man ain't gonna notice if one or two niggas go missing, especially if you come back with a little bit of cash. I hear your county ain't had no good crop for a while. Must be hard finding cash." He looked Lizzie up and down then grabbed her cheek and examined her teeth.

"You lazy like my friend say?" he asked, his face close to hers.

"No sir," she replied, looking down.

"Tell you what, Ace, I give you $600 right here right now, and we don' tell nobody about it, huh? Then maybe if I can get a good price, we split the profit. Whadaya say, Ace?"

The deal was consummated, and the wagons began to move again. Annabelle looked out to see Lizzie following the other captured souls, her hands bound as she looked over her shoulder at the hay wagon with the people she once knew. Ole' Beatrice buried her head in her lap.

Annabelle began to feel her blood rise. She thought she'd seen the worst of what men could do to one another. She had entered villages with the UNITA army and was told to keep the order of people lined up to be maimed, cut, and mutilated. She had seen soldiers taunt hapless villagers with the limbs of their relatives. But this bondage she witnessed now, with not a drop of rain to cool the senses, brought within her a firm desire to end what she was seeing in any way she could. So far, her only strategy had been to maintain her own existence. She had found a way to get here, beyond any explanation, so perhaps she was indeed special in some way. But what could anyone do to end this nightmare, and if not end it, then at least wash it with water and somehow make it bearable? She vowed to tell certain souls that slave days will end. Perhaps that hope would give them comfort, knowing that their children and their children's children would one day be free.

Annabelle knew it was impossible to return to River Hills, that the path home was now permanently closed. She had to accept her fate, just as she had to accept her fate when she was thrown into the belly of the army and forced to march away from Caxito, and everyone she loved.

Over the following days the caravan in which she travelled slept in barns, shackled together, the women with the women and the men with the men with only a few buckets for their human needs. Tomkins himself slept inside the residences of the homes he visited, and they could hear the galivanting into the nights.

Before the sun rose, Tomkins awakened the prisoners with the clang of a bell. They were released from one another in the morning only to relieve themselves in privacy and to perform some chores in service to their hosts in exchange for the night's lodging. Annabelle found herself baking biscuits in the kitchen while the men were sent to the barn to pack the largest tobacco fibers into hogsheads.

Tomkins, now in sole charge of his wards and convinced that he was out of earshot of any authority, drank bourbon in the mornings. Three days passed in this manner. After the third night, Annabelle overheard him say to his coachman that they had traveled over 100 miles from Nottoway.

On the fourth day, the wagon sprang along the roadway, at several points bending left and right as it passed other travelers. They heard dogs barking and the yelping of animals' echo in the valleys. In busier areas, these sounds gave way to the voices of villagers going about their dealings. She heard farmers tending cattle and a man tell a boy to fetch water. She heard men talking and mothers calling for their children, coughing, shouting—all the sounds of a village. Annabelle and the others peered out and realized they were on another plantation. As the wagon came to a halt, they heard Tomkins calling for people he knew and giving orders as to where Annabelle and her fellow travelers would go.

They were led off the wagon and left standing on another slave row while Tomkins disappeared toward a federal mansion that sat down the hill in a valley. The travelers were examined by what appeared to be doctors, and then assigned to cabins. Beatrice and Annabelle were assigned together. Arthur and the other men were assigned to a cabin opposite theirs.

As evening approached, crickets and frogs began their song, and a blanket of darkness dropped over the meager cabins. Annabelle went outside and stood on the porch. She watched the slave people of this plantation carry fanner baskets filled with freshly caught fish. Others carried pumpkins and onions. A small boy walked behind his father carrying a lifeless chicken.

Beatrice came out onto the porch and sat in a rocking chair. Annabelle pulled up a broken chair and balanced her weight.

"Do you think that Calvin is alright? Do you think that they got him?" Annabelle asked.

The older woman shook her head. She had no doubt that Annabelle's brother awaited a cruel fate. Any hint of a Black boy looking at a White girl, especially the master's daughter, was grounds for the most severe of punishments. Annabelle and Beatrice contemplated what they could not see but knew.

"Annabelle," the old woman began, "how is it that you started speaking again when you were quiet for so long? How is that, child?"

Beatrice gazed back at her with knowing eyes. She was as much the woman she met in church on the anniversary of Jemmy's death as she was the Ngaka she had met in the tiny hut behind the initiation lodge back home. The fact that she wore the same wooden pendant in the shape of a crescent moon gave Annabelle a jolt, followed by a strange sense of relief, as if she were with someone who she knew, and who knew her.

"I don't know," Annabelle replied.

"I think you do. Tell me, child. Why do you speak and what is that you have to say? Why did you start talking when we took you to the cemetery to visit your daddy's grave, beneath the very tree where they hang him?"

At Nottoway, Annabelle felt she was living in a fable, but she could not understand the opening scene, the plot, or the ending. It was full of characters she did now know but had somehow met before. It was full of sights she recognized but had never actually seen. It was as if she were singing a song at church about the longings of people from far away, and found herself alive in the verses, lost firmly within the lines of the melody with no idea how she got there, or where she could find the conductor who might point a way out.

She decided to trust Ole' Beatrice.

"I am not from this place, or of this place," Annabelle confided, noticing how strange the words sounded.

The old woman reached for her hand and squeezed it.

"I know it, child." Then she turned her dull eyes toward Annabelle. "Beatrice knows that. But how is it that you came to speak to us?"

Annabelle then began to tell her story.

Beatrice listened as the girl spoke.

Her name was Zarkhanna Cudjo.

She was born in Caxito, Angola, on November 17, 1989. One hundred sixty-five years from now.

Her father had gone to Luanda to find work. He never came home, and no one knew what happened to him. She was eleven years old when he disappeared.

She had many memories of this father, but they all collided into a gush of emotion that simply told a story again and again about a man who loved her and cared for her and took her with him to the river to fish. He had reminded her of an elephant, she remembered. His nose was big and funny. He made her laugh. He told her that she came from a long line of relatives. Some of them were rounded up and taken by force to Sao Paulo, a fortress on the coast of Angola, where they boarded ships and were taken away. It was a long time ago. A few of them had made their way back to Angola from the land they were taken to. When he told her this, they had been sitting on a blue tractor in a field. She remembered that a bird landed on the tractor's bucket. Zarkhanna was four years old.

Then her family was killed and she was abducted. She was ensigned into the army and forced to do gruesome acts to innocent people. One day she was hidden by nuns in a church and was then transferred to the Calito Orphanage. A woman named Mrs. Carolyn White came from America to see her. Soon after, she came to this country on an airplane. Annabelle pointed to the sky. The plane was silver and flew like a bird and people travel in them, all over the world.

Beatrice nodded her head. Her eyes remained dull and she seemed to see nothing. She did not ask questions. She knew that, once, a silver bird had been seen in the sky moving like a machine. The Reverend had mentioned this.

"It has been five years since the rains were last seen...and we all saw the strange silver bird in the sky moving like it were a machine, a year after the hanging of an innocent man and the start of our long drought," she remembered him saying.

Only the slave people had seen the silver bird, and the sight was rarely spoken of. Some had seen the strange bird, while others had not, so that it became a myth that some believed, and others flatly denied. How could a machine bird fly?

Annabelle had found a leather pouch in a crevice on Camel's Hump Mountain. It brought her to this place. By now her family—the ones who had adopted her—would be looking for her in another time, measured in twenty-four-hour days that Annabelle could not fathom, but guessed was likely close to four or five. There was a little boy named Simba.

And she knew why the rains had ceased in Essex County.

And she knew why she was there.

She had no recollection of the years between witnessing the murder as a nine-year-old girl and her return to their world as the fourteen-year-old Annabelle, the very embodiment of that little witness. She remembered that on her first real day in this world she was unable to speak when she had gone with Beatrice and the others to hear the Reverend's sermon, and then walked from the church to the cemetery to visit Jemmy's grave.

"The Old Oak lives in both worlds, Beatrice," she said.

The limbs of the tree were as alive now as they would be in 165 years, nourished by the sun, the rain, the wind, and the dead souls beneath its wooden feet.

Her story told; Annabelle sat back in her chair. The new slave village around her was winding down as night approached.

"We need to get you home," the older woman said. "Help us if you can, Annabelle—Zarkhanna. Help us bring the rains and end the suffering. I know...that you can." She spoke as if asking a question written in a holy book.

Annabelle was given a meal of warm chicken and potatoes provided by neighbors around them. Afterward, she was invited to a gathering in a nearby clearing in the woods where a small fire had been lit by an old man who did not speak. A small group sat around the fire, and a man who went by the name of Monday brought out a fiddle. He was joined by a boy not much older than Annabelle playing a tambourine, and a girl of ten years struck a banjo with an expertise far beyond her years. Through the treetops, a corn moon shone brightly, its yellowish tint casting a warm glow over the revelers.

The shack Beatrice and Annabelle were assigned to belonged to a woman named Sherry, who was soon to be married. She laughed easily and often repeated her phrases twice, the second time under her breath.

"This is our tinder horn, friends," Sherry said. Then, after a pause, she repeated "tinder horn" in a whisper to herself. "This fire has never completely died out since it was lit by my great grandfather," she said as she poked at the logs in the stone fireplace in the center of the shack. “Never completely died out,” she repeated. Her greatest sources of joy were the secret visits by her fiancé in the night. Her lover would come without the required visitation tickets given out by the fat overseers and he would tell her stories of evading patrols and close calls during their nights together. He was always careful to leave before dawn. Annabelle slept peacefully on visions of her hostess’ love stories.

But the serenity of the night’s good food, music, and stories all came to a sharp close when the first light of dawn pierced through the windows and a horn sounded. The shrill note called all these good people to their tasks. Like at Nottoway, and perhaps a thousand other places, African people rushed toward the houses and fields where they were expected to complete their daily tasks before being allowed once again to attend to their own needs.

This day, Annabelle, Beatrice, Arthur, and a few others from Nottoway found themselves together in the middle row of an enormous tobacco field.

A fat man on a small horse gave a steady stream of orders. “Row,” he would yell, startling his own horse, as he called for the fieldworkers to move to the next line of planting. He looked like a man without a neck.

As she worked, she would on occasion look up at the sky and wonder if among the people she saw from the airplane long ago was her own self right now, trapped in the past or an even stranger future.

Days became weeks. She learned that each tobacco plant was like a crying toddler, unconcerned with its mother’s feeble condition and fatigue. The work tortured her back as she bent over with a small knife and picked out the fat worms that housed themselves inside the leaves, making it harder to cut off the flowering apex, which was essential to their cultivation as smoking material.

It was tedious and exacting work. The worms needed to be picked off by hand so as not to break the precious leaves. Equipped with horns, the vermin bloodied her hands and crawled on her feet day after day. Obvious talking was not allowed, only singing. One day, she watched a junior overseer inspect the plants on a row Beatrice had just completed. Filling in for his fat boss who had negotiated a four-day holiday, he was gleeful to hold temporary power. Not yet twenty years old, he had thin hair down to his shoulders. He aimed to use his time as junior overseer to prove to Wappocomo’s masters that his management methods were efficient.

"Let me take a look at your work," the boy-man said. In the mornings, he appeared friendly and talkative to the workers as they followed him toward the fields, but once out of earshot of others, he used one-word commands—"Row!" and "Move!" or "Next!"—whenever he saw one of the workers stretch a back or take a brief pause. Annabelle noticed that the breaks he allowed were always in the hot sun so that the worker would almost crave to return to picking the shady plant, working toward day's end, over being dried alive by the cruel disk in the sky.

"What we got here?" the junior overseer said, carefully picking a tobacco worm from one of the plants that Ole' Beatrice had just moved on from and examining it close to his narrow chin.

She looked at the man with a nonchalant gaze. She had been working as ceaselessly as anyone. "Must have missed one," she said.

The man allowed the worm to crawl over his finger as he approached the aging slave woman. "You may be an old nigga' but our good friend Mr. Tomkins promised me that you're worth the good money the Colonel paid to work on this land. We give you free food and a place to sleep. What you give us is good tobacco plants. Not this!" He threw the worm at her face, but it missed and fell to the earth.

"You miss one, you miss three," he said as he presented another worm on the palm of his outstretched hand. Overhead two hawks circled high and their shadows crossed the path of the scene playing out. "You must like these worms! You must think they're good nigga' eatin' or somethin'! That right? A Sunday supper or somethin' 'fore church?"

"No, sir," Beatrice responded.

"Open your mouth and eat this worm, woman."

"No sir, I won't do that."

"Open wide, I say!" He reached to grab her head so he could thrust the insect into her mouth.

But Beatrice performed such a defensive dance, it was enough to make the young man laugh.

"Scared ya, didn't I?" he said, throwing the creature on the ground and smashing it under his boot. "Next time you remember to grab them worms and get them off my tobacco plants!"

The quitting hour approached as the sun began to slip lower on the horizon. A fellow joined the boy-man overseer, and the men paid less attention to the workers in the fields and more to their evening plans.

Annabelle stood up and met eyes with Arthur, who nodded his head toward her. They were in a part of the fields that required the stalks to be cut and gathered, another careful process to protect the valuable fibers that were to be packed into 1,000-pound hogsheads and stored in the warehouses in exchange for tobacco notes--good for merchandise anywhere in the South, or the world for that matter.

She walked with Arthur back toward the barn.

"Are we to stay here now?" Annabelle asked.

"They must have decided that we were better off being rented out than sold, so maybe one day we go back to Nottoway," he said hopefully.

Annabelle knew only that a road connected the two plantations, but where that road was and how it turned, she had no idea. She remembered the words of the Reverend on the day she returned to the plantation.

*We must have Divine faith, not human faith.*

The words were embedded in her. If she had never come into this underworld, she would have continued living in River Hills and perhaps died there. Instead, she had transformed her life by coming to a time and place where she might also die. Neither fate could define her, and neither could control who she was as a person—a daughter to proud Cudjo parents and a niece to a woman who sought to bring her into a more modern Angolan world.

The sense of purpose that she'd had in the past—to be initiated as a young woman and find her place in her community—had been ripped from her long ago like the limbs of villagers by starving dogs. But she survived and, in this world, she had quickly learned to accomplish her tasks, eat, drink, and live in no less or more separation from others than she had in River Hills, with her friends talking behind her back, Nita keeping her distance, and Carolyn leaving her alone.

Time had been a terrible adversary to her for nearly three years, each chapter worse than the next. It began with the tortured screams of her mother, then came marching armies and unspeakable crimes. She was then taken to church after church and endured interviews with foreign families evaluating her for adoption. Then there were passport interviews with bureaucrats who always mixed up her name. When she arrived in River Hills, she found luxuries she did not need and friends who were not real. Then she traversed into an underworld with new warlords, this time White tyrants bellowing orders toward African people who had no escape.

And now she was at a new plantation, and as terrible as it was to be a slave at fourteen years old with no way out, at least she knew the next chapter of her life could not be worse than the last.

She knew what tomorrow would bring, for she was roped as tightly as the branch of the Old Oak from which a man was hanged for a murder he did not commit. In silence, she walked with Arthur and Beatrice back to the cabin that was the home of the soon-to-be-married Sherry, another dilapidated pile of wood in the belly of the plantation beast, yet a home still, with warm people, good food, and even music.

She had now been in this other world for close to two months. What that equated to back in River Hills was likely moving toward a week, she figured. She was either lost in time, or time was lost on her. Either way, trying to escape was as useless as a rain machine.

# Chapter 11

It was 2:30 a.m., and the light from the television screen flickered on Carolyn and Mark's faces.

A widening circle of news channels were covering the story, now reduced to a headline: *Missing Girl, fourteen years old, last seen in the Tappahannock, Virginia area.* The story was baffling, and irresistible: The as of yet unnamed girl was a teenager from the country of Angola. She had been adopted less than a year ago by a local family, the producer Mark White and former State Senate candidate Carolyn White. Foul play is not suspected at this time. Authorities are following up on all leads. If anyone has any information on the missing child, please call this number. A reward is being offered by the family for any information that leads to her safe return. A news conference is scheduled for later today.

Carolyn had needed to ask her father for the reward money, which he wired into their joint account that morning. The previous evening had been full of calls from people all rephrasing the same question—people who needed to ask and wanted to know.

"When was the last time you saw your daughter?" a reporter accosted Mark when he went out to walk Chowder, thrusting a microphone into his face.

"Where was she last seen, again please?" a dispatch operator inquired over the phone, double checking a form.

"What was she wearing when you last saw her?" Priscilla asked when she came over with an eggplant parmesan casserole.

"Is Anna lost?" Simba asked.

The young boy kept checking the basement hoping she'd magically appear, finding only games and toys, the small trampoline, and the basket that Anna had been weaving. Yesterday morning, he had come running upstairs with the basket, claiming Anna had been working on it all night. He could just tell. Throughout breakfast, he held it as if he had found a lost set of keys everyone was looking for.

“Thank you, Simba,” Tabitha said. “You’re stupid.”

He ran back downstairs in tears.

“We don’t need more problems, Tabby.” Carolyn turned to Nita for help. “Be the big sister, Juanita. We need you.”

“What did I do?” Nita uttered.

As the morning light crept into their bedroom, Carolyn lay beside Mark. She felt that her body was merely pressing up against another, like on a subway. They looked at each other like strangers who suddenly remembered they knew one another, only to quickly look away.

She was still dressed in the same sweatpants and T-shirt she had worn last night. The grayish-blue hint of dawn was going to flush her out of bed one way or another, but she felt her day would be like going to a funeral for someone she hardly knew, forced to drudge her way through the event. Today, everything was going to be based on the sad reality that something was amiss, and no matter what she did or where she went, it was going to be branded on her forehead. She thought about the press that would surely want a comment, and the acquaintance who would want to lend a hand. There would be more questions from Ted. And through it all, there were still details to be ironed out with the Chinese Embassy regarding the new adoption. She could not lose her place in line. She hoped they had not put two and two together.

“Anna is safe,” she whispered to herself. “Be positive. One day at a time.” She summoned the courage to get out of bed and wash up, and when she came back into the bedroom, Mark had gone. She went downstairs where she found him sitting on the sofa talking on the phone.

“What can I expect to be asked?” Mark asked into the receiver. He nodded and gave several grunts of acknowledgement to the speaker on the other end, Barry Kane, their friend, and now, their informal counsel.

The Whites and the Kanes had agreed that there was no reason for them at this point to hire an attorney, despite Detective Washington’s hint that they would certainly be questioned on tape. Barry might have given different advice if the Whites were not good friends, but he did not want to appear accusatory in any way. Still, Carolyn noticed a hint of doubt on Barry’s part. It was not just in her head.

Carolyn made a cup of tea and walked upstairs into Nita’s room. It was barely 7:15 in the morning and the door was closed. She entered the room and noticed Nita still asleep, sleeping outside the covers and perpendicular to the bed. Bags of clothing from The Gap, Forever 21, and Spencer's Gifts were strewn about her side of the room. There was little of Anna's possessions outside of the small pink suitcase she had brought with her and several pairs of her jeans and hairpieces piled onto the white plastic chair at the computer. Since Mark had claimed the guest room as his office, Ronnie slept in Anna's bed. She had agreed to spend the night and help with the children in the panic that had taken over the household. The woman snored audibly. Carolyn peered into the shopping bags, finding a stone necklace, colored socks, and a red beret, all with the price tags still attached. Ronnie woke up with a start when the crinkle of the shopping bags invaded the quiet room.

"Morning, Mrs. White," Ronnie murmured. "Anything?" she asked, then realized that it was the wrong question. She had spoken to the police and given whatever details she could think of. Nita too had been questioned, as she seemed to have the most information about Anna, but all the pieces were not fitting together. What they knew now was all about where Anna wasn't—which included being happy with her friends.

"No Ronnie, not yet. Good morning. Thank you for staying last night." Carolyn sat on the edge of Anna's bed. The Jamaican woman had removed her wig, and her natural hair lay close to her scalp. She wore a long white nightshirt and had cream on her face.

Anna's disappearance was not Ronnie's fault, but it had happened on her watch. Carolyn had left instructions before leaving for Richmond. Juanita could basically take care of herself, but the other children needed to be looked after.

The morning light in the bedroom showed no mercy. Carolyn's mind followed the most improbable of circumstances.

Perhaps after Mark had left for the airport, Anna had snuck back into the house and stole the $300 from the top drawer of Mark's bureau. She had then somehow gotten herself to downtown Tappahannock and boarded a bus to who knows where—D.C. perhaps, or New York City, trying to find an embassy or consulate. Or maybe she was abducted, or picked up, and she was either being driven home right now or in the back of a van somewhere in the Midwest. These thoughts ran into one another like a colony of ants, colliding and heading away from one another in out-of-control directions.

Nita opened her eyes and caught sight of Ronnie sleeping in her room and her mother standing over her.

"What's up?" she muttered, then, remembering the circumstances, simply said "Oh." Carolyn could see the feeling of intrusion on her oldest daughter's face. Although Nita was the last to see Anna, the details she provided were less than helpful.

*When was the last time you saw your sister*? "When everyone else did."

*What was she wearing?* "I don't know, she was in bed."

*Do you have any idea where she may have gone?* "I told you, maybe D.C."

Nita had arrived in Virginia six years ago at the age of twelve. Fernando Henrique Cardoso had taken control of Brazil and, after a brief uptick in services for the very poor, disease, hunger, and corruption began to spread through the once great nation. The girl's father had gone looking for work in nearby Bolivia and never returned. Whether he was dead or remarried, her mother could no longer support the six siblings. The desperate woman had heard through a doctor friend that the Venezuelan Family Welfare Institute was granting releases for children to move to the United States The mother had given the girl up with the unwritten understanding that she would come back one day. It was a bargain that Carolyn never denied, nor agreed to. She had only to give the girl's mother comfort that her daughter would be well taken care of. She would learn English, go roller-skating, swim in pools, even go to college. The girl matched every feature that Carolyn sought in an adoptee, right through the personality profile trait of being gregarious.

She had visited Nita's home—if that is what it could be called, with two filthy mattresses on the floor of a glorified tent on the outskirts of Sao Paulo. A blue tarp separated the sleeping area from the sitting section. The mother was holding the last of her children given to her by her missing husband. On the rutted drive up the hill to the family shelter, the agency people explained that Juanita's fate was either begging on the street or prostitution.

During the exchange, the mother did not have the strength to look at her daughter, never mind say goodbye. It was Carolyn's first adoption, and she did not know why the agency had subjected her to the pain of watching the girl being separated from her mother. She looked around the shanty. The girl would be better off.

"*Obrigado. E nós trataremos sua filha como se fosse nossa, como você faria*, Carolyn had said in the rehearsed Portuguese she had memorized at the Republica Park Hotel, where the room service she ordered that morning never came. She had summoned the manager, but he never called back.

The mother waved her daughter away, and that was that. But her wailing could be heard as their Land Rover made its way down the road, if that was what it could be called.

Nita got out of bed and Ronnie and Carolyn watched her leave the room. She was dressed in sweatpants and an oversized River High School T-shirt covering her squat figure. She did not have a boyfriend, but she was on birth control. While the prescriptions were automatically filled, the talk about sex was stilted and strained.

Ronnie got out of bed and began the process of preparing herself for the day. She was the kind of woman whose appearance changed drastically from slumber to dressed as her curly black wig came to rest on her head. Downstairs, the phone ring and Mark answered it on the second ring. Carolyn looked at the floor as the nanny dressed, listening intently to Mark's one-word answers. Any information at this point was good information. Carolyn walked downstairs and stood next to him as he wrapped up the call and hung up the receiver.

"That was your friend Ted. Our new best friend."

Ted Washington. Her supposed-to-be prom date, but "and?" is all that came out of her mouth.

"He was calling about Juanita."

"Our Nita?"

"Yes, our Nita." He pointed upstairs.

Carolyn looked quizzical. She was now dressed in her battle clothes--spandex workout pants, sneakers, and little makeup.

"Sit down for this one," he said.

They sat together in the kitchen with heavy coffee cups and even heavier air about them given the uncertainties of the day. Chowder sat at their feet, looking for scraps from the other.

"Ted says that Nita has been stealing," Mark began. "She was caught on camera at the mall in multiple locations." He paused and looked away, shaking his head as if he had just found proof the odd noise they had been hearing in the walls was actually the mice colony everyone suspected.

"She's been doing it for a while. She walks in with a bag from the store she's targeting with an item that she has previously purchased, like socks. Then she stuffs..." He began a dance with his arms, "...THINGS in her bag, and walks out. Then she does it again someplace else."

Carolyn looked at Mark as if he had just told her that he was leaving her for a teen actress in his set. She found herself moving through stages of disbelief, like when hearing about a death—denial, anger, bargaining, depression... "All those bags in her room," Mark said. "We are such idiots."

"And what did he say about Anna?" She was not sure why she changed the subject.

"Nothing about Anna. But I need to give my statement today, so I'm heading down to the precinct if you want to drive me."

Carolyn raised her hands in question. "So, what do we do about this?" She pointed toward Nita and Anna's room as they heard footsteps coming down the stairs. Nita came into the kitchen and headed for the refrigerator. They watched her in silence, and then began repeating what little was known about Anna, but their words had a different tone under the banner of the revealed secret.

It did not seem to be a good time to question her, and it did not seem to be a good time to ignore the matter. Nita poured herself a bowl of cereal and sat down, reaching for a bunch of ripening bananas which Carolyn handed to her like an offering in exchange for something that could not be provided.

"Wha?" Nita asked with her mouth full of cereal.

"What are you doing today, Nita? Your father has to meet with the police, and I am going to speak with the embassy again."

Hot bewilderment ran through Carolyn's veins, as if she had been cooking and splatters of oil had hit her face, shocking her, and having no one to blame but herself for her own stupidity and carelessness. She stared at her eldest daughter, her adoptee, and saw glimmers of the girl's mother in her round face, expressive eyes, squat figure, and never-to-be-American features.

"What?" the girl asked again under the glare of her parents.

Mark began. "Nita, we want to speak with you later. We know that you're going through a lot with everything going on with your sister."

Nita shrugged as if being asked to move the car. "Sure," she said. "I'm supposed to work today. But do you want me to cancel and stay home and help with stuff?"

Carolyn and Mark both gave opposite answers and the jumbled words battled to make the call. "Yes," Mark followed up, and Carolyn shook her head in agreement.

"Sure," the girl said, and flipped her phone open.

Ronnie could now be heard upstairs calling the twins and Simba down for breakfast. The sing-song of her Caribbean accent was followed by the children's one-word answers, and the four of them came down the stairs into the kitchen.

Carolyn looked at her children as if they were uninvited guests to a party she never wanted to throw in the first place. As the White clan huddled in the kitchen, less Anna, they collided with one another as if in a game of musical chairs.

Since Anna's disappearance, Wyatt and Simba seemed to discover one another. The two had developed their own theory on the disappearance of their sister. She was, according to the brothers, still somewhere in the house.

"I found her cell phone on the basement stairs," Simba reported inside the fort they built with blankets in the living room.

"Maybe she's in the attic," Wyatt suggested.

The two boys vowed to find her. They spent the days in various conferences deciding where she might be hiding. They checked closets, moved aside boxes in the garage, and looked under beds.

"Anna, Anna. We can't find you, Anna! You win!" Simba called out yesterday.

The hide-and-seek game would last until one boy would collapse at the last spot they checked, and it was now common to find the boys asleep in a closet or under a bed. They began to compare facts about all of their lives; what Nita did at work (played golf), where spaghetti came from (trees), and what part they would play in Dad's movie (a pilot, a driver). Simba began sleeping on the floor in the twins' room. Tabitha began to play the part of their new schoolteacher, scolding and reminding the boys not to throw food away.

"Anna will be really, really hungry when she comes home," she reasoned.

As they finished their meals, the boys would make 'Anna piles' which, not knowing what to do with them, were simply given to Ronnie, who pretended to save them in a special Tupperware container.

"I left some mac n' cheese for Anna," Simba said, holding out the remains of his lunch to Ronnie.

"Anna can have the rest of my sandwich," Wyatt said, offering the crust of his peanut butter and jelly sandwich.

Tabitha had taken to clinging to Carolyn since Anna's sudden disappearance, seeking to provide her mother with all of the daughter that she could need. She had grown dramatically in her ninth year and now towered over her friends. Her height had started to alienate her schoolmates, and a recent boy-girl party had gone without an invitation for Tabitha White.

"I don't like my friends anymore, Mommy," she had said on the drive home from a haircut the day before. The girl gave specific directions to the stylist, stealing glances at her mother's hairstyle in the mirror and emerging with a tight bob similar enough to Carolyn's so that strangers could see they were mother and daughter.

"What?" Carolyn had asked in the car, checking messages on her phone when they were stopped at a traffic light. A driver laid on his horn behind them and Carolyn jolted the Audi forward.

The girl repeated the statement, this time slowly, and spoke in the hopes that her mother would ask questions.

Carolyn looked in the rearview mirror at her daughter. A message had come up on her phone regarding the adoption of the Chinese boy who turned out to be five years old, not seven as Carolyn had requested. "What? How?" she said, shaking her head at the discovery. It would mean different schooling for the boy, and the age would be a stake in the ground that would make Simba an older brother, rather than the youngest, which Carolyn had carefully calculated would make for the best family tree. The news made her swerve, but she quickly recovered control.

"Don't text and drive, Mommy!"

Carolyn glanced at her daughter.

"I don't like my friends."

"Tabitha, there's a lot going on right now. Friends sometimes change as you grow up," she said. Then, after a moment to consider the comment, she added, "Why don't you like your friends?"

"Because they're immature," the girl claimed with a chin turned upwards.

No one spoke.

"I don't want to go to school anymore, so I'm not," the girl stated. "Savannah is being homeschooled by her mom, and she gets to watch more TV and still go to sports at school." She looked at Carolyn in the mirror and the mother and daughter shared a silent conversation. "I could help you look for Anna, too," she said.

"Well, you have to go to school, Tabitha." And that was that.

Carolyn drove faster and ran a yellow light, narrowly missing a motorcycle speeding through the intersection. A silence took over the car and separated the two, like a privacy shield in a taxicab. Carolyn tried to digest what her daughter was saying but saw it only as more chaos in a life that needed no more complexity.

"You have to go to school, Tabitha!" minutes later.

"Well, I don't want to!"

Carolyn tried to remember if she had been clear with the Chinese Embassy that she wanted a seven-year-old child. Now she wondered if the adoption agency also missed the fact that she did not want to adopt any children with physical deformities or were psychologically unstable—difficult was fine, but no children prone to outbursts or seizures. She played with the idea of stopping the process in its tracks. The thought felt freeing but backtracking at this point was akin to abandonment. She needed to push through—for the children.

"We'll talk about it, Tabitha," someone said in a voice that didn't feel like her own. They passed the long curve on Route 17 and Carolyn gazed up briefly at the odd shaped mountain top which kept the River Hills community in its bosom. She looked into the woods where a path began its ascent up the mountain, then turned her head toward the fast-moving waters of the Rappahannock River. She realized she was unconsciously looking for Anna, as if the girl were simply in plain sight, sitting on the edge of the river, or looking down from the steep cliffs of Camel's Hump.

A command center had been established at the Clubhouse, and volunteers for the search party had begun to assemble. The scene resembled a fundraiser for the police department. There were many familiar faces—Mrs. Davidson from the library and a group of local restaurant owners with a picture of Anna on their shirts with the slogan *We'll Have You Home by Supper*. The news of the missing teenager had brought out volunteers who relished campaigns. One man came from Florida with two bloodhounds. Another man in his eighties arrived on horseback as if he had ridden in from the Blue Ridge Mountains

A snapshot of Anna taken at Tabitha and Wyatt's birthday party was now the official photograph of the missing girl. In the picture, she was dressed in a blue velour sweat suit that Carolyn now wondered if Nita had stolen as well. Anna was caught off guard in the photograph with a half-smile that revealed the space between her teeth and her curved eyebrows which now seemed like a beauty mark.

Stacks of flyers with details of the missing girl sat on a long folding table on the Clubhouse porch. On an adjoining table a few local mothers put out packets of peanut butter crackers and pretzels for the volunteers. The snacks drew the attention of the children of the local residents who had volunteered to search the area, and wrappers were strewn about the shipboard flooring of the great porch.

Off to the side, Detective Washington gave a radio interview to Richmond News Radio 1140. Carolyn stood next to him, but she took no questions, as suggested by Ted prior to the interview. The television appearance was scheduled for that night, along with the announcement of the reward, planned to be $25,000, which would take place on the front porch of the Whites' home. Carolyn could think of no preparation for this media nightmare, no words that she even might say. Should she hold Mark's hand? Should she allow herself to cry on camera? Should she?

"Aren't you the same Carolyn White who ran for state senate a few years ago?" the reporter asked when the interview concluded.

"I am," she said.

"Any comment?" the reporter asked.

"We just want her home," Carolyn said with a thin smile that seemed to come from nowhere. She quickly became stoic. Should she smile? The day was playing out like she was locked in a dark editing room, the same scenes appearing before her on a loop, unable to decide what to cut or to leave. Here, the press inquiries, there, the well-wishers, here, the limp handshakes scene, and there, the gentle nods of friends promising their assistance if she or Mark needed anything, anything at all.

"I got your message about Nita," Carolyn told Ted when the reporter had moved on.

Ted shook his head in sad acknowledgement.

"I'm sorry to have had to bring it up to you and Mark at this time. There are a few stores involved. No charges are being pressed right now, given that everyone knows what you are going through, but they do want the items back or paid for," he said. He looked away as if the matter were settled, but Carolyn knew that the remedy would be far more involved than just walking into the Essex Mall and dropping off the bags of clothing. She nodded at Ted, grateful for allowing the moment to pass, but knowing that the matter was like a lighthouse that would keep whirling around until the fog cleared.

Behind the Clubhouse, a police boat hovered on the Rappahannock River near the River Hills Yacht Club. A team of forensic divers stood on board stealing glances at the rowers and small crafts.

Barry and Priscilla had lived up to their promise and now acted as family spokespeople and willing assistants to the upcoming search parties. Although it was a Thursday, people had prioritized the community crisis and made arrangements to get time off of work. Priscilla sat at the table handing out maps of the area, which tended to only be illustrations of the golf holes to which she added small notations to indicate the river, Camel's Hump, and the woods near River Hills High School. Residents gathered around these tables, grabbing the maps and trying to decipher them in small, huddled groups. As 1 p.m. approached, Barry and Priscilla stood on the grand porch and addressed the 100 or so volunteers now gathered on the grass before them. Mary and Cassy stood nearby on the porch, checking their phones, ready to assist but having no idea how.

"Folks, on behalf of the White family, I want to thank you for coming out today. The police tell us that in missing children cases time is the enemy, so speed is essential. Today's search will be four hours, or as much time as you can spare." He tapped on his watch to illustrate the point. "On Detective Washington's recommendation, and many of you know Ted, we are splitting our volunteers into three teams," he said, making a knife gesture with his hands among the crowd. The volunteers began to separate, like a color war, and look around at their appointed groups as if they were new friends. "Group A," he said, pointing to the thirty odd people on his left, "is to walk up Camel's Hump spaced fifteen feet apart." Priscilla then moved the approximate distance of fifteen feet from Barry as a means of example, and Group A mimicked the action. "The center group, Group B, is to begin at the Old Oak and move north toward the river, including the golf course, which has been closed for the search."

Carolyn stood off to the side watching the anxious faces of neighbors she both knew and had never seen. River Hills now had 300 homes within its community of over 1,000 residents, many of whom she would see on her fitness walks with Priscilla, or when Chowder came in contact with another dog. The dogs would see each other before their owners did and run ahead to greet each other, and in this way. Carolyn had learned the first names of many of her neighbors. Today, there was nothing to do but observe her neighbors as she stood behind one of the columns of the Federalist structure that held up the great house. The closing of the golf course felt like a needle in her arm as she realized how the disease was now infecting the community.

*"They closed the golf course for the search,"* people would report, and she felt the humiliation of a River Hills stopping in its tracks to deal with the...failure, yes, *her* failure as a parent to exhibit the basics of mothering—the protection of her own children. She closed her eyes to black out the absurd thought. It was not her fault, it was Ronnie's, but that thought felt no better. She refocused on the appreciation she felt for the people who had gathered, good people who were taking time out of their lives. But the dark humiliation slapped her, and her head collapsed against the marble pillar built hundreds of years ago in another time.

"Group C is to head down to the highway toward the high school and head west from there. Please establish a group leader whose responsibility is to remind their group to keep their distance and call for occasional stops. Our family will be joining the first group up Camel's Hump." People then began to create circles and establish routes. Most wore backpacks and hiking shoes as if planning a day on the Blue Ridge Mountains. The teams then began to disperse without a signal, like at the conclusion of a funeral, and Mark and Priscilla gave Carolyn a thumbs-up and disappeared toward the Camel's Hump trails.

Detective Washington approached Carolyn. "How are you holding up?" he asked, placing a hand on her shoulder. "I can't imagine what you're going through," he said, but the words felt practiced. They had grown up together in Tappahannock, not seven miles from where they now stood. The fact that his football career went nowhere came as a momentary shock to the community, who considered him an outstanding player, but the reality was that he was a high school phenomenon with no chance at the pros. This gave him the reputation of a valedictorian who had gone nowhere in life. Even though Carolyn Jenkins had gone on to marry, run for the senate, adopt children, and raise her own, she realized that Ted—who it seemed just yesterday was a jock with a crush on her whom she easily rebuffed—was now in charge of her fate.

She was not allowed to go to the prom with Ted Washington. She remembered the excuse; she was recovering from an arm injury sustained when the mast of a Hobie Cat she was sailing on suddenly swung to the other side, catching her elbow. He had creatively proposed the date with a series of signs carefully placed along Route 17. *Carolyn Jenkins*, the first sign said around mile marker 319, *Will You*, said the second, *Prom with Me,* it concluded. There was not even a question mark on the final sign, because it wasn't a question, so she thought. She had known that Ted was going to ask her, finally, and she had conveyed that she would accept, or he would have never asked. But her mother had seen the road signs before her, and heard the phone calls before that, and she had squashed the idea.

"I'm OK, Ted. I'm holding in there. I appreciate all you're doing for us."

"Can I give you a ride down to the precinct? I'm sure that Mark must be wrapping up by now."

"Fine," she said, glad for a direction that didn't involve having to choose the right search party.

They drove out of the development in Ted's SUV, passed the group heading toward Camel's Hump, and saw Priscilla and Barry and their girls mixed in with the crowd.

"Carolyn, let's put the issue of Nita aside for now. We will get to that." He paused as if regretting the words. "You should know that Mark is under suspicion in the disappearance of Anna. The morning that she disappeared she had a bruise on her head. That was reported by Nita."

"Oh?" she asked. She intended for it to come out differently. She knew the bruise on Anna's head had come from her falling out of bed shortly after the fainting incident at the Kanes' house.

"It doesn't mean he had anything to do with it, but you might want to hire an attorney," Ted suggested.

"Mark had nothing to do with this, Ted, I assure you."

"I'm sure you're right. But she disappeared on the same day that he left on his trip, and no one has seen her since. We don't suspect you, of course, but we have to eliminate suspects, and right now your husband is a suspect."

The car began to head into Tappahannock and slowed down at the 35 miles-per-hour speed limit. A police cruiser sat in the parking lot of the NationsBank. They turned left after passing the Confederate statue commemorating Brigadier General Richard B. Garnett, who had the distinction of being the first Southern general killed in the conflict. She had passed it a thousand times, but now openly wondered why this modern town could not escape the past. She took the accusation against Mark as another hole in the archery target that had become her life, no more or less important than the other fractures in the once unblemished fabric.

"Can I ask you a question?" Ted asked.

She looked at him from the driver's side seat.

"Why didn't Carolyn Jenkins go to the prom with Ted Washington?"

Carolyn gave out a chuckle, which while audible, was the wrong reaction. Time did not heal all wounds.

"I thought we went, didn't we?" she lied. "I forget."

He stole a glance at her, laughed, and drove on.

Carolyn remembered that the previous morning her father had transferred the reward money to her account. "Can we go back to the bank for a moment? We have to deal with the reward money. I guess that we should put it in a separate account," she said, as if talking to herself.

Ted did a U-turn around the statue, which caught the attention of the officer in the cruiser. The policeman recognized Ted and waved. Ted pulled up next to the cruiser, driver to driver, and Carolyn got out of the car and entered the bank.

Patrons were scattered throughout the roped-off snake line that led to the two open tellers, and Carolyn waited patiently. Her crisis gave her a sense that there was no more important business in the world than hers, and she looked pleadingly at the bank manager behind the counters as he assessed his staff needs. Carolyn's turn came more quickly than she anticipated when one of the customers ahead of her took a call on her phone and hurried out.

"Carolyn White," she said, handing over her ID. "I need to move some money to a separate savings account. Twenty-five thousand." She gave all of the information to reduce the questions and brush off any recognition of her from the media. The teller was an elderly woman who looked like Jean Stapleton, and the strong resemblance to Archie Bunker's wife made Carolyn smile.

The woman wrote down a number on a piece of paper and handed it to Carolyn.

Carolyn looked at it, then looked up at the teller. "There must be some mistake. Can you check again please? Are you sure you have the right account number?"

"I'm sorry, Mrs. White. It's a joint account, so perhaps your husband already made the transfer?"

Carolyn stared at the overdraft amount. There was $80,000 in the account the last time that she looked, not one week ago. She felt a panic come up from her chest into her throat. She caught it before it became obvious and managed a polite smile. She felt the presence of a customer waiting behind her who had noticed that they were speaking, not transacting.

She thanked the teller and exited the bank.

Ted and Carolyn entered the precinct where just the day before she had sat for the voluntary lie detector test. The precinct looked like a restaurant where orders needed to be placed at the counter, and people sat around in fiberglass chairs waiting for their names to be called. A young teenager sat with his mother, both staring ahead. A girl around Nita's age sat next to her boyfriend holding a bandage to her face. Ted disappeared behind a wall, then came back and motioned for Carolyn to follow him. He led her to a room where Mark sat alone, the lie detector machine sitting next to him like a movie projector and a glass of water on the table. She sat down across from him, then moved around the table to sit next to him.

"How was the search party?" Mark began.

"Not much of a party. I'm just...so ashamed...and scared."

"Me too," he said. "This isn't supposed to be happening." He adjusted his glasses which had fallen down his nose. He had not shaved in two days.

"So, what's going on here?" she asked.

"I don't know. I was nervous."

Carolyn weighed the comment. "I know, so was I. They thought that you may have had something to do with all this," she said.

"I know, it's ridiculous, but I understand that this is their job. I just wish they would do...THEIR JOB!" He blurted out over his shoulder for the detectives outside the room. The strategy worked and Ted opened the door.

"Free to go, guys. I'm sorry for all of this. Procedure."

Mark and Carolyn looked at Ted as if they were overheard gossiping about a mutual friend.

"Or you can stay if you wish. We're here for you," Ted offered.

"Thank you," they said in unison, and the detective closed the door.

"I can't handle this, Carolyn."

She wanted the comment to be about their missing daughter, but she sensed it was about more. The adoption, the growing family, the conflicts, the discovery of Nita's stealing, Tabitha now an outcast, Simba turning out to be an extra checker piece nobody wanted to play with. But she could not bring herself to allow his comment to be so easily understood. "What are you talking about?" she asked.

Mark looked at her. "Carolyn, they suspected that I had something to do with Anna's disappearance. They asked me a million questions, about where I was, when I left, what I did. I guess some of it came out wrong." He was sweating and his eyes were darting around the room. He grabbed the glass of water as if he were going to swallow the entire amount, but then only took a sip, placing it carefully back on the table as if showing he was in fact in control.

"Mark, I just went to the bank and there's no money in our account. Why is there no money in our account?" As she spoke, she noticed that she was drawing out the sentence.

"I invested it," he said matter-of-factly.

"In what? We need to post reward money! Our fucking daughter is missing, maybe raped, maybe in a cellar somewhere, maybe, I don't know what! There was $80,000 in that account!"

Mark took off his glasses and began to clean them with a coffee-stained napkin. "I told you; I invested it."

"Where is this investment?" she asked, looking around the room as if the bills might be neatly stacked in a corner.

"I made a bet, Carolyn. I was going to tell you. It's for the movie. It's an option play." The sentences seemed unrelated but spoken as if they made perfect sense.

No one spoke.

"What did you do, Mark?" she asked softly.

She thought she could see the blood rush to his face, but all she could clearly notice was that he was scratching his arm frantically as if he were being attacked by a swarm of mosquitos.

"You might as well know what's going on," he began. He faced her squarely and took her hand, like a doctor calming a patient before an injection. *This might hurt a bit.* "First, you of course know I have nothing to do with Anna's disappearance. I have no idea where she is, and that's most important. But..." He now dropped her hand from his and looked around the room for words that seemed to have wandered away. "But I have been trying to make things work with all of our expenses, and still trying to get the film made."

"What's going on, Mark?"

He straightened his back as if the worst of his comments were behind him, then fell back and slumped into his chair. "We may be broke, Carolyn. I've been raising the money and spending it on us. I put a lot of money into Tower Records. They had a strategy to go...digital. It's the newest trend in music." He looked at her for understanding. "Digital," he repeated as if the word would defend itself.

"What are you saying?" Somehow his brief words left enough dirt in the yard to know that a deep hole was hidden right in front of her eyes.

"The trips, the movie, the fundraising."

"You are telling me that you gambled away the money? Our money? The money?"

"I think I have a problem."

"What do you mean a problem? Oh God, Mark, tell me that..." She broke off.

Mark drank the glass of water. The now spoken words gave him a visibly lighter presence. He shook his head as if scolding himself, but then found that the confession gave him a certain confidence. He turned toward her.

"It's gone," he said.

She looked at him and spoke evenly. “We have a press conference tonight.” She looked around the room for any sign of comfort but saw only old cups of coffee on the table with cream beginning to curdle in the cold liquid.

When they walked out of the conference room together, they were called into Ted Washington’s office.

“Guys, nothing new on Anna’s location, but there’s some good news.”

No one spoke.

“Ambassador Franca has made additional contact with the relative in Luanda. He’s on his way from D.C. now. He has suggested that she might be able to help provide some insight into Anna’s history, past interests, and behaviors, that sort of thing.”

“Has Anna been in contact with someone?” Mark asked.

“As I said, nothing from Anna, but the ambassador said he had some information. Why don’t the two of you grab some food and go home. When he arrives, we’ll come straight to your house, promise.” Whenever the detective spoke, his attention was always directed at Carolyn. His adoration of her had nowhere to go, only to keep knocking on her door, which she neither answered nor ignored.

Mark and Carolyn drove home in relative silence, avoiding topics that would light fires between them. They came to the long curve approaching River Hills. The dimming light of the day created a haze across the river into which a few sailboats disappeared. The steep face of Camel’s Hump created a granite buffer between the busy highway and the tranquil development that lay on the other side. She thought she could see someone searching in the woods, but the movement was just a rock bouncing off a high crevice and splitting itself as it crashed into the earth.

Mark parked the SUV in their driveway and shut off the motor. Both sat in place.

“How are we going to live? I assume that the rest of the money from the film is gone with your...investment?” asked Carolyn.

“I have it under control.”

“I need to know everything.”

His hands remained on the steering wheel, and his thin frame and oversized glasses made him look like a teenager coming clean about his sexuality.

"So, the trips to raise money, was that a lie too? Is there anything else you want to shock me with?" She could hear her mother in her voice.

Mark looked away.

"Is there anything else you want to tell me, Mark?"

He held onto the steering wheel.

"Mark?"

"I might be with someone. Someone I never expected."

There is a certain knowing within a woman that indistinctively radars the sexuality of a man. Carolyn looked toward the man she had married and gave him a forlorn smile. She loved him in the inexplainable way that love tends to grow. Two people with gnarled roots that could never be separated, no matter the circumstances. Life was no one's fault.

"I'll make it right," Mark said, and they held hands.

She looked at him and gave a thin smile, squeezing his hand that was still grabbing onto the steering wheel. "Well, there should still be $12,000 coming in for the adoption of...of...the new boy."

"You can't seriously still be thinking of adopting another child now, Carolyn. You can't actually think that this family, with all that's going on, should even consider..."

She cut him off. "Considering that their father is a fucking thief who stole investor money and put this family at risk of...of..."

"NO ONE STOLE MONEY!"

"Then what do you call it? Oh God, Mark. What are we going to do? We are the laughingstock of Virginia, we can't even take care of our own, and if anything happened to Anna, I could never forgive myself!" Her chest was heaving, but the tears would not come. "How could you?" It was all that she could say, the toss of blame landing on her closest target.

"We need to be united at the press conference tonight. We're still going to offer the reward. We'll get the money somewhere."

She looked at him and reached for the door handle. *Somewhere.* That was all the hope she had in the world now. Anna was *somewhere.* The money was *somewhere.* Her life was *somewhere.* She walked into the house alone.

Simba met her at the door. "Hi Mama Bama," he said with his arms apart like wings. "I'm an airplane looking for Anna!" Behind him the twins sat on the stairs exchanging light punches that were growing stronger as the stakes of their game rose higher. Nita sat at the kitchen table with one leg draped over the other, flipping open and closing her phone. Ronnie was cooking burgers on the stove and the smell of onions hung in the air.

Mark entered the house and threw his jacket on the loveseat. An impromptu family meeting began to form in the kitchen. Wyatt and Tabitha sat at the table next to Nita. Simba pressed himself against the refrigerator and bounced against it as if it were rubber, causing the ice box to shake slightly.

"Everyone, there's going to be a press interview tonight here on the front steps of our house. We're going on TV to tell everyone to look for Anna. It's what you do in situations like this."

"Situations like what?" Nita asked flatly.

Carolyn ignored her. "There's nothing any of you need to do. There are already people looking around the neighborhood. The police are asking questions and even the Angolan ambassador is involved."

"Anna will be found," Mark said with confidence.

"Do we have to go to school?" Tabitha asked.

"School has nothing to do with this."

"I don't want my friends to think that my half-sister is dead!"

Simba stopped his bouncing. "Anna's dead?" He started to cry.

"Everyone calm down," Mark interjected. "No one has said anything happened to Anna. The ambassador will be here soon and he may have some more information."

The sizzle and smoke of the burgers began to spread through the kitchen and Ronnie swatted it with her arm. "Sometimes girls run off," she offered. "Don't mean nothing. Anna is a good girl...a good girl and she be home. I prayed to my Master..." She looked up at the ceiling with her hands in a prayer position.

Mark jumped onto the hopefulness of the moment. "We think there's a perfectly reasonable explanation for where Anna went and where she is now." Nita looked up from her phone for the answer that Mark was offering, but none came.

"Anna will be home soon," Carolyn said. For just a moment, she felt like a substitute teacher lecturing a class she didn't recognize; the island-born Ronnie, a transplanted Bangladesh boy, and a Venezuelan girl from the slums of Caracas. She looked at the twins as if they were witnesses in a kangaroo courtroom.

"Very soon," Mark said. The tone of his words ended the family meeting and he went into the garage. Wyatt and Simba descended into the basement. Tabitha and Nita, newly connected by their sister's disappearance, went upstairs to their rooms while Ronnie continued the dinner preparations.

Carolyn gazed out the window at the empty neighborhood, soon to be overrun with media trucks, cameras, reporters, and microphones. A limousine adorned with the two flags of Angola and the United States appeared first. The young aide whom they had met at the Clubhouse was checking the house numbers, and upon locating the White household pulled over, blocking the driveway. The man, Marcus, hurried to open the rear doors of the limo and both Ambassador Franca and Detective Washington emerged into the evening light. Running out to greet them seemed unnecessary, so Carolyn watched the men come up the walkway before disappearing up the stairs to her bedroom so as not to seem too—too what, prepared? She heard the visitors enter the home without knocking, like relatives, and busied herself with touching up her make up in preparation for the press conference. She heard Mark come in from the garage and attend to the guests, and from the bathroom at the top of the stairs she listened to them converse.

"Good afternoon to you, my friend," the ambassador began in a practiced voice as Mark escorted the group into the living room. Carolyn descended the stairs and stood on the landing. She could see the four men in the living room, their backs to her. Marcus sat in a wingback chair taking notes as the ambassador addressed Mark. Ted looked down at his feet as the diplomat spoke, his powerful frame fighting to break out of his suit.

"We are ready for this nightmare to end, Ambassador Franca. Detective Washington mentioned that you might have some additional information?" asked Mark.

"Anna, Anna, Zarkhanna," the ambassador shook his head. "Zarkhanna Cudjo by birth, a common name in my country." Marcus nodded vigorously. "The name implies pure power, either from an animal or from the spirit of a human. It is a fitting name for a strong girl from my country."

Ronnie entered the room with drinks, and the quartet of men were quiet as she placed the tray on the side table. "Anna is a strong girl, yes," she said, as if she had been part of the conversation. She stood in the room as Carolyn joined the meeting.

"Mrs. White," said the ambassador, standing up in reverence. Marcus and Ted greeted her with a nod. Mark reached out a kind hand to her and she sat on an ottoman beside him. Ronnie took a seat on the edge of the couch.

"What are we supposed to say at the press conference?" Carolyn asked Ted.

"We have not exhausted the possibility that she tried to get to D.C. or perhaps New York, and simply got lost. The fact that there was money missing from the house..." He paused as everyone considered the dwindling answers. "With respect to the news conference, you can say whatever comes to your mind, Carolyn. Speak about Anna, ask for help in providing any information. It's best to speak from the heart."

"But since she is so obviously not our natural daughter, will it look..."

Marcus interjected. "Adoption takes place all over the world, Mrs. White. There is nothing strange about you adopting a child from another country. You do not need to refer to her as your adopted daughter, but if you prefer, you may." His yellow tie was manicured into a Windsor knot.

Carolyn and Mark weighed the options.

"We just want her home," Carolyn said.

"As we all do, Mr. and Mrs. White," the ambassador said. "As we all do. And it is now confirmed that the aunt who wrote to me recently is formally requesting custody of Zarkhanna upon her return." He had been looking away as he spoke, but now confronted Mark's eyes. A warrior turned politician on the lookout for lost refugees.

"Our daughter?" Mark asked.

"Ambassador Franca," Carolyn began. "There is no basis for what you are saying or accusing us of. Her name is Anna, no longer Zarkhanna, and we have legally adopted her and brought her to this country and given her a good life in a loving home."

The reality of the lost child hung in the room, and no one spoke.

She felt blood rushing to her face as if she had been slapped. Her voice rose and she noticed that she was almost screaming. "How dare you try to take her away when she is already...and we are in a crisis...and the TV cameras! You sit here and calmly tell us that some...woman in Angola has suddenly emerged and we are just supposed to find Anna, put her on a plane, and say goodbye? Is that what you're saying, Mr. Ambassador?"

Chowder waltzed into the room with quiet yelps, and everyone watched him take a place directly on the detective's shoes.

"Chowder! No!" Mark yelled.

"It's OK, Mark, I don't mind him. I want to clarify that what the ambassador is saying is not a demand, just something he has discovered. The Red Cross is reuniting children with relatives, particularly those who were forced to serve as child soldiers." He looked at Carolyn. "Like Zarkhanna," he said.

"Anna," Carolyn whispered.

Marcus now spoke up. "Our country has been through terrible times, and it is thanks to people like you that we are on the mend. His excellency comes here today with the news that Zarkhanna...Anna, as you have welcomed her to America, may return to her homeland if that is in the best interest...of all parties." Marcus looked down at his paper and made a note. "Once, of course, that we find her."

*To give up Anna after she is found*? Carolyn felt the eyes of the ambassador on her and thought she saw a flash of anger in his eyes. Mark nodded in agreement as if a solution had been found. Carolyn wanted to ride along that road with him, but then, remembering the shock of his financial deceit and the financial demands of the next adoption, felt like they had crashed against the guardrails, and everyone was slowing down to rubberneck the damage.

"What about the reward? The press conference? What do we say?" Carolyn asked.

"It's up to you," the detective said. "It is probably best if I mention the reward rather than you. What amount are we going with?"

Mark did not meet her eyes, and she motioned for Marcus to supply her with a pencil. She grabbed a notepad on the side table and jotted down some figures which she showed to Mark. He looked at the pad as if straining to recognize a photograph, and he nodded his head.

"Ten thousand dollars," Carolyn said, and dropped her head.

They took a break and Ronnie served the burgers to the children. The house had the feel of a party no one wanted to attend. To Tabitha and Wyatt, the men were strangers, Black men speaking with funny accents occupying their home. Ronnie moved about the house as if serving one more glass of water or fetching the ketchup would help the situation. As press vehicles began to assemble in the front yard, young men in ties and perky blond women moved wires and microphones around the grounds. Simba watched from the window at the satellite trucks parked outside and likened them to flying saucers. The twins watched TV in the kitchen. Bright lights from the cameras streamed through the windows and a knock came upon the door. Nita observed the commotion like a school assembly she was mandated to take part in, then sensing she had a choice, headed up the stairs.

"Nita, your father and I would like to talk to you later, when all of this calms down," Carolyn said.

Nita looked down at them from the landing. "This isn't calming down, Carolyn...Mark," she said.

The detective, the Angolan contingency, and Mark and Carolyn stood in the foyer beside the loveseat and watched Nita disappear up to her room.

"Are you planning to speak, Ambassador?" Carolyn asked.

"I will say only that Anna is an Angolan who has been through much turmoil, and we call for her safe return home."

Carolyn considered the comment and steadied herself. Mark took her hand and opened the door to the flash of lights.

"Showtime," the detective said.

# Chapter 12

As the summer of 1824 rolled into September, Anna found herself one month at Wappocomo Plantation. How the time translated to actual days back in River Hills she did not know, but she sensed that time was not her friend. She thought of Carolyn now and then, grateful for her good intentions, but unsure of which world she belonged to, and whether it mattered anymore.

She paused at the end of the row of tobacco she was tending to stretch her back, only to be called out by the fat overseer as he galloped toward her. There would be no rest between rows. She jumped to the next line of plants to escape his fury. The sticky gum of the plants coated her body, and even her bedstead showed its residue each morning when she awoke predawn to report to the fields.

September was the most labor-intensive time of tobacco production, and the crops cried out like babies. Annabelle found herself part of a small squad of scrutinized workers driven to eat, sleep, and work together on a task that could never be complete. Besides herself, the group consisted of Beatrice, Arthur, Sherry, three men who had been part of their transport, as well as four children. This group worked six days per week under the fat overseer's eagle eyes. When he would leave to inspect other tracts of the vast plantation, his excitable junior would step in and quicken the pace, only to exhaust his squad and lower the quality of work, which he would attempt to rectify with growled threats and an occasional flogging.

The plantation, located outside of Hampshire County and achingly close to the free state of Ohio, was owned by a friend of Leslie Kane's named Colonel Parsons. Some said that the plantation had once hosted Lewis and Clark on their way back from their famous expedition in the Pacific.

The rain in Hampshire County was plentiful and Wappocomo Plantation was awash in downpours that would appear out of nowhere. It was up to the overseer whether the slaves would work through the rains or return to the shacks, losing yet another day's product. The stalks needed to be laid in the fields to dry for hours before being taken to the barn. If the rains came, it confounded the workflow and wreaked havoc on the system, trickling down to the overseer's pay, which he could not afford. There was something wrong every day; either the skies spilled too much water, the slaves moved too slowly, or the plants did not wilt and dry properly enough to fetch a glass of gin at Mrs. Malone's whorehouse.

As with Nottoway Plantation under Leslie Kane, a task system ruled how everyone toiled. As full hands, Annabelle and Arthur were required to tend to forty-eight plants per day. Beatrice was a three-quarter hand with applicable quotas, and so it was with each man and woman in the fields, including the children who worked their way from one-eighth to one-quarter hands, and in the case of one strong ten-year-old boy everyone called Rooster, a half hand.

While the Mondays or Wednesdays were indistinguishable from Tuesdays or Thursdays, the workers found ways to pass the time and talk with one another during the nine-hour workday. Beatrice's slower pace allowed Anna to approach her as the older woman moved slowly through the rows. Anna also took whatever opportunity she could to assist the children. The youngest ones, riding on the wheeled harvester that trailed the work squad, were handed the valuable leaves to pile onto the wagon. The overseer encouraged the team approach and allowed Anna to assist Beatrice as long as all tasks were completed by quitting time.

"Tell me if this ends, if freedom will come, and when," the old woman implored as she cut the plants and tossed a worm into the dirt. Her headdress was stained the color of sweat.

What she knew about the future was something Anna wasn't always sure if she should share. What benefit would it be to speak of automobiles, jumbo jets, or small communication devices when they were hundreds of years away and she had no idea how to construct any of them. How would knowledge of any of these things help an enslaved person avoid the biting tobacco worms today?

Perhaps she could tell them that engines would soon come to power the farm equipment, or how nets would eventually be put over valuable crops to keep out the dreaded parasites that tormented their bodies.

"One day, machines will do this work, and there will be no slaves," Anna confided.

"What sort of machines?"

"They move by themselves with large wheels powered by motors," Anna responded.

"How long, Annabelle? How long will we work...in the fields...in the houses...as slave people?"

Anna thought back to the American history she had learned in school and recalled the emancipation took place toward the end of the 19th century.

"Forty years. There will be a war, and the slave people will be set free." Anna considered her age and resigned herself to the fact that she would be in her fifties by the time she saw freedom again. Perhaps she would marry, like her host Sherry, and have children, like Beatrice had. But the world would be full of wars and terrible events, and she wondered what good it would do to tell the old woman anything about a future that was as cruel as the present, only in different ways for different sufferers.

Even if she returned to the year 2000, should she somehow manage to return, would she have to relive hearing her own mother slaughtered? Or seeing Auntie dragged away? Would she herself be forced to march and watch as babies were hacked in half in front of their mothers by young soldiers stoned on marijuana?

In what ways was the future any better than where she was now? If this was to be her fate now, perhaps she could advise people on how to avoid infection and help lesser-abled bodies avoid the whip. Even helping the aging Beatrice pick one less worm off of a tobacco plant was worth the pain and confusion that had become her life.

"Why have you come here, Annabelle?" Beatrice asked as she battled with the low, broad leaves of the plant that slapped and marked her face with its sticky dark sap. The crescent moon amulet hung from her neck, and for a moment Anna reflected back to the initiation lodge where the Ngaka woman appeared in Beatrice's form.

The urgency of her question gave Anna little time to ponder. She had scolded herself a thousand times for ever coming back to the cabin after witnessing the murder of one young man and the blaming of another. She had watched as the events of that terrible night catapulted A.C. Tomkins into a place of leadership he scarcely deserved. Whatever curse Jemmy had spoken had manifested itself in Essex County, as it had not rained in five years. No one was safe in these counties. Anna thought of Madia, who had endured so much, only to be ushered off the property to become the property of the killer of her own husband.

"I just know I have work to do here," Anna responded. "If I could just tell Master Kane the truth…" She stopped in the middle of her thought. The improbability of making any difference in this locked and loaded world seemed to overwhelm her. Annabelle stood up in the row of tobacco plants she was tending. The overseer noticed and gestured for her to return to the backbreaking task.

Beatrice spoke. "Your father's words were directed at Tomkins, not toward his own kin nor anyone else. I knew your father, he was my friend, and he would never intend…." The old woman lost her balance and fell into the soft dirt.

Anna wished that whatever Jemmy had tried to say had been said but undoing his words from years ago—a time Anna could not remember in the slightest—was as inconceivable as her own mother marching out of the woods right now and taking her home for dinner.

"We must get you home, dear child," Beatrice said softly. "To wherever that home is. You must not stay in these times. These hard times." The old woman looked up toward the darkening sky. "While the rains come here all the time, the suffering in Nottoway continues. I know, I feel it."

The young girl and the old woman spoke until the plants they tended called for them to separate. Annabelle worked the soil with her hands and a sickle, grabbing the worms and beetles with her fingers caked with mud. The day ended with the long walk back to the shack she shared with Beatrice and Sherry. As the slave village came into view, Annabelle saw a man wearing a long black frock sitting on their porch.

"Good afternoon, ladies," Reverend Cooper said with a smile.

The Reverend was such a familiar figure that for a moment Anna felt she was back at Nottoway. "Please, take your time cleaning yourselves up, then we will talk." He spoke as if he were suggesting chicken for supper.

When the women returned from the brook, the Reverend was nowhere to be found. They busied themselves preparing a supper of corn and a chicken, one of the many raised by the village in a coop behind the cabins. The Reverend appeared as they were finishing their meal, and they sat inside together near the fire. Annabelle heard a stirring in the loft and when she looked up, she saw someone quickly step back out of view.

The Reverend followed her gaze. "It's alright, Calvin. You are among friends—even your own sister."

"Calvin!" Anna exclaimed. "How...?"

The boy swung his legs from the loft, so they hung down on the ladder. His frame was powerful and his thick stubble gave him the appearance of a man of twenty-five instead of eighteen.

"The Rev saved me, Annabelle. He sent word for me to run away to his church, and I did. I hid in the basement and have been hiding ever since."

Anna looked at the Reverend for confirmation. "But why is he here?" she asked the clergyman.

"I only trusted myself to bring him this far. Beneath my coachman's seat is a drop compartment he climbed into for the journey. Several times I was stopped to show my free papers, and only once did I become concerned. Wappocomo Plantation is near Ohio, where they don't take to slavery. It's a free state, and my intention is to get Calvin there, where he can make his way to Canada, God willing."

Fear had been Calvin's traveling partner since the Reverend had picked him up and his eyes continued to dart to and fro even in the loft. The evening was quiet with only a puppy yelping in the distance and the occasional clucking of the chickens.

"I was tipped off about the plan the Kane girls were plotting against me, so I had to move out quick. It was bad enough that Mom and you all were taken away, but at least I knew that you would live."

The Reverend added the details. "It was not hard for my team to spring into action and meet him in the woods the day you left. When he did not show up for work the next morning, there were search parties all over Essex County for days. A fugitive report was issued in Richmond, but this is not the first soul who has ridden the Railroad."

"I will never go back," Calvin chimed in.

"I thought it safe for Calvin to travel with me as nobody would think that a runaway would head west rather than north. Still, we have no time to lose. Tonight, I've arranged for a friend of mine, a White preacher, to hide Calvin in the crawl space beneath the church here in Hampshire County until the next tobacco transport takes place in October."

"I am to lie underneath the crops until we reach Cincinnati," Calvin said as if memorized. "Then, I will go to Canada and maybe one day make my way home."

No one spoke.

"Where is home?" Anna asked.

"Where our daddy come from," he responded.

"Angola," Anna whispered.

As the name of her country was uttered, it felt as foreign to her as speaking Mbundu. It was like a Christmas pheasant on the other side of a long table and that she couldn't reach.

"But why did you come here to this plantation, Reverend?" Beatrice asked.

Sherry was busy preparing coffee. Although she had never seen the Reverend or the boy, she instantly understood the language of secrecy that was the common tongue of slave people.

"The morning you were abducted, I came down with a terrible flu," the preacher said. "Doc Kiley came to see me but by the time he arrived, we had already found the arsenic in my tea kettle. When we learned that you and the others had been whisked off, it didn't take us long to figure out that Mr. Tomkins had a hand in all of this. Masta' Kane may forget some things, but he remembers others keenly, and he expected Annabelle to come see him when he asked. It's been a month of recovery for me, and I've had to allow Pastor Wilkins to run the church in my absence. When I had a conference to attend in Richmond, Masta' Kane asked me to stop over at Wappocomo and collect the sums owed to him from Colonel Parsons as well as to bring Annabelle back to him, which is what I intend to do. Miss Cassandra is also aware of her father's request."

"I've been in the hiding space the whole time," Calvin added from the loft, referring to a nook behind a trick door in the church used for these purposes.

The room became quiet, and Sherry rolled the tinder horn, an ageless fire-soul that neither grew up nor died. The woman handled an iron tool and rolled over the flame, adding cut logs of Virginia pine to her family's light.

"And what of Madia, Reverend?" Beatrice asked.

Anna swung her attention from the flame to the eyes of the Reverend. His sleek whiskers caught tiny fibers of firelight.

"Madia...Madia," he repeated.

This answer pleased no one, so Beatrice continued. "Reverend, did the masta' say that I was to join you back to Nottoway? I want to be closer to... my chil'ren." Her tears no longer had the strength to form.

"The Lord be with you, the Lord be with you," Beatrice whispered. Then, rising from somewhere within her, Beatrice spoke of the need to get Annabelle back to Nottoway. "She did not speak for so many years, Reverend, because she saw things, and maybe still sees things."

Annabelle felt removed from these last few words. To her, traveling back to Nottoway meant only the chance to speak whatever truth she knew and then immediately return to that other world, Carolyn's world. Was she supposed to travel backward in time and recite some unknown words under the Old Oak? They were words she did not know, words she had never heard. And to what end? The crime committed has long passed. Would the dead soul of Jemmy suddenly be revived? What was she supposed to do? She was just a child of God with no other business on this Earth than to tell the truth and try to ease whatever suffering she could, as Jesus did, as any other person should, in any other time.

But then she thought of A.C. Tomkins, and she felt anger rise in her, like someone was pulling her hair and not letting go. Revenge, eye for an eye, she knew these were against the teachings of her own God, yet a fate for Tomkins ached in her belly like an unchewed meal. God's Earth may well be full of love, but the world was also full of cruelty, and cruelty had consequences. To this she had only to think of her own mother, the kindest woman she had ever known, who had succumbed to an unspeakable fate.

And so much more.

Yet through this all, there was...love. There was her church that even on this side of the world existed and had brought to her this kind Reverend.

And somewhere out there, up there, was Simba, who was looking everywhere he could for his only true sister.

"Did you bring anything, Reverend? Anything from home?" Annabelle looked up at Calvin.

The boy shook his head. She had not shared with him where she had hidden her possessions. No one else knew of the leather pouch.

"As a matter of fact, I have," replied the Reverend as he reached inside his case. "Something I've seen you hold close every Sunday of your childhood." Anna stared at the object, the heirloom, the time traveler that started it all. The red ruby eyes of the Ndimba doll gazed back at her. She took the treasured object in her hands and touched the heart-shaped amulet around its neck.

"Do you know what that symbol is, Annabelle?" the Reverend asked.

"The heart?" she said softly. "Love, I suppose."

"Perhaps," said the Reverend. "But the symbol is more accurately a Sankofa, from the Akan language in Ghana."

Beatrice spoke up. "*Se wo were fi na wosankofa a yenkyi.*"

The room was silent as everyone took in their own meaning from the foreign words. The Reverend translated. "It is not wrong to go back for that which you have forgotten."

The conversation went on and eventually turned to stories of outsmarting overseers. They remembered when Martha and Beatrice had disciplined Arthur's sons for foul language by threatening to wash their mouths with the wood ashes they were saving for soap. The boys begged for mercy and the women ended up giving them slices of Bundt cake they had taken from the kitchen in exchange for their promise to be more respectful. They all laughed at this and other stories from Nottoway and the night ended with tastes of carob the Reverend had brought as a gift from Martha. When Annabelle finally went up to the loft, she could tell that Calvin would only be able to close his eyes and drift nowhere except toward hope.

"How well do you remember our father?" Calvin asked in the silence that had fallen over the cabin.

"I'm not sure."

He rolled over onto his back. "I remember him well. He told me so many things, Annabelle. Many of our friends at Nottoway went to him to get cured. To me, his deep voice was enough to keep me calm when I was scared of not makin' my tasks. He would tell me...you are not alone, Calvin. You are never alone. He'd say that to me."

Annabelle listened quietly.

"Do you remember the time that you fell into the pond when we were fishing? You had a fish on the hook and Daddy wanted you to haul it in yourself. You stood on the shore, and when you thought the fish had stopped biting, you got mad and started to walk into the water. Then it suddenly yanked and you got scared and fell right in!"

Anna could see the story as he related it, but she had no memory. Still, she went along and smiled.

"I wish it were all different, Annabelle. I know that we are not the first family to lose one another, but we are the only family I know."

She reached out and touched his face. "We will always be family, Calvin."

"We may never see one another again."

Anna held the Ndimba close to her chest and could feel it breathe with her.

"Calvin, I want you to take this with you on your...journey. It is very important that you keep it with you for protection." She held it out to him. He hesitated a moment, then took it into his arms. He had brought nothing with him as there was nothing he wanted to carry to his new life other than memories and hopes.

"This was given to you Annabelle, for your babies. You should have it."

"It means family, and I want you to protect our family, so please take it with you." She hugged her brother, and he took the Ndimba in his arms.

"Annabelle, come with me!" he offered. "Let's go together and find our way, maybe back to where we came from! Let's go together Annabelle!"

Anna could only envision his words, and her direction was no more assured than his. Crickets took over the night sounds. The sweet smell of his skin gave her a feeling of safety. At one point, she opened her eyes and saw streaks of tears, visible in the light of the moon shining through the window.

"I love you, my brother. It will be alright," she whispered. She repeated the phrase again and again, often only to herself, as they drifted off to sleep.

The night passed evenly and when she heard the morning calls to report to their tasks, she instinctively began to stir. She could smell rising dough coming from the stove as she stretched her arms toward the ceiling. She moved carefully so as not to awaken Calvin, then turned to find that there was nothing beneath his wool blanket. She sat up with a violent motion, and then remembered.

"Good luck, Calvin," she whispered to the air.

The Reverend was downstairs looking up at her. Outside, the plantation was coming to life. There were calls for eggs, milk, and water as the slave people began to prepare for the day. The Reverend gestured for her to come downstairs, and they all shared a breakfast of boiled eggs and bread with a marmalade that Sherry had made with a mortar and pestle.

The second horn sounded, and Sherry and Beatrice began to head toward the door.

"Beatrice, no, we are heading home today, remember? We are going back home!" Anna spoke as if the old woman were a child who needed to be reminded to button her shoes before stepping outside.

"*You* are heading home, child," Ole' Beatrice said sadly.

Anna looked over at the Reverend who only shook his head.

"But...you said..." Anna pleaded.

"I only have orders to bring you back to Nottoway, Annabelle. She must endure here longer until the debts are settled between the plantations."

Anna looked at the Reverend. "But why then didn't Beatrice go with..."

The two women as well as the Reverend raised a finger to their lips. "Shh, we cannot speak of him anymore...he is in God's hands."

"I would only hold him back. I am old and will die a slave," Beatrice said, and looked at Annabelle with a knowingness. "He will live free and die free."

"Lord Jesus, we pray," Sherry said.

"Amen," the Reverend added.

Beatrice stood at the door of the shack as the workers began to move down the dirt row toward the kitchens, forges, stables, baskets, laundry, hospitals, and fields that called them day after day, decade after decade.

"Remember, Annabelle, you do not belong here," Beatrice said. "We need to get you home." She stroked the girl's hair. "I sure could use that rolling machine you promised," she said smiling.

Annabelle shook her head and hugged the old woman tightly.

"Give a kiss to my chil'ren for me," she said, then whispered, "*Horatio. Caesar. John.*"

"What machine is that?" the Reverend asked.

The older woman and the young girl smiled at one another.

"Remember why you came here, Annabelle. Go and do what needs to be done. You will know what to do," Beatrice said. "It is not wrong to go back for that which you have forgotten."

Sherry pulled Beatrice away from Annabelle and the two women exited the cabin. Beatrice then looked up at the sky for the coming weather and started her march toward the fields. Anna watched her go until she moved behind a barn to enter the rows of tobacco plants.

The Reverend and Annabelle climbed aboard the cabriolet that the Reverend owned and began their three-day journey toward Essex County. The carriage had a canopy to protect it from the sun and was pulled by a four-year-old Morgan horse named Molly. He was careful to wear his clergy clothes and had a sign on the side of the two-wheeled chaise that identified the driver as coming from the famous Rappahannock Baptist Church. A side-by-side shotgun sat in plain view of any robbers that dared confront the religious man escorting a girl along a public thoroughfare.

When they stopped at a private spot along the road to eat some lunch and drink from the brook, Anna peered into the tiny compartment that had hidden Calvin. It seemed impossibly small for a good-sized male such as Calvin, but it was designed so that the occupant's legs could extend under a sleeve built beneath the chaise itself, through a hinged door.

Still, as Negroes alone on a highway, the Reverend knew to have his papers at the ready, including his own manumission with minute descriptions of his dark skin shade, hair texture, and even the placement of the scar on his calf that he had earned from the kick of a horse when he was eleven years old. He also had a ticket in Master Kane's own hand for the legal transport of Annabelle Cudjo along public thoroughfares. A.C. had no knowledge of the plan.

The two travelers were in fact stopped two times by slave patrols and the Reverend produced the necessary documents on both accounts, reprimanding both patrols in the righteous tone that only the Reverend could conceive.

"I am sure you had better have good reason to stop a man of God and his lamb on this day, good sir," he said to one man as he rifled through the papers. He was neither a sheriff nor a policeman and had the weak character of a man who had never achieved his law enforcement validation.

"I am truly sorry, Reverend. It is just my job," the journeyman said. The Reverend had kept his side-by-side rifle on his lap during the episode.

The second of the slave patrols was a retired overseer with a stub for a leg. This man called for the papers as if he were sure that he had found contraband. His eyes moved from the documents to Anna a dozen times, and he took his time.

"Do not trouble me with your inquisitions, sir. Unless you would like to receive a fine from the owners in Essex County. What is your name, Sir?" The Reverend then aggressively pulled out his old Bible and held it toward the man like a weapon. But the overseer was more interested in riding the final three miles to have supper and sleep soundly. As the man addressed the Reverend, his horse came close to Molly and the young mare's ears went back in fear and self-protection.

"Control your horse, man!" the Reverend called out, but it was too late. Molly reared her head and startled the man's horse, who then kicked Molly in the rear leg. The horse whinnied and rose up, sending the cabriolet off balance. The overseer backed his Mustang away, but the sudden rearing had injured Molly, and she lifted her rear leg before gingerly placing it back down onto the firm road.

"Be gone with you, man!" the Reverend said, and with a weak apology the old overseer turned and headed in the opposite direction.

Anna learned that the Reverend buried hints and secrets in his sermons that all the slave people knew. The preacher would condemn desertion from the pulpit, arguing that servitude to God and to man was of the same nature, and that slave people should put their faith in the Lord to deliver them and not to take it upon themselves. But it was the tone of his voice rather than his words that his congregation understood, and all of his listeners picked up the hints that were embedded in his words.

"Do not run away, my friends, for you cannot run away from the Lord! He will find you!" he echoed one Sunday years ago, and sure enough a family consisting of a man, wife, and seven-year-old girl were ushered into his church basement the following week.

To date, he had assisted fourteen slaves who fled their plantations. Calvin was his fifteenth.

As they bounced along the highway, the two travelers spoke of everything from the critters along the scenic path to religious study, but there were hours when neither would say a word. At one point, the Reverend discussed what to say to Master Kane.

"What you say to Master Kane will be of interest to him, but words can't change much. I don't want you to have expectations."

"But what about A.C.?"

"He'll get what's coming to him, somehow, someway. And now Miss Cassandra is onto his plan to try and marry Mary Louise and take over Nottoway."

"Did A.C. purchase Madia. Is that true?"

"It is true, Annabelle. He has a farm across the river, and if he were not a drunk who takes advantage of good women, he might make for a decent landholder. He has a sister there who is known for being a decent sort, so it is my hope that she is safe." He looked at Anna and patted her knee. "Rest assured that I am inquiring."

"Reverend, I should tell you that he has visited our shack on many occasions. He has an attachment to...my mother and talks to her as if they are together."

"Your mother is a good woman. She remains the wife of your late father in the eyes of God unless she chooses another. But this situation is grim. A transaction took place between A.C. and Masta' Kane for Madia, and there is nothing good to come of it."

No one spoke.

"Change g'wine come," he said aloud. "People ain't got no business trying to be God."

And then they were silent except for the squeaking of the wheels and the polite greetings to passersby, including a Butterfield stagecoach headed for Charleston, packed with luggage.

The Reverend broke the silence. "Last night when you were sleeping, Beatrice told me the secret you shared with her." He looked straight ahead as if he had just mentioned that Mass takes place on Sundays.

"What did she say?"

"Your secret, Annabelle. As well as your God-given name."

Their eyes met.

"Tell me your name again, child?"

The words had difficulty finding their way to her lips and the Reverend was patient.

"Zarkhanna. Zarkhanna Cudjo," she said softly.

"You are from Jemmy's family?"

"I suppose so. I think I saw him in my own time in the woods besides a cross once."

"And from what year of our Lord's world are you a visitor?"

Now the distance between the young girl and the aging preacher diminished into nothing, and Anna had nothing to hide or fear. In a way, whether she stayed in this world or returned to hers was irrelevant. She could breathe, she could eat, she could help lessen the pain of her brethren by knowing more than anyone should. And what of it if she died? Even by the whip. Life had already whipped her in ways that hurt more deeply than any kind of physical pain.

Or maybe she could still make it back to a world that enticed her only by the love of a five-year-old boy. What difference did it make, really?

She decided to speak freely.

And so she did. She spoke for hours, then days. She told him of her native land, her family, the wars, the soldiers. She spoke of the orphanage, and how she had come to Virginia to live in another kind of orphanage that was similar to the first in all but name. She told him about the leather pouch. And she spoke about her faith in Jesus Christ and how she had come to understand that she had no purpose here in 1824 other than to tell the truth about what she had seen and to ease whatever suffering she could.

The road held long stretches of highway where Molly pulled the cabriolet at a speed that made the scenery pass in slow-motion, yet the miles occupy vast distances. The horse was now visibly limping.

"How did you come to be a free man? Are all clergymen free?"

The Reverend took a deep breath, removed his hat, and fanned his face.

"My grandfather's father purchased his own freedom on New Year's Day, 1700, by tending tobacco fields and sleeping four hours a day. He was also able to purchase his wife before he died of smallpox just six years later. Their son, my grandfather, continued the priesthood and built the Rappahannock Baptist Church with the help of local people, including slaves, overseers, and even masters. I'm fortunate to be a steward of this land, a free man able to continue the Lord's teaching with the support of the good people of Essex County."

Vehicles passed by with slaves conducting errands and ladies on visiting trips to luncheons. At times, it seemed that Molly's leg had healed itself, while at others, the horse would stop on her own, lift her rear leg and then continue along.

But as words and travelers passed by, the Reverend began a conversation that Anna could never have considered, and when she heard it, her body stiffened.

"Why not stay here, Annabelle? Not as a slave, but as a free person. I have the funds to purchase your freedom and you can live in the church and assist me. You could receive so much and give even more."

And with these words, Anna felt for the first time in a long time that she could make a choice, and that the choice would be hers. It would not be the army's or the Mother Superior's, and it would not be Carolyn's. If it were true that she could live free and help the people of Nottoway who needed it so very much, what life back home would she be giving up?

"I suppose," Anna said without realizing the words left her lips. "How would it work? Where would I live? Would I have friends?"

The Reverend laid forth a life for her that she could understand, and when he came to the part of continuing Jemmy's work, which the Reverend felt she had the skills, she felt an excitement. As they passed a sign indicating that they were in Essex County, Anna had all but decided what to do. It was only the memory of Simba that stood as a roadblock.

The Reverend hurried the wagon along. He knew that he must at all costs get the girl to Nottoway safely. He moved along the highway as a courier, one whose valuable cargo was a visitor, and he could think of no greater calling than this. He had to keep her safe, mostly from the wrath of A.C. Tomkins, whose world was about to start falling in, as he would surely seek his own kind of revenge.

Reverend Cooper would take Annabelle's lead, and she would take his. As they rounded the curve of the long highway that bordered Nottoway, Camel's Hump Mountain came into view. Molly was now limping with every step, and although they could skirt Nottoway completely in order to get to the church, it appeared that the poor animal could not travel another mile. A quick change of horses at Nottoway would take little time, and they could take Tidewater Row as a shortcut through the fields directly to the church.

"We are going to have to stop at the barn quickly. I do not want anyone to see you, so let's get you into the compartment." The Reverend stopped the transport and opened the hatch below his feet. Anna got in and lay on her back with her legs curled to the side. How Calvin was able to travel this way, she did not know. There was barely enough room to make it possible.

She felt the uneven steps of Molly giving her final pull, and the wagon took a turn into Nottoway. She could smell the familiar dirt and the livestock of the plantation. She peered out through a small hole in the planks and could see they were now on Tidewater Row heading toward the barn.

"Not a sound, child," the Reverend whispered.

# Chapter 13

The Reverend had placed a blanket in the hidden compartment to protect his stowaway's skin. Still, the awkward steps of the injured horse caused Annabelle to hit her head against the wooden slats.

Breathing holes had been drilled into the sides of the wagon, decorative in their design, so as not to arouse the slightest suspicion to onlookers, and Annabelle peered out of these as best as she could. The branches of lifeless trees reached toward Tidewater Row, clamoring for water that wasn't there. She watched critters dart back and forth in their own desperate search. She felt her legs tingling as they began to fall asleep in her moving prison.

Annabelle and Calvin were by no means the first to occupy this cubicle, built by an obviously skilled carpenter to offer maximum comfort in the smallest possible space. As there was no room to turn around, she imagined the Reverend must have given Calvin a code to tap when his muscles cramped, and he needed to shift position.

It was two o'clock on a Wednesday, and everyone at Nottoway was tending to their plantation tasks. Annabelle wondered which shack they were passing, and the glimpse of a chair rocking on a porch gave her the answer.

"Ole' Beatrice" the Reverend said to no one.

On their journey from Wappocomo, Annabelle had recounted to the Reverend how Lizzie had been sold on the highway to slave traders. They both considered how the old woman no longer had anyone to make her tea and keep her company. The Reverend had listened, storing yet another task in a basket already overflowing with urgent requests.

"I'll see what I can do," he said, mostly to himself. It was a phrase too often repeated. "In the world you come from Annabelle, maybe talking and convincing is what you are used to. We will speak with Masta' Kane about what you seen with Mr. Tomkins, but you need to know that it won't change much."

This truth nagged at her like an insect lodged in her ear. She now had no idea how she could help these people she had come to know and love, yet her very presence—in this underworld made a difference that no longer had words—let alone relaying them to an old and senile Master. There was a sense of belonging that was as real to her as the rumbling of the wagon traveling on the uneven dirt.

Annabelle could see they were passing her home on Tidewater Row. While she had now firmly decided to stay as a free person in this world, she still felt she needed to retrieve the leather pouch she had left behind in the loft. She wondered if new people lived in her cabin. As if the Reverend read her mind, he whispered.

"Your home is empty of people, Annabelle, but not of your memories."

Annabelle felt the weight of his words. She would never stay there with Madia and Calvin again. She knew she had to move forward. But she wanted her peculiar item back. It may have served its sole purpose by allowing her to travel from one world to another, but she hoped it might guide her in this next one. Yes, she would stay with the Reverend, live in his church, perhaps even study the ministry, but...if she ever wished to leave, she wanted that choice to be hers and hers alone.

It was only the love of a small boy that caused her hesitation. Simba's whole life had been one full of *withouts*. First it was without food, then without shelter, and finally, without family. Carolyn White may have saved him from this latter fate, but it was Annabelle who gave it meaning. How could she abandon him?

She had no answer to this question other than to find a way to retrieve the leather pouch and keep it with her, just in case she ever decided to go... home?

She doubted she would ever have another chance to retrieve the item, but she could not find the words to ask the Reverend's permission. Soon, another family might move in, and perhaps the item would be found, misplaced, or worse, discarded.

She felt the cabriolet turn and the sunlight through the wooden slats gave way to the darkness of the stables' interior. "Howdy, Rev," somebody said. The air was heavy with manure.

"Hello there, Renty! I'm afraid that Molly here needs a long rest," the Reverend said. "We had an incident along the highway. Right hind leg."

The stable hand walked over and began to unhitch the horse from the wagon. Molly winced at the stable hand's touch.

"Whoa there, girl. Take it easy. We'll get ya fixed up," Renty said. "Where are you coming from, Reverend?"

"Charleston. Then I stopped at Wappocomo to attend some business for Masta' Kane."

"Ain't that where they take our people?" Renty asked. When he disengaged the horse, the lack of frontal weight made the coach tilt backward. Annabelle pushed her feet against the hinged safety latch. She tapped it lightly with her foot and saw that the ground was just inches away.

"How Big Arthur holdin' up?" asked Renty.

"Well, they got him on a field crew with Beatrice and the others. They don't have a drought in Hampshire County, but they are behind schedule, so the overseer, he is a bad man, makes them work too hard. I spoke with my friend Preacher Tom and asked him to make a complaint with the Colonel, but I am not sure it will help."

"Change g'wine come," Renty said.

Now others who had either heard or seen the Reverend approach started to come into the barn.

"Welcome back, Reverend," someone said. "Can I get you an iced tea?" It was Martha, the woman who had rivalled Annabelle's speed in the weaving room. Annabelle could just make out the woman's shoes.

"No, no thank you. We—I best be going. I have got a sermon to prepare for Sunday."

"Sunday ain't but days away," Martha argued. "Now you just follow me right now and we get you a cool drink to welcome our good Reverend back."

"I really cannot...I must be on my way..."

"Now now, Reverend, we won't hear of nothin' like that," another woman said in a tone that was not to be argued with, and Annabelle could see the Reverend was being pulled out of the barn by his friendly parishioners. Only Renty remained. Sensing that his secret traveler might be discovered, the Reverend called over to the stable hand.

"Renty, you come too. You don' do my work! I need to pick my horse!" And with that,

Renty placed Molly in a stall, closed the latch, and joined the group.

"I guess I can afford ten minutes!" the Reverend said, clearly directing his words toward Annabelle.

It was now silent in the barn. In the distance, Annabelle could make out the soft singing of the field workers passing the long day with hymns and folk songs. She could just make out the sound of hoes hitting the earth, likely clearing another channel to reroute the river toward the people, animals, tobacco plants, trees, flowers, and grass that thirsted for water.

Annabelle estimated it would only take her three or four minutes to run to the shack and she would be back before the Reverend had his first sip of iced tea. She pushed on the safety latch, and it quietly squeaked open. She put one foot on the earth.

It was early afternoon, and the overseers, Negro or otherwise, would be attending to their duties. Besides the Reverend, no one knew she was back at Nottoway, so nobody would be looking for her. She placed her other foot on the ground. With a final push off of the headboard, she wriggled herself out of the compartment and fell to the ground. Her legs felt like pins and needles as she awkwardly ran out the back of the barn, finding herself standing on an empty Tidewater Row.

Up the hill to her left, the chimney from the house kitchen let out a steady stream of fragrances, and she could see the figures of the Reverend and his friends sharing the refreshment. As she hid behind the nearest cabin, she caught sight of a delivery wagon coming down the road and heard two people talking as the wagon drew closer.

"We got fifty gallons of molasses," a man said. "Forty pounds sugar, 1,000 pounds cotton..."

"We don' need no 1,000 pounds cotton. We make do with half that." The second voice was unmistakably Glennie's.

"I don' know if you or yo masta' know 'bout the price of cotton, but we selling for far higher to the English, so if we got it, I rec'mmend you buy it."

Annabelle held her breath when the wagon stopped in front of the shack she was hiding behind and she thought she could feel them looking in her direction.

"We don' have no need for 1,000 pounds cotton," Glennie repeated. "We'll take fifty pounds of sugar, though." When the wagon passed out of range, Annabelle ran toward her former home, about twenty-five yards away.

She came upon the shack on Tidewater Row, and carefully opened the door.

It appeared that the people who lived there—her own family—had only left for supper and would return any minute. She looked around at the room, which housed little more than a fireplace, a bedstead, and a woven rug. The white ceramic jug still sat on the three-legged table propped up by a makeshift post. Several woven baskets, some she herself had made, were strewn about the floor. Only the people were missing, and the Ndimba that once hung on the thick nail—the heirloom that was now traveling with Calvin on his treacherous journey. She stood frozen with the memories of the small family she had come to love. She did not know how much time had passed, but she knew she had to hurry.

Suddenly she heard fast footsteps approaching. She raced toward the ladder as the door opened. The Reverend looked at her sternly.

"What in God's name, Annabelle?" he whispered loudly, his body quivering in anger, fear, and apprehension as he closed the door carefully behind him. He held his shotgun at his side.

"I'm so sorry, Reverend. I left behind something important that I need...for me...to...Please forgive me," she said, realizing the danger she had put them both in.

"Then be done with it," the Reverend whispered forcefully, "and be quick. Hurry!"

Then came the sound of horses. The pace of the riders was swift, and Annabelle and the Reverend could feel the earth pounding with their approach.

There was no way for them to run and no place to hide. Should she dive under the bed or try to make it up to the loft? What exactly was she avoiding and who would she be hiding from?

Her answer came soon enough when A.C. Tomkins kicked the door open and entered with his cohort Wendell close behind.

"My my my. Now whadda we got here?"

No one spoke.

"Hey Wendell, I think we got here the Second Coming of Jesus and his little coon-gregation!" Wendell held the door open. The cane-backed chair sat off to the side and Wendell kicked it over to make their presence, and mood known.

"Second comin' and his coon-gregation!" mimicked Wendell. He spat tobacco, then revealed a toothless smile.

"Maybe we shouldn't be disrespecting this here learned man of the

Lord. He might go and tell some nigga' tale to Jesus Christ himself!" A.C. said.

"Can I help you, gentlemen, with something other than taking the name of our Lord in vain?" the Reverend said with an icy gaze.

"Oh, so you a helping man now, Reverend? Helping nigga' girls run away?" A pistol hung at A.C.'s side. "I see you bring back one of our young ones," he said, walking up to Annabelle. A bandage covered some of the oozing blisters on his face.

"Reverend, 'scuse my disrespect," A.C. continued, "but Glennie told me she might have seen one of our own here just now, and we come down to investigate. I am sure der' is a perfectly good explanation. Can I see the ticket you got for her legal transport? And while you're at it, do tell us why you armed there, preacher? You out shooting ducks or somethin'?"

"Ducks!" Wendell laughed, closing the door.

"I am not beholden to you, Mr. Tomkins, and Masta' Kane himself sent for the girl with a legal ticket," the Reverend responded, holding his shotgun in one hand, pointed down.

"You on my plantation travelin' free with one of my nigga's, and by law I am the only one who can sign tickets 'round here, even if the crazy old man sign one himself. By law!" Now Tomkins pulled out his gun. "You will stand down, preacher, while I take hold of this 'ere...possession of mine," he said, glancing at Annabelle with a handsome smile and a wink.

"Like hell you will," the preacher said. He brought the shotgun into both hands and held it like a barrier in front of him. "She is not and has never been your possession. In fact, I am on orders from Master Kane to deliver her to him imminently."

"That so, Reverend?" A.C. said.

"That so?" his accomplice echoed.

"Reverend, why are you pointing that gun at the overseer of this 'ere plantation, owned and operated by Masta' Leslie Kane, who has retained me under his employment to administer all of his property. Why that, Rev?" The blueness of his eyes flashed as he spoke.

The Reverend now pointed the shotgun, fixing the muzzle not on either man, but at the dead space between them. "As I said, Annabelle is not your property. In fact, Masta' Kane is expecting us at the Great House, where I fully intend to purchase her freedom so that she may study the ministry."

"Freedom? The ministry?! You full of gospels! Stand down right now, old man. Or I guarantee you won't be preachin' on Sunday," A.C. growled.

Annabelle no longer knew where to look. The blistered face of A.C. Tomkins instilled hot anger in her. The rough rungs of the ladder she held onto provided little relief. She only knew that her only real choice was to make it up to the loft, grab the pouch, and leave this place for good. She looked up the ladder but remained still.

Wendell took a stance toward the Reverend. A.C. nodded to give him the go-ahead and Wendell lurched at the preacher with force, knocking his shotgun out of his hands onto the floor. The men now wrestled while A.C. and Annabelle watched. The shotgun was kicked toward Annabelle, who studied it as if it were alive and crawling toward her. She knew guns well, too well, but still, she let it lie at her feet.

Wendell got the better of the aging Reverend and now stood over him, delivering a swift kick into his gut. The preacher cried out in pain.

His white collar was covered with dirt from the floor. But he was a man who had become an expert in escape. "Annabelle! Go from this place! Go now, child!" he cried out.

"What are you there saying to my little flower, Reverend? Huh?" A.C. stepped toward the preacher with a heavy foot.

It was then that Annabelle launched herself up the ladder, climbing as fast as she could.

"Hey!" A.C. yelled.

He grabbed her ankle and her shoe clumsily fell off and struck his head. Slightly dazed but more angered, he reached his other hand to yank her to the ground.

She kicked him off and made it all the way to the vantage point from where she had first seen A.C. and Kestin enter on the night of the murder, where it had all started. A.C. now clambered up the ladder after her, but she swiftly kicked his head and he fell backwards onto the floor, stunned.

She leapt over to the loose plank in the wall. On the opposite side of the loft was the small platform that would take her back home. She pushed the lower part of the plank, but it stayed fast against the wall. She recalled there had been a trick to dislodge it but could not remember the motion. *"Merda!"* she swore. She began to frantically punch at the plank. Nothing. "*Deus, por favor!*" she implored. The board still would not budge.

Now A.C. was ascending the ladder again. Even though he knew there was nowhere for her to go, he was not a man to be disobeyed and he would enjoy dragging her into his employ. No slave of his was going to tell Master Kane anything about him.

As he made his way up, Annabelle felt the quiet rage in her that was her companion these past years, constantly bridging the distance between her own sense of right and wrong. She stepped swiftly to the edge of the loft and, with a force that had become a lost acquaintance in her bones, she kicked A.C. in the head.

The man fell backwards onto the floor again, but this time cried out in pain. His pistol had fallen and slid across the floor. "Bitch! The worst kind! I swear I will do to you what I do to your mother every night! Get on down and get on your knees before I put an end to your life, as is my right! You just don assaulted your overseer! Now git on down 'ere!" he ordered.

Annabelle watched him as if she had thrown a rock into a pool, sending waves in all directions.

He lay on the floor, his head bleeding, his leg sprained, and his hat knocked halfway across the room.

"Git down 'ere!" he yelled again, grabbing his limb.

Annabelle calmly walked over to the wall and, remembering that she only needed to tap the top while pushing on the bottom, the plank dislodged easily. She grabbed the soft leather pouch and felt its odd contents—the wing of a bird, the bark of a tree, stones brilliant with red and blue colors.

She looked down at A.C. one final time.

"I am not of this world, A.C. But I witnessed you murder Kestin Kane in this very room and then blame an innocent man for your crime. I have not been able to tell Master Kane myself, but I've told someone who will. You are the one who will be hanged from the Old Oak, not just for the murder of Kestin Kane, but for the crimes you commit against Madia and the good people who work under your cruel hand."

A.C. looked up at her like a schoolboy caught fighting by the headmaster. The truth, when it finally comes out, is as visible as a scar on a man's face.

"My father tried to say something before he was hung from that tree." She pointed in the direction of the Old Oak. "He said, A.C., you will burn in suffering as these slave people suffer.

"But he was trying to say something else. He wanted to release these good people from any similar fate and undue suffering, but even with a rope around his neck, you would not leave him in peace. Now, before I go back to my own time, I can tell you that your time is up A.C. and you will hang for your crimes. Go eat a tobacco worm and chew it well. Those worms will be swarming under your skin soon enough."

"Who do you think you are, talking to me like that, girl?" A.C. looked up at her with a smirk. "You crazy as that whore of a mother you got! But she is in my bed every night now! Ha! Just like you will when I get cha!" He looked at the Reverend moaning in pain on the ground. "Wendell! Get on up that ladder and fetch this nigga' girl who won't listen to what's good for her. I got a special treat for her she gonna' like!"

Wendell, who had been injured in the tussle himself, hobbled over to the ladder and went up it one rung at a time.

Now Annabelle approached the small platform that served as the portal between the two worlds. One step, and she would be free.

"Go to Hell, A.C. Tomkins. Burn, burn, burn!" she yelled as she put one foot on the platform and shifted upwards.

But nothing happened.

She put her other foot onto the platform so that her head reached the ceiling.

Nothing. She only heard the barn swallows above the roof's peak finding their way to their nests.

In desperation, she switched the pouch to her other hand.

She tried holding it in both hands. She held it to her chest.

Nothing moved other than the bouncing of the thin boards under her feet as Wendell made his way up the ladder. The pouch was as useless as beeper. She jumped on the platform one last time, but only hit her head on the ceiling.

She felt Wendell's hot hand come down on her shoulder and whirled around.

She quickly put the leather pouch in the pocket of her dirty dress before she tried to fight him off, but he had already enveloped her in a bear hug despite her kicking and screaming.

"Time's up, little lamb," he said as he hauled her toward the ladder while pressing his gun into her abdomen.

Lost in hopelessness, Annabelle could only do what the man told her to do. A.C. stood up slowly, shaken, but able to walk. Prodded by Wendell, and A.C.'s gun now pointed at her as well, Annabelle made her way down from the loft. A.C. glared at her with livid determination. He was done playing games and had a fate for her that she could scarcely comprehend.

Battered and bruised, the Reverend began to move on the ground, but A.C. paid him little mind as Wendell and Annabelle stepped onto the dirt floor.

The Reverend had crawled his way to his shotgun and raised the weapon in the direction of the others, but Wendell was quicker. He pointed his revolver at the preacher and pulled the trigger and the bullet caught him just below his shoulder. The preacher cried out in pain as he collapsed on the floor and blood began to ooze out of him. Annabelle ran over and crouched next to him. His black frock was torn and his face was caked in dirt and sweat. "I'm so sorry I'm so sorry, Reverend," Annabelle cried. She sobbed as she pulled a large piece of cloth off the bed behind her, rolled it up tightly, and used both hands to press it firmly against the wound.

"Annabelle," he murmured. "Why do I still see you, child?"

"I tried, Reverend, but it didn't work. I can't go back anymore."

He looked up at her and shut his eyes tightly. "But you must, Annabelle. You are not of this world. You only came as a visitor. Go back and go with God." The words came out in gasps.

"Boss, he pointed at me with that dat' dere gun!" Wendell shouted, waving his pistol. "I don' want to shoot him. I don' want to shoot nobody, let alone a preacher man!" Annabelle could see that Wendell was but a frightened boy who acted only at the direction of the overseer and was not someone who could handle the consequences of his own decisions. He dropped his gun. "I go get the Doc!"

The Reverend paid no attention as Wendell jumped over him and ran out the door, leaving the preacher, Annabelle, and A.C. behind.

"A.C.," the Reverend said, his breathing labored. "You are a man the Lord is coming to judge. You can't escape the Lord...you can't escape."

"Best to save your breath now, preacher. Wendell go get the Doc. You just lie still there." Tomkins sat down on the bedstead and all he saw was a bleeding man gasping on the floor.

"Annabelle," the Reverend whispered. "Promise me that you will tell Masta' Kane the truth. Even if it don't change nothin', the truth still matters."

"Yes, Reverend...I will," she cried, watching the cloth beneath her hands slowly turn red.

"And go to the tree, Annabelle. You know the one," he murmured, thoughts tumbling out of him in bursts. "Our people say the curse is buried there and the wind spreads it every night." He paused as a shot of pain went through his body. "Five years now."

"Yes, Reverend." These were the only words she could utter.

"Have no fear, child. Have faith in our Lord, who protects us." The Reverend closed his eyes. Annabelle sobbed as she could barely find a pulse with the tips of her fingers. Her tears fell on his face as she placed his head on a pillow that A.C. himself had offered.

"Don't give up, Reverend. You're needed here." There was no response. In the silence, a mouse scurried in the corner, capturing a meager crumb to bring back to its nest. Outside the winds swept through nearby magnolia trees. The Reverend lay quietly, his breathing shallow. Annabelle prayed for him.

A.C. smirked and shook his head before leaning over Annabelle's shoulder and hissing in her ear. "Now you listen here, girly girl. You ain't gonna say nothin' to nobody about none of this, you got that?" His breath stank of tobacco. "What we're gonna do is go for a walk and get to know each other. You learn like your mama did that A.C. Tomkins, I ain't that bad." He stood up and grabbed her, jabbing his pistol in her side. "Now we walk," he said as he pushed her through the door. The Reverend lay on the ground, alive but in stifling pain.

"The doctor is coming for you!" Annabelle called out to him.

As A.C. led her along Tidewater Row, Annabelle could make out the familiar sounds of the slave people returning from the fields and workhouses that commanded their bodies by day, leaving them to piece together what was left of their families by night. She knew their fate, and she was coming to understand that hers was not dissimilar. A life of bondage, and if she lived long enough, an old woman sold twice.

She felt a tug at her side as A.C. led her behind the cabin once belonging to Ole' Beatrice.

"Where are you taking me?" Annabelle objected. "Master Kane is expecting me!"

"You giving the orders now?" he said. He was limping from his fall and as he pulled her along he half leaned on her for support. "You ain't talking to no master, cause you are going away from this place forever." His pistol dug into her ribs.

Annabelle realized they were heading toward Camel's Hump.

"I'm gonna take you to a special place I took your mama after that nigga' of a father of yours killed Kestin! Don't worry, little girl, you gon' like what I do to ya!"

Annabelle struggled, but A.C. was stronger, and even if she were to wrestle herself free, she knew he would not hesitate to shoot her and she would forever die here in 1824. As with the Reverend, for her to die at this time...that would suit no one. She needed to stay alive if she had any hope of seeing anyone who meant anything to her ever again.

Madia. Beatrice. Arthur. Simba.

Her homeland.

She remembered that a march under the command of an armed soldier can provide unseen opportunities. She wanted to break free and run to the Great House where she would burst in and call for the old master, who would surely protect her. What fate would come after that, she did not know, but she was certain this world would be much better without the weight of A.C. Tomkins bearing down on everyone.

If Madia could return home, even if Annabelle died in the process of freeing her, that alone—to help a single person in this wicked world—would be enough for her.

So, she walked.

The two trudged the steep path to the summit of the odd shaped mountains. A.C. grunted in pain as he walked, his prisoner at his side, for the man was not a man in his own eyes without a helpless prisoner. Here was a man who had power but lacked everything that he deemed important.

"So I'm gonna hang for killing that coward Kestin, huh? Who gonna tell him now? Kestin gonna rise up like dead Jesus?" he laughed, and then winced in pain.

He pushed her and she fell onto some rocks on the steep path, drawing blood. When they reached the summit, she could see the Rappahannock River winding its way down to Chesapeake Bay. The Great House was to the west, where Master Kane was likely rocking slowly on the wide veranda.

"Now we go to your mama's favorite spot." He spit on the ground then dragged her onto the same deer path she had found that day so long ago, when she had hiked there with Simba. Sure enough it led to the small rock clearing she remembered. Standing on the open face, they both instinctively took in the vast open view that the clearing and steep cliffs offered.

"Take off that dress, little girl," he ordered. His expression became contorted as he anticipated his reward. His face held a bandage from one of his angry blisters, and he wiped some of the ooze onto his sleeve. Part of the puss fell to the ground in red and yellow blotches.

Annabelle stood in place. As a soldier, she had learned that things never happen entirely as expected. Instead, one moment could pass into another that just might offer a possibility of escape. So, Annabelle looked into the Overseer's vengeful glare and made no move. Over his shoulder she could make out the slave people returning from the fields and moving along Tidewater Row.

"Don't make me ask you again, girly. I got to go on back and make my reports. But we're gonna have some fun before dat, so I tell you again, take off that dress and lay down on that rock." He let go of her and aimed the pistol at her person. "Now, bitch!"

Annabelle began to unbutton her dress, the dirty gray smock that it was. She undid a single clasp then stood defiantly with her hands at her side.

"I am not scared of you, A.C. Tomkins. You can't do anything to me that you haven't already done. You're nothing but a coward and a killer. And as my father told you with a rope around his neck, you will burn in Hell." A laugh came out of her that she did not recognize as her own. At that instant, Tomkins raised the butt of his gun and struck her jaw. She fell to the ground, brought a hand to her cheek and looked up at him.

A.C. stood over her. "I don't wanna hurt cha, Annabelle. You think I am a bad man, but I ain't. I bought your mama fair and square, even if I don' paid yet, I got a deal that she be mine when the bank notes are right. I'm gonna build my own plantation, and she be my property, and I treat her right, like a wife, for she a good woman. Maybe I even got feelings for her." He shook his head as he considered his plan and, for a second, Annabelle could see a longing in his eyes.

"Now I'm gonna buy you too for the same terms, and me and you and your mama are gonna be a li'l family. Don't worry, you won' have to work the whole time, cause we're gonna be happy." The plan set in his mind, he relaxed as he bent down toward her and spoke gently. "Now take off that dress like I tell you and show me what is soon to be mine anyways." His anger then came roaring back and he slapped her with all the force of his hand.

Backwards she fell and the man was instantly on top of her pawing at her clothing. Her shoes came off in the struggle and as he pinned her arms against the open rock clearing, she could feel his groin rotating against her. He grunted in frustration, undid his pants, and brought them down to his knees with one hand. He grabbed at her again, feeling for her small breast, and ripped her dress off her shoulders with a force that had her naked from the waist up. The man groaned in frustration as he still was not yet able to violate her. "It's your fault!" he screamed. "Same as that mother of yours! Why don't ya just want me like ya should?"

Annabelle wriggled her body as he continued to gyrate on top of her with his eyes closed. Her arms out to her side, she grabbed around for an object to strike him with. She noticed a rock the size of her fist, but it was out of reach. She did everything she could with body motion to push him off.

"Stop your fighting!" His hat fell off his head. With a slight movement of her shoulder, she managed to slide her hand under it, concealing her attempts to seize a weapon.

She was able to grasp a stick and pulled it toward her, but it was wedged between the rocks. She began to twist it back and forth as A.C. continued to talk to himself in futile attempts to perform his function. He seemed to think her motions were born of passion, not terror.

"Bitch, tell me something I like to hear!" He opened his eyes to capture the sight of the helpless girl under his control but found instead a fierce glare from a survivor of years of turmoil. Not seeing what he wanted, he punched her face with the brutality of a man who had never really got his way and never would. Feeling in control again, he closed his eyes and continued his spasmatic gyrations.

Annabelle, on the other hand, felt only determination. She dislodged the stick in her grip like an iron knife.

"A.C.," she said softly, inviting his attention. "Look at me."

This gave him pause—was she finally coming around? He opened his eyes at the sound of his name.

"Huh?"

At that moment Annabelle lifted the stick and plunged it into the gaping sore on his face. She had chosen her weapon well—a stick of mighty oak–and it pierced straight through his oozing boil all the way to the bone. The sound was a like a foot stomping into wet mud.

"Ooowwcch!" A.C. shouted. "Whadja do, you crazy bitch?" He groaned as he rolled off her, putting his hand to his bloody, oozing cheek and crying out in pain.

She quickly leapt to her feet as

A.C. sat on his behind, legs askew.

Annabelle grabbed the rock and threw it at his head, but her aim was off and it struck his neck instead. He fell back onto his elbows and looked up at her, stunned.

Standing on the top of Camel's Hump with the man responsible for so much pain in the lives of herself and others, she could feel the raging fire that had grown inside her for far too long.

It had started in Caxito with a small spark of independent spirit weaving baskets her own way rather than the traditional methods.

It had turned into cinders when she realized her father would never return and that her mother would have to endure alone.

It had become flashes as she listened to the desperate cries of her mother and witnessed Auntie's last moments at the hands of drugged-up, laughing soldiers.

It was ignited into fire when she found herself a prisoner inside an army that had no agenda other than death.

It burst into flames when she was taken away from her homeland and brought to a strange country where she was given new parents she never wanted and friends who did not want her.

And finally, it burst into an inferno when she found herself trapped in a hellish past, unable to navigate through the smoke of time, and at the whim of a man who was hell-bent on extracting every ounce of joy from the slaves he ruled. She felt the scorching heat of this inferno as she looked down at this man now.

"A.C. Tomkins, look at me," she demanded in a voice that did not seem to be her own. The man obeyed and looked at her with vicious contempt.

"You are gonna hang like a well bucket for this," A.C. snarled. With those words, she lunged at him, easily grabbed his face, and plunged the other end of the stick deep into his eye with enough force to wedge the organ from its socket so that it hung from bloody tentacles onto his scarred and bloody cheek.

He screamed as Annabelle backed away from him. The man struggled to his feet, completely disoriented with the stick still lodged in his brain as he circled the clearing. Overhead, Annabelle could see clouds beginning to form into thick bushels so that, staggering in front of the gray billows, A.C. looked like a ghost rising up from the rock face. With his bleeding eye socket and the bandage ripped from his boils, he stumbled and swung his fists blindly.

Annabelle watched his frightful dance, listening to his screams.

"You gonna hang! Hang I say!" Still blinded, he swung his body around, reaching out for his tormentor.

Annabelle stepped to the side and after a few moments called out to him. She had found her shoes and stepped into them.

"A.C., I'm real sorry for what I did," she said softly. "I'm over here."

"You better be, you little Black bitch!" When he lunged for her, she only had to step aside.

He felt the earth shift and give way beneath his feet. He lost whatever balance he had and reached out for something, anything, to hold onto. He found a thin tree through sheer grabbling, but at this point his legs had tumbled over the side of the steep cliff.

"Help! Save me!" he pleaded. "We can be...happy together! We can be a family!" His slipping fingers held on desperately to the thin tree.

"A.C. Tomkins, the only happy that will happen is when you are dead and gone from this Earth." She had no idea where the words she spoke were coming from. She looked at the man and only saw the arsonist in her life and the lives of those she had come to know and, yes, *love*.

"A.C., I release this world from the burning hell you have created." She lifted her foot and stamped her shoe onto the man's clawing hands until he let go, falling backward.

At first, he seemed to be floating in space. His one good eye looked up at her as he fell farther and farther away. He did not try to change his position as he succumbed to the pit of gravity. When his body smashed into a protruding boulder fifty feet below, Annabelle thought she could hear the snap of his back, but it was not enough to stop his downward spiral. After a moment, he tumbled again onto another protruding boulder and was catapulted into a wild spin farther and farther down the precipice until his splayed body, outstretched like a broken bird, smashed onto the rocks at the bottom of the cliff.

Annabelle turned away from the sight and, still naked to her waist, fell to her knees. She felt the brunt of A.C.'s blows and the bleeding wounds from her struggle. A dizziness caused her to fall to the ground. Her face slapped against the cold stone of the clearing and she lay still, breathing, breathing, breathing.

She felt something pressing against her stomach and reached into her pocket and found the leather pouch. Now just a useless bag of stones, she felt that whatever powers it contained could no longer serve her. She had done what she could, and it was not enough. She noticed a crevice between the rocks, and without thinking, pushed the leather pouch deep inside the tight opening, and then fell back onto her stomach. It was an item for someone else to benefit and someone else to find.

An hour passed, and she lay there still.

And then she felt something unexplainable. First it was a light tapping on her skin, then it grew in intensity until there was no mistake, and she looked up and felt it on the side of her face.

It was a splatter. A wetness falling over her in tears that were not her own.

A sprinkle, then a drizzle followed by gobs of delicious, fat raindrops. It washed over her evenly. She turned onto her back and looked up at the sky as a torrent of water poured down onto her, as well as the surrounding trees, rocks, plants, and earth. Thick raindrops dripped onto her skin from pregnant clouds above, soaking her thoroughly. She turned on her side so the water would cool her wounds. Then, pushing herself to her feet, she turned and took in the expansive view of the plantation below as the rainstorm intensified.

She watched the people of Tidewater Row out in front of their cabins, their arms extended, their bodies dancing as they raised their hands toward the heavens to catch the healing rain.

Once again overcome with dizziness, Annabelle fell backward, hitting her head against the smooth, wet rock. She felt as if she were traveling somewhere, rising perhaps, or falling–as if she were losing a part of herself that could never be retrieved, and before she had a chance to change direction, she descended into complete darkness.

# Chapter 14

The jumbo jet kissed the runway and settled onto the ground, startling the few passengers who were caught napping. Outside, the sky was a brilliant blue, expanding endlessly in all directions. Two large jetliners coasted slowly in a straight line. One had an Italian flag, the other, Israeli. A third aircraft, small and unmarked, stood before the two large birds as if intimidated. Inside, announcements came over the loudspeaker in many languages.

"Please make sure to take all of your personal belongings when exiting the aircraft."

"Please use caution when opening the overhead bins, as items tend to move during flight."

To the passenger in seat 6J, it seemed like the first day of school when a long list of instructions was read over the P.A. system. She looked at the other passengers seated around her who were fumbling for mobile phones, books, briefcases, and earphones. Across the aisle, an elderly woman stared out the window as if unsure she was in the right place. A businessman had changed his clothes in the restroom a half hour before landing and was now dressed immaculately.

Sitting beside the traveler was a considerable man who spoke quietly into his cell phone, giving directives in short bursts of information. "We will be clear in twenty minutes," he said in Portuguese, then, "I wish to go directly to my hotel," and finally, "Please reschedule the meeting with the labor chief until breakfast tomorrow. Do not give him a reason." The man snapped his flip phone shut and looked at the girl seated beside him. He smiled and shook his head, then addressed another man in the seat forward.

"Make certain the embargo is extended as long as needed."

"Yes sir."

"Also, put in a call to the powers that be regarding the new mines. Remind them that the deal is far from complete."

"Absolutely, sir."

"And don't forget that item we discussed. Make sure it gets into the right hands."

There was a long chime, and the passengers began to stand up. After the lengthy flight, friends who had been seated apart came together and older children, seated toward the back, rejoined their parents.

She watched as the procession of travelers made their way down the aisle. At one point she started to stand up, but the man beside her gently motioned for her to stay seated. It was some time before all of the passengers were gone, and she even saw the flight attendants and pilot disembark. A cleaning crew filed into the aircraft followed by two muscular men in dark suits who stood silently with their hands folded in front of them. The man beside her and his acquaintance sitting in front of him stood up and moved several seats back to finish their conversation.

No one spoke to the girl, and she was left with her own thoughts. The cleaners vacuumed the floor around her as she held her backpack tightly on her lap, her seatbelt still securely fastened. She wore jeans and a sweatshirt and had wrapped a decorative headband around her forehead.

For a month now she could understand everyone yet speak to no one. Only an occasional yes or no had left her lips, sometimes in English, other times in Portuguese. Language was functioning perfectly in her mind, but it no longer connected with her tongue. She would make every conceivable effort to speak, but almost all that came out was a strange gurgling sound. It was as if the language in her head had not yet been developed. But her thoughts were lucid, and she remained completely aware of her surroundings. At the hospital she had undergone tests by neurologists, gynecologists, pediatricians, dermatologists, psychiatrists and other fields she hardly knew existed. To the questions these specialists asked, she could only offer a 'yes' or a 'no' with her eyes. On one or two occasions, however, she had been able to murmur an affirmative, which everyone considered to be a good sign.

She had spent almost three weeks in the George Washington Hospital after being found naked in a clearing at the top of Camel's Hump. There were no clothes around her and she was soaked, as if she had dived into the belly of a deep pool of water before falling motionless onto the cold stone.

Her body was bruised from blows to her face and kicks to her abdomen, buttocks, and chin. Her hair was strewn about, and she had lost twelve pounds.

The first on the scene was a bloodhound named Charlie, who began licking her face and yelping before the search-and-rescue team rushed onto the scene. She did not remember the helicopter hovering over the landscape, testing heat-seeking devices that had been deployed over a twenty-five-square-mile radius from her home, where she was last seen. She was taken down the mountain on a stretcher while reporters, television crews, and local citizens sprung into a frenzy of activity at the news that Anna White, the missing fourteen-year-old girl, had been found. The discovery had been reported by walkie-talkie to the central command set up at the River Hills Clubhouse, where Detective Ted Washington received the incredible news.

It was incredible for the simple reason that the spot where the girl was found had most certainly been checked the day before. They believed that someone, somehow, must have placed her there, and the detective had swiftly moved to close off the crime scene to closely examine the immediate area.

The girl's mother, Mrs. Carolyn White, was informed that, although there were some suspicious contusions, some of the girl's injuries could have been caused by the fact that she was naked in the woods. To the relief of everyone concerned, the experts who examined the detailed photographs concurred that there was no evidence of foul play. Specialists continued to whirl around her, and Detective Washington even called in a forensic botanist to study the flora around the clearing. Indeed, footprints were found nearby that matched those of a homeless drifter seen in the area.

The detective had announced that they had identified a suspect, the FBI was called in to assist, and by the time the girl was released from the hospital, the homeless man was in custody and being questioned. Most people in the tranquil community of River Hills felt confident that the crime was on its way to being quickly solved. However, a feisty public defender assigned to the drifter vowed to have the case dismissed due to lack of evidence.

"Who would defend such a vile creature who would kidnap an innocent girl?" a neighbor of the Whites commented in a live interview on

Richmond News Radio 1140.

"My client is innocent of these charges," the public defender stated in an exclusive interview. "The police had better do their job, because this community expects more than baseless charges with no evidence." His ill-fitted suit hung on his thin frame as he spoke in a way that made arguing with him useless.

To these facts, to these events, Anna had not been able to speak or assist in any way. When the FBI agents questioned her in the hospital room, she could only barely shake her head yes or no. The neurologists, psychologists, and even a psychic had urged the investigators to allow time for her thoughts and speech to resume.

The psychic was a middle-aged woman brought in from Richmond who had been following the case closely. She had contacted Mark White directly and claimed that she had information that would help the case. The police were at this time following up on all leads. The woman submitted her credentials and asked to be allowed in the hospital room. There was no harm in seeking all assistance, the detective claimed, and the Whites had agreed.

Looking like a guest at a Greek sunset party, Kelsey Brockson entered in a whirlwind of colorful scarves and a flowing long skirt. Her white boots had tassels, her dyed-blond ringlets sprung out in every direction, and her dangling jewelry jangled with every move. A large crystal pendant nestled deeply in her cleavage. She exchanged hellos with the huddled group as if they were all old friends before sitting next to Anna's bed.

"Well, hello there, Anna," the psychic said as if she had seen her only yesterday. She shooed away some of the flowers and balloons that filled the sunny room as Anna looked at her with wide eyes. The woman took Anna's hand.

"Can I speak with you, Anna?" Kelsey Brockson asked, and Anna blinked in agreement.

The psychic now closed her eyes for a long moment. Sensing her effort to reach an altered state, Carolyn and Mark excused themselves. Bored by the silence, the detective exited as well. Kelsey mumbled several times as if she were having a conversation with someone who was not present. At some point Anna closed her eyes and fell asleep. Kelsey stayed for close to an hour, occasionally murmuring inexplicable words. Then she stood up quickly, squeezed Anna's hand, and left her alone in the hospital bed. The psychic motioned for the three concerned persons to join her in the hall.

As she had left the door open, Anna could make out most of the conversation.

"Carolyn, Mark, Detective Washington. I think I have your answer," Kelsey declared.

"Please," said Carolyn

There was a long pause as Kelsey seemed to regain her composure.

"Anna was a visitor through a portal in time," she said as she saw Mark and the detective holding back laughter. She forged ahead. "She was able to cross a void that brought her to a place where she lived with people from long ago, people she already knew. She went there to ease a curse that had been set years before her arrival. She was successful in reducing the suffering of certain people. She had to leave behind a great deal more suffering, but she did what she was able." Kelsey paused and took a long breath. Mark and Ted had collected themselves and looked at her seriously.

"That's where your daughter has been," she continued. "She was not kidnapped, and the man you have in custody is not guilty. She went on her own; it was her choice. She cannot talk because her language skills did not travel back with her in tandem through time. I believe the years she went to were sometime in the early 1800s. It had not rained in five years, but Anna was able to fix that. That's why she was so drenched when she was found. Your daughter brought the waters." Kelsey looked at the three of them as if she had just solved a complex mathematical formula that had baffled theorists for centuries.

"Anna made it rain, is that what you mean?" Carolyn asked, wide-eyed. Mark smiled but hid it by looking down.

"Uh-huh," Ted responded. "That is very...helpful, Ms. Brockson. Perhaps I can take your number in case the Whites or I have any more questions?"

"Oh yes!" Kelsey said. "Call me anytime! The truth is that Anna was here in River Hills the entire time, but of course it was not River Hills. It was just in River Hills. Also, her name was Annabelle in this other world, but it was still her. Am I being clear enough?"

"Perfectly, Ms. Brockson," the detective said.

"I have so much more information. Maybe it can help! During her time in this void, she worked as a servant in a tobacco field and had to fight terrible insects with horns that bit her with their teeth. And then a priest—no, no a Reverend—trapped her in a secret wooden compartment on wheels and promised to set her free but only…"

"Thank you, Mrs. Brockson," Mark interrupted. "This has been very helpful. We are so glad we called you."

"Oh, and Annabelle got into a fight with a despicable man. Fortunately, Annabelle got the best of him in a struggle and pushed him over a cliff! The cliff on Camel's Hump! Isn't that where she was found, Detective?"

"Yes. As the newspapers reported, Ms. Brockson."

"But I want to put your minds at ease about the portal. The one Anna slipped through, which is really just a common time-based multidimensional vortex, was located in your basement. But don't worry! Your home is safe and you do not need to do a thing! Perfectly safe!" Her bracelets dangled as she became more animated. "So often people are in the right place but the wrong time. Don't you agree, Mr. and Mrs. White?"

"So often," Carolyn agreed.

"Well, then, OK. Thank you, thank you very much!" Kelsey said and then turned toward the hallway. She stopped and looked back at her audience. "May I inquire about my fee?"

There was some shuffling of papers, and Anna heard the woman spelling her name, then turn away.

But what Anna heard next made her blood rush to the edge of her skin.

"Mr. and Mrs. White," Kelsey Brockson said from down the hall so that the words echoed loudly in Anna's ears. "It is not wrong to go back for that which you have forgotten," and then her footsteps disappeared down the hall.

There was a long pause. "Crazy as a six-dollar bill," Mark said.

The following day when Anna lay in the hospital with her eyes fluttering, hoping that the Reverend survived and was able to bring back Madia, she thought she heard Cassy and Mary come into the room with Priscilla. Everyone had been trying to get Anna to speak, to tell where she had been, and Carolyn thought that seeing her best friends might trigger Anna to come out of the reverie she seemed to be lost in.

"Hello, Anna," Cassy began. She stepped over to the bedside and bent over the patient as if examining a corpse.

Mary stood at the foot of the bed. Priscilla and Carolyn watched from the window, and then, thinking it might be best to leave the teens by themselves, they walked down the hall.

"She can't hear anything," Cassy told her sister.

"Is she in a coma?" Mary asked.

"Why don't we just tell her what's going on at school. Maybe her subconscious or something can hear us and she'll wake up."

"Sure," Mary said. "Hey Anna, last night Port came over and started unbuttoning his pants when he was on my bed."

"Get out! Why didn't you tell me?" Cassy belted out, and the two girls now talked to one another as if Anna were not in the room.

"Well, he did!" Mary yelled back.

"And did you let him?"

"Maybe," Mary replied, "but I was actually not feeling too good." The girl let out her familiar cough. Anna heard her walk over to the blinds and play with them. The slinky sound was as unpleasant as their loud voices.

"Well, tell me about it later," Cassy said. "Hey Anna!" she said as she tapped Anna's foot. "Everybody wants to know what happened to you. Wake up and tell us!"

"Yeah, tell us so we can tell our mom and everybody will stop asking us stupid questions," Mary added. "Like we know something or something."

"Or something," Cassy added.

There was a stillness in the room as their questions drifted through the air and fell flat.

"Anna, can you speak? Are you OK?" Mary shook the bed.

"Maybe she is dreaming in African or something," Cassy offered.

"Ugandan," Mary corrected.

"Angolan" they said, together.

"No, it's Portuguese, Cassy! She speaks Portuguese." Mary turned toward her sister. "Do you know any Portuguese?"

Cassy whispered. "Just *ugga-bugga*."

"Cassidy Kane! Not now." But Anna heard both girls laugh. There was another long silence in the room.

"Maybe she doesn't belong here. She kind of had a tough time at River Hills. There aren't a lot of Black kids. If we weren't her friends, she wouldn't have met anybody."

"Well, Reggie thinks she's pretty," said Mary.

"Well, that figures." They looked at each other in agreement.

"Do you know how many community credits we got for being her chaperone?" Mary asked.

"No idea, but hopefully enough to graduate."

Both girls sat debating their lunch plans, whether they should go to Chipotle, Taco Bell, or Starbucks. They then discussed Halloween plans. Cassy was considering being a bloody bride.

The girls stood up.

"Remember that time Anna said she saw ghosts walking around River Hills, like along the highway?" Mary asked.

"Maybe everything just got to her and she couldn't take it anymore." The two girls tried once more to shake the bed.

"Maybe she's just in shock and she should go back to Uganda," Cassy offered. They turned toward the door.

"Angola," Mary corrected. "Hey, what should I be for Halloween?" Anna heard Mary ask as the door opened and closed softly behind them.

According to the police report of the now closed case, Anna White, age fourteen, of 186 Tidewater Street, a recent immigrant from Angola and the adopted child of Mark and Carolyn White, had run away on her own. The teenager was having trouble making friends at school and there were reports of her being bullied, according to Principal Dumont of River Hills Middle School, who had conducted a thorough investigation with several ninth-grade students implicated in the bullying episodes. Three hundred dollars had been taken from a bureau in her parents' bedroom, and it was believed that during the week of her absence she may have traveled to Washington, D.C. It was determined that the bruises on her body were self-inflicted. (She had injured herself once before falling out of bed, Carolyn White reported). Through the aid of an unknown person, she had made her way back to River Hills, ascended to the top of Camel's Hump, and removed her clothes so as to create the appearance of a crime scene. In any event, she was neither starved nor sexually abused, which was a relief to all parties. She was just a disturbed adolescent seeking attention, a former child soldier it turned out, who was having flashbacks and an understandably tough time assimilating in America. In addition, it was reported that she had experienced an epileptic episode at the home of friends several months prior, which explained her erratic behavior, according to a psychological profile. With no foul play suspected, the investigation has been concluded, and the media has moved on to other breaking stories.

Anna sat in her airplane seat, listening to the sound of the vacuum cleaners being pushed and pulled under the seats while she waited for the signal for her to deplane.

The goodbyes back at Ronald Reagan International Airport had been especially difficult. She was only able to convey the most minimal responses. She could think as clearly as the sky outside, but she could express no words to members of the White family as the gate area. Mark was not there. Carolyn pulled Anna aside and the two sat on plastic chairs next to one another in an empty section of the gate area.

"Anna, I know it's hard for you to talk to me. Maybe there is much that you have to say."

Anna looked down at the Spice Girls backpack Nita had given her as a going away present and fiddled with the zipper.

"There is nothing wrong with you, Anna. You just have been through too much. Too much for you, too much for you to be with us. But you will be...just fine." She put her arm around the girl, who leaned slightly into her body. "We tried hard to make this work, for everybody. But sometimes, it just doesn't." She blew out a long breath. "And I just need to accept that. It is part of it, I'm told." She took Anna's chin in the palm of her hand. "Do you understand that, Anna?"

She shook her head.

"I know you were upset that we were going to bring another child into our home, but those plans are on hold now. Mark and I are going in a new direction, his choice, but maybe it is mine too. We still love each other, but he won't be living at the house full time anymore. We know we have to focus more on the kids we have. Tabitha is having trouble at school, Wyatt has been acting out a lot, Nita definitely needs help, and Simba... well, Simba's just a little boy."

Anna nodded and reached for Carolyn's hand and the mother and daughter, the rescuer and the rescued, let silent words speak between them.

"*Obrigado*, Carolyn White," Anna whispered, but the words could not be heard.

Carolyn adjusted the green-and-white scarf that fit securely around her neck. She had not had time to fix her hair before leaving for the airport, and it looked as if she had just woken up. She wore no makeup, and it was clear she had slept little.

"Mark said to say goodbye. As you know, we've decided to separate for a while, see how things go." Carolyn looked out at the aircrafts scurrying about, trying to find their places. "I think it's best, all of this is for the best," she said, mostly to herself. Anna felt a connection between them—not like between a mother and daughter, but another kind, undefined, but just as human and real. Carolyn kissed Anna's forehead. She gathered herself and stood up, and with a squeeze to Anna's hand, walked over to the others.

Nita made her way over to where Anna sat.

"So you're going, huh?" Nita began. She was coming into her body, while never thin and traditionally pretty, well-formed and confident.

Anna shook her head yes.

"You're lucky."

Both girls smiled at one another. Nita motioned her thumb toward the siblings.

"Carolyn's orphanage," Nita said. Anna smiled and tried to repeat the phrase but the words still could not form. "You'll be alright," she said and patted her on the shoulder. Anna turned toward the plate-glass windows and watched as an Air France plane drifted slowly by on the tarmac. "But don't think I'm not going to miss you, Anna Banana." She reached out and touched Anna's hair. "I'm going to miss our talks at night." The words came out slowly. Then, after a pause, she added, "I wish I were leaving too, but I can't. So, send me an email sometime, OK? Maybe we'll hang out in D.C. someday, check out those embassies for real. OK. Stay cool." Nita started to walk, then turned abruptly. "And don't worry, you are not the crazy one, that's for sure!" Nita waved and thrust her chin at the family, turned, and took her place.

Simba ran to her, jumped onto her lap, and hugged her tightly without saying a word. He was holding a small bag of pretzels.

"Simba, Simba," she managed to say from somewhere in her throat as she felt the boy heaving on her chest. There was so much she wanted to express, but the words were lost in time.

"Why do you have to go?" the boy asked, his head still buried in her shoulder. "You said you'd take care of me! You're my sister, and sisters don't leave!"

"Simba, Simba...shhh," she said without words.

"Will you come back to see me?" Now the boy brought his head up and looked in her eyes.

"*Sim*. Yes," she was able to say.

"I got pretzels!" he smiled at her. "So, we could have another pretzel fight!" He held out the small bag, clumsily took out two, and lobbed them at her. Anna feigned injury, then grabbed one and tossed it at him. It bounced off his nose and landed at their feet where they both stared at it, a heart shape on the floor.

"When you visit, let's make a fort out of the cushions that's just for us, nobody else allowed, OK Anna?"

She shook her head up and down, placed her hands on his head, and her eyes filled with tears.

He fumbled in his pocket and pulled out a small square of a basket he had found in the basement. The distinctive triangle that was her family's hallmark was slightly visible. Taped to it was a photo Simba had taken of himself at the twins' birthday party. "Will you keep it forever?" he asked with his wide brown eyes.

Anna could hardly see him through her tears. She looked at the photo, then at him, and carefully placed it in her backpack.

"*Obrigado*, Simba. Thank you," she wished she could say.

The boy kissed her on her cheek. "You still have weird eyebrows, sister," and he ran to his family without looking back.

The in-flight cabin meeting between the two men came to a conclusion, and they were all escorted off of the plane by the well-dressed team who stood at the jetway entrance like doormen granting them entry to the terminal.

The two men with whom Anna had traveled continued to speak amicably, mostly about upcoming meetings and the notes and documents that would need to be prepared. The pair of escorts walked behind them and Anna could sense the importance of her arrival.

The psychic Kelsey Brockson had given the best explanation of where Anna had been, but while she was accurate about time and place, she was not able to tell her what became of the people she had come to know. Anna knew only that they were long dead, most buried in the cemetery by the Old Oak, their names barely legible on weathered tombstones. Beatrice and her children, Ole' Beatrice, Big Arthur, Jemmy... Their headstones were the only scant proof that they had ever lived, and Anna wondered if—then felt assured—their lives had any meaning.

Madia, the kind, adoring wife and mother who somehow made the simple, thin shelter a home to her children and husband.

Calvin, the sensitive son and brother who was sweet and kind and brave enough to try to return to his people's homeland.

Lizzie, onto a life she would somehow make the best of with new people, and perhaps another old woman to care for. She would marry, Anna hoped.

Big Arthur, gentle and decent, steadfastly finding something good in every day, despite the fact that his days were controlled by others.

The Reverend, who was willing to risk his life for her and so many others.

Ole' Beatrice, sold twice, who spent her elder years watching over her neighbors as if they were her own children. She would of course never see freedom for herself as the war was not for another forty years, long after she had joined her dead children in the graveyard beneath the Old Oak. But Anna was glad that she had told her in no uncertain terms that slavery would end. They were working in the tobacco field when Anna told her and, even as Beatrice's hands were being bitten, there was a kind of joy in her eyes that can only come from understanding.

Anna even thought of Master Kane, sitting on the porch at his doomed plantation, subjected to the whims of his spoiled daughters and the lies and deceit from men like A.C. Tomkins, who carried around jealousy and schemes like the broad-brimmed hat on his head. When A.C.'s body was found at the base of the cliff, and the rains had come, some peace, some betterment surely came to the plantation. No half rations due to a poor crop. No more backbreaking digging of canals to fight the drought. And no one would have to bear the brunt of A.C. Tomkin's uncaged temper ever again. Anna knew that the dark lives of the slaves of Nottoway, who lived so long ago, were slightly brightened. Of this she was sure—just as she was sure of that her love for Madia and Calvin, Simba, Auntie, and her own mother and father—lived in her through days, years, and even across centuries. Love, for what it is, does not know how to die.

But most of all she thought of Jemmy, whom she had seen only once, on that fateful night in the year 1819. His love for his wife and children ran deep and nothing could take that away, even as men tried to steal his dignity, and eventually his life. He never meant to take away happiness, only to give it, and what was said in his final moments beneath the Old Oak needed to be remedied. Perhaps Anna had succeeded after all.

The thought gave her strength as her muscles began to wake up after the long flight. She picked up her pace down the long corridor toward two booths at the end. Inside were two uniformed officers. Anna was motioned to step up to the booth first.

The officer was dressed like a soldier, except she had no gun. She wore a police badge and smiled at Anna. Gentle and nonthreatening, she seemed like a woman who might be finishing up her shift so she could get home to her children to make tilapia and fragrant *funje*.

"Documents please," she asked in English. Anna handed her the American passport she had been issued less than a year ago.

"Please state your name," the officer said.

The larger of the two men accompanying her stepped up.

"Good afternoon, Officer Sanchez," he said, noticing her badge.

"Oh, my, Ambassador Franca!" the officer said. "I am very sorry, I did not recognize you for a moment! How may I be of service?"

"This young lady is with me. Her name is Anna White and she has a speech impediment, so please excuse her silence. I can vouch for all of her information."

"Anna White," she said. "Thank you, Mr. Ambassador. I will be just a moment. I am sorry to hold you up, Mr. Ambassador."

Anna suddenly felt a surge of clarity, a tingling that rose from the base of her belly, then to her heart, and continued up through to her throat. Images of the people she had known came precisely to her mind, and she was now certain about where she had been and why she had been there. They were long gone, she knew, as was her own family, but time could heal wounds, she now knew.

"Officer, Anna has been through a tremendous experience, and I hope you will allow us to..."

Suddenly a voice rose up in her, and she felt a vibration at the back of her throat.

"My name is Zarkhanna Cudjo."

The words, thick on her tongue, felt like the taste of warm milk, wonderful and familiar.

Ambassador Franca looked at her as if she were a cat that had just spoken words.

"I am from Caxito. I am Mbundu. My great-great-grandfather Calvin Cudjo traveled back here from America..."

The officer looked up from the document to the ambassador. "I trust this all makes sense, Mr. Ambassador?" she asked as she handed the documents back.

Ambassador Franca and Marcus looked at the girl with broad smiles. The doctors had predicted she would regain her speech, but no one expected the words to flow out of her with such clarity.

The travelers now passed the customs booths and continued toward two electric doors surrounded by glass brick that blocked all visibility to the other side. Zarkhanna stepped onto the rubber mat and the doors automatically opened.

"Who is Calvin Cudjo, Anna?" The ambassador asked, catching up to her.

There was a pause as she considered the question.

"He was my family," she responded with a smile.

Now they reached the terminal bustling with travelers of all ages pulling suitcases and wearing backpacks and forming lines for the coffee shops banked along one side of the airport hall. Baggage tumbled onto turnstiles and uniformed agents picked through them, checking the tags.

"Zarkhanna!" someone yelled, and she turned toward the voice. She dropped her backpack and started running toward the caller.

And there, separated only by a red velvet rope the ambassador easily unhooked, Zarkhanna fell into the arms of Auntie.

The two hugged one another with an intensity only they could understand.

"Welcome home, little Zebra," Auntie whispered in her ear.

Zarkhanna then looked down and noticed something in Auntie's hand. It was the Ndimba heirloom she had left behind so long ago. She reached for the treasure. Zarkhanna could now see the passage of time woven into its threads, a passage she knew included herself, as well as Calvin, Madia, Jemmy and so many others. She held it against her chest like a puppy.

The Ambassador now tapped Auntie on the shoulder and addressed her.

"You know, our country could truly benefit from someone like your niece who can bridge cultures with the United States and other countries," he said with a smile. "Bring this brave young lady to me at the Consulate for a visit soon, and when she gets a little older, we will teach and help her."

He then turned to Marcus. "See to it," he directed.

"Yes sir," Marcus replied.

The two men departed the terminal leaving the lost family members in the safe arms of one another.

# Afterword to *The Visitor*

by Joaquim do Espirito Santo
Angolan Ambassador to the United States

In August 1619, a decade after the English settled Jamestown, approximately twenty-five people from the West African nation of Angola arrived on the shores of Virginia to begin a life of enslavement. Over the next four hundred years, six million Angolan people would succumb to forced migration, mostly to Portuguese colonies such as Brazil and the Azores, but also to America. While they would never return to their West African homeland, they would remain to outlive the barbarism and become great citizens of the United States, populating the land and helping to build a country, not always of their free will.

Today, it is now estimated that up to 10 percent of African Americans have Angolan blood. The connection between the United States and Angola may have started with tragedy, but it is now a thriving partnership approaching above two billion dollars in imports and exports, including petroleum, precious metals, iron, electronics, and investments in solar energy and other business areas. During our country's dark civil war in the 1990s, the United States eventually helped to bring forward a peaceful resolution that gave our troubled land independence from its colonialist rulers and a place among nations. Angola continues to thrive on the world stage thanks to its strategic location, educated people, and stable government.

I was pleased to discover that the historian and author Eric W. Gershman would choose to tell a powerful story of the connection between our two countries. Mr. Gershman's gift for research and narrative has produced a thrilling tale of mystery, time travel, and explosive story telling.

In short, The Visitor is a book that uses the fantastic to find a deeper meaning in the wounds history has left us with. It redefines what it means to belong.

I hope you enjoy this book as much as I did and come away with a deeper understanding between our two far-away nations, through the eyes of a brave young woman who epitomizes everything it means to be an American, an Angolan, and a citizen of the world.

# Acknowledgments

I never intended to write this book. Writers come up with ideas and hope to strike a chord. It began as a short story about modern families who live on hallowed ground where terrible events may have happened. That research led directly to Nikole Hannah-Jones and her groundbreaking book, The 1619 Project—which enlightened readers to the fact that Angola was the first country whose citizens were stolen and brought to these shores. So, I would like to thank her first. As a Jewish American descended from poor immigrants scratching out a living, I wonder continually how any people(s) end up on these shores, and what stories they bring. The Angolan story is especially painful, but I hope that the telling of this story brings it notice. I would also like to thank the late Irwin Allen for his 1960s television series, The Time Tunnel, which fascinated me as a kid. We might consider this book to be an updated and expanded episode.

A special thank you goes out to Fred Leebron, an extraordinary novelist (his novel Out West is un-put-down-able) and MFA Program Director at Queens University in Charlotte, North Carolina. It was Fred who first read the treatment I had written and encouraged the work. This book would not have been possible without his leadership and ongoing friendship. I also want to thank a few of my professors at Queens who steered me right. These include Naheem Burr who enlightened me about character development, Elissa Shappell for her wit, Ashley Warlick for her incredible writing and assistance (her novel The Arrangement is addictive) as well as Patrica Powell who helped shape the manuscript. Thank you to my good friend and mentor Biddle Duke who never judged and helped bring the book to life as well as Reid Krakower for believing in me. Thank you to my earlier readers including Danielle Jacobs, Daria Gershman, Toni Barr, and Heather Bell. Thank you to my early editor Tanya Tabatchnikoff for her insights and publishing assistance. Thank you to Maura Phelon, Founder of Greenlight Literary who gave tons of encouragement. I want to thank my production editor, Gwendolyn Mitchell, for her sharp eye and excellent advice. And that goes to everyone at Third World Press Foundation in Chicago for believing in me, even though the speculative fiction genre is generally not what they publish. This includes Antoine Lindsay for answering my endless questions (I'm not done!), Rose Perkins (who I insist actually runs the press herself), and Relana Johnson for the book's layout and design. I am especially grateful to Dr. Haki Madhubuti for his leadership and steady hand, and Keith Gilyard for his encouragement. Thank you also to Priscilla de Lemos Coelho at the Angolan Embassy in Washington DC, as well as the former Ambassador Senor Joaquim do Espirito Santo for graciously offering to write the Afterword.

I want to thank my late father Norman H. Gershman, who sadly passed before reading this, for instilling the seed of imagination which drives me every day. I want to thank my mother, Carol Sue Gershman, for teaching me about perseverance and being a continuing role model for me. None of this is possible without my family and especially my wife of decades, Robin Gershman, a true inspiration and intuitive person. I am lucky to have her in my life.

# About the Author

Eric W. Gershman holds an MFA in historical fiction from Queens University in Charlotte, N.C. He is the founder of McGraw Hill's custom publishing financial unit, now a Standard & Poor's company. His short stories have appeared in numerous magazines and online journals. *The Visitor* is his debut novel. He resides in Vermont with his wife, Robin.